Trust

THE ALEX CONNER CHRONICLES
BOOK ONE

Trust

THE ALEX CONNER CHRONICLES
BOOK ONE

By
Parker Sinclair

Rawlings Books, LLC

OTHER BOOKS BY THE AUTHOR

The Alex Conner Chronicles
(Urban Fantasy/Supernatural Suspense)

Trust: The Alex Conner Chronicles Book One
Truth: The Alex Conner Chronicles Book Two
Forbidden: An Alex Conner Chronicles Novella
Only: The Alex Conner Chronicles Book Three

Eve of the Exceptionals
(YA Epic Fantasy)

The Dark Angel Series
(Dark Urban Fantasy)

A Darker Fall: A Dark Angel Novella
(Featured in The Aching Darkness Anthology)

KEEP UP WITH PARKER SINCLAIR

Webpage: *www.parkersinclair.net* SEP

Amazon Author Page: *https://www.amazon.com/Parker-Sinclair/e/B00Q33GTQM* SEP

Facebook Fan Page: *www.facebook.com/ParkerSinclairbooks/* SEP

Instagram: *@ParkerSinclairauthor*

Twitter: *@Parker_Sinclair*

Join my newsletter for free fantasy/Sci-Fi books:
http://eepurl.com/b9q07X

Rawlings Books, LLC
Visit our website at
www.Rawlingsbooks.com

Cover Art by Jessica Tahbonemah
Edited by Meredith Tennant & Stephany Wallace
Book Design by Stephany Wallace

Paperback Edition ISBN 978–0–9908565–0–4
EPub Edition ISBN 978–0–9908565–1–1
Mobi Edition ISBN 978–0–9908565–2–8

For Lyla and Ella, my beautiful, creative, and intelligent daughters who help me to live life more fully each and every day.

For Mom, whose visit in Arizona made this book possible. You brought me back to the woman, mother, and writer I was always supposed to be.

ACKNOWLEDGEMENTS

To my friends, family, and early readers of a very rough and typo-riddled draft. Your encouragement and pursuit of wanting more and more from me kept me going through all the self-doubt.

To my editor, you helped me give this book more life. This would never have been possible without you.

To Jessica Tahbonemah, for her patience and artistry.

To Lulani, for suffering through some choppy chapters and inconsistencies in order to keep me on track.

To **Above & Beyond** for being a support and a class act. Your music inspires me—your lyrics move me.

To my family. We keep moving forward despite our loss, and I know we will always have our memories and our love for each other, both of which have carried me through the creation of this book.

And to my husband, for the support and enthusiasm you provided as I reached for this dream.

CONTENTS

"Evil, in evil, he may pine and die.
And for myself I pray, if with my knowledge
He should become an inmate of my dwelling,
That I may suffer all that I invoked . . ."
—Sophocles: *Oedipus Rex*

CHAPTER 1

Alexis, Wake Up!

Journal Entry:

Being observant has been my blessing, my curse, and my destiny. My grandmother always told me that I was the most perceptive creature she had ever known, aside from her cats. This focus and intensity have brought about my ability—my power.

I remember smells that would have been foreign to any other five year old, but not to the daughter of Stacy Conner. A pungent mix of bodily fluids, industrial drugs, suntan oil, and stale food. My mom was sprawled out on the floor, while a man I had just met, touched her roughly, yet it seemed that she found it to be in an acceptable manner. A bag of pills lay on the bedside table: red, blue, purple, white, green, and yellow.

"So pretty," I remember commenting after I grabbed the bag and rolled it between my young fingers. I peered over the side at my mom as her pale blue eyes rolled in her cockeyed head, while a goofy smile crossed over her crusted, cracked lips. Her arm slumped away from her chest and blood trickled from her self-inflicted wound. I had come to expect this display on a nearly daily basis, so I turned away and made a slow crawl to the middle of my bed with my little bag of treasures. This vivid memory causes me disgust and a patient, silent inner sobbing.

Regardless of these painful memories, my mother is still the most beautiful woman in the world to me. I assume most mothers are viewed that way. She lay there with her dirty blond hair tied back in her normal messy ponytail. Her beautiful high cheekbones remained, although her skin now held tight to her bones. When she stood, my mother was about six feet tall, usually dressed in tight short shorts, or jeans and tank tops with no bra. Her skin had a beautiful tone despite her drug-induced haze. Our blend of Irish, Spanish, and Italian ancestry mixed the darker shade of her skin with freckles in various locations, but I remember them most on the bridge of her nose, exactly where mine are. The Conner family is a unique blend that no one can really place. We get lots of stares, but not many questions. I guess the mixture of our looks and fear of the unknown lends itself to such reactions.

I emptied the entire bag, and while some of the pills found themselves piled upon another of its kin, the unfortunate ones fell with their entire surface area directly on to the faded, filthy bedspread.

"So pretty."

I picked a few of them up, examining each one carefully before tossing them down to join the others. Soon, I was sailing them up into the air and watching them lose their fight against gravity, as they dropped back on to the bed with me. What a poor place to be, little treasures... you are trapped, just like me. Well, we don't have to be bored just sitting here. Let's try something fun.

My head was turned ever so slyly, my lips curled in a delighted Cheshire cat's grin. Above me, the little treasures spun in the air in a cosmic splendor of colors and a plastic-like glimmer all on their own. I willed the air to move and shift, lifting and turning my mother's prized possessions, spinning them madly around me as if they were planets orbiting the sun. I must have lost track of time, or else time had ceased to exist, when suddenly I took a quick look at my mother and saw her face full of shock and somehow even paler than it had been before. As I lifted my chin in defiance, a pill brushed my ear. Mom gasped, and somehow, even in her drug-induced stupor, she managed to grab my face, the treasures falling all around me like dive-bombing tropical insects.

*Her beautiful blue bloodshot eyes focused on me as if to say, "Tell no one and never do this around anyone else again." And I didn't. Not until my grandmother taught me how to control my abilities and then only with her—till **that day**; the day I had to make him go away.*

"Alexis, wake UP!" It must have been my sore body, or maybe it was the pulsing headache talking to me. They both do that from time to time, neither having any regard for my apparent need of sleep.

Oh, Justin, how sweet of you to stay.

Justin's 600-thread-count–covered form is outlined next to me as he sleeps soundly. It is painstaking as my body helps me recall the evening. Endless hours of dancing, and the soreness of sex, send fire screeching through my thighs and a tense, sharp cramping in my calves. Most people would throw the amount of drinks I had into the mix, but alcohol doesn't affect me the way it does others. Granted, I'm not the least bit like everyone else. Lately, though, I've upped my game, which occasionally manages to keep the nightmares at bay, the only effect I've thankfully received from the numerous drinks each evening.

How long have I known Justin? It's been a little over a year now, and he keeps coming back no matter how many times I push him away. It's simple; he must only want me for my body. The Jane's Addiction song, "Jane Says," runs through my mind and becomes a theme to my misguided thought that it's never love, only the knowledge that someone wants me. I only wish it were that simple—I know Justin loves me. Leaning over, I lightly kiss his neck. He is cold, his eyes open and a look of deep, intense fear spread evilly across his face. His lips don't move, but I hear the words in their sickly whisper all the same.

"Doll eyes."

The rigidity of my neck gives way to the agonizing quiver of hairs as they stand on end. My head whips around when I hear someone scream in the distance. The vertigo makes it apparent that the room isn't really spinning, although I am barely able to keep the evening's remnants at bay. The muffled scream persists, and it takes a few moments for me to realize it's coming from my own lips. My gasps and screams wake me as my feet connect with flesh and bone, and Justin unwillingly tumbles off the bed.

"Damn it, Alex, that's the third time this week . . ." His tirade, mixed with incoherent grumbling fails him, as he teeters ever so slightly while trying to favor the previously targeted leg on his way to the bathroom. Despite the cringing of my teeth, I manage a smile while watching his naked, muscular body disappear behind the door.

I know he's right; the dreams or *hellacious spastic brain episodes*, as I so lovingly call them, are not getting much better. Not even my higher level of self-medication has been able to curb them as well as it used to. I roll over with a deep sigh, covertly wiping tears from my eyes, and open the bedside table drawer to remove my leather-bound journal. Dr. Reynolds has asked, more like required me, to keep a log of these night terrors. It's been an easy enough request for me to follow, since I already religiously keep a private journal. Thankfully, most entries prior to this last year are from my young adult life, that reflect the angst of coming into myself, meeting and wanting the wrong man, or girlhood crushes and fantasies. Come on, every woman needs a good page turner filled with overly emotional exclamations of "Why did I?" and "How could he?" I love my journal from those times of personal gluttony, so I was happy to relive them and ink some memories. The current entries I keep are different. Lately, there have been too many nightmares dredging up dark memories; frivolity has no space on these pages.

Journal Entry:
*I woke myself up from this dream in which Justin lay next to me, dead. Nothing else in the dream seemed incorrect. I had the dirty martini–induced headache, may need to X those from my repertoire—too salty. Or better yet, I'm sure you would suggest I cut back altogether. Be a thinker, not a drinker, ha that rhymes. Oh sorry, tangent. Well, doc, you did request all my thoughts. Justin is here, alive though. I heard that whisper of "Doll eyes" again. The name **that man** used to call me, but that was a long time ago, and he is gone now. I should be past it all by now, shouldn't I? I'm stronger than this, so why can't the past stay in its designated "do not open" time capsule? Why can't it keep its nose out of my present life, and its sticky paws off my future?*

Why can't I eliminate these memories? Trick my brain and go back to pre-nightmare, denial mode? Memories? Well, those aren't *my* memories. They belong to some other girl's life—not mine.

The thing is, I used to love picking up this pen. The Mont Blanc encased in black steel and platinum was a gift from my grandmother years ago. She wasn't usually one for fancy do-dads, but she did always encourage me to write and to keep a journal of my life and experiences. It was something to be kept privately. I don't think she ever intended for me to use it with the doc's mind-dissecting journal, but it's comforting. The pen's cool metal flesh compels my hand to write as it slithers and writhes between my fingers. It longs to stay

4

warm and useful as my pages of irrational thoughts and beliefs come to life through nightmares and mind tricks. Perhaps even the famed psychiatrist, Carl Jung, would have used me as one of his prime subjects back in his day. Maybe we would have shared our disturbing dreams since he had plenty of his own. I guess I should consider myself lucky to not have any golden snake gods in mine.

The sheer weight of the pen causes it to rock forcefully each time my words stop. I stare at the snowflake logo on the end, half expecting it to glide off of its seemingly permanent home and rest upon my nose. Thoughts of the Glenwood Springs' hot tubs and Keystone switchbacks enter my mind, and I laugh at the memory of snow-filled Jacuzzi nights and soreness from failed snowboarding attempts. Helpful hint: have some schnapps before hitting the slopes and some for safekeeping in your jacket. You'll be toasty warm, falling won't hurt as much, and you should become all the more gutsy, or reckless, I should say! I shake my head, and struggle to uncross my eyes as I wake from my daydream.

These days, the pen has become a sign of restlessness, horror, and necessity. The dreams have become ever more frequent, tiring, and mystifying. Journaling keeps me busy most mornings, or okay, with my line of work, they're more like early afternoons. I write about my dreams, and tirelessly find myself casting the gruesome details upon the pages. I have no doubts as to why I could never cut it in the medical field. My own imagination generates a fine deal of queasiness all by its lonesome.

"*Doll eyes.*"

The voice is so crisp and clear in my mind. I shiver and gaze about my loft.

"*Beautiful blinking doll eyes.*"

My head snaps up as the voice seems to be carrying upward and then—silence. Not that birds tweeting in the background silence either, rather a loud silence, the kind that grinds the teeth like ice breaking on frozen glacial lakes.

My body trembles inside and I look to the bathroom seeing the door open and Justin gone along with his pile of clothes. The normal bangs and rustling as Justin rummages about downstairs instantly melt away my fear. I gather myself to look over the railing of my loft. While staring at him I am intrigued, as I usually am, by him. I always go for the swarthy ones. His hair, dark, thick locks, tumble around his eyes. He curses as he tries to swipe some of his glorious stragglers away. With his back to me, I have a clear view of his muscular back

5

and brilliantly colored tattoo. It's an intricate tribal creation his friend designed for him in college. The main outline is of a cross, intended to reflect his Catholic heritage, although I don't know the last time he went to mass. Throughout the cross, patterns of serpent-like vines and strong branches give the impression of a tree instead of a religious symbol.

It makes sense. Justin is at one with nature; his job has him working in the earth every day, although I swear he looks like he should be a North Face cover model. I can never get enough of his striking Italian appearance. Strong chin, large eyes framing dark irises nearly the color of night, and full lips that are both soft and strong. Each magnificent part of him making him hot blooded and hot bodied. It's a good thing, just as he's a good man. Not to mention how good he's looking shirtless in those jeans.

"Looking for something?" Justin jumps, startled at the sound of my voice.

"You're always sneaking up on me, just like that damn cat of yours. At least his loud ass meows find a way to warn me. You almost made me piss myself!" Justin joked as he continued his search amongst my kitchen drawers.

"Now that would be a treat!" I giggle and rush down the cool terra cotta steps, nearly tripping as Pitter, the aforementioned feline, glides along my right leg just as I reach the floor. I swoop him up and scold him for trying to take me down, just to make things even for teasing Justin, apparently his new best friend. His meow is enough of an apology for me, so I set him back down.

"So, what are you missing? Keys? Wallet? These?" I teasingly dance around, waving his boxers in the air. Pitter chases me and paws at the air while doing those fascinating acrobatic moves, only the graceful, stealthy *Felis catus* can do. I bring them closer to his level and he feverishly slashes at them with claws bared.

"I see someone is feeling much better," Justin remarks teasingly while snatching his boxers away.

"No," he goes on, "not what I was looking for, but I'll take these as well." Snatching his clothing from me, he holds back a smile when he sees me appreciating his bare chest. "I'm looking for a cigarette. You never keep any here for me, and when I leave them, they miraculously disappear. Now why is that, Alex?"

"You know I hate when you smoke. What do you expect? Plus, they make that drawer reek of disease-causing, lung-injuring, secondhand, toxic air–spreading cancer sticks!" I snap my mouth shut

6

as I realize I had been on my ranting pedestal again, and it is clearly way too early for elevated blood pressure levels. Justin glances at me in a relieved sort of way as if to say "thank you for stopping on your own."

"I've gotta go." Giving up his search, Justin puts his shirt and shoes on. He moves towards me, kisses me deeply, and turns to leave.

I should say something now. Thank him for staying with me or maybe even tell him that I love him, but I don't. The empty, soundless moment between us does not waver with any such words. Pitter meows faintly, trailing behind him. As Justin bends down to scratch him behind his ears, a smile crosses my face as Pitter slithers along the floor, fully engrossed in feline pleasure. "See ya rat," he says with a chuckle in his voice, and closes the door behind him.

I stare at the door for a while, as if I actually expect him to come back. Then I try to will it so, the pleading echoing in my mind.

"Please don't leave me here. Not alone."

I quickly dismiss these demands as my grandmother's voice drifts into my awareness, "You have gifts. Don't misuse them." It's not only the memory of her words that stops me. I know, as well as he does, that I can't give Justin what he wants anyway—at least not now.

I turn my eyes to the clock and then dance toward Pitter. "Busy, busy night ahead of us, stinky! This party can't run itself. Let's quadruple check our planning, and everyone else's for that matter."

CHAPTER 2

Alex

Journal Entry:

When people think of living in a motel, the associations aren't typically rosy or sweet. Usually, they are linked with poverty, a gypsy-type nomadic life, or some sort of addiction. Well, maybe two out of three hit the spot for my mother and me, but I was still happy most of the time. I always knew that no matter what mistakes she made, or how many difficult times we went through, she loved me, and I loved her.

Now, this motel was one of my favorites. It was a weekly rental in the heart of Ocean Beach. We were so close to the ocean that I could fall asleep to the Pacific waves crashing onto the sand, and to the pleasing tones of the street musicians and peddlers. That was a true beach town. Although it had its rough spots, it was charming, rare, and raw all at the same time.

On that particular night, I had the best dinner prepared for me. Mom had gotten me large chili cheese fries from Wienerschnitzel, and I looked forward to diving into four of our major food groups—cheesy, salty, veggie, and fruity. Okay, so the fruit was the last grape popsicle in our little half-size fridge, but it still counted, right?

I was gingerly eating the fries, letting the cheese spread as far as it could go, when Mom's new boyfriend came stumbling in. Matt. Mom had been seeing him for a couple of weeks now. He smelled like booze and sweat, and I couldn't stand to be near him; in a space this small, it was nauseating. There was only one place to go, so I jumped up and went to the freezer for my popsicle. That yummy little treat and I had a date outside on the sea wall.

*"Hey kid, thanks," said the slob as he took my popsicle out of my hand and ripped the paper off. The paper stuck in all sorts of spots on the frozen concoction, and I could see that it was starting to frustrate him. Hell, if I couldn't have **my** popsicle, why not enjoy this for a minute. Now, as far as my eight-year-old mind could tell, this was a good time to giggle. I know, not one of my finest moments. If I had been more on the ball, I would have taken off like I had intended, popsicle be damned. Instead, I clapped my hand over my mouth too late, and Matt turned his bull-like head toward me, eyes blazing. He was two hundred pounds of muscle and bone, with extra weight hanging over his pants where the beer went to graze. He had receding blond hair slicked to his head that screamed to be washed, while his nose was contorted in a one-too-many bar fights sort of way.*

*"You laughing at me, brat? Do you think this is funny? Well, you know what **I** think is funny?" I knew this was a rhetorical question so I thought the best answer would be to get my bratty ass out the door as soon as possible. I turned to leave, but he grabbed me by my neck and pulled me toward him. His face was so close that I nearly gagged under the hot pressing weight of his breath. At this point, it seemed best to focus on not doing anything to further piss him off. Apparently, I didn't have to. He shoved the grape popsicle in my face and forced it into my mouth, both the coldness of the ice and his Neanderthal-like force causing my lip to crack as I released a cry of pain.*

"Take it then, you little bitch. I know your scrawny ass doesn't mind a little paper, and I'm sure you have a mouth like your mother, so it should be easy for you." I tried to claw away from him, but I felt the heat and the sting before I could get away. His palm connected with my cheek, and I crashed to the floor. He was grabbing for my feet as I tried to crawl away, when I heard the door open and my mom came in.

*"What in the **hell** is going on in here? What are you doing? Get your hands off my daughter, **now**! Alexis, come here. Matt was just leaving!" She turned her hot gaze on her boyfriend. "Matt, get out **now**—before I call the manager." She reached for me but Matt lunged at her, grabbing her by the shoulders and shaking her. She shook like a hula doll on the dash of a car, her ponytail flying in wild circles, creating a pinwheel-like effect.*

"You think you can talk to me like that after all I've done for you? I've been feeding you and that little parasite for weeks. All I wanted was a little respect and your brat daughter starts talking back to me."

Now I hate liars, never was one. Okay, I imagined a lot, but that's kid stuff and pretty much expected, right?

"I did not! He's lying!" My mom didn't seem like she cared to hear what Matt had to say. She looked at me, and I **knew** she had a plan to get us out of this mess. She had the look of someone who was done taking this kind of shit, and she was in no way bringing her daughter down with her any longer.

Mom moved away from him in a slow, delicate manner that suggested she was preparing to work things out and wave the white flag of surrender. Her intention was to fool Matt, but I wasn't sure he was buying it. She took my hand to help me up when out of the corner of my eye I saw the foot come flying out.

"Mom!" I screamed, but it was too late.

Matt gave my mother a full force kick right into her stomach. She doubled over and fell, landing right on top of me and looking into my eyes. She should have been in pain, but her face wasn't registering it. We scrambled to get up, but he grabbed her by her ponytail and threw her on to the bed. He was closing in on her with his back to me when I jumped up and looked around for something, anything to help me. I grabbed the table lamp and held it in my hand so tightly that my knuckles blanched stark white. I closed my eyes and swung. I meant to hit him square in the back, but my aim was a bit off and it landed, a few inches too high, smacking him forcefully on the back of his head.

"What the fu . . ." his voice trailed off as his eyes rolled backward, and he fell on my mother. She pushed, and I pulled, until we got him off her.

We quickly grabbed the phone, maneuvered the cord into the bathroom, and locked the door. I know we probably should have run, but our whole life was in that room, and we were pretty damn sure that it would all be gone, or ruined, if we left it with Matt, *"the psycho."*

My mom's hands were trembling as she wildly pressed buttons. Her breathing was erratic, and beads of sweat trickled down her face. I knew I had to stay calm for her even though inside I was frightened, and wanted to release a mighty wail. At that moment, we heard a crash, followed by a thunderous BOOM.

"Whatcha doin' Stacy, trying to call for help? Pulled the cord on you, little lady. You'll get no help except from me." WHAM! I could

see the door taking the force but bending on itself. Mom had a death grip on the phone, and I thought I heard her talking to someone.

Suddenly the door burst open. Blood was trickling down Matt's neck and in his eyes shone a ferocious anger that froze me. He had just taken a step toward me when I heard another man's voice.

"Hey, you!" Matt whipped around and was smacked in the face with a bat. The hotel manager swung again, and Matt went down.

"Now stay down, man. This is the least of the power I can use on you." Matt didn't move an inch, whether by choice or by the beating the manager dealt him, I'm not certain.

"Thanks for coming, Hal." My mom managed to get up and out of the bathroom before she doubled over, her breathing starting to become labored. I went to wrap my arms around her while the sounds of sirens broke out in the distance.

When the police came, it was both a blessing and a curse. We had been involved with Social Services for some time now, and my mom was indeed high on drugs that night. They took Matt away, but also found a stash in my mother's belongings that was obviously hers. Mom and I would be transported to the hospital where our case manager would be waiting for us.

I was wrapped in a blanket on the bed, waiting, when I overheard a couple of cops talking as they aimlessly sifted through the mess.

"How did she even call out? The wire is completely severed from the wall. Must have gotten the call out just in time." He shrugged and bagged the wire while I looked at the cord and the plaster fragments from the wall unit. The officer had made a keen observation. I knew my mom hadn't been able to call before Matt forcibly ended the phone's life.

I looked up at her as a paramedic treated her, and our eyes held. I didn't fully understand what I saw at first, but suddenly her eyes sparked into a wild blue blaze of fire. She was someone else entirely, and she seemed to be barely holding it together. Her body was shaking, and her face was wet from a building fever. It was almost as if sparks would start to fly off her at any moment, like mad, mistimed fireworks. She held my gaze, and I started to take deep, slow breaths. She instantly mimicked my pace and I saw the fire's intensity lessen.

Those moments went by as if time was standing still, and there were only the two of us in the room. It felt like we were touching hands, but suddenly the connection was gone. Her eyes calmed to their usual pale blue, and I watched her almost snap back to herself. Her head went limp and her blond, sweat-soaked hair, freed from its

*bondage, was stuck in odd places to her face and neck. She gave me
another look and smiled. That was when I knew her power was within
me. I was my mother's daughter, and we both had a secret.*

I love my vanity. No, see, that came out wrong. In no way do I mean
to imply that I am vain. Rather, I love the old Victorian vanity my
grandmother gave to me. The classic ivory-embossed cushioned chair
is enveloped in deep, cherry wood with a matching mirror suspended
by the most delicate beveled encasement. The cherished wood, which I
care for obsessively and often, is safe beneath its polish. Each carving
forms a plant-like pattern, with runs of vines, leaves, and petals. Very
feminine and in tune with nature, it is just like my grandmother.

How odd it is to stare at oneself every day while going through a
routine that requires such self-manipulation, patience, and careful
painting and placement. I don't consider myself beautiful. My
goodness, this gangly form was taunted and teased from grade school
to high school, and I always stood in the back row with the boys for
picture day. I didn't think my body would ever stop growing, but I
eventually stopped at a smooth 5'8½". Yep, I hang onto that half inch
with all my might.

I didn't even develop breasts or hips until the summer before my
senior year at Monument High in Colorado. I have endured what feels
like an entire lifetime of tiny boob jokes. Trust me, I've heard them all.
In middle school, I had this fabulous idea of stuffing my bra so that no
one would know how small I was. There were these snippety girls in
my school who always made fun of young, impressionable girls who
tried enhancing themselves. Of course, being well endowed already,
they couldn't possibly imagine the horror in others who couldn't even
partially justify wearing a bra.

So the trick these little snits had was to take an unsuspecting victim
into the bathroom and make her lift her bra and shirt in hopes of
watching the devastation as the remnants of well-placed wads of toilet
paper or tissue fell to the floor. It was humiliating and sadistic—kids
can be cruel after all—but it was *not* going to happen to me. I was
done being called flat as a board or crater chest. Instead of carefully
stuffing layers of soft paper between my tiny breasts and my bra, I
snipped the thread and placed the lovely accentuating tissue inside.
The girls cornered me on the second day of school. I happily lifted my

12

Padres T-shirt and when nothing came out, well, their look of absolute shock still stays with me. If only I had a patent. That was one hell of a padded bra.

Things are different for me now. I'm twenty-six, for a start, and there's nothing like the ability to wield wicked amounts of Earthen magic to boost one's self-esteem. That and the mature realization that those girls were in pain as well—most bullies are—and in a way, I felt sorry for them.

I clear my mind of the trip down memory lane, and rise from the vanity to look in the full-length mirror affixed to my bedroom wall. My onyx glass beaded earrings tip lightly against my neck as I do a spin in my new little black dress. The lovely San Diego boutique may stay in business due to my credit card and name-dropping, but this dress is worth every penny. I used to model clothes for my two designer friends when they had nothing but their dreams. Now look; I get to help market one of the hottest stores in town, not to mention watch the delight on Andrea's face as she makes a permanent name for herself in the fashion world.

They must have been in an ultra-sexy, naughty mood when they created this particular dress. The back plunges into a daringly low V, exposing my back in its entirety yet stopping just in time to keep things decent. Two thin straps hold the little number on my shoulders. See, those nearly invisible breasts finally come in handy when one actually *can't* wear a bra! The dress skims my knees, a slit creeping up the right side, exposing my leg before the fabric hugs my hip, helping me accentuate it as my still-boyish figure lacks the envied voluptuousness I will never have. I look up into the mirror after making one last adjustment to my barely there thong. My reflection startles me. Sometimes I can't get used to the change in my eye color. Tonight my normally hazel eyes beam green at me in the mirror, highlighting the freckles on my nose. My dark, long curls drape around my face, reminding me of one of those hauntingly intense characters from the *Crow* or *Underworld.* Kate Beckinsale's glowing blue eyes come to mind, and I take a deep breath before I turn away.

"Doll eyes."

The echo draws my attention back to the mirror, and I shudder.

It's just a memory, I tell myself, *and you knew that with such an act reminders would come, and come at a price.* These nightmares don't care whether it is dark or light outside; things still bump and bother in the daylight, haunting me. Although, to be honest, it's the nights alone that truly are the rub. I can try my hardest not to sleep, but sleep will come nonetheless.

But for now, work is the queen of all distractions and I am truly a ringmaster of the night. I earn a living entertaining people by showing them a level of dining, drinking, and partying that they have only dreamed of. I am the party planner, the event coordinator, the one with the know-how for those who need to be known. My friends are DJ's, dancers, cooks, designers, club owners, and club rats, with a few drunks and druggies thrown in for good measure. I love my job, and it pays well; why *wouldn't* it, with a job that takes all my weekends and fosters my innate vampire-like circadian rhythms, it's like it was made for me. Plus, it is *my* company, with trusted professionals and friends surrounding me. It's fun to get dolled up each night. On days that are solely mine, I am a true tomboy in comfy pants and a t-shirt, but when I'm running an event there are no holds barred. In this industry, it is vital to be noticed. I aim to be approachable while also making it clear that I am not a person to be toyed with, but it also depends on what the event or mood calls for, I guess.

I do a quick check around my apartment. My downtown loft is close to the Gaslamp district in downtown San Diego. I love this place, from the terra cotta tile floors to the earth-toned walls and furniture. A breakfast counter lined with a mish-mash of barstools separates my kitchen from a tiny dining area, while the rest of the downstairs feels like one big room. The open space holds a nice-sized TV with stacks and stacks of movies. Hello, my name is Alexis Conner, and I'm an addict. Movies are my escape from reality; hey, with my history, it could be a *lot* worse!

In front of the TV is a cushy brown leather couch that has been snuggled and passed out on enough times to make it comfy. Right now, Pitter is sprawled out on an ottoman in front of a matching brown leather oversized chair, draped in a chenille throw of greens, blues, and browns. There is a half-bath downstairs and a *very* small "room" that holds a futon and works well for both overnight guests and for storage. A door off the kitchen leads to a small outdoor patio, walled off and draped in lush, hot pink bougainvillea.

The upstairs portion of my apartment has a good-sized bedroom loft with a full bathroom that houses an old-fashioned clawfoot tub as well as a shower. My bedroom has always been my sanctuary, and the feeling in this one is no different. To top it all off, I actually have an upstairs balcony right off my bedroom. The building is on a hill, so if I stand on my tippy-toes, I "think" I can see the faintest glimmer of the bay. San Diego is truly different from most cities, although bad things have happened to me in the past here, I still love San Diego. This is my home.

Justin's phone calls started around 5 P.M. I wasn't in a complete rush yet, but if the calls kept coming, I would be.

"Alex, you need to consider some alternatives. This quack "shrink" is not helping you, and I'm not sure this job is either. You're always out late, and I don't know if you're sleeping at all anymore." I'm sure this is coming from a place of good intentions, but I hear it differently and immediately go on the defensive.

"You know, if you don't like it or can't stand it, then why do you keep coming around? Nobody is asking you or making you, are they?" So childish, I know. Justin just kind of stumbled into all of this, not knowing what he was getting himself into by dating me. I've been having nightmares for the last year now, but they certainly have gotten worse lately.

"Let's see, Alex," he says, with an irritating condescending tone, "last night I was just fine hanging with my friends, having a few beers, and you begged me to come out and meet you. I believe you asked *then,* and there was also last week…

"Okay, enough!" No one could ever tell me that I don't know how to cut someone off and end a fight, even if there is no substance to my end of the argument. "Fine, I *won't* call you anymore and then you won't have to deal with any of it." This is pure bona fide Alex, defiant to the end, but part of me feels that he deserves better than what I am and what I can offer. Love is hard for someone like me, and trust is even harder.

"Is that what you think I'm doing, Alex? 'Dealing' with you? I'm in love with you, you miserable, selfish, beautiful, crazy woman! I don't want to 'deal with you.' I want to help you, damn it! I want to help stop your nightmares and maybe even save myself some mental and physical battering in the process."

"When was the last time that happened? Weeks ago, maybe even a month, and I wasn't attacking *you,* I was attacking, oh, never mind!" I throw out some colorful language and stomp around the house, feeling frustrated as I hunt for the shoes I want in the same spot for the hundredth time.

"Attacking what? Who? Why won't you tell me what's going on with you, so that maybe I could help you?" Justin sounds exhausted at this point, as he always does. He can't stand fighting with me. I always wear him out and cause him more strain than an hour in the gym would. That's his version, anyway.

"Look, Justin. Ah, there you are." I snatch up my heels and slip them on. "Dr. Reynolds *is* helping me. She thinks that if I don't allow the dreams to happen, I won't get to the bottom of them. If I take the drugs, you know, that shit they keep pumping into children who are bored and adults who are even worse? I'll change. I won't be me. But hey, maybe that's what you want. Look, I gotta go."

"Alex. Alexis, listen to me." God, I love his voice. He may very well be the most real, honest person I know, and I lie to him *every day.* "All I want to do is be with you, but I don't think you will ever *really* want to be with me until what you're going through gets resolved. I'm willing to wait for that, for you."

"I know." My voice is barely a whisper as I stare at my keys, flipping and twirling them in my fingers. The radio blares Oceanlab's "Satellite" as I waver in my next comment.

"Justin, I have to go. You know I need to be there at least two hours earlier than everyone else. You know how crazy these things can be. I'm all right, I promise, and I'll be even better soon. I'll call you later, okay?"

"Okay, Alex. Be careful tonight, and please get some sleep."

"I promise," I lie. "Bye, Justin." I don't wait to hear him sign off; it already hurts enough when I can't say the words back. I take a look around my loft one last time. Pitter is snuggling on the couch now, only looking up to give me an appraising look along with his usual goodbye noises.

"See ya, rat," I say, mimicking Justin as I swoop out the door.

My back rests against the outside of my oak door as I think. I think about Justin. I think about what he says and what he means to me. My feelings for him are real, but then I remember all the ugliness and secrets I have trapped inside, and I wonder, how can he possibly love me.

CHAPTER 3

It's Just Another Party

Journal Entry:

People say the West is the best. I felt the real sting in that saying as I headed East, away from the Pacific and into landlocked territory. I felt myself sever in two that day; it was as if my soul was ripping apart. I could practically feel my toes clinging to the ocean sand even as my head and my thumping heart were being yanked away.

My heartbeat intensified as I curled my toes and gripped them tightly into the sand, but Grandmom just would not let go. No matter how much of a fit I threw, she held on tight. You would have thought she was a 300-pound beast of a man by the way she held onto me, but no matter how hard she held me, it never felt cruel. She enveloped me and tried to quiet my screams with the sweetest voice. Even though she wasn't loud, I could hear her over the crashing waves, over the sound of the diesel Winnebago starting up, and over the wind ripping through the air as I held my curl-ridden head out of the passenger window, wailing my little girl heart out.

I cried for my mother, for the part of my spirit that was being left in San Diego, for the salt air, for my ocean cliffs, and the waves my legs used to kick through so that my body could effortlessly glide atop. What would I ever have or learn to do in Colorado that I didn't already have in California? Gone were my skyscraping palm trees, endless summer days, the dreamy sounds of pounding waves, and the coarse warm sand that felt to me like down pillows. I didn't want the rivers or lakes of Colorado, and I didn't want the mountains to replace my soaring oceanside cliffs. The thought of losing all I had grown up with was nearly paralyzing.

I wanted only to be with my mom again, to stay with her by the waterside and to look into her eyes alight with beautiful blue sparks, and talk about our secret. A secret she was never able to speak about before I was taken away.

*"It's for the best," Grandmom would say. "Your mommy is sick and she needs help. She **will** get better, and you **will** be together again—one day." The song in her voice was like a warm blanket, or a hot cup of chocolate on a cold day with those yummy little marshmallows.*

*"Don't worry, my darling. All will be good again, in time. You'll see, my sweet Alexis—I will make this better. Just give me time." Grandmom's soothing voice was winning out, and my tantrums finally began to subside. My screams turned into sobs, my sobs into the tiniest of sniffles, and then my body gave in. The feeling of sand lingered, even though my toes uncurled themselves from its warmth long ago. The only world I had ever known was just, gone. I collapsed into my nine-year-old body—my **whole** body—but my soul remained torn. Half of it refused to leave its West Coast home.*

*Throughout the days of driving, I had lots of time to think; Grandmom is apparently a driving machine. We slept in campgrounds, rest stops, and the occasional parking lot. We played card games, and I learned how to play, well, okay, how to **lose** at poker. Our chips were replaced by saltwater taffy left over from her trip to the Keys. Although we spent a good deal of time talking, we never brought up Mom, and I never spoke of what I now knew. My mom and I had a power, and that scared and excited both of us. Before we were separated, she told me to tell and show **no one**. Looking at my grandmother, I wondered if she knew, but I was too afraid to find out.*

*What if she sent me away? Mom didn't talk about why she didn't see **her** mom much, but what if it was because her powers scared my grandmother? I wouldn't risk it. My grandmother pretty much kept to herself, so I should be able to stay under the radar even nestled above the Colorado National Monument in Glade Park, just outside of Grand Junction. Grandmom said there were lots of hiking trails and hidden gems near her house, so I decided to just keep my distance and work on figuring out this power thing on my own.*

That was the million-dollar question, wasn't it? What was I? Was I just like my mom? I wasn't even sure what I could do, let alone what she was capable of doing, so how could I even answer that question?

Apart from that one night, I never got to ask her anything about her abilities. Worry spiked through me as I thought through all of my favorite books and movies involving witches, elves, sorcery, magic, and the like. Did I fall into some mystical category that I had been drawn to for what used to seem like mere fun and enjoyment? Maybe a part of me felt more alive and less alone with those movies than the reality around me. Oh boy, I hoped I wasn't some crazy goblin king, like David Bowie in "Labyrinth", or the Skeksis from "The Dark Crystal" stealing essences for my own gain. No, instead I hoped that I was perhaps a good witch, the world-saving Gelfling, or maybe a fairy like Flora, Fauna, and Merryweather. I reached behind my back, patting around for wings, scales, or maybe even horns. Okay, an overactive imagination brought me way off track. So I didn't know who or what I was. That didn't mean I couldn't find out what I could do.

In the desert of Western Colorado, I found hills of red rocks to climb and to hide among. Remembering what I was able to do when I was younger, I spent days learning to pull what seemed like pure energy from the earth into my body by mere thought and will alone. The rush of power was alien at first, pushing into my body like tiny prickles of static electricity, filling my mind, and setting the hair on my body on end. Eventually, I managed to harness the wild power, controlling it in small doses. Willing it to impact the world around me, by twirling rocks in the air, yanking small weeds from the ground, and teasing water from a stream and creating small, floating droplets reflecting the light of the setting sun.

With practice, I also found a way to store some of the Earth's magic inside of me, accessing it within my own body. In time, I was able to maintain large amounts, using it on command. A few times I took too much and had to funnel it back into the earth, it caused a frightening sensation, almost like I was overheating, but I managed to control it; though, I admit, for a moment there, I was scared and wishing I wasn't alone in this.

That gift I have for observing everything around me came in handy as I practiced pulling on the energy and searching out what I couldn't see. Eventually, I could feel the movements of small creatures scurrying above ground, underground, and in the water. In time, I could find people as well, but try as I might, pinpointing my grandmother was always tricky.

It was near a beautiful waterfall and swimming hole, locals coined the "Potholes" nestled between Delta and Grand Junction that my awareness of my abilities went in a different direction. Grandmom was getting our lunch set up while I walked along the rocks, enjoying the sound of rushing and falling water. In the largest natural pool, one fed by a torrential waterfall that many people leaped into from various death-defying points, I noticed something splashing around. At first, I thought it was a fish, but I soon realized that it was a young fox frantically scrabbling in repeated attempts to climb up the steep, slick rock to safety. I could see that one leg was injured and wondered if he had fallen and hurt himself, or if something or someone had gotten to him first. Sometimes he stopped and rested against the slippery surface, but he was never able to stay there long before being swept into the current and slammed against the rocks again.

If I was going to help this little guy, I needed to make the jump into the pool below. I wasn't great with heights—hey, who is at ten?— and I wasn't exaggerating about the close proximity of the rock wall, on the other side of the tunnel-like jump into rushing water fifteen feet below. Leap too far and I'd hit the jagged rock wall on the other side; leap too short and I'd hit the jutting rocks just below me. It was a matter of specific calculations, and I feared, an element of luck. I sent my thoughts into the earth and pulled energy into my being, hoping maybe I could elevate myself if I miscalculated. I took a deep breath and jumped.

Cold water rushed up around me as I plunged into the circular pool, and I quickly scanned for the fox. My splash had startled him, and his fear made it harder for him to stay afloat. I sent a tendril of my magic toward him, and he instantly calmed. He stared into my eyes as I spoke quietly to him.

"Don't worry, little guy. I won't hurt you. I'm going to try to help you, but I need you to be still, okay?"

No, he didn't speak back, but he did let me scoop him into my arms as we swam over the last waterfall before making it to shore. He was so little, even smaller than all his splashing and carrying on made him appear at first glance. He was a strong little guy. His front left leg was obviously broken, the bone nearly snapped in half as it protruded from his coat at an odd angle. The wild look in his eyes made me realize he had been hurt for a while, and was maybe even half mad with sickness. I found a wooded area to hide in as I held him close to me, sending my energy into him partly to keep him still and partly to keep him from biting me, he was wild after all, and to see if maybe, just maybe, I could help him. His little heartbeat pounded wildly, as clearly as if I could hear it, and his breaths gradually went from rapid to calm as he

20

relaxed into my body. I opened my eyes to see the bone pulling itself together. Veins and muscles reconnected, and lastly, his skin and hair pulled tightly over what had been a wound just seconds before. His eyes opened and he looked at me thoughtfully. I placed him gently on the ground and he quickly scampered away.

Now that was something, the first something that solidified the knowledge that my power was good. I could heal. That had to be good, right? It was definitely something to hold on to while I was alone in this place, far from my mom and my San Diego home. The odd thing, as if this whole thing hadn't been odd enough, was that after that astonishing day, I found myself coming across injured, sick, or lost animals quite frequently. I chalked it up to my powers of observation, yet in the back of my mind I had the nagging feeling that these critters were somehow seeking me out, drawn to me—or maybe just to my power.

"Stop saying that! You know how I get about these things and just, just look at me. I'm a nervous wreck, and all those boys will be there. Ugh, I think I'm going to be sick."

"You're fine, Nic! You've got this. How many times have we done this type of gig? It's always beautiful, and even if something goes wrong, we'll fix it." How am I going to fix him is the issue. Nic is my lead designer, and he is having a complete conniption. What's new, I know. Watching him pace around in a strutting, peacock sort of way, while I try to avoid his flailing arms is a nightmare. Not to mention the million other requests buzzing in my ear.

"Alex?" The static breaks into my earpiece as Carmen, my event manager and business partner, comes through. "We're T-minus thirty minutes. Are things under control down there?"

"Yep. We're doing fine." I manage between my locked jaw and grinding teeth; I'm surprised I haven't chipped a tooth by now. Here I am, stuck in the ladies' bathroom with a hyperventilating gay man, and a drunk girl who is supposed to be jumping out of a cake to sing "Happy Birthday" to one of San Diego's best receivers in less than two hours. This may seem like a disaster, but I have certainly dealt with worse. Nicky continues to pace, his perfectly spiked jet-black hair looking like it might just fly off his head.

I love Nic; he's a crazy man whose parents came here from Mexico right before his birth. He is obsessively fit, and I get occasional "humphs" from him for towering over his five foot four frame, especially in my heels. Nic is always trying to set me up with random boys he sees. Actually, usually he just wants me to give one of them a try to see if the guy plays on my team or his. I'll admit, occasionally I enjoy obliging him; it's a fun distraction when we aren't tearing our hair out about an event.

"Okay, enough of this crap. We need to sober her up. Go see if she's still draped over the toilet." I watch with mental fingers crossed as Nic steps quickly to the second stall door. He takes a deep breath and enters headfirst.

"Oh no, she *didn't*… she's chuggin' an airliner in here. Where did you get that? Honey, now give that vodka to *Uncle Nicky*. Dammit girl, gimme that!" A struggle breaks out, and I see silver and red boa feathers float up over the stall. Plan C it is.

"Well, I guess I'm on then. Carmen can't find backup at this late hour, and neither of the dancers can sing. I need to get out and do one more walk through, greet our guests, and then get changed." I take a deep breath, a deep calming 'holy shit' breath. "Nic, go to my car, get my bag and, hell, grab yours too. I'm going to need an outfit. Oh, and bring in your bag of good wigs. I need to be on the down low, you know, discreet. Do you even know that word?" I swiftly pace out the door, leaving Nic slack-jawed, preparing to make a snippy comment, but I don't have time for our usual banter. What I need is that girl to get out of the bathroom and into a cab.

One of the most important things in this business is to hustle without *appearing* to hustle. After tearing out of the restroom, I slowly smooth my dress and my unruly curls before making a sweep of the set-up.

The club looks stunning. Tonic sits below the sidewalk in San Diego's famous Gaslamp Quarter. It gives off a New York vibe, but with the class and natural subtlety of La Jolla and life in a beach city. The glass top of the bar, which has a warm golden glow produced by lights under the surface, beautifully accentuates the dark wood. The front room is kicking some jazzy house beats, as the guests begin to arrive and mingle in the cozy chairs and couches that surround an elegant piano. Others choose a different view by snuggling up to the bar. It's a beautiful crowd so far. What did I expect? The main man's birthday is tonight, and all are here to impress.

22

I loop around into the back room and the mood changes. Walking through either side of the front room's main bar has you swiftly knocking through a set of swinging doors. The lighting changes and the music feels heavy, emitting a low, deep throb. The dance floor is bare for now, but the colorful lights play games on the floor, the stage, and on the two podiums that hold my dancers. The girls look good; I give them a quick nod before quickly making my way around to the DJ booth.

Danny is in the booth tonight, and he looks to be having a good time already. I just hope not *too* good a time. During our last party together I found a baggie containing two orange pills on the floor and his *"huh, where'd those come from"* look wasn't selling me. He's amazing at what he does, and loves it more than any other DJ I have known, I just have to check in with him every once in a while. I actually might have to schmooze the security guys coming in with the football team, since my usual security contingent was out. I need to make sure Danny is on the "watch but do not touch" list.

I step through the other set of double doors and the music immediately changes as I pass the main bar, entering the bright glow of the front room. After taking a walk through the middle of the room, among the chairs and by the piano, I make my way to the right and enter the alcove where the stairs lead up to the street. My greeters are up top, gradually bringing guests down in their leather *and spice, and all things not so nice* in their sexy outfits. It's not your everyday party, but this is going to be a kickass night. Sex sells, to most humans, and I kept that in mind when I drafted this proposal. When required, my imagination has no trouble taking a trip into the gutter and this birthday boy didn't seem to mind.

Spinning away from the stairway, I walk back through the alcove toward the main bar. From the bottom of the stairs, through the alcove and along both main paths leading to the bar and the back of the club, small circular amber lights shine from the floor, creating a beautiful glow for the guests to follow. On the way back to the bar, there's a small sitting area carved out, a secret little space tucked away, and darker than the rest of the front room. The nook normally has an oversized chair against the wall, but for tonight I removed it to allow space for a small table and two chairs for my psychic. The theme doesn't really call for one, but I threw one in anyway. Should be fun; plus, she's my best friend.

Sandra spots me and calls me over. Her hair is cropped platinum blond, and she's in a tight gray pinstriped skirt, a barely there white

23

skintight top that accentuates her new breasts, and a bitchin' pair of fuck-me heels. No, I'm not jealous; I swear I'm not. So she doesn't ever have to wear a bra to be perky. Who cares, right?

"What's up, sexy? You look to die for tonight. How do *I* look?" Sandra stands up and does a little twirl. She walks in heels as though they're a good pair of Pumas. Love her, she's insane, but I love her.

"So, are you going to let me read you tonight?" She smirks at me, already knowing the answer.

"I like to be surprised by life, but you already know that. Too much mystery and magic to find all on my own, plus, I wouldn't want to go around getting all worked up about nothing when you start flipping those cards telling me of imminent doom or, for goddess's sake, love awaits me. Blech." At this, her bottom lip pushes out in a pout. I've never let her read me. Partly because of my fear of what she'll find, but also because of my fear that she may already know, only holding off on breeching the subject until I am finally willing to let her do a reading. Maybe someday I will, but not now.

"Okay, I just wanted to check on ya; time for me to go upstairs. You have fun now, but not too much." I hear her laugh, and I spin off to march upstairs. My smile is on, bright and ready to throw a sweet party. It falters only for a second when static hits my ear.

"Honey, I found it! I've got just the thing. Now get your perky ass back down here ASAP."

"Thanks, Nic. Be down in two shakes. I need to be here for the grand entrance."

More limos roll in and the boys from the team start pouring out. Security comes into view, and I get a glimpse at the muscle for the night. Big guys, all in black, slide out of doors and line the walls like mist. You gotta love an entrance. The team is decked out to the nines, and I'm loving the camera flashes as our photographer snaps them all rolling in.

The birthday boy—#3 we call him—comes up to me with a grin ear to ear."Havin' fun already, Marcus? Now, don't wear yourself out. We're just getting started." He gives me a smooth nod and cruises in with an entourage of players, friends and, of course, a line of ladies.

I'm just about to hightail it down the side alley to the back door— thinking how nuts I am to be willing to jump out of a cake and hoping like hell that Nic has a good wig for me—when I catch a glimpse of movement over my shoulder. As I spin around, I come face to face with a well-built stranger whom I've never seen before. He's gorgeous, but a sensation crawls over my skin, like a tingle of electricity, both gentle and warning. A sound escapes my lips, not in the least bit smooth, rather more of a squeak. His reply is a bit subtler as the corners of his mouth turn up slightly. Now, I'm not saying I feel scared, for some reason I'm not, even though I damn well should be. Here I standing here in the dark with a man I don't know who looks like he could punch through a wall without breaking a sweat, but something about him just makes me calm.

"I'm Ryan. I'm leading the security team here tonight. You're Alex Conner, right?" He gets straight to the point, looking as if this is his usual MO, and all I can do is nod. I think I've forgotten how to blink or even breathe. Ryan reaches down and brushes my waist to tap the tiny radio clipped to my slim belt.

"We're on channel five. Let me know if you need anything." And then he vanishes, blending his fine body in with the night.

"Shit, shit, shit," I curse as I barrel into the woman's bathroom, nearly killing Nic as I haul ass into the back stall. Nic follows me in, looking eager with a wicked smile on his face.

"Now, I hope no one needs this stall cause this may take a while. What are you waiting for, girl? Take your clothes off. Wait a minute. What is that look? Where is he? He must have been fine, because you are glistening."

He was fine, over six feet of pure muscle, but not overly so. Hard everywhere, and decked out in all black from head to toe. His skin looked like it had been dipped in a mix of cinnamon and mocha, but I couldn't place his heritage. Latino, or maybe from some remote tropical heaven, or, goddess I don't care, he was gorgeous and terrifying—don't forget terrifying. He was like a taciturn, dark-eyed stone God, but the air around him seemed to crackle with a promise of squashing anything or anyone who causes trouble tonight; and those hands and lips.

"Damn it. Why is it so hot in here?" I am pulling my clothes off and putting the barely there clothes on, rambling about dark eyes, skin, and almost peeing myself.

"Alex, girl, he sounds fine! I think I need to go check him out myself. I might be more his type anyhow." He turns to leave, but I grab him by the neck of his shirt.

"No way! We need to camouflage me. You know, make me look different. Make-up and hair, please. Now!"

Okay, in times of panic I wish I had a surefire crisis cure. Some girls eat candy, cake, or cookie dough. I would prefer a drink; hell, even a shot would work, but I don't have time for that, and watching *little Miss Thing* in the bathroom floor makes even a sip less appealing than it would have been an hour ago. Later, yes, after this, I'll curl my fingers around a nice cold vodka drink in a dark corner somewhere away from this madness. Nic gives me tea. Ugh, I could go for my grandmother's whiskey, honey, and lemon concoction over this drab drink. Next, he places a cordless mic in my hand. I do some warming up and try my best not to panic. I throw in a few "why me" sobs and take deep breaths for the next ten minutes.

Crazy thoughts start swarming around in my head. *I mean, so what if there is no singing girl jumping out of a cake. What girl? Was there supposed to be a singing cake girl? Huh? I don't remember that. Who came up with that dumb idea?* Earth to Alex, it was *your* bright idea! Stupid, stupid, stupid! Okay, breathe, you can do this, and no one will even recognize you. It's time to get into the act. When you run your own company, you've got to be ready to do nearly anything to make things run smoothly, so get some courage dammit!

This outfit is unreal and way too tight! The long, straight, blond wig with blunt-cut bangs and blue contacts are fine, but it's the tight black leather bustier with matching little spank-me shorts that have me shooting death glares at a giggling Nic. I take one quick look in the mirror and freeze. My mother stares back at me in the reflection. I know we look a little alike, but this is unnerving. I have her high cheekbones and the same sprinkle of freckles across the bridge of my nose, but it's the hair color and eyes that are startling. My head starts to swim and an intense warmth causes beads of sweat to break out on my forehead. I think vertigo has settled in, but I don't have time for it to stick around. Nic's voice breaks through, and I tear myself away from the mirage staring back at me.

"Okay girl, you're almost on. Time to get in the cake, and I need the boys to help me wheel you out. So let's get you in now, and I'll call them over." After hustling to the back stage, Nic does some maneuvering and helps me into the cake, slamming the top down on me.

"Shit, sorry Alex. What channel again? Five? That's right, three for us on the DL and five for the rest of 'em." I hear Nic's radio static and I know my time has almost come. "Hey, any boys there? I need some help backstage. It's cake time!"

Thunderous steps signal their arrival, and I feel the cake start to roll. Danny's music starts while I continue to remove the image of my mother from my mind. The feelings keep swirling inside me and I start at the power that I rarely use around other people unfurling from my being—sparked to life by memories of my mother in the reflecting glass. Just a little can't hurt. Focusing on the energy stored within me, I use it to create just a bit more camouflage from my everyday appearance, and then *Bam!* I'm out. I don't see a single face in the room at first, but I begin to sing all the same. Suddenly, I hear a crackle in my ear.

"To the left, he's on the left, you're looking in the wrong-ass direction!" God, this is humiliating. "Hey girl, that doesn't even look a lick like you. Am I good or am I good?!"

I step out of the cake and lower my gaze onto Marcus, the lucky birthday boy. Yep, he's had more than a few drinks. I only hope that his dazed look means he won't recognize me. My magic soars through me, making my features flutter and shift so that I never look quite the same. I'm like a desert snake in the shifting sands, there one minute and gone the next. Now, a little dance here, there, and the song is almost over. I ease down to sit on Marcus's lap, giving him a light touch on his face. Almost done. I sing the final "TO YOU!" give Marcus a smooch on the cheek, and hustle my ass back stage.

I feel an invisible tug as I fly through the curtain. Looking to my left, I see Ryan; well, part of him at least. His back is against the wall, the rest of him nearly melting into the darkness. He's looking out through the side curtain with his arms crossed in front of him, my breath catches when I see a glint in his eyes, as he looks my way. Ryan holds my gaze for two long, deep breaths before giving me a slight smile.

"Hee, hee, that was great!" exclaims Nic as he comes running up, spinning me around. I look over my shoulder, to find an empty space. He's like smoke, sexy-ass smoke.

Nic briskly ushers me into the back office and I let the magic wash off me while trying to extinguish the fire in my eyes. I know they're blazing green fire, and even though no one else can see it, the energy charging the air in this small space will make him uneasy.

"We got kicked out of the bathroom, so here we are." I do a quick change and look at myself in Nic's hand mirror.

"Cool. I'm *sooo* glad that's over. Move the channel back to five and let's see what's going on out there." Only Nic and I were on channel three; well, maybe Ryan was too.

The party goes right along and the crowd has a blast. I stay in the back, hiding in the shadows, sipping my cucumber-infused martini while the event unfolds around me. I'm ready if I am needed, but my crew is damn good, so things go off smoothly without me having to lift an extra finger, having done most of my work on the front end, well if you don't count the cake incident. Most people hate working late hours. I honestly don't really wake up till about five or six P.M., so this two A.M. stuff is great for me. True, I can't do it *every day*. A girl has to be able to enjoy the beach and not sleeping face down, working on a burn instead of a tan. I take another sip, before I notice Nic heading and hiccupping in my direction.

"I can't find this mystery man of yours. Are you sure you saw him? None of his boys will talk to me—so serious and not very friendly—hot, though. Hahaha."

I agree with Nic. I'm no longer sure if I had seen Ryan for real, either. The man is a ghost; I haven't put eyes on him since the song of humiliation.

Things wind down and I make sure the guest of honor is carried out unscathed to his limo.

"Best birthday ever! Alex, you rock. Oh, and tell the cake girl to call me!" Geez, I'll make sure to do that.

Catering is nearly broken down, and Danny is thumbing his albums back into some sort of sensible order that I'd never understand. I say goodbye to Nic and walk out with Sandra. The valet brings her car first, so I give her a hug goodbye.

"I'm reading you soon, girlie. You'll be so much more aware of what's going on in your life if I do. Something's happening with you, and I just *know* I can help. Don't you want to get rid of your nightmares? Don't you trust me?" One of the ball players comes up behind her and gives her a little tap on the butt.

"Oh, he's coming too. Thanks, the party was great. Always is with you, Alex." She gives me a wink and slides into the driver's seat.

My car pulls up next, so I pop the trunk and load my essential event bags of mystery. As I move to close the trunk, I feel a tingle of a presence in my awareness, like a warning buzz before a static shock. The perception stills me, and soon after I feel heat on the back of my neck.

"Hey, party girl. Are we done partying?" I spin around and find myself face to chest with a gorilla of a man with no neck, no hair, and no idea of what is what.

"Ah, nice to see you. I'm so glad you enjoyed the party, but it's time for me to head home." Trying not to tremble, I move away from the trunk and reach for my car door, but his big hands around my waist stop me. I'd seen him with the group, and recognize him as one of the players. He comes in close and I dig into my purse. I have pepper spray in there, and I'm not afraid to use it. I come out swinging with it, but he catches my wrist before I can hit the trigger.

"What the hell?" He growls. His next move is too quick for me as he gives me a ferocious smack across the face, knocking me ferociously to the ground.

"Now, that's not a nice party girl. What's the matter? You get all sexed up and now you don't want to share? Come on, let's get back up and start this over."

He reaches for me, but then I see him seize up. His eyes roll around a bit before he falls in a heap beside me on the ground. I struggle to breathe and an uncontrollable shaking takes over my body. Just then, a pair of warm, firm hands grabs me, lifting me up gently. My vision is blurred, but I barely make out deep, dark eyes. My fingers slide along my face and come away slick and warm.

"I think there's blood," I mumble. Then the world spins and everything goes black.

CHAPTER 4

"Lex"

When my eyes start to open, I realize that I don't know where I am or how I got here. I try to focus and stare up at, well, my ceiling. I am in my loft. Am I alone? What the hell? What happened? My fingers creep to my face. Ow, my chin, no wait, my entire face freakin' hurts. I groan like a pissed-off lion whose sunny spot disappeared and roll my ass out of bed. My throat is dry, and I can smell something yummy downstairs. Ah ha! Justin must have come over. My feet hit the floor and I freeze. Wait, how did I get home?

Quietly, I creep down the stairs. I catch a glimpse of an arm, and I jump back. Not Justin, definitely not Justin. Get a grip! I do a quick body check; I have on my underwear and a big t-shirt. Oh man, I don't remember putting this on! Okay, don't panic. I'm not sure how or what happened, but I need to stay calm. Everything is going to be okay. Peeking around the corner I nearly scream when Ryan moves into focus.

"How are you feeling?" He asks so matter of factly I think, hell, I'm not entirely sure how I feel. A strange man is in my apartment; he had obviously brought me home, and clearly I had been half naked at one time or another. Shit, did I drink too much? Is that even possible? Nope, that's right, no I remember the big ape guy.

"Hey, what happened to that guy?" Ryan looks over at me, and I nearly faint again. He has deep radiating eyes; no, not radiating, piercing eyes that send warm heat laced tendrils all over my body.

"Don't worry about him. He won't be bothering you anymore." Once again he speaks in a straightforward tone like he knows me, or is giving me an order. I'm not sure which one it is, but it's different, and kind of a turn on.

"Um, okay, so what exactly happened or would you have to kill me if you told me?" What the hell? Am I being playful, flirting with this guy? I don't even know him, but somehow he makes me feel safe, like I already know him. Dangerous yes, but not directly toward me.

"I taught him a lesson with my Taser. You fainted after taking quite a hit, so I brought you home, got you cleaned up and into bed. I slept downstairs with your furry friend here." He shoots Pitter a look, and I swear that little sneak starts to purr on cue. "Want some food?"

"So...when you say 'got me into bed,' how did that go exactly?" Dirty thoughts have taken over my mind. I can't help it, he's gorgeous and he came to my rescue like a knight in shining armor. Hell, I owe him dirty thoughts, don't I?

"I slipped a shirt over you, so there was no looking and only necessary touching." Matter of fact and to the point. Guess there's no rattling him. Should I be insulted?

I sashay closer to him and grab some toast and fruit; the bacon and eggs cooking are next and my stomach growls in anticipation. After taking a seat at the counter, I watch him work in the kitchen. He still has on his black shirt and black pants from last night, but now he's wearing some scruffy, little black facial hairs beginning their five o'clock shadow. I long to trail my fingers along his milky brown skin and he looks like if he did sleep, it was sitting straight up. He doesn't look tired, he looks perfect. Hair, nearly pitch black with only a hint of brown, is slicked back. Yet, it looks soft and warm and, oh God, am I drooling? Get it together Alex! You don't drool over men. I snap out of it as he sets a steaming plate in front me.

"Well, I gotta go. Let me know if you need anything." Wait, he's leaving? Just like that? "Here's my card. I'm sure we'll be seeing quite a bit of each other as I'm now leading the main security teams for special events downtown most nights." He passes the card to me, and our eyes lock. I feel myself flush, and his set mouth turns into a grin. What seems like seconds pass and I stay frozen while he walks away.

"Are you sure no touching?" I call out, breaking the spell. This puts a crack in his cool demeanor, and he gives a little bark of a laugh and a sly smile. I think he already gave me the answer to that question.

"See ya, Lex. Nice party, and oh, nice song by the way." He says, slipping out my front door.

What in the world just happened? I had this amazing guy save me last night, bring me home, clean me up, and not try anything naughty with me. Damn, I wanted him to try something. Bad, bad, Alex! And then it hits me. I slept through the night. No bad dreams, no voices, I was safe, and for some reason Ryan felt like a big part of that.

It takes me a second to realize a few things.

Number one, I ran down here in a t-shirt and undies and never even looked in the mirror. Number two, my face is aching, and a loud "oh" escapes my lips when I barely touch my chin with my finger. I have never broken a bone, but my face seems to always get in the way of things. Poolsides, roadways, corners of walls, and now apparently it has taken a licking from monkey man hands. Son of a bitch!

Oh, and number three, did Ryan say song? Damn, he did know, and now I'm not so sure it was because my radio channel got hacked. Yep, something is definitely up with this guy. I just don't know what, yet.

I head to my downstairs bathroom and shudder at the look of things. My jaw is swollen and my right cheek is dark purple. But what I see next is even worse. My hair is stuck to the left side of my face, and it feels sweaty and nappy in all the wrong places. Shit! I had a gorgeous man in my house, a man who apparently saved me in one way or another, and I look like Medusa after Perseus—in his sexy *Clash of the Titans* outfit by the way—bitch slapped her before he cut her damn head off. Okay, so I have an overactive imagination as well. Another one of the "Alex curses." Saying the word "curses" in my mind triggers a chill that causes me to shiver.

How embarrassing is this? Okay, Alex get a grip. Why do you care about what a man you barely know thinks about your appearance after all that happened? I mean, he saw you last night, and you threw a killer party. He can overlook this, right? Perhaps I could do my own brand of healing and try to clean myself up. No, I won't use my power right now, especially since it felt like Ryan could sense something about me, and I'm not going to test that theory. Plus, the smell of the bacon is making my stomach growl and I've learned not to ignore my appetite.

Just as I am about to appease my hunger, my cell phone rings, making my heart jump a little. I grab it and see Justin's name flashing on the mini screen. Best not dive into this talk just yet. Half of me wants to cry to him and tell him what happened, but the sane half knows if I tell him, his reaction won't be good. He'll go silent and then the hot-blooded Italian protectiveness will kick in. Not what I want to deal with right now. I need some Advil, ice, and perhaps a nice Bloody Mary rimmed with lemon salt. I pick up the phone again and see five missed calls. There were three from Justin, one from Sandra, and one from my therapist. The latter is most likely my reminder for our session on Monday. Does anyone else get these calls on a Sunday? Most likely it's her answering service, but still, you would think I was crazy or something. "Alexis, this is Dr. Reynolds' office. This is to remind you..." Goodness, of course I remember my own damn appointments!

I feel like taking a nap, but I'm too afraid. Ryan has gone now and perhaps it was just a fluke, I don't want to have another nightmare. He may have saved me from gorilla man, but I don't think he will be coming to my rescue in the middle of a fitful dream. It is nearly 11:00 A.M. and I need to get some fresh air and a walk along the beach. Sandra may want to meet up. Maybe we can get some yummy Chinese noodles, perhaps even that Bloody Mary, and a stroll along the boardwalk. Although, I'll have to do something about this awful bruise, and I don't think my big shades will cut it.

Journal Entry:

Colorado was nothing like I expected. My feelings of being trapped and stolen away slowly began to fade, but never completely because a part of me stayed far away in the Pacific Coast breeze.

The thing about Colorado is that it's not all about mountains, snowboarding, and snow. We were in the desert; I mean cactus, sage, and actual fucking tumbleweeds that I had to pull out of our gravel driveway with all my might, desert.

Believe it or not, it was one of those damn tumbleweeds that brought the conversation about my powers to light. I was playing around in some of the neighborhood's new builds with Bear. Bear was one hell of a black lab, sled dog mix—over one hundred pounds at only a year old—so entirely befitting of his name. That day, I spotted one of the biggest beasts of a weed I had ever seen. I had reached my limit with those damn things, and I began to beat it down with a stick and insults. When I tossed the stick down and moved my hands toward the ground, splaying my fingers as far as I could stretch them and screaming that I hated this damn devil weed of the desert, the faintest whisper of an electrical tingle traveled up my right arm. Bear stopped in his tracks and his beautiful brown eyes stared at me, his head tilting toward me in questioning. Without a thought, I threw my hand toward the tenacious tumbleweed, and instantly I could feel my power curling around the bush, at first almost caressing it in loving tendrils. Then the power started to grow and tighten, lifting the plant as easily as I would lift a pebble. It twirled frantically in the air and vanished. Afterward, there was nothing, not a sound, not a rustle of wind, not a song from a bird. The desert is known for being quiet, but not this quiet.

"Well, there's no question now, is there?" the voice behind me asked as I whirled around to face the source of the query, my grandmother. I was instantly ashamed, and afraid this would be the thing that would separate us, that this type of behavior would tear me away from her as it tore me away from my mother. Instead, she walked over and embraced me while talking softly.

"I wondered when you would come into your powers. You know what, dear? Twelve years old is the right age to realize and begin using your talent, so let's go; there's much to do!" She laughed so softly that I barely noticed, but I did see something right then in her eyes—she was proud, but also scared.

"I guess we both have some explaining to do, don't we?" Her eyes crinkled with the warmth I had grown to expect and acknowledge as evidence of her love for me, but at that moment I was experiencing more betrayal than love.

My body began to tremble while I fought my tears back in my building anger. She knew my deepest and darkest secret; she had always known about the abilities hidden within me, but never even hinted that she had known. All the loneliness and fear of her finding out could have been avoided, but she hid the truth from me, keeping me locked inside myself. Instead of finding reassurance and understanding over the years, here she was trying to give it to me now.

All those years were wasted, as I kept myself from telling her, from telling anyone, and barely accepting myself for what I could do. Years of not knowing who or what I was, and there she was, in front of me, laughing like I had just shown her I could do a back flip. I had to keep the heat from rising inside of me, by moving the intense flow of energy that tried to rush into my body back into the deeper parts of the earth. I had to keep myself in check; I still didn't know what I was capable of doing and I would never forget my mother's face full of fear long ago There had to be a reason for her distress; my mother wasn't easily rattled so I would heed her warning even then. My grandmother must have had her reasons, and without a doubt I knew she loved me, so I

34

breathed in deeply, exhaling and pushing the unbridled energy called by my sadness away. I let my anger go.

"You are like me, my darling, like your mother, but you just know that I will do better. I'll guide you and make you strong enough to handle your abilities. Your power can do such wonderful things; it can save lives, and it can help the earth. Don't worry, I will help you." She had tears in her eyes of regret, hope, fear—it was all there.

"She told me never to do it again. I thought she was disappointed in me, scared of me... My voice was a whisper, but it held great strength, and my grandmother didn't falter as she took my face in her hands.

"Your mother knew? My goodness, child! How long have you been able to use your power? There was no way she was afraid of you, sweet Alex. She was scared you'd be like her, unable to manage your magic, unwilling to work and practice to keep it under control. That, my sweetheart, is the reason she began taking pills. Drugs were the only way she could keep her gift suppressed, away from others and herself. She made a few mistakes when she was young, not as young as you are now, but she was too frightened to try to harness and handle her abilities. She thought numbing herself was the only way she could. She became so lost to me so quickly, that I could never reach her. I could never get her back. I'm sorry for that, Alexis, I really am." Her eyes cast away from me, seeming to search into a distant memory instead.

"Do you even know where she is now? You said that she left treatment but have you heard anything?" I asked.

"No... This time her entire body turned from me as she stared at the red rocks of the distant range. "We have work to do, my darling. So, let's see what you've got."

Grandmom was shocked to hear that I had started noticing and using my power when I was only five, although I did hide it from my mom, until she caught me that one time in the hotel by the ocean. Apparently, no one had ever been known to tap into the earth's power that young. She called the force I harnessed into my being, Earthen energy, coming directly from our earth's goddess, Gaia. It was the power of gods and goddesses balancing the acts of good and evil since time began. Some called it magic, power, or mysticism—it had many names. Though humans who have gotten wind of us coined us witches, we also had very different names. Many of us were "Earthen Protectors" and some of us "Earthen Healers," yet, surprise, surprise, my weirdness continued as I appeared to be both. I was considered

35

"lucky" because only those deeply entwined with the earth, could draw out the energy and use it to manipulate the world around us. My observational skills apparently enabled me to root out even the smallest traces of energy to pull from land and water. Grandmom didn't say anyone could pull Earthen energy from the air, but there was always water and dirt in the air, so I wondered if it could be done. She didn't say much on the subject, but her silence was deafening. A chill passed through me just thinking about that level of power.

On the flip, or evil side, their protectors appeared to be normal human beings just as we were. I'd imagined the sorts of evil horned creatures, demons, vampires, and half human–half animal beings that had always freaked me out in books and movies. But no, they got to hide in plain sight just like we did. For longer than my grandmother could remember, they had been trying to rid the world of mankind so they could take over and run the earth the way they saw fit. They were fueled by hate at the way humans had been "destroying the earth." If you called their ideas of enslavement, superior race wars, and genocide a form of protecting then count me out! The whole thing didn't make much sense to me. I mean, we considered ourselves part of humankind; we just happened to have supernatural abilities. Didn't it make sense that we were all connected? Didn't we need all sorts of people to make this world a better place? Grandmom never said they were the smartest lot. I guess powerful and conniving didn't equal intelligence.

They called themselves the Absolute Protectors, although Grandmom preferred the name Dark Protectors, and if we weren't with them, we were their enemy. Some of them were born into those beliefs while others were persuaded to leave our side for one reason or another. Many found the lure of limitless power, and the methods they use to obtain it, more appealing. Their side learned how to steal Earthen energy, or force from others, some even taking it from their own families and loved ones, to increase their own power. She felt that may be where the vampire lore came from, but she wasn't so certain that the traditional bloodthirsty ones didn't exist. Oh, and the last tidbit she shared with me was that they had their own healers too— best to have a good doctor when at war.

My little fox trick wasn't the proof I needed after all. I could still be a danger and capable of evil like the Absolute Protectors, even with my ability to heal. Yet, my grandmother was the proof I needed. She knew I was good. We came from a long line of Earthen Protectors, and

I could only guess some Earthen Healer had to have popped into the gene pool somewhere along the way.

"My dad?" I asked her. No one knew a lot about who he was, or if they did, they weren't telling me anything. Mom said he died in a car accident shortly after I was born. I was never even shown a picture of him and my grandmother wasn't giving me any answers. All she did was shrug "perhaps" and that was all that passed her lips on that subject. I'd never heard much from my mom or grandmother about my father and she was not about to start talking then.

My grandmother kept the surprises coming, when she told me my real name was Eila, but that soon became my middle name, which of course, I'd been told I didn't have. Apparently Mom felt a name that meant "the Earth" was a target for the Absolute Protectors. Grandmom liked to call them the spawn of Demons, but I wasn't sure if she was being literal in her use of the word "Demon" or if she just meant they were truly evil. She explained that Demons were indeed real, a tricky lot that few had ever spoken to or seen. I liked to use my Darth Vader voice to play as if they were calling the good protectors of the world to the Dark Side, and then gave the big reveal of their parentage. "No, I am your father." The humor didn't seem to translate for her; in fact, she actually preferred not to speak of Demons at all.

It was obvious from her stories about the Absolute Protectors that they were nearly impossible to kill. That meant I had to learn how to remove objects from our world and send them away to alternate places, dimensions you might say, so they couldn't return, unless by my own hand. Both sides used this method to rid each other of their most powerful warriors. When ours had come back from those places, there hadn't been any good tales of their experience. Some relayed feeling like a spirit walking this world, but unable to interact with anyone, which led to intense loneliness and suffering. Others saw only darkness and heard only the sounds of a grating howling wind. The ones who came back in the worst condition, spoke of Demons and tragic lands of torture and pain. I couldn't understand how anywhere else existed besides our realm where good dwelled, but it was obvious that there were many things I didn't know. One thing was for sure; I was not interested in finding out.

My devil tumbleweed had been the first to suffer that fate at my hand, and I was happy to see it go. It seemed easy enough, although it was a bit draining and sometimes painful to move even a small stone. Thank goddess I could use my healing ability in small doses to recover, though it never worked as quickly or as well on myself. I guess that made sense since it took energy to create energy. Something Grandmom reminded me often, when I overdid it and barely had enough in me to lift a twig let alone protect us.

Grandmom kept me on my toes, training me quickly, "trying to make up for lost time" she'd say. It took me a long while before I felt completely in control and comfortable, even when she caught me off guard. She'd sneak up on me, trying to get into my subconscious while I was sleeping. There were a few times I knew of, when she hopped me up on Benadryl or cough syrup to test me and to make sure I wouldn't slip up. She warned me that anything could happen if I were ever injured or unconscious. I would always need to be able to protect myself, and, most importantly, our secret. So I always kept reserved power inside me, and to hold it hidden in case I ever needed it. Harder still was controlling it even when I wasn't fully aware. I understood her concern, and I berated myself for not thinking of all of that sooner. Who knew what could have happened to me before. Grandmom reminded me almost daily that guilt and regrets would only keep a person from moving forward into happiness and contentment. She always knew the perfect things to say.

I remember she smiled and wept when she first saw the emerald glow of my eyes while using my power, something only those of our heritage could see. Her mother had been one of the very few to have that vibrant color, something that had skipped multiple generations. Before her, nobody had seen that green in nearly fifty years. Her mother died young; she had lost her life in the war. Grandmom didn't elaborate, I didn't ask, and we left it at that.

Things became pretty wonderful after that day. I wasn't alone anymore, and I learned more and more each day.

CHAPTER 5

Law Street and Noodles

Journal Entry:

Today I came back to the house, her house, but it's different in here now—empty and alone. My black Mary Jane shoes hit the floor and echoed throughout the bare entryway of what used to be the home I thought I would live in forever. I'm barely out of the eighth grade, and I have to leave because my assigned caseworker from Child Protective Services is waiting for me outside. I was shocked she even allowed me some time alone. I hadn't even been able to stay after school for basketball. What a joke! After only a year since I learned to harness and nurture my powers, when I finally had someone to guide me, the cancer took her and she was gone.

Entering her room assaulted me with sights, smells, and memories of her—her voice, her hair, the rustling of her dress as she walked by. I started to look through the drawers in her room. My hand tingled as it touched the bedside table. Curious, I looked more intently. In the back of the table, I felt a hollowness that didn't hit the wall for a matter of inches. It had a good amount of space.

Hidden in that space, I found letters addressed to me from my mom. Not many, but each one was stuffed with different confetti-like substances and opened like a party, in their own style, and in their own way. There were shiny pastel cupcakes to deep black sparkling bats—a spectacle of color inside. I stared, slack-jawed; I read each and every one of the letters, and then I read them again. A tingling feeling brought me back to the drawer, where attached to the top, I found an envelope with a two-page back-to-back college-ruled letter.

Dearest Alexis:

You're probably at the age where you don't like Alexis anymore. You go by Alex now, don't you? Oh, don't be so surprised; I've known you since birth. I've known you longer than anyone else in your entire life, Alex. I can only hope that you don't hate me as much as I fear you do, or should.

I was always afraid you knew the truth about me using drugs to hide our abilities, or about the awful mistakes I made, but I knew no matter what, I didn't want to be the one to tell you. I figured you not knowing was better than you knowing. Instead, you would believe I was weak—a druggie who couldn't show love to her child. What a shocking tale, so cliché, white trash, and typical. It would keep the public away, and that is all I ever wanted.

There are really two sides to this story. One your grandmother knows, and feels intimately each and every day of her life, just as much as I feel for you. My power was too strong for me, and I couldn't control it, this is true. However, what made me unable to control the Earthen force inside of me were the constant attacks and threats on our lives. When I say our lives, I mean you and me—actually mainly you. You are the purest power in our family for over ten generations. You have a true, angelic, natural control over the world around you. Most like us, have to learn to harness their energy and power. It takes many a great deal of time, sometimes ten to twenty years to reach anywhere near your level. You would be admired, revered, and sought after. Good and Evil truly exist, Alexis, I'm sure you know that by now.

I concluded that the only way to keep you safe was to make it seem as if you meant nothing to me, meaning you were nothing special. So I decided to risk myself by becoming the one thing I never wanted to be—an addict. It wouldn't have been believable if it weren't true, so I gave myself over to the one thing I had seen lay waste so many lives. My first order of business was to ease myself in, so I abused the soft drugs first. Mostly I smoked pot and a little opium and drinks—lots of beer and liquor. By way of those drunken late night evenings I met the true ballers; the tweekers, rollers, and trippers which led

40

me to the many straight up wastes of the earth. They were all like me in some ways. Trying to escape or enhance some part of their lives. Most were pretty smart and dipped in and out. I, however, made myself find some quiet quicksand to lose myself in, dragging you in there with me, giving us the camouflage we needed. I love you that much, Alex.

I bet you're strong. I bet you're powerful, and I hope you hate me, because if not, I didn't do my job and neither you nor I would be alive to read this letter right now.

I am so sorry, sweet pea. I think the world of you. You inspired me the day you were born. You were so curious, radiant, and happy. At many times you were quietly still in all the chaos. You would sit for hours, taking in everything around you. It was as if you saw every movement and understood every shadow; always the explorer, with an independent and wild side. Be true to yourself. Believe in yourself and take the power as your own. I love you, always remember that. Don't be angry and sad now. Be happy. Be content. You, my mother, your grandmother, we're all connected now. Be strong.

Love,
Mom

I was floored, and started to shake with both fear and a tinge of happiness. "Thank you...." I whispered to my grandmother and then walked out of her room for the last time. I would never shake the guilt of not knowing in time, of not having done something, for not having used my skill to save my grandmother. Instead, I felt I had forever—I failed her.

An hour later, I'm tossing food into Pitter's dish and running him some filtered water. I have my keys in one hand, my purse in the other, my hair is tucked in a low-set hat, and I'm sporting some really big shades. The make-up, cover-up scheme didn't go so well, so this is going to have to cut it. Here's to hoping I don't run into anyone I know, well, aside from Sandra, obviously.

I pick her up outside her house and we head off to Law Street.

"What the hell happened to you? I leave you outside for two minutes and you what, you throw your face into a brick wall? I mean, I know you're clumsy, but this is ridiculous! You're lucky we don't have a gig till Wednesday because you need some serious ice."

I want to tell her that I could be healed later tonight if I put my mind to it, but I'm not ready to go there yet. Instead, I tell her the story, tip-toeing around the Ryan part, but she catches me easily. We climb out of the car, dodging some skateboarders with their skim boards, and she gives me the patented Sandra stare. This is one serious look that brave souls try to resist, but mostly fail. For me, I bust up laughing because I can't keep a damn thing from her, so I spill the dirt.

"You didn't sleep with him, did you? I mean *I* may have, but *you* wouldn't. Wait, did you?" Her face is so bright and hopeful that I wish I had more dirt for her. "And 'Lex,' now that is sexy! How come I never thought of that? You go, girl; that's hot! You should get some business cards made." Somewhere inside me I want only Ryan to call me Lex—from his lips it just felt right.

"No! Geez, the only sleeping I did was by myself, in a heap, alone, on my bed. He slept downstairs. Thanks for asking me if I'm all right though!" I cross my arms in a mock pout as we keep walking.

"Well, you know I'm used to you bruising yourself up one way or another, but now meeting a guy like Ryan, this shit is interesting." I don't have the faintest idea what she is talking about. The lost in thought moment goes south when I stub my toe on a crack in the boardwalk, curse to myself, and then direct my fury at my damn flip-flop.

"I don't get it." I can see Sandra is getting a kick out of this, and I've heard it all before.

"You're like a cat on the prowl at work. I mean you're a silent ninja with super stealth and class. Now, when we get you out of there, you're a wreck, running into men's fists and tripping all over yourself. You're a mess. Love you, but don't screw up my image. I have people who know me all over this place, and I can't have them thinking my girl's a klutz. Get it together or I'm leaving you here!"

"But I drove!" No sympathy for the wounded.

"Well yeah, but I bet I could get home faster walking than with you. You'd probably knock yourself unconscious opening the door or something. Maybe I should drive us home." She snickers at my frown deepening with her teasing jabs.

"Real funny! You know you aren't driving my baby; you're hell on cars. I've seen you jump curbs in yours. You think your little coupe is an SUV, well news flash, it's not, you know."

Thank God for small favors as the street heading to the Asian noodle shop comes up, and we are both too driven by yummy goodies in cardboard wrapping to continue the banter. We head into the restaurant, grab some noodles, steamed veggies and little shrimp dumplings, and take a bench overlooking the ocean. It is a gorgeous day. The beach is packed, and the waves are the chorus to our lunch.

"So, about that reading? I know you're ready. What do you say? You, me, candles, tarot cards, and incense, how about it?" Sandra's hopeful smile is contagious even though her question worries me as always.

When it comes to Sandra, you have to know some background. I met her six years ago when we both worked at another production company, Seaside Events. I was hired for all sorts of odd jobs before becoming a sales and design associate. Some jobs were in the entertainment division and some on the production side. Sandra was fully on the entertainment side. She is a 5'4" blond bombshell from San Diego, with a heart-shaped face, big blue eyes, and a deep dimple on her left cheek. Most days she wears 4-inch heels the way most of us wear sneakers.

Sandra married young, at twenty-two, and was divorced two years later. The man was a wanderer and unfortunately, he and the couple that he was with didn't wander out of their shared bed before she came home early from a canceled gig. Hell hath no fury like a woman scorned. The house was emptied of all his possessions and memories in no time. Anything belonging to that oozing ball of slime was tossed out before he could say "what the fuck?" She used to play lacrosse, so she had fun flipping his expensive watches and other trophy shit out the window with her stick. He didn't dare come at her since she played defense and knew how to use her stick as if it was an extra goddess-given appendage. She hired a hot shot attorney, got half the slime ball's money, and bought some brand new, perfect boobs. The rest of the money she has in a portfolio some financial guy is investing for her. He's invested in her as well, but it's nothing serious. They mess around once in a while, but I don't know if Sandra will ever be in a committed relationship, let alone marry again.

She's a smart cookie, and one of my best friends. I feel there's more to her than meets the eye, but I haven't been able to put my finger on it yet. It may have something to do with her parlor trick readings. She says they're just for fun, but her insistence on reading me seems to be led by a desire to truly wanting to help. Maybe there is something to it, and maybe she can help me.

43

I slurp up some noodles and give her a sly grin. "Ouch, that hurt."

"Yeah, you better not move too much there, purple face, you might break something." She puts her arm around me and gives me a hug.

"I'm glad you're okay," she says, looking straight into my eyes. "You are okay, right?"

"Yeah, I'm okay." Trying to give her a smile, a trigger of pain shoots through me causing me to give her an ugly wincing smile.

We sit back, done with our food and enjoying the view. San Diego feels like heaven at times like these. My sleeping time is the only time it feels like hell. We watch surfers of all ages capture waves, hoping for a glance of a playful dolphin leaping alongside them. I have heard mixed reviews about this phenomenon from surf-riding friends. Some find it exhilarating and enlightening, while others, well, they freak the hell out!

"You got his number, right?" Sandra says breaking the silence. "I mean the boy is fine, and you better not let that one go. Knight in shining armor and all that." Her eyes cut to mine, with an eyebrow raised. I try to copy her, but I just can't manage control over that talent. "Tell me you got his number."

I have his card. I almost forgot since he slipped out of my house as quickly as he had into my life. Ryan is an impressive example of the male species—dark, scary, and sexy all in one tight package. *Yum*! Part of me wants to see him again, but another part of me doesn't. Guess it's fate's move. I shove my hand into my purse and produce his business card for Sandra.

"Ah! Damn, you did get it! See, that's the smooth, cat-like shit I'm talking about." She gives me a friendly shove, followed by a regretful smirk knowing it sent a sliver of pain rattling from my face. "Sorry. Well, since you don't have any juicy details, let me tell you about my night. The boy was big I tell you and not just in certain places either . . . uh, uh in the right places." I set a permanent smile on my face, gave a small whimper of pain from the effort, and laugh as listen to Sandra's tale, all other worries slip away, lost in hushed tones of lapping waves.

CHAPTER 6

Dirt, Rocks, Lichen & Flowers

Journal Entry:

I didn't last long in foster homes. Focusing on engaging with the families, following rules, and building any sort of relationship took a backseat to the exploration of my powers. My mother's note and my inability to help my grandmother in her fight against death had instilled a new level of intensity to my practice.

I continued to work on breaking down pretty much anything and everything to its simplest forms before I was able to return it back to the earth, or elsewhere. My ability to sense other life forms became more of a conversation with the earth. I understood when and where she was hurting, so I could heal her plants and the small animals that crossed my path.

It didn't take long before I became fully aware that water was my obvious savior; being near it and pulling the Earthen energy through each glassy surface, ripple, or current replenished me almost instantaneously. It made perfect sense really, since being near the ocean most of my childhood seemed to keep me more balanced than most of the time I spent in the desert. Thankfully, I became skilled at finding the Colorado River's paths, lakes, and waterfalls all along the western slope, and was soon able to easily work on my craft each day.

I guess not many people wanted a fourteen year-old girl who refused to be parted from her dog. The doctors had in fact deemed it medically necessary to keep Bear with me, which was usually a hindrance. So, when the Nestrour family living on large acreage close to the Colorado River offered to take me in, I was thrilled. Freedom on a large acreage of land, access to a wild waterway, and Bear at my side was perfect.

However, the thoughts of perfection didn't last long. I was living with a couple and their two children, an eighteen-year-old boy, Greg, and an eight-year-old girl, Cheyenne. Greg didn't spend much time at home as he was busy with baseball, school, and getting ready to leave for college in the fall, so I never really saw him. I spent my time with Bear, at school, playing basketball, or practicing Protector and Healer skills. The girl, Cheyenne, who always wanted to be tag-a-long, was harder to shake when I needed to have some "me time." Their parents were always busy, the mom with her constant volunteering and the dad lawyering it up over some land acquisitions.

One night when I was outside practicing my skills, the world tumbled down on me. When I thought I was safely alone to work on a broken tree, trying to repair its phloem and xylem that some idiot had carelessly chopped into trying to take the behemoth down, I heard a scuffling behind me.

"Oh, don't stop on my account." It was Steven, or Steve as Irene, my foster mother, called him when she became highly irritated with her husband, which seemed to happen frequently when they were actually around each other. Steven was the head of the household, "Mr. Big Money Bags." I stilled, uncertain of what he had seen.

"Let me tell you how this is going to go." I felt my body freeze, but not by my own doing. It was as if the energy field I used on animals to keep them still while I healed them, or around objects while I shifted them into other planes of existence was wrapped around me. Instead of the soft hum and warmth of my force, this was hot like ice, scalding where it lapped along my exposed flesh. Trying to call to Gaia in my mind was pointless, her energy would not come, my contact to her was blocked, maybe even severed.

"I tracked you down, little girl, you and your beautiful doll eyes. Eyes just like your mother's. Do you think you're here by chance? You're mine now, and you will do as I say, or you will be placed in the farthest alternate dimensional hell, away from your precious waters and this mutt." He struck at Bear and I heard an "umpf" as the air was knocked out of him. Bear lay growling and whimpering as alternating heartbeats pounded in my ears. "Or, would you rather be like Mommy? I can hold you down and pump you full of so many drugs you won't know who you are anymore."

46

His power eased off but was soon replaced by his foul, well-manicured hand as it traveled along my back and pulled at the straps of my tank top. His fingers grazed the top of my jeans and dared to travel along my backside possessively as I seethed in anger.

"Oh, that's good, pull on your power, I relish in it." His nostrils flared as he inhaled and trembled, causing me to feel immediately weaker, nearly passing out where I stood. He had taken my stored Earthen energy right out of me. I was a fool for not having been in my protective lock down mode, a fool for thinking I was safe here on my foster home's land. This was who my mom had tried to protect me from, and I had fallen right into his hands.

My body was paralyzed once again and in a heartbeat he was in my face, the hot air of his breath assaulting my senses.

"You will be quiet, little girl, and you and your beautiful doll eyes are mine."

As I near my loft, I see Justin's white truck parked on the street. He isn't in it, so I keep on going. Why do I feel so guilty? I mean, I didn't do anything wrong and looking and thinking a little naughtily about Ryan is all in good fun, right? Plus, I belong to no one.

I keep driving, heading north, hoping to clear my mind. It seems like forever since I met Justin, although it's only been a year. I met him while looking for new, unique flowers and designs amongst the flower warehouses in Carlsbad. I'd had a dream the night before about going to a new place I had read about.

Have you ever seen those birds that appear to be quite ordinary in color until they take flight? Then all of a sudden the flashes of bright blue, red, or yellow shock you, and for an instant, that little creature takes your breath away. They are amazing and in my dream those birds were singing in their trees, taking flight with their glorious colors revealed that then seeped into me. They landed on rocks and morphed into the most gorgeous lichen patches I had ever seen. They continued that cycle of flying onto a rock, becoming the lichen, taking flight to the trees, singing to me, then flying back down. When I woke, I felt stronger and more alive than I had felt in weeks, and I had this picture in my head for the centerpieces I needed. The gorgeous lichen, flower, and rock centerpieces had to be found and somehow I knew they would be.

There was supposed to be some master botanical magician conjuring up all sorts of crazy concoctions of colors and symbiotic relationships amongst the plant world. One thing I have always been nuts about is mixing moss, rocks, and other plants to make arrangements. What I needed was some brightly colored lichen for an upcoming fundraiser, and I knew exactly what I wanted. Perhaps this madman would have just the thing.

I spent time wandering around the greenhouses and into some hydroponics rooms looking at the fish feeding the plants that were then feeding the fish. Crazy, right? I was transfixed by one tank when I noticed someone bending over one in another aisle. This must be the mystery magician. His tanned skin and toned body unfolded and leaned over another tank to place various aquatic plants amongst the fish. He was shirtless, which was fine with me, and I saw the barest hint of the top of his boxers as his roughly treated jeans fit perfectly down his body, hugging the right places. His hair was tousled and just long enough to allow me to fantasize about how firm a hold my fingers would have in it. He was definitely a brunette, with his hair nearly jet-black in places. Obviously the sun had bleached his hair to a lighter shade, but not in a toolish "I frost my tips" sort of way.

Oh man, I was staring. He didn't seem to notice because he was fully engrossed in his task, caring for the biological process that created the amazing plants and landscapes in this room. No, he didn't notice until I walked into and fell right over a stack of buckets, and then slid gracelessly along the slick floor managing to get some sort of mossy plant stuck to my face. He was so zen-like that he didn't even move at first. It's as if he knew I would do that, knew I was there, and was not alarmed or alerted by my "smooth" move.

"You okay over there?" he called out smugly with the most adorable smile that I wanted to slap off his face. He toweled off his hands and offered one to me.

"You've got a little something right there," he said while pointing at his entire face indicating I needed a full scrub down.

"Ah, thank you, umm... do you have a bathroom? A mirror?" A closet to hide in?

"I'm just kidding. You look great, I mean fine, you look fine." Ha, I flustered him a little. Good! I shouldn't be the only one. "I'm Justin," he said after a few awkward seconds, Making sure one of my hands was free of gunk, I shook the strong, tan hand he extended my way.

We spent the next hour wandering around viewing his plants and experiments, walking through the rows of college students assisting him while the girls ogled and giggled, and the guys asked for tips on their "vegetable" hydroponic gardens. I watched him as he went into his office to work on an idea and a quote.

While Justin worked, I went back to the tanks and strolled around, peeking into each area. In the farthest tank, small crabs were milling around cleaning, eating, and shoving each other aside. There were some larger fish in there, and one was swimming, lying, okay, floating sideways near the top. I glanced around and didn't see anyone nearby, so I reached into the earth with my mind and drew power into my fingers. Reaching over the tank, I lightly touched the little guy. He instantly jolted and darted around happily. I hadn't been doing so well working on my powers of healing, out of practice I guess, but something about this place centered me.

"I see you found the crabby guys; I think their fish buddy, Stitch, is barely holding on. Not sure what's wrong with him. Hey, where is... whoa look at him go." And there was Stitch, on cue, acting like he just got some from one of his finny friends.

"How... what? Well, okay then, Stitch. I guess he's all good." Justin seemed to light up like a boy half his twenty-some years of age. He caught me staring and immediately tried to curb some of his adorable enthusiasm.

"Stitch ha, I love that little guy." I did my best and cutest alien Disney character's grunts and laughs, mimicking his crazy claw movements, trying to ease Justin back into playfulness. He smiled at me and turned back to Stitch with wonder. At least I knew he didn't mind me being silly and unbelievably clumsy.

It seemed like a breath or two, but it might have been minutes before I realized neither of us had spoken in quite a while, and there was not a damn thing wrong with that. I felt more comfortable standing next to him watching the crabs sidewalk about, and Stitch get into the routine with his fellow finny friends. I didn't usually let myself get sucked in too much, but this was different, this wasn't some night out dancing, drinking and flirting with some guy I didn't care to see again. This was someone tangible and real who appeared to love nature as much as I do. It may not seem like it now, with the concrete jungle being more of a home to me than the backpacking trails and pop-up tents of my past with Mom and Grandmom, but I longed for this type of environment and that translated into longing to be around Justin.

I snuck a glance at him and dug deep for the courage to speak. "Do you ever go hiking along Torrey Pines at State Beach? I love that hike and don't venture out there often enough."

"I haven't been in a while, but I do have to go by there for some estuary samples across from State Beach soon. Any chance you like trudging through murky waters with nets?" He asked hopefully, filling me with warmth throughout my body that I never knew I'd been missing.

I left with a plan to meet up with him the following week, and I felt good about my ability to actually meet someone outside of the club scene, someone who made me feel normal, safe, and balanced.

When the day arrived, I met Justin at the parking lot off the Pacific Coastal Highway. "Um, okay, where is the other person who will wear the second space-like get-up? I mean, I love a good rubber overall suit as much as the next person, but that thing is begging for some mending. Are those patches? I'm not going to have some friends swimming up into my ticklish spots, am I?"

Justin laughed out loud and handed me the gear. The dang thing felt soaking wet already and nearly threw me off balance with its damp mass. Dirt-brown rubber boots were attached to the camo-green get up, making it even *more* appealing. We walked down the hill and crossed over the buzzing highway to the estuarine side. Dropping my bag, I slid off my cover-up to slide inside the suit of a thousand pounds. I felt his eyes on me; it made the sun overhead turn up a few notches, and the tingles of a flustered girl trembled through my body. It took all I had to hold back a smile, which I couldn't. Bad idea! Even that slight twitch in my face made me lose my balance and I nearly fell over trying to get into the other boot.

When I did look up, he had pulled off his shirt and made putting on the clunky rubber suit somehow look sexy as hell! I mused on the possibility that this could count as a second date. Yeah, I know meeting him for the first time is not a date, but a girl can dream, right? On a scale of sluttiness, how slutty would I be if I crashed into him right now and kissed those lips in this marshy mess? *Enough! Get it together, Alex!*

Once Justin proclaimed we were done sampling, we stripped off the pounds of gear and walked back to his truck. For the next hour we sat on a blanket in the sand, staring into the waves and eating a picnic lunch. Justin sure knew how to reach a girl's heart through her stomach. We snacked and chatted about his work that made my crazy job seem superficial in comparison. Aside from the amazing plants and flowers he grew, his research in conjunction with San Diego State University's botany department would lead to saving the environment and protecting the wetlands. I reminded myself that I wasn't cut out for the helping jobs I thought I'd pursue in college. It was too hard for me. No matter how much I wanted to help kids, I couldn't get past my own issues; I would get in too deep and lose myself.

One date turned into many, and by the fifth date it was time to see if this guy liked to dance and let loose. Carmen and I went to our favorite club and planned on meeting Justin and her boyfriend at the time, Max. We had our iced shaken tequila shots and were dancing on a pedestal when I noticed Justin walk into the club. I was wearing a short, dark blue sequin dress and three-inch heels, which occasioned many, many nights of practice before I stopped falling on my ass. The music was pulsing, and the lights played colors along his face, which illuminated his eyes, but fire was clearly already in them. The night played out with lots of dancing, cheers, and a cab ride home with Justin coming to my loft for the first time.

"Don't mind Pitter," I giggled as he nearly tripped Justin up. "Do you want anything to dr…" My question was cut short as Justin's lips pressed against mine. It wasn't our first kiss, but none of them ever felt this determined and lustful before. His tongue snuck past my teeth and explored my mouth as I moaned into him. Suddenly I was lifted up, and I kicked my heels off toward the wall, apparently catching Pitter unaware as he yowled and ran away. While I sat on the kitchen island, Justin trailed kisses down my neck and explored my chest. The only way for it to go any further was for that dress to come off right over my head. Before I could even make for the hem, Justin hiked it up, his mouth made trails of kisses along my inner thighs. If I had a weakness, it was the inner thigh, dammit! Following my unspoken logic, the dress came off with a smooth quickness and I shivered at the newfound coolness hitting my skin. His warm hands caressed my thighs as he bent back down, his mouth driving me mad once more.

"Ohhh!" escaped my lips as his warm breath hit the outside of my thong, causing me to clench. His lips grazed the thin fabric of my underwear as his fingers pulled it aside to create a clear path, instantly turning my body to jelly. Whoa! My mind was reeling as he explored me with his tongue, lips, and yipes, a slight grazing of his teeth. It felt painfully good in the most arousing way.

"Do you have anything?" I asked him, a little too forcefully. He grabbed his wallet and flipped through it, finding a condom, and I heard the sound of zipping right before his pants hit the floor. The man was a genius as he kept enticing me, my senses sizzling with need while putting on the condom simultaneously. He lifted his head and his eyes bore into me, making me want him even more. As he slid me off the island, I wrapped my legs around his waist, before he crushed his lips into mine.

"Couch, couch over… mmm… there!" I barely hit the sofa before he entered me, and a hissing sigh escaped my lips. I arched my back in response and dug my nails into his hips. Moving with him, I kissed any part of him I could reach; his neck, shoulders; his body responding to me in turn. It was as if this was all we needed at that moment, the only place we wanted to be. He grasped my hair to lift my chin up and stared into my eyes for a few breaths as he inched teasingly out of me. I grabbed on to him willing him to stay, to move harder when suddenly he smashed his lips to mine and pushed deep inside of me again. I didn't think I was going to hold back much longer when he flipped me onto my stomach and grabbed both sides of my thighs, lifting me into a cat pose. I pressed against him immediately, wanting him and keeping time with his motion. The intensity grew and grew before he fell into me as wave after wave of pleasure rolled through us.

After a few moments he eased back, gently turning me over to face him. I lay on his chest hearing his heartbeat thundering in his chest just like mine. His gentle, sun- and water-roughened hands stroked my hair, and I smiled at the warmth, the satiated way my body felt, and the undeniable safety of being in his arms.

As this memory slips through my mind, it stirs up a multitude of emotions as I find myself nearing a T in the road. A decision needs to be made: do I turn left and back home to Justin, or do I turn right and explore northern Pacific Beach, allowing myself to drift along the 101 hugging the ocean into Del Mar? I know Justin; I trust him. He loves me and has always taken care of me, has always forgiven me. On the other hand, I can't escape the feeling that I am missing a huge part of what my life and love could be like if I were able to completely be myself, with my powers and all. I can't shake the feeling that meeting Ryan wasn't a coincidence and that I responded to him in a way I never had before. I recognize something in him; something I know is inside me as well.

A horn blares behind me, and I turn on my signal. The wheel turns clockwise as I make my decision. I travel along the coast, the sun casting an orange glow along my left cheek, warming me as I drive.

52

CHAPTER 7

"What's up, Doc?"

Journal Entry:

It danced in the moonlight as it slashed across my wrist. The blade I toyed with and admired longingly was finally grasped so tightly in my hands that there seemed to be no turning back. I would not be locked away, I would not end up like my mother, and this was the day I would end his reign and the pain raging inside me. I meant to finally do it; the scars of previous attempts had healed but would never really go away. The scars would always serve as reminders of the hell I endured at the hands of Steven. He was an Absolute Protector—one of the very evils I was warned about—and I let him overpower me.

My hearing has always been downright eerie. The words "no, stop," rang like an alarm in my ears. It was three A.M., and my last perimeter energy sweep of the house showed no movement. Chey's breathing was steady, signaling her sleep. I let the knife slip slowly to the bed and moved to my door, quietly opening it to the hall. There was a barely audible muffled noise and a thump. I reached out with my power, trying to sense what was going on. I only sent a slight amount toward the sound; it was the most I could muster without setting Steven off. It had taken patience and practice, but I found a way to use it without alerting him.

Suddenly I heard something. "Chey." The name rolls like "Shy" off the tongue, the name I gave her, but it was said in such a way that my bones turned cold and the hairs stood to attention on the back of my neck. "Look at me, doll eyes, it's me. Chey, don't be afraid." I knew in an instant that Steven was in her room; he had her and was using his soft, soothing voice along with the name I had given her to calm her down. What in the hell was he doing here anyhow? He was supposed to be away for work. I was taking care of Chey while her mother was on some woman's retreat, and Greg had already left for college. Irene had been spending more and more time away from home. I truly think she wanted to get away from Steven, and who would blame her. Who knows what torment he had put her through with that sweet, loving wife-and-husband look plastered on their faces so hard that it couldn't possibly be real, but only I was observant enough to know that.

It took all of my anger, hurt, and forced silence to focus on another new form of power; one I had also been working on those past few painful months. It had been long and tedious, but I had found a way to set my power's tone to match his. I knew that somehow I could trick him into thinking my Earthen force was his, just long enough to get close to him. Breathing deeply, I slowly sent tendrils of my force to search him out. I called on the earth, on Gaia herself, and asked her bones, rocks, detritus, invertebrates, moisture, and power to conceal my magic and to carefully cling to him. I held my breath as my force crept towards him; crawling up his legs in an attempt to cover him without him realizing it was actually my vengeful power. I reached deep down into the earth again as I sought out the deeper parts of Gaia, pleading with her to take him, to drag him down into her being, to bind him away forever. I begged her to remove him from this place, this plane of existence, to take him anywhere but here, I didn't care where, I just wanted him gone. I broke out in a sweat, my body shaking uncontrollably in the hall where I stayed hidden. Slowly, I drained the invisible parts of him through the carpet, warped wooden floors and into the cold, dark, calm space in the body of Gaia. His energy, bits of his soul, slowly, so slowly, so he wouldn't sense me; wouldn't know a thing till I had him, till it was too late.

I felt Chey trembling within the energy of the room as Steven kept talking, trying to soothe her, to take her in a way no man should ever with a child, his own child. He was too focused on his own trap, his own pursuit, to feel the slight difference in his energy, to sense any part of me. He would not hurt her, her beautiful soul, or her innocence. I can and will stop him; I am my mother's child, my grandmother's child, and I was meant to fight his evil.

A gasp broke the silence and then a scream. Chey ran out of the room, and she locked eyes with me, but only for a brief second. At that moment, she held the eyes of a frightened doe—doll eyes. My finger moved slowly to my lips, mimicking my mother's silent prayer, she blinked rapidly, and then Chey was away like a silent breeze. Bear peered around the corner at me; he always sensed the change in the air when Steven or I used our power. I shook my head at him and nodded my head in Chey's direction, making sure he went to guard her. It was only Steven and I this night, and it would all end here and now.

I gave a silent prayer to Gaia that I could heal Chey's mind, that I could help her forget what had nearly happened to her—what had been happening to me—but right now I was going to make that man pay. That man who had terrorized me for months, who had shown me his own power that I hadn't yet been strong enough to combat. I couldn't risk going against the force that he held over me for fear of him doing to Chey what he dared to try this night. All that time I thought I was protecting her when she never had a chance of ever being safe from him. But I knew I had him. All my work to channel my energy to subtly match his at such a low level had really paid off. It's not always the big guns that win the fight. Steven never understood that, and it would be his downfall.

My power had reached his neck, and as I slowly squeezed I heard a gasp of response. I sealed his lips when I heard a grunt in the room, signifying that Steven had fully realized his error. I reveled in his terror for a moment, almost reeling at how powerful it made me feel. It must have felt like that for him each time he controlled me, and I immediately felt disgusted with myself for even tasting the dark side of my abilities. That monster in Steven skin knew: he knew he was trapped, and I let my power ease off his mouth for a moment as I glided into the room. I toyed with him for a while, using my ability to tighten, squeeze, and buckle his knees, pulling him down to the floor. Then I let my mimicry of his force fade as my power's resonance fully took over.

"How dare you!" he spat, as I lifted my chin to stop the trembling caused by my hold on the difficult task of concealing my power, and the tendrils of fear he unleashed in my being. I would not be weak in front of him, not this time. I would show him what I had been planning, what I was capable of.

"It's over, Steve!" I bit his name off so forcefully that my teeth felt the intense grind from the clench of my jaw. "You are over. You will never hurt me again, and you sure as hell will never lay your hands on Chey or anyone else **ever again**." The green glow of my eyes swirling

55

with waves of power lit the darkness of the room, reflecting the intense storm brewing.

Steven cried out as his body started to fold in on itself. His legs begin to fold in on themselves, as bones snapped and muscles popped amongst his blood-curdling scream. I turned my power back to his mouth so no one would hear him roar. There was no blood, no body parts falling to the floor; I gave all of that back to the earth. He would never be whole again, and the look of terror on his face at that realization made me smile wickedly.

"Goodbye, Steve. Rot in hell you sick son of a bitch!"

His face was the last thing I saw as it caved in like a sinkhole, and I felt an enormous burst of force fly through me. My body reabsorbed my power, like humming vibrations on my soul. I felt a new tingle, something foreign, then a warm, loving feeling. An icy blue glow appeared and enveloped me in a recognizable hug. I heard her then, my grandmother's soothing voice.

"That's my girl... "

That night, I spent time with Chey and eased her mind, literally, by pulling out the bad and only leaving the good. For all she knew, she'd had a bad nightmare and then snuggled in with Bear and me for the night. I hoped she couldn't feel the waves of Earthen power still rolling and humming over me. What I had done was intense, and it took all I had not to shake so intensely that I knocked her awake. I finally slid out, padding softly to the bar area where I downed some of Steven's crystal-encased vodka, willing its warmth to stop the trembling so I could fall asleep.

The days that followed were intense to say the least. Since Steven was supposed to have been on a business trip, nobody knew that he had ever been home. His car was found near the cliffs of the Colorado National Monument, and eventually his disappearance was ruled a suicide. The life of my foster family completely changed after that night. I changed as well. I knew then that I was stronger than I had ever thought possible, and that I would never let myself be trapped, tricked, or used by anyone ever again.

Time and time again I have been told that a therapist can only lead you to solve your problems, they can't actually solve them for you. Well at this point, I'm wondering where those people are hiding that *do* solve problems, now that I am willing to pay dearly for. I guess Ryan can solve problems, or rather take them out and let them drop to the ground. Part of me wouldn't mind seeing him on a regular basis, that's for sure.

Dr. Reynolds's office is classy, dim, and usually comfortable when she isn't digging around in my brain. She's the third therapist I've seen and the one I've stuck with the longest. She asked me to keep a journal, but told me I only had to share what I wanted with her. We've gone over the parts about my mother, my grandmother, and my foster care, but I omitted all the stuff about my power. I know that she's fully aware that I'm holding something back, but there's no way I'm going to share that information with her, and my stubbornness is telling me that my abilities have nothing to do with the nightmares. Denial is always the first step to inevitable acceptance, isn't it?

I lean back in the cozy leather chair and close my eyes. Taking a deep breath, I enjoy the smell of her burning candles and the sound of the waterfall that trickles down her wall. The room is large, with two doors and a big window overlooking a garden. One door leads to the waiting area and the exit, while the other door opens into a private area for Dr. Reynolds. I sometimes wonder if it was a huge set-up and a rush of people would come running out one day and wrestle me into a strait jacket.

She has a matching cozy chair in soft brown and a large sofa in green tones. Our surroundings are very earthy and in tune with nature, and I know this adds to my much-needed feeling of comfort. On the walls are pictures of nature. She enjoys photography, and most of the photos were taken on her own trips and with her camera. There are incredible icebergs and penguins from Antarctica, big black bears and moose crossing rushing waters in Montana, and brightly colored tropical birds from trips to Florida and Hawaii. In a way, I wish I were in those places at those times. I feel that even the animals, and nature as a whole, are comfortable around her, posing even.

Dr. Sharon Reynolds herself is a lean five foot seven. On occasion we talk about our exercise routines. While mine tends to fall into the nighttime dancing category, yoga, running, and weights, she is up at the crack of dawn rollerblading, kayaking, or running. She can be both quiet and intense, so she knows when to be soft and when to tell me how it is. Her hair is bright red and stick straight, and her slim oval face carries the tiniest nose and small, light brown eyes. Some days, like today, she dresses in designer jeans, heeled pumps, and a solid colored button-up top. On other days, her full arsenal of power suits can be seen. I am sure it depends on both her mood and her subject.

"Alex, care to share what you're thinking? What's reeling in that head of yours? At least it looks like a pleasant thought. Care to let me in?" How I long to share my secrets with someone, but I can't, the last time someone found them out, I nearly took my own life.

Make-up hides my remaining bruising fairly well now after a couple of days, and a touch of magic I did last night while hiding in the closet of my bedroom with a flashlight and mirror. I'm still too jumpy to heal myself fully, half expecting to see Ryan around every corner. Dr. Reynolds's eyes quickly travel to the bruise, and she falls in line with Sandra's snarky remarks.

"Well, despite one of your obvious run-ins with a wall, door, or floor of some kind, you look a bit more rested than usual." She taps her finger to her chin and gives me the questioning look.

"Actually," I announce, the words tumbling out of my mouth, and I perk up like I'm telling my grandmother about a good grade I received on a school project. "I had a solid six hours of sleep Saturday night and not a single dream, good or bad. It was blissful. Short lived, but I may have caught up a bit. At least I feel more refreshed than I've been in about a year."

"And what was different about that night?" More like who was different.

"I won't beat around the bush, and this may sound like I'm grasping at straws, but a guy, Ryan, was the difference." Her eyebrows inch up a little, revealing that she's intrigued with an added glint in her eyes that seem to be hoping for some dirt. *Why Dr. Reynolds, are you trying to get some naughty tidbits?* Well hell, she's human after all.

"Nothing like *that* happened." Ha! I catch her off guard and she shakes her head slightly trying to rebut the idea that she's thinking such a thing. Busted!

"He sort of helped me out of a jam Saturday night, and yes, he did stay, but on the couch." If he even slept down at all, the gorgeous machine-of-a-man. "Nonetheless, I woke up feeling like I had slept for days. It's as if a switch went off and all of the stress and fear from the nightmares vanished. I don't even remember dreading that I would have one, and even though this little love tap hurt like a bitch, it wasn't hard enough to knock me out that long. When I woke up, I felt normal. I nearly forgot about the nightmares existing at all."

The Doc's answering smile is genuine, she cares and that's something that's kept me coming back. "I've always felt your fear of abandonment and your inability to truly trust, especially men, are two focal points from where your nightmares stem. If this Ryan truly makes you feel safe, then your meditation training to stay focused and grounded in the present, will only continue to help you adopt the feeling of trust and love for a man, or men. Which will overpower the traumatic feelings associated with the abuse you suffered at the hands of your foster father, his suicide, and the loss of the two important women in your life."

I know what she is saying, and I know part of it is true, but I have Justin, Carmen, Sandra, even Nic, and any of them would have my back in a heartbeat. This thing, whatever this is or was with Ryan, is different. I don't even know him, but it feels like we have a connection. Maybe it's some past life mojo coming to the surface between us.

"Well, whatever the reason, I'm happy you got some real sleep for once. Make sure you journal about how you felt yesterday morning; it may help you find some answers. Do you plan on seeing Ryan again?" My chest flutters at the prospect.

"I'm not certain." I have a feeling no one plans on seeing Ryan, somehow he just appears.

"Well, today I thought we would get you prepped for a possible hypnotherapy session within the next few weeks. Now, I know you don't really want to do this, but I think at this point it's the best option. You have a high level of trauma that may require some tinkering to rid your mind of the damage it's doing, causing your headaches and sleeplessness. I know you think you will be under some sort of mind control, but that isn't what is going to happen. Hypnotherapy relies on you being present; that is why I have been asking you to work so hard on your meditations. You won't be retelling or reliving the traumatic events themselves; we hope to get you to the point before they began and then reset your timeline, or remove the events from your memory. You are stable enough to handle this technique, and I truly believe it is your best option."

Not even realizing I'm biting at my finger, I drop my hand and give her a weak smile. I hear what she's saying, but I can't shake the worry or the fear of blurting something out, or reliving the other event she can never know about, or accidently displaying my power. What if I exile her or the hypnotherapist away? Now, I know I am being irrational, as that would never happen. She said I will be completely alert while reliving my past, and my grandmother's teachings and my practice are engrained enough to keep my real secret safely locked away. What would it be like to completely forget something ever happened, to rewrite history for oneself? Is it even possible? Would it change who I am?

Dr. Reynolds continues on and I do my best to look as if *this* time I may cave and agree to undergo hypnotherapy. If I do this, another doctor will put me under, partially in their control, as my memory is scoured. My fingers instinctively caress my left wrist. The scars are old and healed, yet the skin still tingles from time to time, a constant reminder of a painful past.

"I get the feeling that one of your worries is about the man I want you to work with. He's a close personal friend of mine, and I know he is the best. I can't put you under, but I will be with you in the room the entire time. How does that sound?"

Terrible is how it sounds, but what's been happening over the last year isn't any better. "You know what? I'll think about it, seriously this time." Giving her a thumbs up, she gives me an eyebrow raise. "You know my main worry is if removing the actual event, or my reaction to the event will change me in some negative way. I know I have abandonment issues with my mom. The loss of my grandmother, and then being in foster care with that despicable man have all taken a toll on me. Maybe I need that weight lifted, but I also think it has shaped me, and I really do like who I am, you know. Plus, he's gone, so I think continuing the meditations and focusing on how wonderful life is now is the key to shutting these nightmares down. I'm safe, loved, and I need to let the past go. Easy enough."

It hasn't been easy, how could it be, for me or anyone else? The doc's eyes squint with the crease in her brown and I back peddle. "Okay? And of course, work on my obvious detachment and relationship issues, I know, I know. I need to work through those and move on. Piece of cake!"

I don't think my little tirade is selling her. The doctor slumps back in her chair and gives a sigh. Even her sighs are comfortable. She does well to not sound annoyed with me. Being annoying doesn't sit well with me; I can be a pest, but I don't ever want to be annoying.

"Alex, have you read the literature I gave you?" *Um... no.* "People don't change who they have become by using this technique, that is, when they commit to the proper preparation. This is why the work you are doing to keep you grounded in the present is crucial. I'm telling you that you will not change in a negative way, only positively." She makes it sound so appealing, but I shift uncomfortably in my chair all the same, moving a non-existent strand of hair behind my ear in a nervous tell.

"We'd start by focusing only on removing the memory of the abuse you suffered," she continues softly. "We'll leave the memories with your mom and grandmother for you and me to continue working through together. Steven is the voice you hear in your nightmares; he and his destruction are what I want to help you annihilate so you can have some peace." Peace, the word warms me from head to toe. I can't help but picture "Buffy the Vampire Slayer" when I listen to her. She embodies the *saving the world from the hell* mouth level of intensity that I love.

"Alex, you know I'm concerned for you." She leans forward, worry creasing her brow once again. "You're barely sleeping more than three to four hours at a time, if at all, and your dreams are getting worse. I don't think the journal is going to be what creates the breakthrough that you need. We have gone over the history of the abuse you endured with your foster father, and maybe the trauma of his suicide made everything worse. There isn't much closure in violence." A persistent nudging taps at my mind with the words "breakthrough," and the "doll eyes" whispers hits me in such a way that my head even swings back. Dr. Reynolds' eyes widen but she doesn't pry.

Yes, there was a full investigation and his disappearance was ruled a suicide, but I'm clear on what truly happened. I did it; I exiled him from this place, bound him to another plane of existence. Steven isn't dead, and I gave Chey the peace of mind of knowing that he would never be able to hurt her, not like how he hurt me anyhow, but binding is mystical; it doesn't equal death.

The doc notices my eyes glaze over, or maybe she smells something burning as my brain takes flight. Shifting from her relaxed posture, she's now perched on the edge of her chair, ready to pounce, to drag out every last detail. I break my contact with her eyes, shutting the door, most likely frustrating her though she doesn't show it.

Maybe erasing the control and damage he did to my psyche is the key, but I know without a doubt that I cannot let the memory of the binding completely disappear. Somehow I feel that would make it not exist; that it may even set Steven free. How can I allow them to remove the awful memories and not this one? Is that even feasible?

"I can't explain it," I say, half lying, "I just feel like something is surfacing, and perhaps that is a good thing. Maybe during one of my dreams it will all spill out, and I will be better." I shudder at the thought. Nothing I have been dreaming about should spill out anywhere.

Closing my eyes, I take in the sounds and smells of the space once again. The waterfall soothes me, its tones rhythmic and the power within the droplets sings to my stored Earthen energy. This is a safe place for me. Now I just need to trust Dr. Reynolds enough. I know that if I continue my efforts to use my abilities, to observe everything quickly and effectively in a different way, by staying in the present, then I will be ready to maneuver this technique and work only on the memories of my abuse.

I need to rid Steven of that power over my past, over my body and my soul. I'm working in a time very different to when the Earthen energy itself originated, which was pretty much at the beginning of existence. Nightmares develop in the brain, thoughts, memories, images—this is purely psychological. I need a professional to help work parts of my past out while the older than dirt abilities try to sort it out as well. I already know I can conceal my magical side deep within, and far away from even the deepest psychological probes. Over the years, I have pushed so much of that side of me away that it has become a commonplace for me.

"Okay, I'll do it, but you will be with me, right? And who is this guy? Can I meet him before? I don't feel all that comfortable with a man putting me into la la land having not even had the opportunity to shake his hand." She eases backwards in her chair as a smile of relief crosses her face; I feel like she truly wants to help me and finally feels like we are getting somewhere.

"Yes, of course you can meet him! Early next week? How does Tuesday sound?" She reaches behind to grab a date book off her desk. "And don't worry, I think he is scheduling sessions a week or two out so you'll have plenty of time to think about it, and maybe even speak to him a second time, if you like. His name is Dr. McAdams, and you will learn all about him once you read the literature I gave you last time." Uh, oh, busted. She doesn't even have to look at me to get her point across, and I give her a little salute in acknowledgement.

"I'll have Darlene make you another copy," her words tumble out neatly despite her smirk. "Please try to hang on to this one this time. The more knowledge you have on the technique, the safer you will feel which will make you more open, and the process more effective."

"Got it, I'll read it over this time." No fingers crossing aloud this time. "Oh, and yes, next Tuesday sounds good. That is my one day between events and I can manage an hour." Ugh, am I really going to do this? "We're meeting here, right, in your office?"

"Of course, Alex. We will always meet in here. I know you're safe and comfortable here, and neither Dr. McAdams nor I would want it any other way." She scribbles in her date book before snapping it shut, leaving it lying on her lap. "I know you'll like him, and maybe he can help us get to the bottom of things. I'll have my service give you a reminder call on Wednesday." Knowing the session is over; I stand and gather my purse. Dr. Reynolds moves to me, giving me a hug, before I sweep out the door.

I can do this. It will help. I need answers, and I need Dr. Reynolds, and possibly even Sandra. My mind drifts a bit—maybe even Ryan.

CHAPTER 8

Pills, Pop & Sizzle

Journal Entry:

I was finally moving back to the west coast. Bear and I were loaded up in my old Jeep and headed back to San Diego. Classes at UCSD—the University of California at San Diego—started in a couple of weeks, and I was going to get settled in with my new roommate Carmen.

Carmen had a house in Encinitas where Bear would have a yard, and we would have hills to hike, and the ocean was mere miles away. Carmen was a student at the college of life and a program manager for an event company called Seaside Events. She had two rescue dogs, a pit bull, and a German Shepard, so I knew we would get along perfectly. Dog people were my favorite people. I rarely trusted anyone who didn't like animals. Animals were truly at our mercy and I didn't understand how someone could neglect, abuse, or destroy a living thing whose sole purpose was to be loved and to please their owner, or in Bear's case, his mommy. Yep, he looked just like me!

My academic advisor had helped me find a roommate in a place I could afford. My dedication to my schoolwork had paid off, and I earned merit scholarships since any money my grandmother left me was wrapped up in a bond I couldn't access until I was twenty-three. I wasn't interested in living on campus anyway; I needed my privacy as you could imagine, and dorm life just wouldn't be the place for someone like me, or Bear for that matter. To be honest, the fewer people, the better. All I really wanted was to be involved in school, spend time with Bear, and learn more and more about my abilities when I had time. I had declared psychology as my major, with my lofty goals intensified by my need to understand how the brain worked and maybe even how I worked.

Heading down the Pacific Coast Highway is spectacular to say the least. I rolled my windows down and half expected Bear's tongue lolling out of his mouth to be an exact mirror of my own. Oh, how I had missed the Pacific. My body soaked it all in, the salt air, the coastal desert wind—I was home.

I drove a little further south to give Bear his first taste of doggy heaven by stopping at the Del Mar dog beach. Even with just the windows down in the Jeep, I could tell the energy was different there. I was sure it had something to do with the conductivity of the salt and brackish water surrounding the area. Once we hit the beach, my body tingled as though I could feel the positive and negative ions moving from higher to lower concentration levels. I loved the feeling; I felt stronger and more powerful with each step on the sand, and the feeling intensified once we hit the water.

"Whoa," escaped my lips, and Bear stopped mid chase, after a wily terrier, to come back and sit next to me. Even my stroke of his ear sent a shudder through him that I hadn't had to focus on preventing since we were both younger. Okay, I know seventeen isn't old, but for what we had been through it felt like it had been ages. Being back at the beach brought a whole new variable into the game. It was almost like starting from scratch with keeping my abilities under control. Water in Colorado may have replenished my energy, but something about the ocean made the level of power I was able to pull into my being intensify, to the point of being overwhelming. Well, if I could harness my abilities while being close to, or actually in the ocean, then inland would be a piece of cake. As the saying goes, if you have to eat a bowl of frogs, start with the biggest one first.

Carmen and I hit it off instantly. She was easily the most organized person I'd known, but she did it with style and grace. She wasn't overly type A in her personal life as much as she may have to be with work, so we got along well. Carmen was five foot three, with beautifully long, thick, black hair, a slim frame, and gorgeous skin thanks to her Hispanic heritage. Her family lived in San Diego where her dad was a master chief in the Navy, and her mom worked hard at her own baking business out of her home. Needless to say, we weren't starving college students, not if her mom could help it.

Carmen earned college credits in high school through a marketing program, and being the top student in her class two years in a row.

Seaside Events recruited her before she could even start college. She took courses here and there at the community college, but with her hours, it was nearly impossible to maintain her career and attend school. Event management was perfect for her; she had a voice that could soothe even the highest tempered person. I had seen her use these skills to both get something she wanted, and to keep someone from flipping out over even the most trivial of reasons.

Work kept her busy most weekends, so I had plenty of privacy. When we were both off from work and school, we would take our dogs hiking or to the beach. Those became our favorite things to do. My plan was to be out of college in four years or less and enroll in a master's or Ph.D. program in the field of behavioral psychology. Dream big was my grandmother's motto, and it soon became mine.

Pharmaceutical companies have a tendency to splurge on their parties. It's good for business, but sometimes I wonder how they use it frivolously instead of helping more people. I mean, they have so much money for little pads of paper, pens, desk clocks, tote bags, and parties; why wouldn't they help those in need of medicines they can't afford?

Mantar must have hit it big with the sales numbers this quarter because they rented out one of the swankiest clubs in town. Yep, Allure was all ours tonight, and full of mostly the rich and young sales reps from the company. Everyone was partying with no strings attached, and some I believe were using the "what happens" line for Vegas before they even finished their first drink of the night.

To my surprise, and obvious enjoyment, I hear a familiar voice in my ear as I switch to channel five.

"Hey Lex, looks like you heal quickly." I don't know why Ryan's voice startles me; I was hoping to hear it.

My chest jumps all the same, and I do a quick scan to make sure nobody saw, after all, I do have a reputation to keep. That's right, all calm, cool, and collected here. On the outside, maybe, but inside, Ryan's deep, penetrating voice makes me want to squeal.

"Yeah, I'm good with the ice and I have some old Chinese recipe my grandmother passed down to me from a generation of healers. It smells nasty but sure does the trick." Hee, hee, I crack myself up sometimes. In fact, I had to use a little bit more of my magic since the dang bruise wouldn't heal quick enough on its own.

"Yeah, something like that, I'm sure." He seems to keep a hidden agenda in everything he says. It's always so to the point on the surface, but reeks of mystery. Now, how do I keep him talking without making a total fool out of myself?

"So… are you from around here?" God, I wish I would shut myself up sometimes. Why don't I just give him a "come here often" cheesy-ass line? Ugh, can't stop me after I start. Shit, here I go again.

"I mean who is, right? I'm sure you're not, I don't even know why I asked." Nice save, idiot! I stand there cursing myself silently, and I can almost feel him chuckling and shaking his head at me when I hear the click of a reply.

"I've gotta take a look around downstairs. One of those suits wanted to arm-wrestle one of my guys earlier. I'll see you around, Lex." Click and he's gone. Nice work, Exlax! And what's with the "I'll see you Lex" crap? The statement makes me feel slightly exposed, as if he's seeing me more often than I ever see him.

Now, I have actually watched an arm wrestling competition on TV once, and it's nuts. I was working out at the gym one day, and it was the only thing on. Okay, that's a lie, but hell, if you have the choice between crazy men rocking back and forth trying to snap a guy's arm over the threshold and the "Hour of Power" which would you choose?

I snap out of my little arm-wrestling dream where I think I may have inserted Ryan a time or two with a tight shirt ready to wrestle me with any body part of his choosing. I've got issues, and an overactive imagination, which is leading to sexy Ryan thoughts. So sue me, and damn that Ryan!

I spend some time walking around the club that some genius created from an old bank. No, he didn't completely gut the bank and destroy all remnants of its previous use. Instead, he kept some of the obvious clues that it used to be one to accent the atmosphere. There are multiple themed rooms, from the richly decorated masculine vault room turned into a billiard space, to the secret room under the stairs for the VIPs wanting to be deep underground and unnoticed.

Patrons have a street level entrance that leads into the immense first floor room with its perfectly placed, huge rectangular bar barely off to the left. The bar glows with soft golden light, its dark wood offsetting an iridescent floor. Off to the right, an elevated level is roped off for VIPs who want to have a nice vantage point of the dance floor. The dance floor itself is nothing short of gigantic, with three elevated dancer platforms amongst the throng of sweaty patrons. To the left is a small sushi restaurant with flowing curtains to create a sense of separation without completely cutting off the diners' view. The restaurant serves to-die-for rolls, and no-holds-barred pieces of sashimi to tantalize the taste buds. I have to admit, I usually come here for it all, the sushi, drinks, and to dance my ass off.

If one wanted to proceed downstairs, it could be done one of two ways. One way is the main stairway on the far end of the bar away from the front door; the other is behind the screen of wildly fantastic lights and video shows to complement the music, on the outskirts of the dance floor. The main stairway leads down to an open hallway, lined and lit with large glass blocks along one side of the hallway, and a bar nearly its full length making up the other side. This is the hip hop area which, I am happy to say, gets plenty of the Golden Age of Hip Hop from the 90s along with current artists. If you choose to go under the stairs, you would be led into and charged a hefty fee to enter the VIP room, which is heavily guarded and enveloped in the sickly smells of sweat, top shelf liquor, the buzz of unmonitored drug use, and sensual flirtations.

Past the hip hop hall is the first vault door into the billiard room and the other side is the second vault door leading into my favorite room. This one is decorated like the ship from *Hitchhikers Guide to the Galaxy* with its plush white sofas, random cushy pieces to sit upon, and a glass bar with blue lighting underneath creating a glowing enigma to serve fantastical drinks upon. The music is always the loungey house I love, and on some nights, such as my event tonight, a percussionist accompanies the awesome beats. He puts his love and talent into various instruments designed to entice even the most wary dancers to partake. In short, Allure is the "It" club these days, and it can prove difficult at times for me to keep from being sucked into its tractor beam of frivolity, even when I am working.

I haven't been looking *all* night for Ryan, just part of it. By part of it, I mean the part between quarter after every hour and the halfway point. I'm smooth though. No one has any idea—I hope. I only used my tippy toes a few times. At around eleven, two hours after our start time, I notice the temperature around me change and a soft, smooth warmth cozy up the back of my neck.

"You seem to be looking for something, or someone. Anything I can help you with?" How about you soak me out of the floor since I believe I just turned into liquid mush and sloshed all over the marble tiles.

I can smell Ryan so clearly, an intoxicating mix of raw testosterone, old world wood-burning heat, and the scent he has on in teasing amounts. Okay, play it cool. I slowly spin around to face him, meeting those dark, intense eyes. Shit, please don't say something stupid!

"Oh, I thought I saw someone I knew, but I haven't seen them since, so I can't be sure. I'm thinking it's best to just give up on that; I'm sure it wasn't him anyhow." Nice. I smooth my hair down, smiling at my ability to not make a constant fool of myself.

"Well, let me know if I can be of assistance." His smile slips a fire down my belly. "The night has gone smoothly. Nice work, Lex." I see him getting ready to turn around, and I have a raw desire, no, a definite need, to stop him—to keep him with me longer.

Even if it's just to smell him, maybe touch him. Yep, I would definitely like to just touch one part of him to see if the clothes truly fit the man, because they are fitting good and showing the tightness of his arms, chest, stomach, oh god, I think I feel a little moisture at the corner of my mouth, again! *Damn it, Alex, get it together! You're acting as though you've never been in the company of a gorgeous, delicious, yummy... ugh!*

"Um, actually, maybe we could do a walk through together? We're winding down so I would like to do a quick sweep and see if anything is out of order. Typical routine, but an extra set of eyes wouldn't hurt." Excellent! That was very professional and fully along the lines of a normal working relationship. Nope, no ulterior motives going on here, no sir!

He turns back toward me and takes a long draw of me. I feel like he tastes me as if I am a velvet dark red liquid, from an uncorked bottle of wine he's slowly enjoying from a glass.

"Sure, let's go." Okay, easy enough.

We walk along the outer part of the bar and head toward the back stairs. As we enter the lower house music room, I hear a soft, sensuous hum and a deep bass rumble. Then the song begins to play. The lead in is insanely passionate and makes me quiver inside. I stop in place, my back against the far wall, and watch the DJ move her head slowly while she works her hips in a sensuous twisting grind. I feel Ryan slide in next to me along the wall, and when I look up at him, I see his face intent on her as well. He doesn't appear to be moving on the outside, but I notice the rise and fall of his chest intensify. We are close enough that his shoulder grazes my hair causing a wisp to slightly tickle my ear. Butterflies shoot through me, and the hauntingly beautiful lyrics unfold.

Stop karma come back to me
A lesson always to learn
Feel, forget, hold fast to me
Silently unfulfilled.

Is there a way you can come and dance with me?
A soft and timid thrill
Turn, now twist, can you match me?
Something so strong, so hard, it has to be real

Becoming a part of each second
Hold fast, stop, now rewind
Ripples move my body
Teasing and impatient for what I must find

Stop karma come back to me
A lesson always to learn
Feel, forget, hold fast to me
Am I silently unfulfilled?

I can't help but feel more passion
With each turn of time
This can't be real, just a distraction
I'm sure to wake to a world where you aren't mine

As selfish as this sounds
I'd rather you were a figure of my creation rather than share you with
*   anyone else*
I feel it in my fingers; your body feels so right against my skin
The music beats and moves within me—my hypnotic thrill.

Stop karma . . . you have to come back to me!
This lesson I don't want to learn
I felt and won't forget how you held fast to me
I scream for you—you have to be real

Have to be real
Have to be real
Have to be real

Karma holds fast to me
Baby, you have to last with me
Karma comes back to me
My soul will be revealed.

I don't know when it started to happen, but the truth is it's happening all the same. I am somehow caressing a body part that isn't mine, and I feel firm, hot hands on my waist. I look up to see Ryan staring straight down at me. His eyes are so focused, so intent and they hold my gaze for three long seconds. I try to turn away, but his hand gently touches my chin, my body responding as my eyes dart back to him. We are dancing face to face, and my hips are gliding into his. Somehow my left leg is slightly between his, and the other is moving rhythmically on the outside of his thigh. My nipples are grazing the bottom of his pecs, and I don't think it is cold in here, but they are responding all the same. The music is a low throbbing hum, and the smell of Ryan is inescapable.

I drop my left hand off his arm and bend back slightly as he cradles me in his right arm. I feel his breath on my chest and then a sudden rush of heat and fire. His kiss, an inch above my breast, is like a flame licking along my skin. He brushes his moist lips along my heart pendant and dampens it as it swings back along my chest. I gasp and drop my body gently, roll my head, and press my hips into him. Ryan eases me back up till I am an inch from his face.

His breathing is deep and rapid when he lightly brushes his lips along mine. My tongue instinctively touches his bottom lip, lightly running along it before settling back in my mouth. Ryan presses his body harder into mine, and then, then he's kissing me. It starts light at first, and I respond to him. His hands urge my body; they caress my waist and back before he lifts me slightly to kiss me deeper and longer. His tongue passes between my lips, sending fire shooting through me again. He moves his right hand to touch the back of my neck, to the base of my hair, yanking it ever so slightly yet with enough force to cause me to moan into his kiss, wanting more. Every synapse in my body is firing on overload. The floodgates are open, and the positives and negatives of all sorts of ions are running through my system, creating an overflow of endorphins—a happy serotonin cocktail.

The song intensifies as it reaches its melodic climax and then slowly begins to fade. I am so insane with need and want that I don't take notice of anything else, or anyone else, around us. Once the song ends, I feel a sudden jolt and Ryan quickly moves away from me.

Coldness creeps in from his absence until our eyes meet and I see a silvery fire flicker madly in his. He stands there motionless for ten of my rapid heartbeats, and then quickly slips away.

CHAPTER 9

"Paging Dr. McAdams"

Journal Entry:

I still can't believe the only option I had for working on a behavioral study was some form of torture on a poor, unsuspecting animal. Flipping through the undergraduate wanted, or rather lowly peon wanted, ads, I couldn't find anything in line with what I was hoping to start researching with one of the graduate students, or better yet, a professor.

Through all that page tossing, it became apparent that the descriptions were of studies on rodents. Electrocution of a mouse, ingestion of amphetamines by rat, dissection study of a mouse brain, and the doozy, electrocution of a rat when he injects amphetamine. Oh geez, I bet that is a spectacular sight. I'm sure the outcome was a fried rat who couldn't say no to the drug as he constantly pressed the lever for more. Addiction at its worst, even with the intense pain he suffered. Being the daughter of a junky and knowing how hard it can be to break a habit—even one you walked into knowingly—it didn't sound like a study I wished to partake in. It was time I visited some of those labs to see what I was up against with the chemical engineering and the pharmaceutical companies. They promise mental healing but the side effects can be drastic. I grabbed a couple of flyer stubs with email addresses on them, and was heading out when I bumped into a guy who came out of nowhere.

"Umph, oh sorry there, I wasn't looking where I was going very well now, was I? Here, let me help you with those." My stubs had

started to drift and float toward the ground in grand twists and twirls, fluttering in a manner that made them remarkably difficult to catch.

"Looks like you've found some research in our psych department. I was just getting ready to post a new one for Dr. Rosen in the animal behavior specialty if you're interested. A little off the path from the lab-based ones you've picked here... oh wow." My stomach dropped knowing what he must be thinking. "They're testing the effects of household cleaners on rodents in the neuroscience department, eh? Fun stuff."

I blushed immediately, feeling unfounded shame, as my true reason for picking that study was to work on healing those little buggers if I could. Call it my own act of defiance and sticking it to the man. I would practice my healing and work on my stealth and escape artistry. Yet, to this guy, this cute and probably intelligent guy, it must have appeared as though I was into inflicting pain on defenseless animals. All I could do was allow the little girl inside of me to jump up and down at the mention of Dr. Rosen and her work with animal behavior on birds of prey. So there it was, a real opportunity staring me in the face, and all I could see was an expression on the guy's face of stomach acid boiling in his mouth as he glanced over the eight different stubs I'd selected.

"You know, these are part of my own research on how many studies involve the cruelty toward animals versus the understanding of them. Cruelty seems to be winning of course, but hey, Dr. Rosen does incredible work with aves, and I would be extremely honored to work with her, and you, if it is you, or whoever it is, that's fine too." Oh geez, shut up, shut up! I couldn't help it. Not only was working with Dr. Rosen a blessing in itself but this hot, intelligent guy was standing right in front of me, dark brown locks nearly hitting his shoulders, framing a warm face with gorgeous doe-brown eyes, and long eyelashes. He was wearing relaxed cords and a long-sleeved shirt, as though he was modeling for the Sierra Club. His lips were so red and soft looking that I finally had to fumble with my bag to unlock my eyes from them. He carried on the conversation apparently unaware of my inner turmoil.

"Oh, awesome! So, we're working on a new hawk study, their feeding and mating patterns, as well as areas they've been nesting in, for environmental protection purposes. It can be long hours of fruitless observation and dull data-logging, but it's the first step to getting into a possible grad program." He smiled at me and handed me a copy of *the flier. I was so excited that I didn't care about the cheesy grin on my face. This was what I was waiting for—the study, not the guy.*

Carson was a graduate student, and he quickly became my mentor. In some of my spare time, I interviewed for the rodent research jobs to see the labs and meet the subjects. I was taken in by some of them, but after spending time dabbling in a few here and there, healing some animals and releasing others, I had to take a break altogether. Not due to feeling like I was going to get caught. The real reason for leaving was the toll it took on me as I increased the use of my healing power.

I was exhausting myself. It even got so bad that Carson sent me home one night during an observation as I found myself stumbling to keep up in the canyons, and once sitting, I was nodding off. I was glad he knew of my dedication to my work well enough to know it wasn't a partying lifestyle that was affecting me, but something else. He assumed it was illness, but I started to feel like there was something else going on.

I've never been the "drink till you stumble" type of gal. For some reason, drinking doesn't faze me even close to the way it does other people, normal people. It must be the whole one-with-the-earth, powerful, angel of mercy, witchy thing I have going on. Hey, vodka is natural—it's wheat or potato, right? I've gotten good at pretending, since downing shots and cocktail concoctions and never getting beyond a giggly buzz can lead to some questioning from noisy-ass Nancy's. I tell you though, not being on my ass most nights or bumbling like an idiot sure has its perks!

Despite the fact that yeah, I do like the taste of vodka, and mixing and muddling drinks is kind of a hobby of mine, it think it's been the vodka keeping the worst of my nightmares at bay. Maybe my little synapses in the noggin get a little over-giddy, and either don't let the big bads in, or they can't find the door.

Needless to say, I have upped my consumption and this upping my nights out lately is not sitting well with certain people in my life. Justin and Carmen are in the "Alex, you're worrying us with your drinking" club. I get a bitter taste in my mouth that Justin may be jealous of the nights I've been spending without him. We used to see each other more often, and nearly every late night event led to me calling him afterward, and inviting him over. But since the night I met Ryan, I haven't seen Justin much at all. Instead, I have been going out after work events, and then heading home alone. Sometimes we don't even talk, or I miss his calls. I'm not trying to avoid him; at least I don't think I am.

Carmen is more concerned about the pesky way alcohol can destroy a person's mind, body, and soul, and I swear one time she insisted I was diving into the harder side of the party life. Been there and done that, not going back. Talk about losing your mind to nightmares; drug abuse is a living nightmare for some of the addicts, both in and out of sobriety—that I know. I tell you, brain chemistry is nothing to mess around with, and neither is lack of sleep. It's no secret that I don't need any help in that department. Nor do I need to touch, rub, and smooch on strangers that I suddenly love, stare at walls and then watch my face melt in the bathroom mirror, or find myself awake all night only to crash and burn for a week after. Nope, I'm all good with my unnatural attachment to muddled fruit soaked in vodka, and the occasional iced and shaken tequila shot.

Well, I guess it's time to focus on the paperwork I need to fill out for Dr. McAdams. It's his damn question about how much alcohol I consume that started me off on this tangent in the first place. Sitting in Dr. Reynolds's office does make this meet and greet a little less stressful for me, yet I continue to stare quizzically at the question in front of me.

"Do you drink alcohol?" Um... yes. *"Do you drink: rarely, every week, every day?"*

Does the questionnaire have a box I can check for "whenever I fucking feel like it?" which lately is almost always.

"How many drinks do you have per week? 1–3, 4–6, 7–10, more than 10." I check 4-6, which feels like an appropriate comparison to the "normal" person's ingestion with the same results. I think circling 'more than 10' is a way to throw them into a tizzy about what they think is the real reason for my nightmares.

There is a light knock on the door, and Dr. Reynolds comes in. She is looking sharp as always in a pencil skirt, and button-down shirt tucked in with a shiny, hook-buckled belt. The turquoise shirt really highlights her skin color and swept back glossy red hair. Her well-done professionalism shows my real class as I clash her sophistication with my ponytail, jeans, sneakers, and Avenger's t-shirt.

She sits down across from me, crossing her legs and leaning toward me in the standard active-listening, empathetic counselor pose. I'm used to it, but she never does it in a way that makes me feel claustrophobic. She has always been able to put me at ease, and in a relaxed state in which I don't feel like I have to be "on" all the time. In my line of work being "on" is a constant.

"Well, don't you look well rested and refreshed; any chance you ran into your mysterious Ryan again?" The glint in her eyes pulls a grin from my lips. "Though, obviously, this time without any facial damaging incidents, so I think we can cross off the possibility that your nightmares were curbed due to your "love tap" that evening."

Of course, as always, she is dead on. I slept wonderfully after the Mantar party and for the following two days. "As a matter of fact, I did run into him a few nights ago, at an event. I've slept like a baby ever since. Maybe you're right, doc; maybe he is somehow filling in the parts of me that have been too afraid to really let someone in and completely trust them. But I don't understand why Justin doesn't create the same reaction. I care for him, and trust him with my life."

She smiles in a way that makes me think she's familiar with this little love triangle I have forming in my life. It is as if parts of Ryan mingle with parts of me and tune to the same frequency. I am definitely having a hard time controlling myself around him. It's getting to the point where Mr. Dark and Enigmatic and I are going to have a little heart to heart about what's really going on.

"It has a lot to do with our chemistry and what the body and mind need." Her words seem to mimic my thoughts. "Even when you don't know it, the brain is running the show; it's the boss telling you and your body what to do. Perhaps Ryan is someone who is more in tune with what your subconscious wants and needs. Justin may be that wonderful guy you can trust, but apparently your body and mind have someone else in mind."

Yep, there is definitely something my body wants from Ryan, but hopefully that carnal need isn't clouding my judgment. And there's that *magic living inside of him* thing he has going on.

"I'm going to go out front and check if Dr. McAdams is here. I'll be right back."

The knock on the door stops her mid-rise. My mind starts to race, and I can hear my heart beating in my ears. I try to do some breathing exercises; in through my nose and out of my mouth. True to form, Dr. Reynolds touches my shoulder lightly and smiles down at me, reassuring me without even so much as a word. At that moment, I know that something about my decision today will change things; that the torment I have been suffering will all go away. That I can finally move past Steven's memory. This may be the way to keep him from punishing me for what I did to him, or maybe the way I'm punishing myself. If I'm lucky, this has all been in my head. But I've never been that lucky.

The paranoid part of my brain kicks in and my faith takes a tumble. This idea is totally batshit crazy! What in the world do I think I'm doing even meeting with some doctor that wants to hypnotherapize me? Okay, that may not be a real word, but it's a real concern, right? I can already feel him digging into my brain. This feels so invasive. What if my powers react in protective mode and I'm not as prepared as I think I am? I know I've been able to let them idle and run without anyone noticing. The power cycles through me and into the earth before I go into overload. That is easier and easier to do now as I am pretty much forced into being around people all of the time.

My reverie is interrupted as Dr. McAdams enters the room. He is shorter than Dr. Reynolds, and the way in which he carries himself makes me feel as if he is even older than the ten years his bio said he had on me. It doesn't have anything to do with gray hair—he obviously dyes it to keep it that blond—or wrinkles on his face since I barely notice a single one. No, his demeanor is what makes it obvious that he is highly intelligent, successful, and motivated. I know he is from San Diego, an avid surfer, scuba diver, and thrill seeker, and from the wet hair on his head it looks like he's been out enjoying the waves.

His golden eyes are set atop a narrow nose and his smile looks so genuine that I can't help but like him instantly. The power swirling inside me sparks with recognition in the way that my *spidey sense* used to know my grandmother was nearby, or how I know the instant Carmen needs me at an event, when Sandra arrives on site, or when choosing who to work with and who to trust. I'm in tune with them, it feels right, and I'm usually on point or just very picky. This common ground makes me feel at ease, and hopeful that this is going to help. It's my mind's way of giving me the green light for him to proceed.

I've read his bio thoroughly, and I know he is discreet and highly recommended. He has worked with many poor souls who either suffered terrible acts of torture, abuse, trauma, or committed those acts themselves. He helps them find the truth, and has healed the most broken of lives. His work with soldiers returning from the countless wars raging in our world is remarkable, and allows many who had no hope to move on.

"Good afternoon, Alex. Is it okay if I call you Alex?"

I nod, smiling. "Absolutely, Dr. McAdams."

"Great. I've been looking forward to meeting you ever since Dr. Reynolds consulted me on your case. I hope you don't mind my appearance. I couldn't pass up grabbing a quick jaunt with my father on the waves this morning. My mother recently passed, so I'm trying to see him every chance I get."

I can see the pride in his eyes when he mentions his father, something I have never felt for any man, let alone my father whom I never knew, and never for my foster father who I hope is enduring unfathomable amounts of pain in a hell dimension somewhere. I smile a little at that thought, and Dr. McAdams smiles back. What a reminder of how freaking odd I am that I am smiling about basically killing a man, who was somewhat of a father, and Dr. McAdams is smiling at the memory of spending some good father/son time in the Pacific ocean's glory. Yep, my life is officially a walking, talking freak show. *Get your Tickets, tickets, anyone?*

I hold my 'just a normal looking chica here folks, nothing to be concerned about' look plastered to my face.

"Not a problem, Dr. McAdams. It's nice to meet you finally as well." I stand, shaking his hand before all three of us take a seat.

"As you may know, I'm formally a physiological psychiatrist, but after moving away from pharmacology to find other ways to change behavior, I now specialize in hypnotherapy." He's relaxed in his chair, and I see the ocean water dripping along the back, down the arm, and only the floor. "Our memories, even the most repressed ones, can be manipulated and adjusted through my techniques, and in some cases, eradicated altogether. I'm not sure where we'll end up with the memories that are obviously creating your nightmares, so we'll start slow and see how you respond."

Easy enough. I just need to keep myself in check, but what if I can't?

We sit and go over the medical basics; no concerns there since I refuse to take any of the medications that had been suggested, so I don't have to wean myself off anything. The doc didn't seem concerned with my self-medicating trips to the bars either.

"What I would like to do next is have you come here again, if that is okay with you, Dr. Reynolds, and use our first session to see if you can indeed be hypnotized. Some people cannot. In my experience, individuals who have suffered intense trauma and subsequent nightmares or night terrors, may be on too high of an alert to allow themselves to relax enough for hypnosis to take place." Well, that sounds like me to a T.

"I hope it won't be too much of an issue. I've been working on my overactive defense systems, and constant worrying about having a nightmare through daily meditation and breathing techniques before bed, and during my more stressful times." I cringe knowing my job can always be pretty stressful. Maybe I'm not as centered as I claim to be. "My fear of losing part of who I am, or of not being present enough or aware during this, has significantly lessened after reading more about the process. I now know that you'll shut things down if I appear out of sorts, right?" I'll also have an added amount of Earthen energy for a super-powered alarm system just in case.

"Absolutely. Typically, some control is passed over to me since your mind is the one creating the terrors. It needs to be released somewhat so I can help you navigate through your past." Dr. McAdams has a thoughtful, almost apologetic look on his face, like he knows what it feels like to fear losing control. "I try to help you find a way to break into the dream creation source, which is hard enough without the patient being in the driver's seat. If the defenses you have in place have already been broken down through your work and practice up to this point, then I feel confident we can find your trigger memory and work on either removing it, or creating a new timeline for you."

"I have been working on dropping my shields after Dr. Reynolds suggested I was exacerbating the issue by being so worried about having nightmares each night." Oh, and of course, the need to enjoy life more as it happens, and focus on the good I have accomplished. Meditation is not easy in my line of work. It's hard to keep my brain from bringing up ridiculous thoughts of flowers, linens, music, locations, but I have gotten pretty good at it.

I don't want to say or do anything that will give me away. No need to let everyone know the real reason why I can't let everything go, or why I even have these damn nightmares in the first place. What if I say something that leads them to think I killed Steven? Okay, maybe this is a bad idea, but nothing else is working and I'm pretty much winging it with all the magic stuff anyhow. It's not as if anyone is around to help a twenty-six-year-old party-planning, closet go-go dancer, power wielder, and trust me, I've tried to find them. I smile despite my nervousness.

"This is also the trickiest part as we try to decide if we need to let whatever is causing all of this mayhem be shifted or removed completely." Dr. McAdams continues on. "Your mind and body reactions while we are in memories before your trauma was created, will help me decide on what I think is best. In my opinion, ridding your mind of it for good may be the best option, since creating a new timeline in which to store it might only create a temporary bandage that will dissolve over time. Removal might be harder though, since it can require events, or feelings surrounding the event, to be partially relived and then rewound. This assists us in getting an exact starting and ending point for the extraction." Ugh, at those words, the alien that popped right out of Riley entered my mind. Get it out! Get it out of me!

The whole thing sounds like some haphazard bandaging, coming undone from a massive wound. But I nod and smile, like a good patient while keeping my jitters at bay. "Sounds like you know what your doing. I've read about the process, and your successes. Plus, Dr. Reynolds promises I'm in good hands." We all smile; Dr. McAdams gives a thumbs-up and then discusses some logistics with Dr. Reynolds while my mind sets adrift.

So basically, my choices are to face the music, do the dance, and get my ass kicked by some uber-dream-creating bitch of a memory now, or wait for it to slowly creep up on me again in some unknown moment in the future. Part of me wants to say the hell with it and get this shit over with, but another part worries about reliving even the smallest part of that time, especially in such an exposed state, and with the possibility of what I did to Steven surfacing.

Am I really secure enough in my ability, to covertly use my power to protect me from further emotional damage, while Dr. McAdams is basically tapped into my brain? Even more frightening is to think this is all about Steven coming back for me. Am I being paranoid? How can he possibly be released? Every lesson with my grandmother taught me that I had to consciously undo something like this, and I know that will never happen. Maybe I can use this technique to my advantage and somehow secure the bind while dipping back into my memories. I wonder if that's possible. Damn, I wish I had someone to ask. I wonder if my senses are on target, that maybe Ryan is someone I *can* ask. Shit, Alex, you can't ask some stranger to help you, no matter how hot he is!

If only someone had been there to guide me on what the hell I was doing when I bound Steven away, maybe this wouldn't be happening. Yet, there is always the possibility that this has nothing to do with his binding at all, not really, just my own memories of what he did to me and the resultant helplessness and powerlessness I can't completely shake. But, I doubt I am getting off that easy. I better work on

81

strengthening myself the best I can, with modern techniques, and repairing or removing his damage can give me that power. The memories, both physical and mental, of what he did to me have impacted my ability to trust many people, and I've developed some bad habits as a way of coping. Perhaps the most apparent is that I never allow myself to be loved fully and honestly, or permit myself to return such affection. If I can just remove even the feeling of what he did, the sounds, the horrific pictures in my head, I may be free, or at least feel less like that scared, powerless little girl. That broken girl will never have existed.

My fingers move towards my wrist, stroking the scars in a soothing motion.

No, I will keep the loathing of him, the deep, burning hate and rage, without the reason for their origin. That is the power I already have, and need. It's nearly settled in my wheel-spinning head; I will continue to practice, keeping my ability to draw on the earth's force grounded while I keep the stores of reserved energy in my body hidden away and locked down, only to be released if need be. That way I can always protect myself, or shut myself up from letting something slip about the Earthen Protector and Healer in me. No need to give the good doctor a glimpse into what I am really hiding. I have worked on this technique since what seems like forever now, but since my grandmother's passing there has been no one to help me keep my practice on point.

It isn't like I could ask Carmen or Sandra to drug me and see what happens. I wonder if anything would even work, since alcohol has no effect, and my only adventure with other recreational options led to some never repeated interesting side effects. Regardless, I trust that I can stay aware, and if I do feel myself slipping, I'll end this hypnotherapy option and find another way. There will have to be another way, a lobotomy maybe, or a good hook-up to a power line to create a reset. I think of Sandra and wonder if I should let her read me before I get into all of this. I know her, really know her, and more importantly, I trust her with my life. What do I have to lose?

Ah, it seems as though Dr. McAdams has been talking to me while I was in my reverie, but true to my abilities I can focus on two things at once, or at least appear to do so. "Alex?" Oops, apparently Dr. M. can tell that I was off in Alex land. "If you aren't comfortable going this route we can always wait. It'll be at least a week before I can set up our initial appointment anyhow, so we have some time. On the other hand, if there is something about me that is causing any concern,

Sharon and I can always make a recommendation to someone else." Hey, wait a minute; can I start calling her Sharon? I look at her with an impish smile, and she shakes her head in a way that tells me she knows what I'm thinking and not to even think about it. We both laugh a bit at the shared exchange. It was much needed with how dramatic this all seems.

"Not at all, Dr. McAdams. If I'm to move forward, it will definitely be with you. However, you're correct, I am a little hesitant about having someone guide me through my brain. Sometimes I don't even like it in here." I shrug and drop my eyes, remembering when someone else had control over me and I was unable to break free. I'm stronger now, and this is not the same situation, not by a long shot. Yet, I can't help but be wary.

He smiles warmly at me, and not in a "you poor thing" way, but in a manner that tells me no matter how broken I might be, I am strong. It is a supportive smile. One hell of a smile actually. He looks good for an older guy. I wonder briefly about how close he and Dr. Reynolds really are. My eyes turn to her, the idea playing around in them and she looks at me with a quizzical look. Oh if she only knew, the vixen.

"Please, call me Ian from now on. There's no need for formality between us."

I think the doc has had some work done on his chompers, perhaps as a result of some wild surfing accident or from getting knocked around saving kittens from a fire. His track record is solid, and he is a friend and trusted colleague of Dr. Reynolds. Nothing I am doing is really working. How much am I willing to drown myself in the drink to keep these things at bay? I don't think my liver can stand it for much longer. I have to at least set this up and then, I think, dive into a reading with Sandra. I feel only she can give me direction, if she can do anything at all. Dr. McAdams, I mean Ian, now he can help me end the constant, vicious reminders of the past for good, or at least make them tolerable.

"Okay, Ian, I'm ready to set something up. This has gone on long enough." And with that he reaches for my hand where it grips the arm of the chair. Geez, I didn't even realize I was doing that.

"Are you sure?" Yes, my mind screams, the power inside buzzing around my fingers in response to his touch, and my fingers relax.

"Yes," I say confidently, "let's do this."

Before I leave, Dr. McAdams gives me some homework that involves delving into the past—to a specific memory, in fact. A time when I was with the Nestrour family, when living with them felt safe, normal even. I think I can do that, I mean I remember being happy when they took Bear and me in with all the open land, and of course, Chey. I loved the idea of having a sister. Moving around so much had made it hard to make friends, and Chey and I got as close as if we had known each other our whole lives. It may take some uncomfortable journeys into parts of my life I have compartmentalized and locked away to find that happy place, but I know it's there. Focusing on Chey should get me to a safe memory, maybe even a joyful one.

When I get home, I'm exhausted. I catch a yoga class just in time, but even with the relaxing meditation practice and breathing exercises, which usually boost my energy, I don't remember ever being this tired. Trying to decide about the hypnotherapy must have been weighing so heavily on me that the final decision released a wave of hidden stress, and I need my bed now! With Pitter fed and cuddling in the crook of my arm, my eyes close when my head hits the pillow.

My dream is different, missing the usual death, gore, and violence I am used to. Justin is here, but he is staring at me in a really vicious way and there's someone sitting in his lap as he sits on a couch of some sort. Where are we anyhow? This place is dark, gothic looking, and my skin breaks out in gooseflesh as I shiver. Wherever I am, I have never been here before, and I hope to leave and never come back again. The music in the background sounds like ice cracking and grinding mixed with nails dragging along a chalkboard. I glance around to see throngs of people rubbing up against each other in time with the harsh sounds.

Justin is holding a young woman around the waist with one hand and caressing her legs and arms with the other. He is looking right at me with that sinister smile as if taunting me, and for some reason I can't turn away. His wicked smirk looks foreign on his strong, intelligent face, but it is Justin; I can feel it. I don't recognize the girl at first because everything is hazy, and I wonder if someone forgot to give the smoke machine a rest. Her black-leathered body turns slightly in his lap, and she glares at me while mouthing something I can't understand.

I'm shocked to see that it's Chey, dressed out of character for sure, but unmistakably her. She seductively slides her hand over Justin's chest, and my mind finally catches up with my rapidly beating heart as I make out her words, *"Doll eyes."*

She stands with quickness, my eyes struggle to follow as she slowly saunters towards me, a menacing glint in her eyes. At first, I think she is going to touch me; my mind screams at me to move, but my feet are cemented to the floor. Oh God, the floor is so dirty and disgusting—focus, Alex, focus! I try to bring energy into my hands but to no avail. Instead of touching me, Chey puts her fingers to her lips before mouthing those two fear-inducing words again.

"Doll eyes."

Man, she is frightening to look at, no longer the little girl I remember. Her skin is ghostly white, and her hair is cut in a sharply angled, midnight black bob that barely brushes her chin. She is shorter than me, but by only an inch or two in her knee-high heeled boots. Chey's body sways like a cobra waiting to strike as she continues to close the distance between us. Suddenly, a low buzz I had mistaken for music hits an intense and loaded climax before it explodes in my brain. She takes the last remaining steps toward me with amazing speed.

"Chey, is that you?" I squeak at her, trying to make some sense of what is happening while looking at my foster sister with fear, something I never dreamed I would feel toward her, ever.

She throws her head back with neck breaking speed and lets out a laugh so chilling that clutch my arms around myself, trembling uncontrollably. Chey's head snaps upright and her eyes are once again nearly level with mine. Hot, menacing breath hits me for a brief second before she snatches both sides of my face with her sharp, piercing nails. With lips nearly touching mine, her mouth opens wide while she lets out a hellacious scream.

"Where is my father, you *bitch*!?!"

CHAPTER 10

"Sandra, What Do You See?"

Journal Entry:

Away from the focus of academia, college life was full of excitement, and the "buzz" my foster mom spoke of as students found themselves. Okay, so sometimes they found themselves lost in bushes high on psychedelic mushrooms, or in the drunk tank after some serious public intoxication, but that was college life, right?

Carson was the only guy that I felt really close to anyhow, and even though he was five years older than me, he didn't make me feel like a child; he didn't make me feel desirable either, but I felt close to him in a professional way.

One Saturday night I was hanging out with a group of my guy friends, and a couple of girls I had grown closer to over the previous months. Shane was my best friend; we had the same sense of humor and the same drive for our education. We hung out at parties, in the library, and at each other's houses watching The Simpsons, and hitting up the 7–11. I always knew something was up when he would disappear at a party and literally ditch me for a half hour or so before coming back. I could tell what was going on. He had that look, the one I grew up knowing. Being the daughter of Stacy Conner, I had a feel for what someone was on and this was a stimulant for sure, with his dilated pupils, euphoria, and wild energy.

On this particular night he'd been gone for an hour before popping up out of nowhere. He swung me around and dragged me towards the keg without so much as a "what's up?"

"Okay, shit, chill out! You're going to pull my arm out of its socket. Where were you anyhow?" He stopped and spun quickly around, nearly touching his nose to my chin.

"Don't come looking for me ever, do ya hear me?" His jaw was set sternly, then a fleeting look of regret passed over his face. "Ha, ha! I'm just messing with you; I had to help out a friend and take a piss. Let's get a beer."

I followed his short stocky frame and light brown head to the keg. He was stronger than most guys twice his size and was a killer surfer and wave boarder. Girl's heads turned as he walked by; he was giving off his amazingly energetic vibe and flashing the patented Shane swoon-worthy smile at the onlookers. Shane was everyone's friend and an overall genuine person.

I knew the timeline; in an hour he'd be heading back to wherever he came from and this time he wouldn't be alone. There would be consequences for following him into the belly of the beast, but I was too intrigued to care. I never knew everything about my mom's habit, not the social side of it anyhow. Most of my experiences lay in her comedowns and those great one-on-one moments with boyfriends when I ended up sleeping in closets wearing my headphones.

I had recently discovered my ability to hold my liquor despite keeping pace with the boys, and I had already clocked their patterns. Shane would be heading on his way soon, and he would have a tail.

Right on cue, he told me he had to use the bathroom again. I was playing bones with the girls, and one of our tattooed biker friends as Shane excused himself. I gave him a good minute and then went after him. I sent my energy outwards, using it to sense him, figuring he was downstairs I kept following him until I hit a wall in the basement. It made no sense that my road ended there. There was no door, and I checked the rooms and bathrooms to be sure. Huh? I went back to the wall and I heard a giggle and thump on the other side. This wall had built-in shelves and a small stereo system. I pushed the buttons, but nothing came on. Following the cord, I noticed it wasn't plugged into anything. I pushed, heard a click and a whoosh and then the wall revealed a door that came about an inch toward me. I opened it wider, revealing darkness, and went inside. After walking about twenty feet, I started hearing laughter and seeing flickers of light. The dark, narrow hallway opened up into a large room decorated with twinkle lights, lamps, and scattered pieces of furniture and beanbags. On the far wall was a DJ table. Some people were up dancing while a large group was on the couches, hovering over a glass table.

I heard Shane whisper, "oh fuck" in the cluster of bodies and some grunts and "heys" as he clamored over legs before rushing toward me. The table was covered in an intricate pattern of white powder, and each couch patron took turns following the line with his or her rolled-up bill. It was mesmerizing, but it also made me queasy thinking of my mom. I felt an unexpected anger rise toward Shane. How could he do something like that? I must have unknowingly let some power leak because he stopped in his tracks and held his hands up in an act of surrender. Shane knew about my mom's drug use, and I know that's why he tried to hide his extracurricular habits from me.

"Save it, I'm not here to judge. I'm here out of pure curiosity." Pushing past him, I moved towards the table with Shane on my heels.

"Don't, Lex. It's not what you think." I spin in my sneakers, placing a hand on my cocked hip while shooting him "yeah, right" glare. He started to rant about stopping me, but some of the other people down there were joyfully waving me over to the table.

"I'm a big girl, Shane, and I don't lie to my friends." Putting my back to him once again, I worked my way over to the friendly calls, sliding onto the couch, my skin prickling from the high levels of electricity bouncing off of everyone. So this is what it's like, I thought, almost as if the act was more of a high than the drug itself. The process, the sharing, it was addictive. I told myself I was only trying it once. That it was just an experiment.

I checked on the energy stored in my body, its intensity at the ready just in case, and then bent down to inhale the powder. My eyes stared back at me from the mirrored table and blinked at the sudden spark and swirl as they cycled quickly between blue, green, and brown. I inhaled and then sat back slowly.

In an instant, I was so in tune with my body and mind, so much so that I swear I felt the rush of dopamine come to life in my brain. Within the next few minutes, I was dancing to Finn spinning on the tables while wearing a girl's platinum blond chin-length wig of the Daisy variety. Time seemed to flash by in small bursts and fits of laughing, talking, dancing, and making plans with complete strangers who were now somehow my best friends. The energy in my body danced around to the music and the life of the room. I felt happy, confident, and energized all at the same time.

But in what felt like the next instant, a stern, commanding voice roared within my head.

"Alexis Eila Conner, get out of there now!"

I didn't wait to hear more; instead, I jerked into motion and quickly moved toward the secret door making a beeline out of the house. As I walked out from behind the secret door, a new group of partakers was coming in. I was incognito in the wig I apparently "borrowed" so Carson was oblivious to my presence, but I sure as hell knew who he was. I stood rooted in place outside the door for a moment before sending my power down the passageway behind him. The sounds of greeting confirmed my suspicions that he wasn't a newbie like me. I barely had time to register it all since Shane was hot on my heels, nearly taking me down as our limbs tangled when he didn't notice me in my statue like state.

"Alex, wait, are you okay? Man, I told you not to follow me. That's it, no more. Never again for you, or for me for that matter. Oh man, you don't look so good. Okay, I'm calling a cab and getting you home. I'm going to call Carmen too."

Getting home was a blur, although I vaguely remember Carmen putting me to bed. I think she was reaming Shane out in the living room about my obviously drugged state. I didn't care. I was dead tired. My constant critter healing had been wearing me down, and this one little experience made me feel like I had been up all night. With my eyes closed, my body began to sink into a deep sleep.

*I woke in an emerald-colored forest, curled up against a tree. My feet were bare and being tickled by soft moss and sprinkles of dew on fern leaves. Grabbing my head in a moan, I rubbed the sleep from my eyes. When I looked up, I came face to face with a fox—not just a fox, **the** fox. The very same one I saved at the "Potholes" years before. I had never forgotten the color of his fur, his markings, or his eyes, and now here he was as an adult, no longer the kit I saved from the rushing waters.*

"So, how was that?" he asked in a rather condescending yet sing-songy voice. "Satisfied now? Are you done with your little experiment?" Holy shit, he was talking to me. I reached out to touch him, for a couple of reasons. First, um yeah, he's a talking fox? I had to touch him just to know that he was real, and second, he was so stinking cute I just had to feel his soft coat. Ha! Bear will go nuts when he smells me.

The fox let out a sound of aghast astonishment as my outstretched hand neared his jet-black nose surrounded by brassy blond fur. "Easy there princess, I'm not your pet pooch."

"Easy Vex, don't scare her now; we need her, remember? Come here child, let me look at you." Now where in the hell was that voice coming from? And why did it sound so familiar, ah yes, my motivator ringing in my skull at the party.

"Up here, child. You are lying on me, you know, so at least give me a little courtesy and let's have a chat." My eyes darted around trying to locate the source of the enchantingly female voice echoing in my head. Actually, I couldn't truly tell if it was my mind or my ears that were taking in the sound first.

I squinted at a shimmer I saw in the bark of the tree, trying to make out what I was seeing. A woman's form appeared in the ancient bark, taking on the appearance of an old hag. She smiled toothlessly.

"Well, hello there my darling, welcome. My name is Terra, and the talking fox is not a hallucination. His name is Vex." Vex let out a chuff of sorts and moved further from me so he could see Terra and me easily. *"How are you feeling? Quite disoriented I'm sure. You know that's what the human drugs can do to our kind, my dear. You need to be very careful, very careful indeed."* Her form melted back into the tree, and I felt a slight hitch in my throat, fearing that she was leaving me. Her form materialized again, but this time she was lying on her back on a thick branch with her body arched so that her breasts protruded seductively from the rest of her body. Boy, Shane would have lost his shit if he saw that.

"You know, I do understand the allure, we are not immune to the promise of feeling unlike ourselves, of living in a different state, orientation, or presence of the mind." Her hair tumbled down in a cascade of branches and leaves. *"I can see why you wanted to try it."* Terra's voice began again, throatier and softer while her hands trailed along her stomach and her sides. *Maybe it was to connect to what you experienced secondhand through your mother during most of your young life. So, what do you think?"*

She turned her face toward me when she finished her questions, whereas before she had only been looking up through her branches and into the glowing night.

"I... I was only trying this one time. I had to know. I've been so off and tired lately. It felt something needed to change. Maybe I was being held down or drained over the pain of my mom being gone from my life for so long. Maybe I was trying to connect to her in some way, but I know I'll never do what she did, even though I know now why she did it. I'm not afraid like she..."

"Oh, but you should be!" Terra's form dissolved before instantly reappearing and shooting out at me. We were eye to eye now and even though my mind screamed, I could not turn away. Her face crawled with clicking and scurrying insects, dark beetles, bright red centipedes, and maggots, while her hair writhed along the hard bark like tunneling worms.

"Easy Terra," shouted Vex. He moved close to my legs and leaned against me, sitting on his haunches and staring up at the woman's face. Terra softened immediately, and her frightening form disappeared into the hard ridges of the tree bark.

A little girl formed next, tiny on a small branch just above my head. For some reason, I felt an emptiness, but only for a moment.

"Sorry dear, we just can't risk losing you as well. A power as strong and unique as yours must stay with us—on our side. We can't afford to have you go the way of your mother, or worse, following the others to the wickedness of the dark." That caught me off guard. Were there others with my level of power who had turned evil? How? Why? And did she know where my mother was? Was she okay?

"Yes, yes, who, why, where, and when. I hear your questions spinning in that quick-as-a-whip mind of yours, but no bother; you are stronger than any of them. Even those with your blood weren't and never will be as strong, but rather weak and, dare I say, simple minded and easily manipulated by the promise of frivolous and vain things." Terra's matter-of-fact tone and the air in which she held herself looked out of place on the child-like form she reflected. It reminded me of the young vampire Kirsten Dunst portrayed in Interview with a Vampire. The memory causing me to shiver at the memory of her screams in the sun.

"Just know this my dear." Terra went on, oblivious of my unease. "The harsh industrial drugs damage us, drain us more easily and more potently than the humans. You must know that somewhere in that pretty little head of yours after living with your mother." Being lectured by a ten year old was starting to grate on my nerves, and I couldn't help but think that it's what Terra intended.

"But that isn't the only reason I have brought you here, little Eila. You are also creating a great imbalance and disruption that will not only alert those wicked Dark Protectors to your presence, but also drain you of your abilities, silly girl." I haven't been called Eila since my grandmother passed, but it didn't hurt to hear someone else call me what, I had only heard from her lips. Instead, it soothed me in a way that made being in this weird-ass experience, in this strangely

91

remarkable place feel comfortable. Yet, that ease left me when my mind caught up with what else she had said.

"What? I'm causing all of this to myself? How?"

Vex spoke up. "I thank you for saving me, Eila. I was a test for you on that day so many years ago. I told Terra it was a bad way to go about it, and I knew with your hyper-observant nature and the uncanny way injured animals find their way to you that it could be disastrous." His fox eyes glared at the tree-girl, yet she only shrugged and picked at her nail of bark and lichen allowing Vex to carry on after a long inhale. "You cannot heal all of them, Eila, you just can't! You are draining yourself and upsetting the balance. I know you want to help, but seeking out lab animals in addition to the ones you find in the wild is tipping the scales too far. We needed to warn you before it's too late, and you lose everything." Vex's words sent a shiver up my spine, and a strong feeling of possessiveness filled me, as if I were Gollum clinging to his Precious. My powers clamped down, and my energy began to build within me. The Earthen power rushed into me quickly there, wherever there was, more readily than in the real world. Vex watched me, twitching his nose frantically and flicking his ears wildly.

"What? What is it Eila? Danger? Are there Dark Protectors here? How?" My hand reached down toward him automatically and stroked his fur. He immediately calmed before yanking his head away from me.

"Hey, cut that out, I'm not your fairy dog friend, Aurora!" He didn't take off too quickly though, allowing one last caress on the top of his head before flicking his tail and trotting a good ten feet away. Disney princess my ass, look who's talking—literally.

The air rumbled, and Terra's little girl form vanished, leaving no trace of her. A torturous humming began to swarm inside my head and I held tight to my power, ready for a fight. Terra's voice echoed all around me as if she was trying to ease my tension, but I was wound far to tightly in fear. "Easy, Eila, we are not the enemy. We are only here to warn you." I knew that, I thought, but my body was reacting to something. Was it a test?

"See, you have fear; fear of losing your power, the one thing that has always been with you, your one true constant. It is good to feel that fear and to learn from us so you don't lose control. However, too much fear, and the mistrust you have lingering in your soul toward even those you love the most, that is what you must try to overcome. Always stay on your guard, yes, but trust yourself. Trust love, it is *what sets us apart from them." I knew she meant the Absolute Protectors, and I knew she was right—about all of it.*

I couldn't find her at first as my eyes followed the trunk of the tree all the way up its thickness. Legs began to form, followed by a waist, breasts, and her head. The branches and leaves above became a beautifully awe-inspiring sight as they flowed from her and created a mesmerizing image of gorgeous, intertwining curls of hair. She looked at me, her eyes glowing emerald green. They were an exact reflection of my own, and I stood before stumbling back a step, sensing the power in them, knowing her power was a part of me.

*"It is time for you to go, my dear, my Eila. Heed our warnings, stay strong, and accept the help we send you. For if you do not…" her voice started to reach a crescendo and her leaves and branches reacted as if taken up by gusts of wind in a hurricane. Terra's strong wood-covered arms flew out as her back arched, and she threw her head back and up toward the sky, "**all will be lost!**" she sang out to me in a heart-clenching wail.*

I woke, drenched in sweat, my mind reeling. What had just happened? Where did I go? And lastly, she said those of my blood weren't strong enough to resist the lure of the Absolute Protectors, didn't she? So, who in my family turned to the darkness, and why?

I jolt awake, feeling sweat drip slowly from my hair, leaving a chilling trail along my back. I don't know if the sweat caused the tremor or if it was the residual effects of the mind-jarring nightmare. My body aches, like it typically does after one these dreams.

I am so over it and what the hell was that anyhow? It makes me want to text Chey and see if everything is okay. What do I say to her? *Hey sis, been spending any time freaking people out at strange jaded clubs?*

Settling instead for a test, I send her a quick message before heading to the bathroom for a shower. I plan to work out this morning, which will require a shower later, but I have to remove whatever that nightmare left on me. I feel filmy and overheated, so a nice cool shower should do the trick. I'm sure Sandra will love to hear about this one. Tonight I am finally heading to her house for my reading; good timing if you ask me.

Looking in the mirror treats me to quite a sight. My hair is damply sticking to my face here and there, and knotted as if I had rubbed it against a hundred balloons before lying down. The dark circles under my eyes might give way under some heavy make-up, but it's the impact on my thinker muscle that takes the biggest hit with each nightmare. My brain is nestled in a thick fog, and it takes more than caffeine to get out of the haze and squash the throbbing headache. The sun is up, and I have a couple of hours before I need to be in our office. A nice run on the beach and maybe even some bodysurfing might recharge my soul and give me some clarity. I am looking forward to talking to Sandra tonight more now than ever. A shiver runs through me when I look in the mirror again, my eyes connecting with the woman looking back at me. For a brief moment, my eyes spark a pale emerald green fire as I pull from the earth in an attempt to bring myself some balance and peace.

Chey and I text each other throughout the day, I realize I haven't been keeping up with her enough, and the shade of her in last night's nightmare leaves stings of guilt and worry that take all day to shake. She is doing well, of course, in her senior year and working on college applications. All is well; it's only my jacked-up mind that's in turmoil.

The rest of the day is a slow motion walk through hours of phone calls, emails, and designing. When evening comes, I head to Sandra's for my reading. I asked to meet at her house, as I need a little distance from mine. With everything transpiring at my loft lately, a break will be good thing. Plus, for some reason Pitter acts utterly nuts around Sandra; he won't leave her alone, rubbing all over her legs and jumping into her lap. Not to mention, that I swear he will not shut up. Doesn't he understand that we do not speak meow? Well, maybe Sandra does because he actually seems partially appeased when she speaks back to him. Crazy animal—I guess he has to be since he's a part of my life. All aboard! I'm driving the crazy train!

Sandra's house is stunning, even though she refused to keep anything from her ex that wasn't trashed during the nasty breakup— worthy of Angela Basset's *Waiting to Exhale* rampage. She did, however, get enough in the monetary compensation department to afford herself a beautiful single-story home in La Jolla. The air always seems fresher and cooler here, as if Mount Soledad chills the hot Pacific Beach air as it rolls down from its steep precipice.

Sandra greets me with a genuinely, gleeful smile, instantly making me happy. It's one of the reasons I bonded with her so quickly. She waves me into the entryway, and I catch a scent from the six gardenias floating in a large glass bowl of water and shells. I recognize the design from one of our events; I guess she took off with one of the florist's set, the little sneak. Sandra sees me looking and gives a little smirk and shrug of her shoulder. Every group has someone that's a little klepto, don't they? Hell, guess I'm happy to have helped her decorate, and I do love gardenias.

Sandra's house is a three-bedroom home sprawled out and open, with natural travertine floors and cool-toned walls. Photographs in black and white with occasional shocks of color from a bracelet, animal, or car adorn her entry wall. It is perfectly tranquil, with bamboo growing in large ceramic pots, and the sound of trickling water falling along her fountain wall. All of this is made even better by the large cushy slate-colored couch to flop down on. She places a tall glass of vodka and soda, muddled with oranges and lemons in my hand as my grateful tush hits the cushion.

She wears a t-shirt so tight it could make a priest blush with no need of a bra to keep the girls perky. We're both wearing our favorite comfy yoga pants that we buy in sets of two for each other every Christmas. I tuck my feet underneath me and take a nice, long, and well-deserved gulp from her delicious drink; nope, no dainty sips going on here. Momma needs her cocktail!

"So, how's Ryan?"

I nearly spit my drink into her face. Of course, she's no-holds-barred, going right for the jugular with a sly grin and wicked flash in her eyes. That damn arched eyebrow makes me feel instantly guilty. I shift a little, feeling the lingering tingles from his touch and trying to keep my body calm. Get a grip, Alex, he isn't even here.

"Ah, damn girl, you don't even need to say a word. You're in trouble with this guy. Does Justin know? Carmen?"

"Geez, nothing is going on that needs to be reported to the authorities! We're just friends. Coworkers? Acquaintances, maybe?" My all-knowing best friend just shakes her head while I try to label what Ryan and I are.

"Okay, give me a break! We work together on occasion and fortunately he's tolerable." Nice try Alex, there is no way you're going to convince Sandra when you can't even convince yourself.

"Okay! I don't know what's happening, but he has me twisted in all sorts of directions." I feel the heat of her stare, and see her sideway glance giving me those "oh ya?" eyes of hers.

"Directions, Sandra, not positions. Can I please get this out? I'm trying to have a real conversation here, so get your mind out of the gutter!" She chuckles and takes a sip of her drink.

"Hey, you're one to talk. I don't believe *I* said a word."

We laugh out loud and lean back, enjoying our cocktails and nibbling on the edamame she set out for us. Three drinks in and then it's time to bite the bullet and let her perform her little trick.

"Okay." She says perkily and turns to me on the velvety couch, tucking her left knee under her right. "Let me see those beautiful hands and relax. Open your mind to me."

"What? Why? Where are the cards? Candles? Smelly shit?" I look around, half expecting the candles elegantly placed around her open living room to catch fire in a spectacular fashion.

"Oh, that whole bit is just for clients, girlie, theatrical showmanship you know. I don't actually need any of it to *really* read someone."

She takes my hands, and the air around us changes and charges, like a storm brewing. I've always known there was a magnetic pull to Sandra. She's the type of girl everyone is drawn to, while I, on the other hand, slightly scare people. Smoother than silk, Sandra can make the slyest con artist give up everything before he even knows what hit him.

Without warning, my power pulls from its hiding spots in my body and gives her a jolt.

"Ah, there you are." I give a start, looking at her with wide eyes, and I'm fairly certain my mouth is gaping open like a frozen fish. Either I just electrocuted her, or her hair is literally floating around, all mystically, on its own. My hands start to pull away, but I know Sandra, and I trust her immensely. Hell, she isn't heading for the hills after obviously feeling the shocks of my power running through her. Honestly, it feels like it does during my ebbs and flows with Gaia. It is such a strange sensation to have with another person, when I have only ever felt it from the water and earth.

Memories come to mind. I smell salt air, the scent of Colorado sage, and the gardenias mix together and flow around us in a fragrant haze. There aren't any noticeable sounds other than our steady breathing and the faint rustling of her hair on the fabric of her shirt. It has been too long since I have felt this aware, this observant. It's a gift I used to focus on constantly while learning about my power with Grandmom, and when I spent time alone, plotting out how I would give Steven his final demise. I take in the happiness and pain of it all, and just continue to breathe.

"I know you aren't scared, Alex, but can you ease off a bit? I can't funnel as fast as you're sending."

"Oh, am I the one doing that?" It would make sense. I've always felt the need to connect with Sandra, and I took time to nurture our friendship. It's taking tonight for me to realize how much I don't want to hold back from her, how much I want to share what is hidden inside me with somebody I can trust, and I do trust Sandra.

"You know, I bet Ryan has some ideas of what to do with all this power, darling. Hahahaha!"

"Very funny there, *Little Miss full of surprises*. Are we going to get to second base anytime soon or are you just going to enjoy holding hands forever, you prude!"

"Patience, young Alex, you must first learn to hone your use of the force." Normally, our Star Wars references to each other would make me giggle, but the apparent elephant in the room is keeping me from lightening up. The room silences even further, and she begins to speak in a distant voice.

"The vision is starting now, I've slipped into a part of your past. I see an older woman, sixties, blue eyes. She looks familiar, but I don't know her."

"My grandmother!" I blurt out.

"Yes, that's her, I recognize her from your pictures. She's with another woman close to her age, Diane? Dana?" My brain ticks around in my head, working through memories, dusting off the silence that I have clung to since her passing.

"Ah, it's Dana. My grandmother spoke of her friend Dana many times. She always sounded a little batty, but maybe she's a bit more like us than I thought. Hey, what is all this anyhow? Are you a clairvoyant or something? A mind reader? Voodoo priestess? Oracle? There is no spoon." I don't know what other beings there may be in the supernatural world, but knowing about my existence and those before me, I don't doubt for a second that there are all sorts of people with amazing abilities.

"Shhh blabbermouth, there's more! Geez, take a deep breath; this is work you know, not just a snap of my fingers sideshow. We'll settle all the "what are yous" later there, sparky. You've got some wicked freaky power thing going on yourself, so let's save the chit chat for later when we can both spill it." She's right, of course, so I zip it

97

quickly and take deep breaths, reining in my power while easing off the clutch a bit.

"Okay, so we have Grandmom, Dana, and it looks like they're cooking. They're definitely following some sort of recipe. Did either of them have glaucoma? Because those don't smell like plain ole brownies to me." Wow, all her senses are triggered during a vision, as if she's really there. It reminds me of my nightmares, and I a sliver of dread wriggling its way inside makes me shudder.

"Oh, okay that's gone. Ah, the bunny. Seeing this little guy symbolizes trickiness. Little bastard, he always gives me the briar rabbit slip, trying to lure me into his spiny patch. I'm not your tar baby tonight, you twitchy rodent, nor am I Alice, you tease."

"What in the hell are you rambling on about, Sandra? Ouch! Okay, geez. No need to get violent about it. I kind of need my finger for, well, everything." My finger cracks a bit, and Sandra continues without seeming to notice a thing.

"Things seem to be fading out now, that must be it. Oh wait. What the…" Sandra takes a deep inhale and I brace myself. I sense something unbelievably powerful creeping into my body. My ears begin to thump with the humming from my nightmares as blackness encroaches on the rims of my sight. It is starting, right here with Sandra. Am I awake? This can't be happening—unless this isn't a nightmare? Is this real? Shit, I knew this would happen. Why did I agree to this? Now I've brought Sandra into my mess as well. What a selfish decision, one I made in desperation, a motive that never leads to happy endings.

I'm not in Sandra's house anymore. Rather, I'm somewhere else entirely, but it's too dark to tell exactly where, and I can't seem to move. Am I tied up? I hear wicked laughter within my thoughts followed by that voice—Steven.

"Got ya, little girl. It was all a matter of time, and only you could help me." Pain lashes through my body, but I am still frozen. Not a single muscle responds, and my mind can't focus long enough to urge power into my fingertips or pull it from inside me. My mind is mush; I'm unable to gain control of myself long enough to hold on to even the smallest tendril of power. I remember this feeling, this powerless entrapment I vowed never to let myself succumb to again. I should be stronger than this. I have to be.

Suddenly, another presence arrives and my senses tell me I am safe. A new energy resonates just like mine, telling me I'm going to be okay. Ryan? Maybe it is Ryan. For a minute the pain subsides, and I'm aware of a cool hand on the back of my neck. At the same moment, something warm and velvety soft tickles my hands. I regain some control over my body and look down to see a jet-black rabbit.

Pain explodes in me again and nothing can keep my guttural screams at bay. Just let it end! I accept my punishment for what I've done. I should have known there would be a price, even after all this time. An icy coldness slaps me in the face and I'm pulled from the nightmare. My eyes open to the sight of Sandra's ceiling fan rotating above me where I'm sprawled out on the floor. Blinking water from my eyes, Sandra's frightened face comes into view.

"You're lucky I shocked you out of your freaky trance with the ice bucket; I nearly resorted to slapping the shit out of you. Damn it, Alex! You scared the hell out of me. All that glowing green eyes rolling in the back of your head, zombie-like shit. I mean seriously! What in the hell was that? Is that what you've been going through? I never realized it was as bad as that. Shit, shit, shit! Two rabbits, an unidentified big bad of some sort who is pissed as hell at you, and some crazy old lady making pot brownies with your grandmother? First things first, we need another drink, stat. After that, you need to start talking, girl. You're not alone in this anymore. We'll figure this out together." I hear her loud and clear, but I'm still having a hard time fixing on where she is exactly. My vision swirls in and out of focus, and all I can do is try to blink the haze away. I finally sit up and see her clearly for the first time.

"How about a hand so I can get up? Oh, and a towel would be nice. I think next time a glass of ice water will suffice and not an entire bucket. Oh, and bring me the bottle of vodka will you? This may take a while."

After a few minutes of banter back and forth, mainly me quoting *The Matrix* with all her oracle-ness and no-spoon-having ass, she schools me on the ways of her kind of magic. Sandra draws on Earthen energy, as I do, but she takes it within her, listens to it, looks within it, and sends it right back. She is very direct about not holding onto the pictures and thoughts that come to her; others have gone mad keeping them. They don't belong to her; they are other people's pasts, presents, and futures. No one else, not even someone with her gifts, should keep them. She and her twin brother are both Seers. He lives in Virginia, working as some super-secret FBI agent on a national security gambit, and more than twice she tells me she doesn't know exactly what he does, so I might as well stop asking. I should count myself lucky that I even know about him, or maybe unlucky seeing as she doesn't linger on the subject of him for long. I get the feeling that though twins, they aren't close.

It's amazing to know there are other people out there with unique gifts to help do some good in the world. Even better to know that one of them happens to be my best friend. I don't think I believe in coincidences much anymore—no, her friendship is meant to be.

We have an intriguing trip into all things Sandra the Seer, which includes understanding her ability to emote feelings in others by showing them glimpses of their past, present, or future life. In some cases, like with our session, she can feel and sense as much as the other person does. We then turn the discussion to my lineage, and not surprisingly, Sandra knows of the Earthen and Absolute Protectors very well. She had sensed the power in me for some time, but let me take my time to open up to her completely. She had known about the abuse I suffered at the hands of Steven, but hearing that he was an Absolute Protector and what I had done to him, versus the story of his suicide, doesn't make her turn pity upon me; instead she takes a hold of me. We cry together, and she tells me how strong I am fighting him on my own, and that from now on, I am not going to be alone. It also doesn't surprise me that she knows of Terra the Tree Goddess. Sandra explains that even though we have different powers, Seers and Protectors both pull from Gaia, and the Tree Goddess is one of her most famous emissaries.

After hours of digging in my brain and finishing off her liter of Kettle One, it comes down to this. First, my grandmother's friend Dana knows or has something to tell me or show me. Hopefully, it's more than a long, strange trip while watching the Yellow Submarine and chasing off Blue Meanies.

Second, there are two tricks I need to watch out for, which have me second-guessing myself and everyone else in my life. So much so, that my brain is about to explode under the pressure. Trust has always been an issue for me, something abandonment and loss created, topped off with the trauma from Steven's abuse that cemented it in place. Now, Sandra and I agree that continuing my preparation with Dr. McAdams is still the best step for me to take toward getting some focus and clearing my head. The strides I've made with my meditation practice, may be the only reason I'm functioning at all, so there is at least one thing I'm doing right! Not to mention, we both think a peek into the past might be helpful for what is to come, since last but not least— and what I truly need to face—is the cold, hard, fucked-up truth that Steven is somehow breaking free from his exile.

Worse yet, I will be the one responsible for letting him out.

CHAPTER 11

"Watt the Hell?"

Journal Entry:

After that intense drug-induced dream with a Tree Goddess, when I found out that I have the ability to speak to creatures—well at least one—a lot changed for me. I guess that is an understatement since I spent the next day trying to talk to Bear, and finding odd pieces of foliage and fox hairs all over me.

Bear went crazy with the scent and looked everywhere for the intruder. I stayed in my room with him most of the day, since I didn't want to get mauled and drooled on by Carmen's dogs as well. One thing was for sure, that was one majorly trippy dream; I had been good and warned about the dangers of sampling any more illicit substances, but I also now knew what had been draining my energy. Even though my good deeds were saving the lives of plants and creatures big and small, I just couldn't save them all. I had to back off on my mission to save every one I came across, and I surely had to stop searching them out.

Even though I didn't partake ever again, I still hung out with my friends on their wild adventures. I knew that, sooner or later, Carson and I would cross paths again outside of school. The night came as springtime led to outdoor get-togethers. One Friday night, Shane had a party at his house. It was a small crowd, and we spent most of our time on the back patio listening to music and grilling out. Shane coined it his famous Grill and Chill. Of course, the Grill and Chill always turned out to not be as chill because the crazy characters that came by.

One such character, Cleef, set up shop in the Jack and Jill bathroom. I didn't know when he went in, but when I went in the bathroom to fish Shane out, Carson was there with a bill poised under his nose. When I looked down into the mirror I saw his pupils dilate as his brain registered my face. It was a good thing Cleef was quick to realize Carson was about to flip out and quickly moved the mirror away to avoid sacrificing his bounty.

"What the fuck, Cleef? I was up next!" Shane was so oblivious sometimes. It was then I realized I was happy that he was more of a stoner. I think my evening of craziness kept him away most of the time.

"Alex, hey, oh.... how're you? Wow, I didn't know you were here. What are you doing here?" Carson's bazillion questions were as scattered as his eyes. They darted from me to the mirror and back again, searching my face.

"What do you mean what is she doing here, bro? Is there a problem? Cause this is my house, Carson, so if there's a problem with you and Alex, you can take off." Ugh! Shane's tact was awful when he was high, aggressive even. It was time for an intervention to bring him back to the chill guy I knew.

"It's Carson, Shane, remember? We spoke about Carson and my research, remember? Geez, I'm fairly certain you're good for, well, forever. Let's grab a beer instead." I grabbed Shane's hand and gave one last look at Carson before I turned away. He followed us out, catching up to Shane quickly so he could talk him down and apologize.

The night got much chiller after that. Carson and I hung out after the awkwardness disappeared. It was cool spending time with him to talk about non-school-related matters. By the end of the night, he was telling me how glad he was that he wasn't my supervisor anymore, and that all he wanted since the day we met was to ask me out. We sat curled up together on a papasan chair, snuggling and slyly watching Shane work his magic on a couple of girls. Girls loved Shane; he was easy to talk to, cute as hell, and wicked smart. He deserved a nice girl, but boy was he a player. I hoped that nice girl didn't come around too soon, or he would miss out. Deep in my thoughts, I hadn't noticed that Carson had stopped snickering and watching Shane with me, but instead was staring at me with a lopsided grin on his face.

"I'm going to kiss you now, Miss Conner. I hope that's okay with you." His hand found the back of my head and I nodded my approval as he slowly and passionately kissed my lips. His mouth was so soft, the curls of his long hair tickling my cheek. My power sparked and sizzled within me, and for the first time I really longed for a man, this *man, my mentor and friend. I really don't know what came over me when I allowed Carson to carry me downstairs and into Shane's roommate's room. He was away in Hawaii for the semester, so it was kind of the guest room, and oh, it was missing a door, so a shower curtain sufficed.*

Carson's warm, soft hands traveled all over my body as we kissed. My thoughts had raced for a moment. This wasn't considered a one-night stand, right? I mean, I had known him for almost a year, and I felt I could trust him, and boy could I feel the rest of him loud and clear. The real question was, could I allow it to go any further? Not because I didn't want to, but because something in me was broken after what my foster father had done to me. I tensed at the memory and Carson immediately stopped to look into my eyes. He kissed me again before he whispered in my ear.

"You're the most beautiful, intelligent girl I know, Alex. I can wait if you want us to." He brushed the hair from my face and kissed me gently again. Wow, were his lips real? My goddess they tasted like fire and ice cream all at once. I worshipped his lips, and my body apparently wanted more than that as I rubbed myself against him suggestively.

"I don't think I want to wait." My response was lost in his next lustful kiss, and then my clothes were lost too. Our bodies fit against each other like perfect puzzle pieces... That feeling of connection was amazing, as if we were perfectly in time and rhythm with each other. Our first night together was intense, passionate, and, honestly, a little scary. At one point I thought my power would boil over, so it was a test of will, as it wasn't something I had ever trained for. I also don't think some of the things we engaged in were ever mentioned in health class, or in Judy Blume books. He was very giving and exploratory of my body, and I tried not to let my shyness and inexperience shine through, but at times that was a bit difficult. He was apparently a huge proponent of using everything the goddess gave him to satisfy me, whether it was his lips, tongue, fingers, or his very erect weapon of choice. I'm sure I blushed quite a few times, but more like flushed with pleasure as I found comfort in knowing him, even if this was our first intimate time together.

After that night, we were inseparable. We went to dinner, cooked, met up, or went together to parties, and for a while, I trusted him completely. One thing I had blinded myself to, was the fact that Carson had the same illness as my mother, the same addiction, and that was what drove us apart. He became dependent on using some sort of upper when we went out; he couldn't even have a few drinks and call it a night. Soon, I started to go home before him and left him to his partying. I tried not to worry at first, as a lot of my good friends went in and out of that rabbit hole, but I felt Carson wasn't going to come out of it, and our relationship suffered as a result. The mood swings were the worst. Once the increase of mood elevation was spent in his system, he'd be angry, irritable, and overall vicious and mean. It was a side of him I hadn't seen before, and the contrast between his sweet, seductive self when he was high, versus the come down was tortuous on me, and even worse, he couldn't see it for what it was.

The ending was painful for both of us, and I don't think he ever really knew why. It's hard when someone can't see their own addiction. I nearly dared to heal it out of him one day while he slept in my bed for twelve hours straight after being up all night on a bender. The idea of healing his body and mind, of ridding him of that disease danced around in my head, and I knew I could do it. I'd healed Chey; I'd brought animals back from addiction in research studies, and even some from the brink of death. But Carson was different. I questioned each selfish and manipulative thought. Could I do that? Should I do that? It meant altering his life plan, taking away his free will. Just because I couldn't live his lifestyle didn't mean he was a bad person, right?

I hovered over him, the magic tingling in my hands as sparks of my power pull from my finger tips, touching his cheek delicately to release a moan from his lips. All I had to do was touch him further and envelop him in the energy. I would start by removing the drugs from his system and then the idea of doing or enjoying the drugs from his mind. I'd never done anything quite as intense as that—what if I did something wrong and changed him forever? I wouldn't have been able to live with myself if Carson were somehow damaged by my selfishness. Chey was different; I only had to remove a moment in time, whereas Carson was engrossed in the world. The people in it were his friends, my friends. How could I tease it all out? I might cause irreparable damage, and that was all I needed to tell myself. My heart and mind slowly backed out of the plan. My power had already subsided, the goddess energy already knowing what shouldn't be done. I couldn't; it was as simple as that. It was too close to the dark side of my abilities, something perhaps an Absolute Protector would do.

I bent down, kissing Carson gently on the lips before moving to my desk and drafting a letter. The note, I left on his clothes, and gave him one last kiss before leaving my house. I didn't go back till later that *night, and by then, Carson's car was gone. Nothing was in the house when I returned, no note in response, nothing.*

A few days later I was asleep in my bed when I heard Carmen talking to someone. The other voice was subdued at first, so I didn't immediately recognize it. Once I sent my magic out, I knew instantly that it was Carson, and I found that I couldn't move. I was frozen in bed, not knowing what to do or expect. My letter had pretty much spelled it all out, letting him know that this was the best for us. He didn't need to change for me, and I needed to be away from that whole scene and what it was doing to us. Not much time passed before the front door closed and Carson was gone. Carmen knocked on my door lightly before entering with various items in her hands. A hoodie of mine, some CDs, movies, and Bear's spare leash and collar set. Seeing our relationship in her arms, I began to cry while Carmen moved to comfort me. Carson was the first boyfriend I had ever had, and I let him go. I could have made it different, better even, but I didn't. Instead, I grieved for the loss of my first love, for the emotional and physical joys and pains we had together, and for the awful truth that even though I had powerful gifts, I'd have to sacrifice what I wanted for the sake of using it justly.

"I'm so sorry, Alex. I know how much he meant to you. Is there anything I can get you? A burger? In and Out? Ice cream? I know, so cliché?" Carmen wiped a tear from my face and held my hand. "Carson wasn't a dick about it. He brought back your things and took the pile you set out for him. He said one album was missing though, so he grabbed it. Oh geez, I hope that was okay, he caught me off guard."

Eyes wide, I jumped off. "What album? I already gave him the Bob Marley one, and that was all I had of his, the rest are my father's collection. That collection is the only thing I have of his, my only connection to a man I never knew, and Carson knows that!" I ran to the bookshelf in our living room that doubled as the movie/music storage. I thumbed through the ten albums, the only remnants of my birth father, my only link to the person he was. My breath caught, and I knew what was gone.

"The Wall," I whispered and tears streamed down my face. I moved the other albums aside to feel the empty space where the Pink Floyd album used to rest. A piece of paper brushed against my fingers and I took hold of it.

Dearest Alexis:

I know how this must feel, treacherous I'm sure, but I need this piece of you. Please let me know when you're coming back for it, coming back to me.
  Love and miss you more,
  Carson

How dared he keep hostage something so important to me? My teacher, guide, and mentor had taken his skill in psychology to a whole new level by thinking that game would work on me. The drugs had obviously made him mad for him to stoop so low. I knew I would never be able to trust who Carson had become and, true to the coincidences in my life, in that moment, I began to put another brick in the wall—rebuilding it around my heart and mind once again.

Not coming home from Sandra's house till the next morning really put Pitter in a fine mood let me tell ya. He is bitchier than a bumblebee in a silk flower shop. Not to mention Justin's texts that he apparently sent all night long, left unanswered, which resulted in how much pissier they get as I scroll down. I have some explaining to do—to both of them. But for now, I have a bride and a wedding in a hot tent in the So Cal desert to attend to. Loads of fun as Bridezilla has already been driving Nic completely batty—not the longest of trips by any means.

Don't get me wrong, I do love creative, batty Nic, but not "I'm gonna killa bitch" crazy-as-hell Nic. I have so much on my mind that I'm honestly having a hard time deciding where to start. Sitting cross-legged on my balcony, I follow my breath in a guided meditation. I need to calm my mind. It is the one thing I look forward to in the session with the soul-surfing Dr. McAdams, some peace with the removal of bits of the past that will help me focus on my future. Feeling refreshed, I gather my things and head out to the desert.

One thing about remote locations, aside from the natural beauty and splendor, is the need for power that isn't always readily available. Generators are a must, so our electrical game has to be on point and capable of handling even more than the anticipated, due to the inevitable add-ons, or "oops, I didn't tell you about that" moments from the clients. Oh, and boy do caterers love cooking and serving in the heat. The Pacific may cradle San Diego, but it is a scorching desert, people! One only needs to go a mere two miles inland, over cliffs and hills, to find air quite devoid of even a single flutter of salt air breeze. Carrying a table for twelve on your shoulder is a bitch on its own, let alone trekking it fifty yards over the heated terrain from the catering tent to the wedding tent. All smiles on their way in, but boy do the sailor mouths come out when they return. I think they even made Carmen blush.

"Why didn't the bride tell us she needed extra wattage for a huge fountain attached to her ginormous cake? I mean, does her cake need to match the size of her ass?" Matt is fuming, nearly pulling his hair out. I can't help but replay Doctor Emmett Brown's crazy reaction when he realizes he needs 1.21 gigawatts to get Marty back to the future. Matt leads my lighting and power distribution department, and he is beyond livid. Carmen nearly drops her entire folder, full of lighting gels at his not so discreet comment about the new bride. Nic's chuckling is obvious as he lounges on the catering crates, getting surly with his cocktail. His job is done for the night, even though at times I wondered if he was going to make it. A few too many mock-chocking pantomimes behind the bride's back if you ask me.

Carmen is my fire engine, but also my flame retardant. She prevents fires and puts them out, all in one tiny little body. She knows how to work our team and she somehow has Matt wrapped around her petite fingers. Her incredible road-racing legs don't seem to be a hindrance either. I once thought she and Matt may have been tumbling around in the sack, but that hasn't been confirmed, yet. She is very discreet, which is one of the reasons she's my number one. She can make hardass clients happy, and the easiest ones euphoric. I wouldn't trade her for the world, and I make sure she knows that. Plus, who else is as crazy as me to love this work and these insane hours? Thankfully, the power add-on turns out to be a minor hiccup, and the event goes smoothly, but Matt isn't letting it go just yet.

"Hey, Matt, at least you didn't have her slobbering hugs and kisses all over you. She saved those for me after kicking my ass all day." Nic's slurring speech may be the only reason Matt isn't pushing his ass off those crates right now. "Weddings, bah! Alex, can't we do fewer of these and more company events? I can't handle the stress. Look, just look at my hair, it's falling out."

"Easy there, Nic. It's just a chunk of your décor feathers, you spaz!" I lovingly smack him in the arm and refill his drink. Normally, Carmen and I head out before striking an event, but after everyone's nerves had been grated today we're staying to make sure everyone is taken care of before they quit on us.

After downing another drink, Nic catches a ride with Matt and gives me his patented "don't call me for this shit again" sarcasm-filled smile. Carmen still has her headset on and the usual spark in her eyes after an event is fading. I had been hoping to grab some food and a drink after an event like this, but I can tell something is off so I break the silence.

"What's up, girl? We've endured worse; why so glum?" It's easy to understand why we work well together. I can be all scattered and harried during the design process while she is the picture of Zen—that is, until event time. Then I am the more visibly calm and cool director, while Carmen is on high alert putting out fires right and left. Good thing we're both excellent problem solvers, which covers our jitteriness at differing times. She is still abuzz now, which is weird since the event is over. Whatever is on her mind, it has nothing to do with work.

"I'm worried about you, Alex. Justin and I are both worried." Here it comes. She doesn't even look at me when she says his name. Nice little chats they've been having about me, I see.

"Wait, you guys have been talking about me? Well, this is perfect! Where is he? Hiding in the bushes somewhere waiting for the intervention speech? Did you prepare something in advance? You're always so fucking prepared!" Whoa, where did that come from? So much for having my emotions in check. I really need to get some better rest, especially since I never sleep well away from my home; I tossed and turned all night at Sandra's house. Funny to say that since I never sleep well in my bed anymore either, but I sleep even worse elsewhere. I always have. Must have been all those times meandering from place to place with my mother and then from home to home in foster care. Once I had my own bed and place, I nested big time.

"See, there you go, that's a perfect example of how you've changed. You would never have gotten so upset by a comment like that. Anytime we bring something up, your defenses pop up automatically. It's like you're constantly preparing for a fight."

Well, she's right there. Too bad I can't tell her who, why, or that I'm worried it may be my life at stake. *"hey Carmen, guess what? I'm like a descendant of some mystical earth-protecting goddess and I think I'm losing my shit over the level of magic I wielded on my foster father years ago. Even better, I think that same uber-baddie is coming back to get me."* Yeah, let's tell her that one!

Nope, instead, I lash out at her and Justin. Ugh, I need to go on serious damage control and mend this situation. I can't let them become a part of this, and fighting with them, or showing the effect this is having on me is only dragging them in further. I need to at least give the appearance of having my shit under control. It's too dangerous. Maybe I should really distance myself from them; that would be much safer. This mental baggage, or whatever I'm actually dealing with, isn't safe for them or good for me if I hope to salvage my relationships.

I mean geez, why would I get flustered just by them talking about me? It's not as if I'm worried about what they would say. And I wouldn't be jealous, would I? That would mean I didn't trust Carmen, and that just isn't the case, right? Oh man, I need to figure this out before I lose my shit. My normal self would never be questioning any of this. What I do know is that obviously Steven isn't accomplishing this on his own, and hopefully who or whatever is assisting him doesn't know the people I'm closest to. I don't want to hurt either of them, but I do need some distance. I guess it's time to set up a plan to put some safe space between us, while trying to appease everyone at the same time.

"I know, I know. I just need sleep, and hey, I agreed to try the hypnotherapy in a few weeks. It requires me to do some mental cleaning and meditational type soul mindfulness. You know, some Buddha time needs to be kicked up a notch before the good doctor can begin. So I guess that means I need a lot of 'me time.' I may need to be off the grid for a bit. I've got this. Don't worry, okay?" I give her my winning Alex smile. Damn, I don't think it's as effective as it used to be, or maybe she just sees through me.

Soon, her shoulders visibly relax, and I know I've accomplished a small part of my plan to keep her safe. I wonder if Justin will concede as easily.

"I just want you to be happy and healthy, Alex. It's so hard to watch you go through this and be completely useless. You've always drunk me under the table somehow, but it seems like you're going out even more these days, and not with Justin or me. I know you're with Sandra, and that's cool. You know I love her—stop wiggling your eyebrows at me, not like *that*. Geez, be serious for once!" We both take a break to crack up. It feels like the same as it always has, as it did when we first met, effortless.

"Well, don't worry, I'll be calming down and focusing on me for a while. I'm working this out, I promise. I know the drinking isn't the answer to taming the nightmares, and I totally agree with you. I see what I've been doing and I'm aware. That's a good sign you know, it's when a person doesn't see an issue that friends need to worry." She gives me another partial *I'm not so sure about this* look.

"Well, at least tell Justin, will you? He's really worried about you. He loves you, Alex. You know that right? I know you really care about him. No, I won't use the "L" word, God forbid the great Alex fall for a man that hard. I swear Nic is the only man you've ever trusted, and even he thinks that's a stretch!" She turns to look off into the distance where Matt's car sped away. "You know, he wears more make-up than you most days, and don't even get me started on the accessories. How many scarves does that man own?"

She's right, but hey, who can blame me? I shudder at the thought as a whisper glides through the stunted desert flora. Even thoughts of Justin invoke chills after the dream I had, one I can't seem to shake. It's cooler now, but my goose bumps are not from the shift in the air.

"What? Do you hear a mountain lion?" Carmen swivels her head around and steps a bit closer to her car. If I didn't know her better, I swear she might hightail it out of here, kicking up dust for me to spit out of my mouth while she saves herself.

"No, I just caught a chill. I know, I mean, I will, I'll talk to Justin. Maybe he's still up and I can call him on my drive home. There are a good thirty minutes ahead of me anyhow." I step closer to Carmen and hold out my hand for her to take. "I love you, Carmen. You're one of my best friends. I'm really feeling good about what's coming. Things will be better soon, I promise." Liar, my mind screams at me. Man, I'm being such a pessimist. Fear is getting to me, that's for sure.

"Okay, Alex. I know you're trying, and I know this is hard for you. I'm glad you've decided on getting some more help. I'm sure it will work." At least one of us is! "Let me know if I need to call in some backup to cover some of the events so you can have all the time you need. You've planned pretty far in advance, so we can take on some of the actual day of coordination without you. Just let me know."

Even better. I will be around her less that way, and with my solitude endorsed RX, I can keep Justin out of the front lines as well. We say our goodbyes and agree to just head home, opting to not stop for our usual unwinding routine. We snacked on enough of the catered food anyhow, and there's some ice-cold vodka, and my bed, calling my name at home.

CHAPTER 12

Sweet Dreams

Journal Entry:

You know what doesn't pay jack shit? Research and apparently all things educationally related. Kind of a kick in the ass if you want to solve the world's problems, gain knowledge about her treasures, or brighten the minds of young learners. Apparently we don't invest much in all that vitally important stuff, but boy do people expect the world with few resources and a short staff.

Carson had moved to Washington State to study some of the birds of prey in that region. It was nice to know I had a good two-state buffer between us. We didn't run into each other after he left with my album, and his phone calls were either ignored or answered by a very pissed off Latina who threatened his genitalia if he didn't return it. He never did return it, and I was just happy to stay away from him rather than play his little game.

Apparently, it was obvious to Carmen what I needed to do when she came into my room one day and saw me staring at the wall. My music was blaring, which to some people might be distracting, but the louder the better for me to think through things.

"So, I need an extra cocktail girl tonight, a quick $150 for you to work the whole night. What do you say?" Oh boy, I had seen those cocktail girls and their costumes, or the lack of them, and I was not feeling up to it. Realistically, not ever, but $150 was a lot of money for groceries, and I didn't want to keep sponging off Carmen or eating grilled cheese and tomato soup every night. I needed the cash, but I was not committing without seeing what itty-bitty outfit she had

planned in that mind of hers. On cue, she pulled the get-up out of the bag I hadn't noticed that she brought in with her. Okay, at least there were pants, or what could pass for pants or tights I guess. The top was more of a bra, but there was a cool belt for the waist that was in turquoise-y colors to contrast the black pants and black top.

"Oh, that goes around your belly as well, kind of a bandagy look. I also have these." She pulled out two long rope-like bracelet glove numbers for me to wear as well. Okay! I could work with that. Kind of a warrior goddess look; very fitting I would say. Carmen gave me a huge hug after I agreed while telling me how much fun we're going to have, but I still had a doubt-laden lump in my throat when we got to the venue.

The night went well one night, playing cocktail server turned into something else when one of Carmen's podium dancers didn't show for her dance club–themed birthday party in the hills of La Jolla. That party was immaculate, and Carmen was brought on as a designer and sales consultant rather than having her solely manage the event. I knew Carmen was a better fit for the management portion and not as comfortable with the design process, so I offered to help her. I wasn't surprised by how well we worked together, but I was amazed by how much I enjoyed the process.

The end product was an entire club created in a mansion on the hills. One room was solely devoted to music, and it had three podiums set up for go-go dancers, but one girl failed to show up. We thought about removing it, but then Carmen looked at me with that glint in her eye.

"So.... do you feel like changing your role tonight? Oh, don't look at me like that. I've seen you get lost in music in your room or at your friend's DJ parties, so come on, it'll be fun. Plus, I have her outfit. She was gracious enough to have her friend over there bring it with her, in case we could find someone." Ugh! She had that look on her face that made it very clear to me that she thought I could get roped into this.

"Come over here and meet Sandra. She's awesome, and she can help you get dressed and make you look amazing." She stopped her quick paced heeled stride to turn back to me. "Not that you don't always look fantastic, but she can make you look different, so maybe you won't feel so exposed. How's that?" She gave me a hug, and I was starting to wonder if she thought I always kind of looked like I needed one. Maybe she was right.

Carmen motioned to a gorgeous blond woman walking around one of the podiums on the other side of the room. Her make-up was as

113

perfect as her hair pulled back in a long ponytail. I had seen her at other parties. She was kind of known as a chameleon. I knew she did some other work as well and that this was more of a side gig, but I'm not sure what it was, something in real estate I think. Sandra was easy to like; she made anyone she spoke to feel special, and she seemed to be completely in tune with what they wanted and needed. I liked the blond beauty instantly, I allowed her to lead me off to the bathroom dedicated for staff, and let her get to work.

About an hour later, I could barely recognize myself in the mirror. The one-piece black shimmery get-up was very freeing, with shorts and a crisscross in the front that connected to a tiny—yet not letting my parts go anywhere—top. We started to head downstairs when I instinctively inched back into the wall of the stairwell. The house was a stucco mansion paradise and all glitz and glammed up for the party, but I was rooted in place. Sandra hissed in my ear.

"Hey girlie, I told you, you look awesome. So what's up?" Dr. Rosen and what was obviously her date canoodling at the bar was "what's up"! Clearly Dr. Miranda Rosen liked to party, and with younger men, as that was most definitely Carson on her arm. My power sparked within me and Sandra, whose hand was lightly touching me, jerked away. Oops, that'd never happened before. I needed to keep myself in check. Jealousy wasn't something I really had to deal with much before. It was hard to be jealous of someone when you didn't let many people get close to your heart.

Carmen's heels clicked quickly toward me with a grim look set on her face, which vanished to a glimmer of wicked surprise when she took in my appearance. She grabbed my arm and took us off the stairway and quickly around the corner toward the dance room set up with those cursed podiums. Did she really think I was going to continue this little charade? My ass was getting out of there and fast— ooh and maybe with some of those shrimp, yum! Carmen whirled me around to face her, excitement and a bit of cleverness glinting in her eyes.

"Look, I know how bad this all seems, and that you're ready to hightail it out of here, but let me make two points before you haul ass." She paused as if waiting for my permission which was all for show, she was going to tell me whether I wanted her to or not. I gave her "a get on with it" wave anyhow. "First, you look fucking hot!" She gave Sandra a no-look high five and continued.

"Second, that douchebag Carson won't even recognize you like this, no earthly way he will know. Hey, maybe she doesn't dance, or I

114

can get the bartender Spence to get her all trashed so then she can't dance." Carmen was so giddy I wondered if she was sipping on some Spence cocktails as well. Something she said stuck with me though: the word earthly. I wondered if I could change the way I looked for a short time, just to keep those two from recognizing me. It was worth a shot. Carmen was bouncing excitedly on her toes, so I had to let her off the hook.

"Look, it's fine, I'm fine. Let me just run to the bathroom and then I'll be right back to help you for the night. I can handle it, and you're right, I'm sure they won't be able to recognize me." More like I hoped, but there was no time like right then to see if the trick would work. I rushed upstairs to make sure I was out of sight and then tore into the bathroom, locked the door, and stared into the mirror. Energy tingled in my fingertips as I focused on making small adjustments to my appearance. I started with my eye color, the hazel pushed all the way to startling blue. Okay cool, that was a start. Then I made them go back to normal, not realizing I was holding my breath as they returned to the ebbing and flowing hazel color, flashing bright blue before settling. I spent the next couple of minutes arranging the appearance of my bones, without actually moving them. I held the idea of subtle differences in my mind, and the magic created it. I hadn't done much of that with my grandmother. We had spoken of camouflage and having the ability to do so, but we only made minor hair adjustments. This was a whole new level as I began to feel even more safe and protected now that I knew I could change how I looked.

It didn't take much energy, but I knew I would be worn out after a night of keeping it up. I practiced moving quickly between the magical changes, and looking like my normal self for the times I would be close to Sandra and Carmen. Tricky yes, challenging hell ya, but I was confident I could do it. Plus, the practice was good for me. My grandmother warned me never to get complacent. "You never know when war is coming," she would say. Well, all is fair in love and war isn't it? Ugh! I was not going to think about those two now or what that meant for my work with Dr. Rosen. The betrayal gnawed at my stomach with acid and boiling anger. Not right then, I was there to help a friend, and she was more important than any man and his Mrs. Robinson.

I slipped back downstairs, gave Sandra a wink before getting on the podium, and let myself go. It was fun to be this new girl; my senses were heightened as I kept myself aware of the people around me. Knowing my luck, this party would be some UCSD professor reunion.

The music was pretty good, cycling from current dance hits to disco to keep all generations happy on the dance floor. Sandra and I played off each other, and my long fake ponytail was fun to flip around as we looked like twins twirling on our tiny stages.

I felt Carson before I saw him; he had the same energy spiking off of him that I had grown accustomed to identifying as his high-as-hell self. I wondered if the good doctor knew about his extracurricular activities. Whatever—not my problem! As I hawked him moving around the room, I made sure he saw the different me. I watched him as he prowled; he seemed different, more intense. The drugs can make a person permanently edgy, and he was totally wound up. His eyes caught mine and I took a short, sharp breath. God, this hurt a bit more than I thought it would. Love and hatred all welled up at once. A deliciously evil idea popped into my head as I thought of luring him to me and then crushing his little man ego, but before my plan could take shape, I had a tap on my foot as a cocktail server pointed me toward Sandra who motioned for me to take a break. Man, it's like she knew what I was considering. Oh well, probably for the best. I hopped down and headed to the bathroom. Boy, I didn't know I had to pee that bad.

"Hey, excuse me." Holy shit it was Carson. My power tingled and poked at me; yep, it was working, so what the hell did he want? I turned to face him with my hand on my hip.

"Ya, what?" I gave my voice a nice annoyed accent and held the illusion in place.

"Sorry, I don't mean to bother you, but you just really remind me of someone, the way you dance, it's just like her. Oh God, I sound crazy, I'm sorry to bother you." Oh crap, my dancing, of course, that would set him off. How many parties did we go to together, where some nights he would just sit and watch me dance? Now here I was, same body, but a different face dancing right in front of him. When my back was turned I must have looked exactly like the girl he watched those many long nights. I felt a little guilty, but that was soon squashed. I remembered his note, my dad's album, Dr. Rosen whispering into his ear. He deserved a little pain.

"Look, buddy, I don't know you." I put a little too much behind that statement as it was one of the reasons I left him, and was nearly the same wording in my final letter to him. "Anyhow, I have to get going. Break is only a few minutes long and I need to pee." He looked at me closely as I took a few nervous breaths before turning away. My power dropped immediately as I ran into the bathroom and broke down in tears in one of the stalls.

Damn Carson for being here, and for dragging up all that hurt and how much I had loved him again. Why couldn't people just stay gone like they were supposed to? The thought sent another wave of grief through me as I thought of my mom, still gone who knows where, my father, who I'd never met or had a chance to grieve for, and my grandmother, who I wish had never left. I gasped for air and the sobs racked my body before a knock sounded on the door.

"Alex, hey it's Sandra, are you okay?" Sniffling sobs were the only answers I could manage. "Can I come in? I brought you something to drink, and I snagged us some shrimp!" That made me break from my reverie and laugh out loud at how perfect that all sounded. I opened the stall and forced a smile her way while my arms wrapped around my middle.

Looking into the mirror I laughed a little too hysterically, this time as I saw how all the make-up painted on my face stayed perfectly in place, just as Sandra said it would. Make-up of the stars she said, sweat and sob proof. My hair was another story. The tightly pulled back ponytail was askew and pieces were flying this way and that. I unclipped the extension and turned to face Sandra. She took me in for a moment and then lifted her small silver tray of goodies. When she said drink she meant a bottle of mandarin vodka, glasses of ice, and some soda water. Now as if that wasn't superb enough, I think she snagged an entire buffet bowl of shrimp. Okay, I loved the woman! I might have been mentally in shambles, but nothing healed me like a night of dancing, and damned if I wasn't going to take some cocktails and shrimp with me!

It's warm in here, and damn does it smell good. Sitting by the picture window staring out at the desert, a roadrunner zooms across my line of sight along the red landscape. More like a road chicken if you ask me. The thing looks like it runs every second of the day for fear of its own shadow. Nothing like the cocky Warner Brothers version, I bet these guys get picked out of coyotes teeth on a daily basis. I rap on the window to get his attention. Huh? On second thought, wow, he is fast. Guess I underestimated the little desert chicken.

The Pozo Redondo Mountains in the distance must have some excellent hiking. Did I even bring my hiking shoes? How do I know the name of these mountains? Where am I, and what is that wonderful smell? The light sounds of shuffling, bowls being moved, and spoons tapping complement the reggae music drifting from the stereo.

"Okay, dear. I need you now." I am vaguely aware of my body uncurling from the window seat, moving toward the voice, and stopping next to a shorter woman whose white hair is pulled back in a loose braid. Wild flowers are placed haphazardly amongst her hair like a vine growing throughout the thick white locks.

"Sure, Dana. What's next?" My mind is momentarily in shock, but we continue mixing, sifting, pouring, folding, and chattering about all things, normal things. It seems like hours tick by; the sun starts to set before we sit down and enjoy a batch of various baked goods stuffed with meat, cheese, fruit, and chocolate. I feel her touch lightly upon my hand, like a feather that drifted in on the breeze. When I look up, her eyes seem to bore into mine.

"What are you doing here, young Alex? Not here, not in my home, but in my dream, dear?" Her voice is so sweet and soothing, it reminds me of my grandmother's and I choke back the sobs threatening to break free. I try to hold myself steady as my heart breaks with sadness and longing.

"I, I don't know," I stammer, feeling a sudden dread that a nightmare is going to take hold at any moment. Very few of my dreams these days don't end in that manner, so who can blame me?

"No need for alarm, my dear, all are safe here." Her hand still lies atop mine, and I feel a slight chill when she moves it to gesture around her room. I take in the multitude of crystals, candles, and dream catchers decorating every window, wall, and doorway; I'm astounded by the beauty and variety of shapes, animals, feathers, and plants.

"The Arizona desert protects me as well; we have an understanding, she and I." She gives me a wink that makes her seem younger, more like a child than someone around my grandmother's age. Her eyes twinkle, and she lays her weathered yet soft hand back upon my arm.

"I knew you would come someday. Your grandmother and I spoke of the day you might need a guide and if she were ever unable to be here, that I would fill that position in her absence." She looked away into the distance, as if seeing someone in the empty space. "Oh, how I miss JoAnna. She is my best friend, as you know. Such a caring, wise, strong soul, much like you, my dear."

Realization hits me like a sledgehammer to my heart as my dream-self recalls Sandra's reading. I know this woman is *that* Dana, my grandmother's most trusted—if a little off kilter—best friend.

"You reek of fear, my dear; you will need to work on controlling it and your anger if you are to beat this impending darkness away with your light. Plus, it's not becoming, child. Well unless you're kicking ass, in which case use your arsenal of rage at will, dear." I look into her eyes and smile.

"I know you, I mean of you. My grandmother spoke of you all the time. You are, I mean you were, her friend. You're Dana." She smiles brightly while shaking her head.

"*Are,* my dear. I'm still friends with JoAnna. We talk all the time. You will be able to as well; you just need to listen for her, my dear."

I recall the night I bound Steven away, and the calm that flowed over me when my grandmother's presence eased the intensity of my act and engulfed me in her warmth and love. Since then, there have been times off and on when I knew she was with me, but I feel so empty lately. I haven't sensed her in so long. The guilt and sting of jealousy hits me simultaneously as my cheeks flush, and I turn my moistened eyes away from Dana's gaze.

"You have something blocking you. How is she supposed to get through?" She squeezes my arm kindly and I blink away the tears before meeting her kind eyes. "The very thing you sent away, through impressively powerful means I might add, is attacking your mind. It appears your assaults are to be in the form of nightmares. Am I right, my dear? Ah, and migraines I see." Geez, what is she doing? Taking a tour in my head? She smiles before going on.

"Continue to focus on the present, Alexis. Don't let Steven and his dark power drag you into those dark places of your past and haunt you still. You are granting him time in your waking life and thereby setting up this vicious cycle. He has caused you to live in fear and mistrust most of your life, which is understandable after what he put you through, the bastard." Her other hand smacks the table and I grin at the strength in her despite the old woman appearance. "But the more recent nightmares, the intense ones that have stolen sleep and sanity from you for what, about a year now, right?" I nod wondering if she's a Seer like Sandra.

"You must remember he is a master deceiver, my dear. He plays on your fears, creating them visually in your dreams and then you suffer those fears tenfold in real life. You begin to doubt even those you count as friends and loved ones, few as they are. That doubt then carries over into your sleep where he feasts on them and forms even more fodder for your fear. Hold on to the love and trust of those who have helped you and cared for you. Focus on the success of your

119

professional life, on how far you have come, of all the fun you have had and continue to have. Love life, my dear. That will carry over into your sleep and then your grandmother can come to you. When you fill your days with happiness, not dread, JoAnna will come. She has to come; we need all the help we can get." She grabs my hands in her own and the warmth envelops me, spreading from my palms and traveling up my arms and throughout my body.

In the distance, a coyote howls. Knowing that a single voice rarely pierces the darkness, we wait for and are greeted by another howl and then another. How do they always seem so close even when they are miles away?

"We don't have long, Alexis. He appears to have a stronger hold on your dream state than I realized." I start to shake as the warmth of the room vanishes, except where her hands remain on holding mine. The howls grow incessant and her voice barely echoes in my head while her lips stayed planted in her warm, reassuring smile.

"Let me take care of him tonight. You sleep, child. You will need your strength. I will be waiting my dear. Follow the howls, I'll be waiting..." Another coyote in the distance cuts off her voice as my body, which is preparing itself for the onslaught of a nightmare, releases its clenching muscles as the vision of her home drifts away. The comfort of her touch upon my hands is the last sense to fade, replaced by Pitter's rumbling purrs against my chest. I know I am home, in my bed, and for one of the few times in the last couple of months, I feel safe and so very tired. My eyes never take the opportunity to open before I am asleep once again.

When I finally wake, it is noon. The sun is high in the sky, but even Pitter lies next to me snoozing versus giving me his normal impatient meowing about this and that, and why can't I get up in the morning hours like normal people. Key word, being normal. What is that anyhow?

My fog lifts and I bolt upright. "Dana" escapes my lips as my sudden action sets Pitter into kitty panic mode—claws out and back arched as he bounces around searching for the source of danger in a poof ball of claws and canines. He is my cat after all, and we don't run away under beds around here.

"Ya, you're real intimidating. I think even the neighbor's dog might have soiled himself looking at your cute little ferociousness." I try to smooth his fur but he flicks his tail, moving to the farthest end of the bed where he begins to groom himself, pointedly ignoring me of course. He gives me one more mid-lick look of annoyance before turning away from me completely. I see some tuna sashimi in my future to make up for hurting his puddy tat feelings. I shouldn't be discounting any of my protectors—even the littlest. My brain drifts to Bear and my heart tugs at itself. Why must I constantly be missing the ones I love?

I grab my tablet off the nightstand and begin to surf the web, piecing together Arizona and coyotes. Oh geez, thousands of pages to scour. What am I missing? This can't be what Dana meant. Pitter makes an "I've found a bug, mom" howl and pounces off the bed in pursuit. My brain ticks slowly before an idea finally hits me, and I type in Arizona and Coyote howl. An onslaught of audio clips and pictures pop up, but a few spaces down is a link to Coyote Howl's RV Park. I click on it and find the slideshow. As the pictures of the park and its surroundings slowly fade in and out, I hit pause when I find the mountains from my dream, the very ones I saw right outside of Dana's picture frame window. I read the description out loud.

"The Pozo Redondo Mountains. Pitter this has to be it! I have to go!" My sense of urgency nearly lands me flat on my face as my feet entangle in my blanket as I scramble out of bed. Pitter comes racing in after a spider before looking at my traveling bag and then at me questioningly.

While I was throwing my stuff into the bag, I thought back to my conversation with Justin last night. I had called him when I got home told him all about the preparation for my hypnotherapy being taken up a notch which equated to me needing some "me time." Of course, I threw in how it would help me be more in tune with the present, meaning being more accessible to him and our relationship once I feel better. I believe it to be true, and I know that came out in my words to him.

Justin is always so easy to talk to, easy going. I could nearly sense his natural earthy smell and feel his smooth skin as if he was snuggling next to me instead of talking over a cell phone. At one point in the conversation I knew he was going to ask to come over, and I can't lie, part of me really wanted him to. Though I doubt I would have been open enough to have the type of experience I had with Dana if Justin had been here. This understanding makes me feel as if my decision to keep my distance from him is a smart one, not only to allow for the security of knowing he will be safe, but to keep the lines of Earthy communication open.

He wasn't pushy about wanting to come over. Justin never is. He is very in tune with what I need, and his question elicited feelings of needs and wants within my body and mind. I think growing up with three sisters has given him a strong understanding of femininity. He did tell me he misses me, and I wasn't surprised at how much I wanted him to not only miss me, but to hear that statement formed with his perfect lips. His words made me shiver as my imagination took over, and suddenly, those lips were right next to my ear, pushing the wind against my eardrum, lightly brushing my lobe with a soft warmth that made my lady parts tingle, and had me longing for his scent, his arms around me, and the touch of his warm skin.

I could tell that he noticed I had gone quiet, and I know he worried that he shouldn't have told me, that he had pushed me when he knew I needed space. I immediately shook myself out of my fantasy and told him I missed him as well. Letting him know that his words didn't put him in jeopardy of being further isolated, at least that was what I kept telling myself.

We ended the conversation with plans to see each other soon, maybe take a hike. Justin has recently adopted his first dog and even though I want to meet his new addition, I don't want to become attached to something else right now. My life is getting way too crazy, and, I fear, very dangerous.

The conversations with Justin and Carmen about me needing space, provide me with some much-needed freedom to work on my dilemmas. It is nice not to have to worry about what to tell either of them as I quietly slip away to Arizona. I'll call Sandra on the way, because I know she is going to want to hear all about this.

After packing my small travel bag, I reach for my phone. There's a text message that was sent in the middle of the "night" from Ryan. Ah ha! So *Mr. Super Smooth Controlled* guy tried to booty call me, eh? Ha, he is going to get it. I open the message and nearly drop the phone to the floor. I have to read it again to be sure my eyes aren't playing tricks on me. I shakily raise the screen back into my line of sight, sweeping strands of hair from my eyes before taking another long, careful look at the text. Yep, I had read it right the first time.

"Lex, don't even think about going alone."

CHAPTER 13

Going Somewhere?

Before I could take my next breath, my body feels a familiar vibration before his finger even touches the doorbell.

When I open the door, Ryan is standing there in all his six feet of glory, coffee cups in hand, looking as if he has been up for hours with his alert eyes, perfect hair, and toned body.

"Going somewhere?" I know he asks in a rhetorical way, but I can't help but ask.

"How did you... whatever. Come on in." I sweep my arm back dramatically letting him walk by me, surreptitiously taking a slight whiff of him as he strides by. His scent reminds me of desert wind mixed with salt water and sunshine. A trace of asphalt and tree bark is the final smell lingering in my consciousness as my swaying body breaks me out of enjoying his presence. I had been getting ready to argue with him, but he's more than a little distracting

My life is full of crazy dreams, talking creatures, long-lost friends, and now this man apparently knows what I am dreaming about. Am I shocked? Not really. Apparently I am stuck with Ryan on this wild goose chase. In some ways, he feels like a second skin, like I've known him forever. Not a bad person to be tied to, I have to admit. I hadn't seen him since our little tango in the club the other night, but as I remember his taste a hot streak of need races down and clenches through me. Ryan turns instantly in my direction, as if sensing my desire.

A normally unusual, but apparently commonplace around this man, embarrassment reddens my cheeks. I had thought the years of working with Nic had chased any last virgin-like wholesomeness out of me. I search for a flicker in his eyes or a movement toward me; instead he works his way to the couch and casually sits down. Pitter jumps in his lap as soon as his perfect backside hits the cushion, instantly turning into a purring mush of fur. Slut, I think, and Ryan's mouth does that slight smile thing again. I don't know what goes off in my head, but I think I have just about had it, mystery be damned! If I am going to trust this guy I need answers, and I need them now.

"Okay, spill it! Have you tapped my phone, put cameras or listening devices in my house? My brain? What gives, Ryan? Why are you here, and how in the hell do you know that I'm going somewhere?" The last part is given with a bit more sass than I intended, but what the hell? I have nothing to lose, shit seems to be getting very real and extremely harried right now. I do want Ryan's help; I know that somehow deep down he's like me—maybe I always knew.

Something has attracted me to him, other than the obvious of course. Seeing his eyes the other night, now for sure I know his secret as well as he knows mine. My grandmother's warning rushes through me. She predicted that I would be attracting the good *and* the evil of our kind. She was right about the evil part, but that little girl is done suffering, right? Sandra's voice cuts in on my grandmother's tail feathers, echoing what she said during her reading about the tricks I would encounter on my quest to keep Steven bound. What if Ryan is one of the tricks? What if he is really a conniving little bunny? The thought makes me chuckle as I picture a milk chocolaty, velvety bunny sitting on my lap.

I must have looked as mad as the hatter because the quizzical expression on Ryan's face is one of questioning, and of someone carefully gauging my sanity. He isn't sure if I am going to flip-out in a rage or start rolling on the floor in laughter. One minute I swear he can read my mind, and then the next it's as if I'm completely confusing to him. Story of my life, I guess.

"Okay, I was going to say don't worry I'm here for you, but now maybe I should be worrying. Are you okay? Here, maybe you aren't awake yet. Drink this." He motions to the covered paper cup on the coffee table, and I gratefully take it in my hands, inhaling the chai latte aroma. Yum, and yes, this guy knows way too much about me in such a short amount of time.

"Yes, I'm fine. Thank you for this." I take a sip and close my eyes for a moment. I need to regroup. "Okay, sorry. I'm fine, and this is great. I'm glad you're here to help, but that doesn't answer my other questions." I stand my ground, hovering above him, as he stays seated petting Pitter softly, and returns to his zen-like calmness. I typically hate when my clients don't sit when I'm seated. It always feels like it is some power play. In my studies, in both school and life, it usually is and in this case, it definitely is. I put my hand on my hip for further effect.

Pitter gives me his hundredth annoyed glare of the day before turning to Ryan with a "just ignore her" look and forcing his head under Ryan's hand again. The dark Adonis on my couch takes a second to look me over where I stand in my shorts, hiking boots, and a tank top. My red flannel is tied around my waist, and my hair is pulled back in a ponytail.

"You look so much like her," he says. "I mean, I only saw her in person when I was too young to remember, but I've seen plenty of pictures. When I first saw you, I knew instantly who you were."

I ease my hand off my hip and stare at him with a thousand questions rolling around in my head at high speed, like molecules of liquid being heated over a fire. I remain silent as my brain can't make my mouth create any sort of coherent questions.

"Your mom was one of my parents' closest friends," Ryan continued. "Well, I guess they would still be close friends if they knew where in the world she is. They met when they were young, before my parents were even married. They came together by chance, during a trip to assist poor families throughout the US and Mexico. My mom always spoke highly of Stacy. They became best friends instantly, and even with distance and over the years, Mom could always count on her." My eyes dart around as my brain works in overdrive, trying to remember a time when I could count on my mom, or even knew where she was. It's been a long time since I'd even received a letter.

My building anger and feelings of abandonment focus on its new target. "Wait! So you've known this whole time about me, my family, my mother, and you never said a thing!" Pitter takes off when the vehemence in my voice hits a new high. About time, you little furry traitor. Ryan rises slowly, looking back and forth between Pitter and me, calculating which one of us is the bigger threat. As I take an offensive stance, Pitter's hackles rise, and boy, are his claws sharp. Ryan raises his hands in a placating manner and his eyes soften.

"Lex, I was asked by my mother to come here and find you. At first I had to make sure your power was still on our side, and if so, protect you at all costs."

Okay, now I'm really pissed. "And what if I wasn't on your side? Whatever side that is for that matter! What would you do then, huh? Destroy me? Well let me tell ya, buddy, I'd like to see you try." My fingers tingle while my power responds to my body's fight or flight response, while I also try to deal with the hurt and confusion swirling in my heart and mind. My power isn't going to wait for me to call upon the goddess for help; I have enough reserved inside me and it is preparing all on its own. It's a good thing I can control the amount of power rushing into me—or at least I used to—lately I have been off in all sorts of ways.

"Whoa, whoa! Lex, come on now. Slow down. Look at me." Hands by his sides now, his eyes plead for me to take a moment and think. I know I need to hear him out. I have to. "All I knew was that one of my mom's best friends had a daughter, who may or may not be the most powerful Earthen Protector in ages. The first powerful blend of Protector and Healer we've heard of in centuries. No one knew for sure how or even who you would be after living unchecked for so many years, not to mention after what happened with Steven Nestrour. The use of that much power, even with the best and most necessary intentions, can drive the most well-meaning of us to the other side."

Nice, so I've been hunted down by this mystery man for fear of me being some psycho Absolute Protector. Real nice! What's going to happen next? Am I finally answering for what I did to that bastard?

"He deserved it." My nails stab into my palms, both out of my fury and to keep myself in check. Ryan may be fishing for info, and I'm not about to give it to him that easily.

"We lost track of Steven around the same time we lost track of you as a child. We never thought to look for both of you in the same place. How he even found you at all is a mystery. It shouldn't have been possible with all the protection your mother and grandmother possessed you with."

Now I'm floored. Ryan and my mom knew I needed to be protected, and her friends were worried about whether or not I had turned evil, yet no one bothered to help me. Man, the F-bombs are about to start dropping on Ryan any second now.

"Well, if you know so little, but oh so much, where were you twelve years ago? Where were any of you? Do you know what that man did to me? What he almost did to Chey and who knows how many others? You all knew about me, you knew I was alone and scared. Protection, my ass!" My body is overheating, and I know the power is blazing in my eyes. "Well, newsflash, sorry, but it didn't work! First my mom leaves me, then my grandmother–nobody was there to teach or guide me! Why? Why, Ryan? Why are you just *now* trying to help me? Little late don't ya think? I'd say a good deal of damage has already been done, and I hate to break it to you, but there's worse to come. If you and your little family were too scared to help me then, you sure as hell should be now!"

My body trembles as tears roll down my face. Ryan stands and takes a tentative step toward me, his hands up as if approaching an injured wild animal. I am damn near close enough to that, since the wild Earthen energy pulsing through me is creating a breeze like effect; my hair tickles my face as it flows around. Even Pitter bows out of this one and hightails it up the stairs.

"Lex… Alex… Alexis, please understand, I can explain everything on our way to Arizona. We do have somewhere we need to be, remember? Is there any way you can trust me enough, right now, to let me help you speak to this friend of your grandmother? At least let me take you there, you're in no shape to do this on your own. Lex, use your powers, sense me out, I know you can tell I mean you no harm. We're on the same side, and I have over five hours to tell you all you want to know, but right now, we really need to get in the car."

Ah, I was wondering when he would shut down the free for all on information. The man has never been much with words, and this was a freaking lecture series by comparison. I look up at him and I am amazed at the softness around his eyes and mouth. He has always been on alert, stealth mode around me, with the exception of the brief dance we shared at the club. It's nice to see this side of him.

My power unfurls from my body and reaches out to check him out once again. It laps along his being and sparks with recognition of his power. It feels safe, familiar. Even though I'm pissed as hell, I do have a long drive ahead of me, and I'm wasting daylight here. Plus, if Ryan wanted to hurt me, wouldn't he have done it by now? I mean, the man was in my house while I was unconscious, for goddess's sake.

"All right, boss, let's head out, but you better keep talking because I need a lot more information from you and your nosey power family." I make a move to get by him but he gently takes hold of my arm.

"Lex, I know this is a lot to take in, and we *will* talk about everything, but there is one thing I want you to understand now. I'm here to help you; you're not alone anymore."

His touch is warm and caressing, while still giving me the feeling of a burning heat. My anger eases a bit as my own desires take over. His arms had held me not long ago in the club; his lips had touched mine and the memory brings back the sensation. I turn back to him and run my fingers along his other arm. He reacts with a sound deep in his throat, and I take that as an opening to continue touching his arm, chest, and taut abs. My eyes were following the sensuous path my hand travels, but now they seek his. The silver spark in his eyes is undeniable, and I go up on my tippy toes when he dips his head to mine.

This kiss is different. Maybe because I am kind of ticked off, but I also now know that this powerful person holds information about so much. I'm attracted to him, yet also drawn to what he can teach me and what he can help me learn about our kind, maybe even about my own mother. My lingering anger and frustration make me bite his lower lip a little too roughly, and his reaction has me slammed against him so tightly I lose my breath. Yet, as abruptly as he turned me on, my mind shuts me down. I know nothing but what I am being told by the very person I know nothing about. Get a grip, Alex! You need to be a bit more careful these days. I break from our embrace, daring him to complain by looking him right in the eye, knowing my sparkle of emerald green power is lighting up my gaze.

"Okay, let's get one thing straight. I may need your help right now, and I sure as hell may obviously want a little more than that, but I need to find Dana, so let's get a move on."

The sizzling tension in the air drops significantly as I move away from him, gracefully walking on my toes and maneuvering to the bathroom. Of course I put a little extra sway in my hips for effect, not the easiest and smartest thing to do in hiking boot, and the grips on the bottom of my shoes hit the door transition, leading me into one hell of a sexy trip. I barely manage to grasp the doorknob to steady myself before slowly closing the door behind me. His rumbling chuckle fills my ears while I curse my clumsiness and glower at my boots.

After making a more graceful exit than my excellent entrance, I holler a goodbye to Pitter while setting his eating and drinking machine. Then I grab my bags and follow Ryan outside. I nearly run into his wall of a back when I spin around after just locking the door.

"What the fuck, Ryan? Good thing I'm wearing these boots. You nearly broke my—oh Justin, umm, hi!" I smile a little overly enthusiastically, trying to cover my guilt. Well, this is just great! Can you say *awkward*! So much for him honoring our "Alex needs more alone time" agreement. My anger boils, but is quickly doused with icy guilt when I remember what I had just been doing in Ryan's embrace mere minutes ago.

Ryan is all business. He takes my bags, gives Justin a quick yet respectful nod, and heads for his black SUV. Ah, a hybrid, so he is a nature lover, a well-built, sexy as hell nature lover. Remorse bitch slaps me again and I quickly silence my thoughts and turn to Justin, giving him my full attention and my sweet as pie guilt-free smile.

"Going somewhere?" he asks. "Guess alone time is over, eh? Who's the Vin Diesel meets The Rock lookalike, Alex? Not your hypnotherapist I'm guessing."

Ugh. I give Justin a mental eye roll. I don't have time for this shit, but then shame hits me for being so callous. We were never really formally exclusive, although up till now I'd never thought of being with anyone else and I am pretty sure he hasn't been. Not to mention, Ryan isn't a thought at all. Being around him is kind of all action and no thought.

"Look, Justin, it's not like that. Ryan is the new security guy for the company and we're heading out to look at a new event space. He's also a driver, and with my lack of sleep lately, I feel safer hiring him than risk going it alone." Yep, smooth and typical Alex, giving good lip service. I'm not sure Justin is falling for it, but he really has no reason not to believe me. I'm always honest with him, for the most part, and my rational response is also somewhat true. Ryan does need to take me at this point. Truly, I am in no shape to drive, or to go on this mystical scavenger hunt alone.

Geez Alex, are you going to screw up everything with Justin because you can't control yourself around Ryan, who is truly a stranger to you? My guilt factor cranks up a notch at the notion. I can't fault Justin for being on edge. I mean, if I was watching a female version of sexiness walk away from Justin's house right now, my blood would be boiling. My angel/devil sides take turns playing around in my head as I call up the fact that Justin was not following the Alex-time guidelines. I need to revisit the OutKast "I'll Call Before I Come" lyrics with him sometime. I've never been a random drop by fan anyhow; I'm too edgy for that. Of course, I take the high road and refuse to go on the defensive.

"Look, my nerves are rattled, but I still need to work or I'll go completely mad. You can't drop everything to come with me, and I do need some "me" time. Why do you think I'm bringing that guy? He barely says a word, and I think he may be all brawn and nothing up here." I accentuate my statement by tapping my right temple after throwing my head in Ryan's direction, as the obvious brunt of the conversation. Is that a loud guffaw I hear coming from the SUV?

Shields up Mr. Sulu, can he freakin' hear us from there or is he in my head again? I allow a little energy to creep into my mind and order it to guard the gates. It feels odd at first, but a few brain freezes is better than having Mr. Nosey over there rootling about.

Justin backs down a bit, and I finally take a good look at him. He is holding something in his hands that I hadn't noticed before.

"I was only coming by to drop this off on your steps. I know you need some time and doing something different, even if it's some hypnosis mumbo jumbo, is better than nothing. I want you to know I support you wholeheartedly." He hands me a container of flowers with their delicate white bulbs shut-up tight. There's a card placed inside, which I carefully unfold.

Alexis:

For those late nights after work or when you wake from a nightmarish dream, these evening primroses will be awake with you when I can't be. I hope their beauty and fragrance brings you peace, and reminds you that you are always loved.

Yours always,

Justin.

Well, damn! Now my freaking eyes are burning, and the tendrils of shame pull at my heart and my soul. I must not be paying attention since I unknowingly let my energy create some sort of connection with the resting flowers, and I quickly catch a glimpse of a primrose opening, now, at a very inappropriate time. Damn curious goddess. I quickly draw the energy back into myself and the flower closes as if exhaling a gentle sigh. Inwardly, I curse myself for letting my guard down, and once again, a low chuckle escapes the silence of the SUV.

"Did you see..." Justin starts shaking his head, "hmm, must be my eyes playing tricks on me, but I could have sworn that... never mind."

"Thank you, Justin. I love them. They're just perfect." Just like he is. So unlike me, with my jagged edge of a past full of sharp, harsh memories and secrets. "I'm going to put these on my bedroom balcony right now." I turn to go back inside and then swivel my head back in Justin's direction.

"Do you want to come in for a minute? Maybe show me the best place for them? I'm sure Pitter will want to see you." I smile gently at him, feeling like a normal person again, like someone who can be in love and in a relationship with a normal guy.

130

"No, I've got to head out. I'm meeting some new students at the SDSU library to go over some project plans, and then it's an early day tomorrow in Mexico. Where's your new site of interest?"

"Arizona. I found a family friend to stay with while I scout out the place, as well as a to-die-for spa to visit that has all sorts of meditational, yoga, and sleep therapy options. I thought it was a perfect plan for me so I can work, and focus on myself as well. The big guy over there has some lady friend, or friends, waiting—so he says." My shields are up for that one, but I kind of wish Ryan could have heard that jab.

I place the flowers down for a moment and give Justin a hug. Putting all of my emotion into it, I once again feel I can love this man, but can someone love me, really love me when they don't know the real me? When they *can't* know the real me? Keeping Justin safe is my main priority, so telling him how I feel is not an option. It may never be.

CHAPTER 14

Dana

Journal Entry:

Graduation day, and my guest list consisted of my foster mom, Chey, Shane, Carmen, Sandra, and Nic, my new friend at Seaside Events. Why in the world they wanted to sit through this long-ass ceremony was beyond me, but being short on family, I was grateful. And so I should be since I did have more than others in the world. That line of thinking didn't erase the pain and loss, but on occasion, it told me to buck up and keep moving forward.

The ceremony led into an amazing party at one of our favorite clubs in the Gaslamp Quarter. A good deal of the production company crew was there as well, from electric to design, so I guess I shouldn't have been surprised when one of the Seaside Events owners, Martin, dropped by to either send me well wishes or to check on us. Martin was kind of a shady guy, but he normally stayed out of our business and left us alone to do our jobs. He was the spoiled rich boy who never grew up, and one of the two owners of Seaside Events. Jarvis was the other, the more elusive and much older owner. Jarvis spent most of his time in Europe trying to set-up an "international office." In my opinion, he was really spending time scoping out his retirement home.

I wondered how long it would all last before Martin threw a major hissy fit and the company broke up. Maybe that was what Jarvis was waiting for; I was sure he'd get more money that way. He milled around for a while and then made his way to me. He didn't hide his intention as he looked me up and down, always one to comment on *how tight my clothes were at work, they felt better that way, so he could shove it. Tonight was no exception with my snug red romper. My skin seeming to crawl with a million tiny sickly waves as Martin's eyes started at my fuck-me heels and up my legs to the beginning of the short number. Before I could even glare, he snapped his gaze to my eyes. Yeah dude, that's where they should have been to begin with.*

"I have something for you that I thought you might want tonight. I'm not sure why it was sent to us and not your home address, but it seemed important since it came by evening messenger just as I was heading down here from the office." He handed me an envelope that was addressed to me, but one thing that stood out was the way it was addressed. Instead of the usual Alexis Conner, it read Alexis E. Conner, something I never went by. Nobody alive knew about my middle name, well, truly my first name. That was, nobody except my mother.

"Thank you, I need to... I'll be right back." I turned and made my way to the upstairs loft, which was now empty as everyone was off having all sorts of merriment and mayhem below. I sat down slowly and with shaking fingers peeled open the letter. There was no mistaking my mother's handwriting, and apparently no helping the tears that began to fall down my face, snatched by my fingers at the last moment before they could dampen the letter. It had been years since I last heard from her. Mom sent me a short letter after Steven's "disappearance" and I remember the way it tingled when I touched the ink letters formed by her hands. It was freeing and soothing at the time, and even in its crypticness, she was proud of me but also wary of what the future held for us, mainly when we might see each other again. When I got into UCSD, she sent me a hodge-podge of UCSD gear and a new journal. There wasn't a card included but the tingling of her power on the items was obvious.

I wasn't sure what she would say in that latest message. I had finished college, my full time job as program manager/sales assistant was lined up for me at Seaside Events, and the life I had forged for myself was pretty low key—for the most part, normal. The letter in my hands felt like a shakeup of the poorly formed fabric of that world I created.

The beginning was the usual congratulatory well wishes and great jobs, but then the next paragraph had me stopping and staring at the final sentence.

Please come outside, turn left and walk one block. I'll be waiting.

133

I knew exactly where she was, so I bolted out of the club and ran toward Rosa's Restaurant. She stood there like an angel, seeming to glow in the light of the lamp. With her head turned away from me she took a few steps away to round the side of the building. After following her, I ran to embrace her as soon as she turned toward me. We just stood there, holding each other in a way we never had before. It felt a little strange because in my heels I was nearly even with her six-foot frame, whereas I was a child—not even four feet tall—when I was last clutching her and fighting against being taken away. Tears began again, this time unbidden as they fell down my face, and I tried not to make choking, sobbing noises like a child. She smoothed my hair back with her hand, and then lifted up and out of the embrace.

"You're all grown up aren't you, Alexis, so beautiful and strong. I'm so happy for you and all you've accomplished, and I'm sorry that I wasn't able to be with you... that I couldn't help you when you needed me. I will never forgive myself, believe me. It's complicated, and I'm sorry to say that I'm only here for a brief moment before I have to leave again."

"No!" I yelled angrily, betrayal boiling up inside me at the thought of how long she had been gone. "Why do you have to leave? Where have you been? Do you realize what it's been like for me without you, without Grandmom? I've had to figure all of this out on my own! I've had to do things to keep myself, and the people I love safe, and I didn't even really know what I was doing. Why do you have to leave me again? Why?" My fingers balled into fists and I felt like a child once more staring at my mom as I was taken from her,, yet, this time she seemed to have a choice.

"I can't explain everything, Alexis. There isn't time, and I'm really not supposed to be here." She looked around cautiously, and I heard a faint whistle call out, and then again, like a pattern.

"Oh, Alexis, I have to go. I'm so sorry dear. It won't be like this forever; I promise we'll be together again, but right now, please know I'm leaving so I can protect you. It's the only way. Believe me." The trembling began to roll through my body and it wasn't from the cold.

"Bullshit, we can protect each other, I can protect myself now! I have before, and I can do it again, only this time I won't be trapped in the first place. Together we can be even safer, we can help each other, stay... please." My tears began to fall again, and my mom embraced me. Rigid in my ire at first, but then my muscles gave way and I sunk into her warmth.

"Shhh... it's okay, you're doing marvelously here. I cannot be here, not now, but you need to stay. Stay with your friends, your life, your new job, but always stay aware. Steven wasn't—and isn't—the only one looking for you, for all of us. He isn't alone on his mission to upset the balance completely and wipe us, and all of humanity out. We must do what we can to find them and end their attempts to control us all."

Man, when she said it like that I couldn't help but either want to go with her and join the fight or feel really lucky about being where and who I was right then. Even though getting there had been rough, I loved my life, the good I was doing with my powers. I guessed being off the uber-danger radar was a good thing.

"But, I love you, Mom. When will I see you again? How do I get in touch with you?" She wiped the tears gently from under my eyes and from my cheeks. As she lifted my chin, I could look into her eyes aflame with her blue light, as they were the night I first realized we shared a secret.

"There will come a day, Alexis, when we'll need you. When you'll really have to join the cause and possibly leave this behind, but for now—at twenty-one—enjoy yourself. Keep making those wonderful and beautiful changes in the world. I love you. I'll see you soon."

Mom kissed me on my cheek and softly moved my head downwards to kiss me on my forehead. She squeezed my shoulder, smiled through her tears, and turned away. As I watched every second of her silhouette walking into the distance, I noticed another join her before they both disappeared like drifting smoke into the cool San Diego night.

The small town of Why, Arizona is home to the Coyote Howls RV Park. It's a little-known area, and I think the residents like it that way. The trip is going to take us five and a half hours, so I take my laptop out to work on an event proposal while Ryan drives. The mood changed after the encounter with Justin, and I really just want something to take my mind off all this power, darkness, and magic for a while. Ryan and I don't talk about Justin at all, which is just as well. I don't really feel like explaining what's going on in my head or with my body's attraction to Ryan and feelings about Justin, and to hell with all of Ryan's secrecy. He doesn't need to know everything that is going on with me, no matter how much he seems to know already.

I'm not sure when exactly, but at some point I doze off and awake to Ryan's voice announcing our arrival. The sun dives under the desert horizon and sends intense bursts of reds, oranges, and yellows across the sky. I take a moment to stare out of the window at the landscape, which to some might appear desolate, but to me, seems full of life. The desert is a magical place, and my senses tingle from the newfound pockets of Earthen energy.

"Wow, that was fast." I rub some sleep out of my eyes and cringe when I touch the mangled mess of my hair. Apparently it came halfway out of the ponytail during my nap.

"Yeah, it's real fast when you sleep for the majority of the drive." His smug smile irritates me into sassiness.

"Guess you think it's a compliment to have a girl fall asleep on you… not on you, near you, oh, whatever, smartass!" His snickering is not easy to ignore as I distractedly untangle my limbs that have somehow gotten caught in the arms of my flannel. When I manage to get free, I reach for my purse.

"No nightmares I gather?" Ryan's question stops me in my search for a hair clip and lip-gloss. Of course, he is right about that, and by the sneaky smile on his lips I suspect that he is also responsible in some way. It isn't the first time I'd had that thought. On top of it all, I had slept away hours I could have used digging into Ryan's brain. Wonder if he was involved in that, too.

"How in the hell did I sleep that…?" I trail off as my eyes catch the sign on the left. Its large white blocked letters spelling out **Coyote Howls RV Park**. We're here, and the answers to my questions will have to wait once again. Ryan starts to get out of the car when I press my hand against his chest. Goddess, he is like a flesh-covered statue.

"I've got this. You might make some old-timer swoon, or be prematurely laid to rest with all of *this*." My hand makes a quick air motion to imply him in his entirety, and with a grin of satisfaction, I hop out of the car.

The office attendant is a pleasant lady who offers to ring up Dana for me, but before she can grab the old-school, twenty-pound cordless phone, equipped with a large telescoping antenna, it rings on its own.

"Coyote Howls, this is Barb. How can I help you this evening? Oh Dana, just the young lady I was looking for. What's that? Yes, yes a young woman is standing right here. Is your name Alex, dear?" The last comment is made in my direction, and I nod with a dumbfounded

136

look on my face. At this point, nothing should really surprise me anymore. Barb smiles and continues speaking with Dana.

"Why, yes, Dana, I'll send her to you now. Okay, dear, bye for now." Barb presses the large rubber End button and places the phone back on its charger with a "thunk." She pulls a map and a highlighter out of the drawer from beneath the counter, and proceeds to draw the route to Dana's site. I thank her and head back to Ryan's SUV.

We drive along the gravel "road" to Dana's site, taking notice of the various people strolling around the park, or sitting outside their RVs to take in the sunset. It is peaceful with gentle murmurings of conversation, laughter, and the smells and sounds of campfire and propane cooking.

Beautiful rocks, some large boulders, and various forms of cactus surround Dana's mobile home. A "river" of rocks begins its trek from the left, through the front of the "yard" and takes a U-shaped turn to the right where it joins another rock river to the road.

Before I manage to completely escape the car, Dana comes out of her door with her peach dress billowing in the breeze, as is her long, grayish-white hair that cascades down her back. Crystals, feathers, and glass figures sparkle enchantingly in the windows of the RV as they catch the rays of the sunset's mingling of colors, twinkling like stars. I am caught up in the vision as she nears me, holding her hands out to take mine.

"Oh, Alexis. Dear, aren't you a sight to behold! I see so much of my closest friend in you, my dear, especially in your eyes." While her hands stay connected to mine, her eyes shift and widen at the vision over my shoulder. "Oh, and you brought muscle, excellent thought my dear. Isn't he an Adonis in the coming night?" If I didn't know better, I swear I see Ryan blush. Hard to tell with his deliciously dark skin, but it is more the way he appears to be taken aback by Dana's eyes roving over his body that signal his discomfort. Dana doesn't seem to notice, or care, so she carries on.

"Well, come on you two, losing light out here." Dana enters before us, and we follow her up the three metal steps into the RV. The inside is precisely as it was in my dream last night. Even the smells of baking are the same. Only one thing seems out of place: I notice an open spot in her picture window where I'm certain a crystal hummingbird with a red beak hung in my vision. Small crystal shards of glass sprinkle the window ledge below, and I turn to Dana with a question on my lips.

"Yes, we had one fatality I'm afraid. Steven is quite a powerful dark soldier indeed. How interesting that a young girl led him to his

137

demise. Don't worry, Alexis. If we can't prevent his escape, we will definitely make sure that next time he doesn't have the opportunity. Isn't that right, big guy?" She gives Ryan a solid hip bump, startling him to retreat to the other side of the RV.

"Well, he sure is jumpy for such a big guy, isn't he?" Dana and I share a laugh as Ryan turns to her with not a hint of laughter on his lips or in his eyes. Instead, he seems to be looking straight into the woman's soul.

"Seems someone is extremely astute at camouflaging *their* power." He says launching into his interrogation. "I didn't even sense you as we drove into the park, not even right outside your home." Funny, I felt her. Wonder what that means about me, about her, and about Ryan. All at once, the small space inside Dana's home fills with an intense amount of power unfurling off both Dana and Ryan. Oh geez, are we having a pissing contest now?

"I happen to know when to hold it, and who I need to hide it from." Dana says flippantly, while giving me an obvious wink. The loaded conversation comes to a halt, which appears to appease both of them. The reduction in the tension—which was palpable in the confines of the RV—was immediate. Well, this is just great! Now I have two extremely powerful, zen-like warriors to deal with! Not a problem really, just an obvious fact having felt the amount of Earthen energy these two can wield in that little display. Quite the bold move for both of them in front of strangers, in front of me. Either they trust me, or they are a couple of over-trusting fools. These thoughts make me feel warm and fuzzy inside, while simultaneously bringing to the surface my own doubt of being just that, a trusting fool.

Dana places a plate of delicious-looking baked goods in front of us, with a small glass of bottled milk next to it. I smile, grabbing one and taking a nibble, but I don't lose my focus on what just happened. I take a moment to lightly send my magic out to do a more in-depth check of the RV and its surroundings, something I should have already been doing, but I hadn't felt any concern about this place. Actually, I am more relaxed now than I have been in a while. I take another bite of one of Dana's cookies and stop mid-chew before looking at the baked goodness with an accusing look. She didn't, did she? Ha, well they're damn good, so I'm not complaining, although I will clear this up with her later.

"So, let's get down to it, shall we? I have a feeling we're on a short time line before Steven and his minions make their final push to free him for good. I'm at your service as a mistress of both potions and

138

weaponry, Alexis. Some also call me *the keeper of secrets* as so many confide in me, and my Dreamwalks with others give me access to their thoughts and experiences, such as we had, my dear." Dana gives me a knowing smile and I once again look down at my cookie. Potions and weaponry, eh?

"Oh, only extra love and a little something to ease your fears," She continues on, before the question comes to the surface. "You're safe here, so give your body, and the poor goddess a rest for a while. My father always talked about time, wasting time, killing time, buying time, needing more time, never enough time. We are all so afraid of not having enough time that we don't live in it, don't make the most of it. So scared we are of wasting it, that we fill it with too much crap, and never allow ourselves to be in the present, in what is the now. Remember that when you find yourself worrying about what is to come, what has happened, and what everyone else is doing." She has me pegged. With all that is going on, waiting to be tricked by someone, or something, as well as trying to hold my fear in check, it's all an exhausting use of my time. She must be able to see the look of stress on my face.

"I know dear, it's a hard task, especially when we become activated as Earthen Soldiers. We are, you are, fighting a war against Steven and his allies, but you need to know that you're not alone. I have the wisdom of your grandmother, who told me one day that you would need me, and that you would need to see with a clear heart, clear mind, and clear eyes. In that knowledge, I made you a special potion to help you see the truth. You'll need it when you don't know who to trust, but also trust yourself and be wise. Some people are worth believing in without the use of magic. You can only use the potion once, so choose well."

More Alice-like talk, just what I need. All these riddles! Why can't I get some straight talk!?! She hands me a Wonderland-like "drink me" bottle and a padded pouch. I stare into its swirling contents. It resembles the view from space of a massive storm brewing, clouds circling and converging, all of that power and madness in one little bottle. Blinking away my fixation on the small cylinder, I quickly put it away.

"Thank you, Dana. What did my grandmother say exactly? How did she know?"

"Well, she came to me in a vision, so it's a little fuzzy. I did know you would be seeking me out sooner or later, and that I needed to tell you that your fear and your lack of trust for those close to you *will* open the door. The door for Steven to be set free, but that even a small opening cannot be breached without a part of you. You see darling, he must have your blood to truly be set free."

Eww, geez, of course he does! Why does bodily fluid always have to come into play when power and magic are involved? That's why our human title, witches, always gets a bad rap. Movies portray us as needing blood of innocents, eyes of this and that, so cliché. Guess they got the cat thing right though.

"Okay, so that's great. I just need to keep my blood in my body, I can do that." I think, with my clumsy track record it may be easier for him to get his hands on it than I think. Dana doesn't look thrilled by the worried look on my face, and Ryan harrumphs in the corner. "And this potion is to help me with those tricky rabbit things from Sandra's vision? I'm sure you know the whole shebang since you were in my head soon after." Dana nods in agreement and I take it in stride. My life is no longer my own. "Sandra told me I'd be tricked somehow, twice in fact. How am I supposed to suppress my fear and trust anyone at all with all these warnings? It's a crappy catch twenty-two is what it is!" There's my temperature-raising jitteriness again, and I try my hardest to keep it together.

"What I'm trying to do is protect the people who don't need to be involved in this, and in order to do that I'm trying to distance myself from them. Which so far is hardly working, I may add, and others just somehow find their way to me." I send a poignant head nod in Ryan's direction, and give Dana a knowing look before they can object.

"Not to mention, sleep is a luxury right now and my exhausting, edgy waking hours are wreaking havoc on my psyche. I'm pissy as all get out, and yes, I'm afraid. Afraid to sleep, afraid of failing, afraid of my past, and of being that powerless little girl again if Steven gets his hands on me." At this point I am trembling and can only think to take another goody from the tray, hoping its contents will take me down a few notches. Some of this stuff I haven't even admitted to myself yet, and here I am pouring my guts out in front of the female version of Gandolf and *tough as nails, sexy as hell,* Ryan.

Dana's answering smile isn't of pity but more of knowing. "But don't you see, Alexis dear, you are fiercer and more aware now. You are more of a match for him than you think, and you've also sought out excellent resources, both modern and magical. Not to mention, I believe I can help you with a solution to getting more rest." Her eyes shift to Ryan. You've got to be kidding me. "You know you have the answer right in front of you. *Mr. Communications Expert* right here

140

can block Steven from getting to you from a hundred feet away. You don't even have to sleep with him to get what he's sending! Hahahaha!" Oh my goodness, how many of her own special goodies has she been eating?

Yep, this time I definitely see Ryan flush. It eases my stress enough that I can speak, well for the most part.

"So, how many nights have you been close enough to block Steven and when were you planning on letting me in on this little trick of yours? You know, oh yeah, of course you know, I could have used you more than a few times lately." The only shift in Ryan is a slight turning of his shoulders in my direction. The rest of him remains leaned back nonchalantly against the far wall. He looks so much like a statue that I actually jump a little when he starts to talk.

"Some nights you needed your dreams, didn't you? With all the power circling around you from different people, it's been hard to tell when to intervene and when not to. Even at Sandra's house I had a hard time staying out of things." His lips close and the statue is again once more.

"Stalk much? Geez! Guess I better make sure I'm not sleeping in the nude anymore, Mr. Tom." My arms subconsciously move to cover my breasts in more of a way to keep him from seeing my excitement than to project a mood. Wow, thinking of him lingering around to protect me, and possibly catching a glimpse of me undressing, really won over my happy spots and it is downright embarrassing.

Is he smiling at me? Damn it, of course he is. He's picked up on my damn arousal despite my attempt to cover up the evidence. My cheeks may as well stay heated around him on a daily basis.

"No need to stop on my account." He gives me his smug smile and uncrosses his arms, turning his full attention to Dana, whose head has been whipping back and forth between us with a gleeful look in her eyes. Somehow, I doubt she gets this much entertainment very often, out here in little ole Why.

"So, Dana, Mistress of Potions and Weaponry, Alex takes the potion to see the truth of who or what is tricking her, but it could be too late if she doesn't figure it out before Steven really gets a firm hold as her bind breaks down on this side." Ryan pauses before turning his head in my direction. "Alex, you really are stronger than you think, you just need some rest to be on top of your game, and yes, I'll help as much as I can, but you have to trust me. Together we'll find out who else is playing in Steven's game. While we head into Scottsdale tonight, we need to have a serious talk about the people who are close

141

to you, both old and new." Ryan's eyes reflect his intensity as he speaks that I truly feel compelled to believe him. Dana touches my arm but keeps her eyes on Ryan.

"Yes, hopefully she's strong enough to not fall into the traps, which may or may not be someone she knows, but the potion will be her confirmation. With there being two issues at hand it may be hard to tease out, yet the potion will be definitive. It is so influential that no one, or no thing can hide in its presence." At this, she turns to me while my fingers fiddle with the sleeves of my flannel.

"So, Alex, trust yourself and know when to use the extra boost I have given you. Use it too soon and you may miss something; use it too late and Steven may have already turned the odds in his favor." Okay, now I am royally confused.

"Do you two hear yourselves? Trust, but stay on guard, sleep but don't have nightmares, take the potion but don't take it too soon or too late? This is crazy. You both see that, right? Crazy! If I see Steven again, I swear I'm going kill him myself!" Dana moves from me when she sees Ryan crossing the distance between us. He places his strong, warm hands lightly on my shoulders.

"No, Lex. I won't let you carry that. Steven is my responsibility and trust me—he will die." Oh goody! Potions, rabbits, tricks, trust, and death; this would make an awesome party theme. My head drops under the weight of his gaze, and I move into his chest as his arms wrap around me.

Of course, Dana takes this opportunity to put some goodies in a bag and hum a little tune. Is that Naughty by Nature's "OPP"? Oh boy, this woman. Yep, I love her.

"Some free-of-any-additives treats for the road—the empanadas are my favorite." She hands the bag to me when I break from my embrace with Ryan. "And for the muscle here, some weaponry worthy of the man you are. Use it well, and let me know what you think." She says this to him with a wink, and I think her hand twitches a little as if she is going to give him a good-old-sport pat on the butt and yell, *go get 'em tiger.* The duffle bag she hands him is large enough to carry a couple pairs of shoes, but that's about it. I wonder what's in there. Or do I even want to know?

Dana continues to stare at Ryan for a while; her hand touches his elbow, which takes his focus away from the bag and onto her.

"You mustn't keep her completely in the dark, you know. That will only cause her unease, which can lead to suspicion. Is that what you want, dear? I can read you fully, and as skillful as that may be, those who can't will be led through needless struggles, and right now we have enough on our plate, don't we?" She moves her hand off him, but I swear I see her squeeze slightly, causing him to jump a little. I think she may have just zapped him. Hahaha, how delightful. One way or another I'll have to whittle him down to get the information he's hiding from me.

"You two take care of each other now, and try to focus on the task at hand. If Steven comes back to his full power again, the balance could turn in favor of the darkness, and even those Dark Protectors that have not yet rejoined him may not be able to resist. Who knows what Steven can and will bring back with him? Best if we don't find out." Agreed! I hug Dana, inhaling the flowery smells of her hair and comforting ones of her bakery-filled RV.

"When will I see you again? What if we need you?" She is the closest person I have to my family, and I am leaving too soon.

"Don't worry, darling. I'll always know when you need me, and trust me, I can always find you." She gives me a kiss on the cheek and one last hug before moving away to let Ryan and me make our exit. Ryan gives her a wave that looks more like a salute, and she returns it in kind, looking more cunning than I thought possible. Don't underestimate the older ladies; they are usually more than meets the eye.

The drive to Scottsdale consists of a lot of conversation about the people in my life. I mean, when the hell is his exposé? I neatly breeze over the Justin details, but they're even hazy to me right now. Carmen, Sandra, Nic, and Shane are easy and fun to talk about. My purely professional relationships and contacts are really only that, professional and respectful—not personal. Talking about my therapy and Dr. Reynolds is stickier as I open the vault to the details of my past with Steven, and the subsequent issues to my mental state. I don't give much detail about how I bound him away. I'm not sure why, I guess I feel like I need to keep some of my cards to myself. Ryan is thoughtful as he listens, only tensing a few times and allowing me space. After a while, I cease speaking and close my eyes, hoping it somehow takes me away from fully reliving the pain.

"Lex, I'm pissed as hell at my family for not having found a way to intervene and help you sooner when your grandmother passed away. I know my parents said they tried to find you. They had always been on the lookout for Steven, but his power blocked them from getting a location on him, so it must have kept them from you as well. I was just a kid then." I was just a kid as well, but he knew that. I turn away, staring into the darkness outside the window, unable to look at him as memories force their way into my mind. "I remember the stories about Steven and how he was one of the darkest ones out there. So much so, that he left his life as a Dark Soldier when he felt his side wasn't hitting us hard enough. If I had fully developed my powers like you obviously had back then, I would have gladly joined the hunt to find him, to save you." His knuckles flex under the pressure of his clenching hands, wrapping them tighter around the steering wheel. It is a signal to me that he is telling me at least some portion of the truth. His stance on fighting the evil side of our kind is flowing through him; I can nearly see his silver power coming to life within him.

"Lex, you're obviously a strong Protector as well as a talented Healer. You won't be alone in this. We can stop him together—and for good this time."

My grandmother had touched on these specifics, but we didn't get very far before her death. Exile was as much as I could master, and was the only thing I knew to do to Steven, or even had the stomach to do. Could I really destroy someone completely? If I could, would I be able to when it really came down to it? I don't know if I have to worry about pulling that power trigger, since I don't doubt Ryan can and will. The thought makes me tremble a little, but I'm surprised to realize that it isn't with fear but more like a bit of morbid excitement. I've apparently had enough of this Steven bullshit. He had his chance to stay in his personal prison, so the fact that he has the balls to come out and render me powerless against him again has me daydreaming about the day Ryan will end him for good.

"So, I'm a Protector and a Healer, but you're solely a Protector, is that right?"

"Yes, my powers are used for hunting and protecting, but you, you may have abilities from nearly every form we have ever seen, maybe even some we don't yet know about. You're rare, Lex, rare and incredibly powerful." Well, when he says it like that I can't help but feel pumped up, and a little turned on.

"So, what kinds of things can you do exactly? I mean, obviously you have some control over my mind or emotions in order to help me sleep, but I swear you can read my mind sometimes. Are you reading my mind? Oh shit, are you reading it now? Have you always been?" I straighten up, holding my hands to my head as if I am trying to block him out. Why had I let my guard down? I'm beginning to seriously consider wearing one of my hard hats from work around him, or maybe I should carry a box of foil. I don't feel anyone rooting around in there, but just to be safe, I focus some energy around my consciousness and lock it down again. She can be such a blabbermouth and really quite visual and imaginative when it comes to Ryan. His laugh is a rumble, but light and not arrogant.

"Yes, I can pick up on some of your thoughts, which is odd since normally I can hear almost everything from others, so much in fact I have to filter it out so I don't go crazy. You have good shields built into your mind, no doubt from your need to survive and move past such a difficult past. Not during your dreams, however, well, these days, your nightmares. It's like watching a movie, a horror movie where I'm helpless to assist you unless you're near me."

"Within one hundred feet to be exact, right?"

"Yes, it seems to be somewhere around that distance for now, but I've been working on casting a larger net. That way if you ever need me and we're far from each other, I'll know it." The thought is meant to be kind, but it only makes me shiver at the idea of being away from him when I'm really in trouble, and once again, alone. Possibly not even close enough for him to know I need him.

"But if I'm blocking you, how will you know?" A chill wrestles its way through me, though the car is warm. Covering my shiver with a play at a loose strand of hair, I can only hope he doesn't notice.

"Just like during your nightmares, you must try to be open to me when you need me, at least enough to let me know. I know your first instinct is to lock down, especially if it's something with Steven, but try to send a tendril of your power to me, just me. Work on finding and recognizing my power so you can lock onto it." Yep, done and done. But once again, I keep that to myself and give him a nod. My grandmother told me there were lots of special powers in our world of supernatural abilities, so I'm not totally surprised by his reveal.

We move back into conversation about the people in my life. The referral to Dr. McAdams and his techniques intrigue Ryan. I think Ryan considers himself an expert on human behavior with his abilities, but reading minds and using our powers on our enemies is different from truly understanding those of us who don't live our whole lives knowing about, and being a part of, the Earthen powers and magic world, surrounded by family and friends to learn from.

Most of my life was lonely, and solitary, and has caused some perhaps irreparable damage. Those are all things that Dr. McAdams has seen through his work with patients like me, something he knows how to fix. That portion of the conversation brought to light how different Ryan and I are. I had been telling myself that I've found someone like me, but I haven't, and I doubt I ever will.

We make it to Scottsdale before ten P.M., and into our two-bedroom suite. The hotel is actually a mansion converted into an amazing spa with hotel-like accommodations holding only twenty rooms. Luckily, we are here for a couple of weeknights, so a suite is available.

Even in the darkness the moon highlights the amazing view of Camelback Mountain from the common area and my bedroom. Its massive rock formation appears smooth in the distance, and I look forward to some early morning exploring before venturing to the spa. Now, it's time for sleep. Driving and talking to Ryan about everyone from work to friends was exhausting. I say goodnight to him, and close my bedroom door, too tired to even think of him being so close to me while we are so far away from the chaos of my life, and from my devotion to Justin. Yep, that is the icy shower thought I need. I close my eyes and drift off to a peaceful sleep.

CHAPTER 15

The Sun, the Moon, & the Stars

Journal Entry:

"I'm going to kill Janice! Sorry Carmen, I know she's been your mentor and whatnot, but pardon my French; she has totally fucked us!" I was in rare form, scurrying down steps, and over low rock walls from atop the hotel's mezzanine outdoor patio. Carmen, Nic, and I were shimmying and climbing as discreetly as we could, up and down levels, and amongst ferns and vines to the back stairway leading us to the hotel's interior. When we made it inside and dusted off, I started in again.

"Look, yes, look one more time for me, Carmen. What is the time she listed for the cocktail hour?" I pointed at the paper on my clipboard, turning it toward her and tapping it forcefully at the indicated start time of six p.m. "Not five, not even five-thirty, but six! How many times did we confirm with her, sit with her? I had to stomach sitting with Janice, and you know I can hardly stand her, but I did it for you! I wasn't even supposed to be on this gig. This nearly impossible sold-out gig that didn't start when it was supposed to. Now whose fault will it be, Carmen?"

"Ours," she mumbled. She was as irritated as I was, but Janice— one of our Event Sales Representatives for Seaside Events, with all of her asinine faults—had been mentoring Carmen in one way or another since she was in high school. Believe me, I understood some of the allegiance, but come on, now! People change or show their true colors

147

at some point, and that is when the cord needs to be cut, severed, burned to ash for goddess's sake!

Ah man, the anger was boiling in my stomach, and I felt it rising up and drumming in my ears. Carmen and I had finally talked about the state of things in the company. Not only about the subpar leadership from Martin and his obvious Peter Pan issues, but also about my feelings about Jarvis and his waiting game for the company to implode. With all of our connections—the ones I had established during the previous eighteen months, and those of Carmen's over the previous six-plus years—the vendors, crew, and entertainers who I knew would come with us or contract with us, we could start our own company. Yes, it would be small, but it would be exclusive and classy and, not to mention, the only one in San Diego with two female owners

Shane had been living the glamorous So-Cal life. He had already told me he would lend support for our little start-up, and I could match him dollar for dollar once my twenty-third birthday hit, and my grandmother's inheritance became accessible. I'm not sure that she ever envisioned me using it for that line of work, but I think she would be happy that I was enjoying my life, doing something that was challenging and fun, well, usually fun. With our own company, we would also make it a point to work with nonprofits in support of the earth, her creatures, and resources. See, doing my protector job in the twenty-first century looked a lot different than my grandmother's and our ancestors' time.

"Carmen, we're going to turn this set-up into the most professional, badass-looking event ever, and once the dust settles, we'll be praised and thanked for saving the event instead of shooed off a roof when the guests arrive an hour early!"

The hard work paid off, no thanks to Janice or the owners. Instead, they came blazing in on the second night taking credit for all our work. We were friends with many of the bartenders they hired, and they heard it all.

Weeks after the event, Carmen and I sat down with the other production company's owners, as well as the owners of Seaside Events. The other company owners knew about the opening night screw up. They wanted answers, and someone to hang it on. Janice had saved herself from total annihilation by checking into a mental health facility, feigning stress-induced exhaustion, which was the excuse Martin and Jarvis used for her total screw-up. The owners had heard through the grapevine about who was really to thank for the outstanding outcome, so we were highly praised and asked if they could use our styling and design for some of their events. I jumped in as Martin was taking a breath.

"Of course, but please credit them as Feelyne Productions and Design." And that was the end of our time at Seaside Events and the beginning of a whole new adventure.

After a great night's rest, I'm ready to go hiking before the blasting summer sun can melt me in the scorching desert. Then I'm going to enjoy a nice relaxing day at the spa. I kept hounding Ryan over breakfast about dashing into Phoenix this evening to check out a new club that I heard about, and the hotel it is housed in as well. I want to expand to more venues in Arizona, and this trip can easily serve two purposes, dang it!

Instead, he was having some sort of stick-up-his-ass moment about being here to relax and that it isn't going to work that way if we go out in the Phoenix club scene all night. My assurances that it would be purely a professional outing, while talking about shopping for a killer outfit that is easy to dance in the next minute, did not win him over. Oh well, I still have time. It is only seven A.M., which is probably why Ryan keeps looking at me like I am crazy as I stretch out in my hiking gear, on zero coffee or tea. Some things just don't require much of a pick me up; I mean, the view of the mountain in the daylight is enough to get me moving. The guided hike leaves in fifteen minutes, and by the looks of sleepy bear in his robe, I am going alone. I bet he heads back to bed as soon as I leave.

The hike is a couple hours long, and my sweaty body is grateful for the shower once I return to the room. Ryan has gone, leaving a note that he was heading to town to look around and that he had some friends to catch up with. A small twinge of jealousy wraps its way around my chest as I imagine a female friend, but then I push it quickly aside and focus on getting my spa bag together, complete with a swimming suit, a super comfy yet cute dress, sunscreen, books, and my music. I've heard of this spa as a place of mysticism and enlightenment, and I'm psyched to finally have time to check it out.

As I walk into the spa, Tanya, who is apparently my guide and aesthetician for the day, greets me. We climb beautiful stone stairs to the second level and into a room with an indoor mineral pool. The lights are down, and the ceiling is alight with thousands of stars glittering above us. There is a small fountain attached to the pool containing beautiful crystals and multi-colored stones. The pool appears to end at the wall, but Tanya informs me that it continues to a large outdoor bathing pool for spa guests. She produces a velvet bag, and encourages me to reach inside, chose a stone or crystal before making a wish or a hope for what I want to accomplish today, before tossing the item into the fountain. Hey, I'm on board with this, magic comes in all forms, and this place definitely generates some holy place vibes. I grab a crystal and hold it tight in my hands. All I want today is peace, some peace to take with me, and some reassurance that I am not alone in this fight—that I can somehow persevere. I toss my glittering gemstone into the water, watching it sparkle as it catches the glow from the twinkling lights above us, during its descent.

After my wishing well is complete, I prep for my treatment. I opted for the detoxifying body mask, so I am down to nothing under my robe except plastic undies—yep, comfy. Tanya instructs me on getting into the bed and what to expect. The bed is warm and toasty, which matches the adobe look of the treatment room walls. I want to cleanse my body and my aura of all this bad mojo. I want to feel free. Tanya speaks very little during the treatment, but most memorable is what she says when she finishes wrapping me in a cocoon. Right before she leaves, she asks me to open my mind, my awareness, and to allow the cleansing to occur. This is a good place to practice, so I focus on the moment, on my breathing, and try to keep thoughts from bombarding my mind.

But I keep going back to thoughts of my grandmother, about missing her, about not having her in my life, and wondering what will happen if I ever have my own family? My children will never know her, and most likely not even my own mother. I won't ever be able to seek her guidance in what to do as a mother, as a wife. She is gone forever, and my mom is apparently still in hiding. Graduation was over four years ago, and I haven't heard a word from her since. Tears trickle down my face, and they are going to stay that way since my arms are wrapped and strapped against my sides. My heart breaks as I see my grandmother's dying face in the hospice bed. It's taken me years to stop seeing her this way; to only remember her healthy and strong, not her last moments, not like this. That was the cancer, and I don't want that illness to hold a picture in my mind.

I try to clear my head by counting as I breathe in and out, focusing on the feeling of the air coming in and out of my chest, as the numbers roll up and down in my mind. I felt lighter all of a sudden, and my chest swells with feelings of love and warmth. As I open my eyes, I look down at my cross-legged position. I am somewhere very bright, cozy, and warm. Something soft and of flesh and bone squeezes my hands, and I instinctively squeeze them back. When I look up, I meet my grandmother's gaze, her beautiful hazel eyes look back at me, and her lips are curved in a gentle smile; lips that don't move as she speaks inside my head. She sits across from me, in the same pose, and we just hold each other's hands, she smiling, and I crying. Her fingers feel so soft against my hand. I rub mine along hers, feeling the wrinkles and lines, every knuckle, and even her nails. This is Grandmom, all right; I'd remember the touch of her hands anywhere, anytime.

"Don't cry, Alexis. You have to know that I am here with you. I may not be there in person, but I am in spirit. You have made me so very proud. Please let go of the pain of thinking you have lost me and that I am not with you. I am here; I am always here as a part of you. Your sadness and fear of more loss keeps you from loving, my dear. I need you to accept love; to know you are worthy of being loved. You have so much to offer, but also so much to experience and to learn. Open your heart, my dear, you deserve to be happy, to be loved." She squeezes my hands in hers once again, and their warmth is undeniable. How I miss this amazing woman, but I also feel a new sense of happiness, and love that has been missing, locked away inside me for so long.

It's as if my heart bursts open, breaking locks and busting open barred doors. I sense an immediate lightness in my very being, as well as a change in the overall form and intensity of the power I have inside me. When I look into her eyes again, they are heavy with tears and yet, their spark of power is unmistakable—an icy, silvery blue. I have never seen her power shine through before; with years of mastery it had never betrayed her. When I look down at my hands, vines of emerald green flow around me, touching me lightly, a vision of my power that I had only ever felt and never seen. Her nearly translucent Earthen gift flows out like silver tears, turning to dandelion seeds and flitting around the green vines on my arms. They circle and twirl with each other in a dance that fills my eyes with sparkling light.

"Now, I have protected you better than before, my sweet Alexis. Your power has been shifted slightly—a camouflage of sorts, ever changing and confusing to those who would prey upon you by using your own power against you. This is my gift. I love you, my dear. Be safe and please allow yourself to be loved." My eyes close and I nod to her, tears rolling down my face, silently thanking and promising her at the same time. Her hands squeeze mine a final time before my mind slowly rearranges itself, returning my awareness to the spa table as if waking from a dream. My eyes open slowly and I am alone, lying on my back, staring at the ceiling. A lone green tendril of my power shimmers and fades, dropping a dandelion seed just as it bursts open like a tiny supernova in the dimness of the room. I smile and weep, happy to know that she is with me, a part of me even more now. My heart swells as if a heavy weight has been lifted and sent far, far away.

When I return to the suite, Ryan is sitting on the couch working on his laptop, his hair still wet from swimming in the pool. I wonder if he has changed his mind about visiting the club; I know I haven't. The little number in my bag is hollering to be let out to play. Waving the bag in his direction, I give him my winning smile. He bolts upright so fast that the hairs on my neck stand on end.

"What is that? You seem different. What did you do? Did something happen?" Ryan is in front of me faster than I can answer. I wonder if he is going to pick me up and sniff me, by the way he's looking at me.

"All's good, big guy. I just had a little experience with my grandmother and maybe, just maybe I got some help. Now, if you will excuse me, I need a little nap before heading to Phoenix. It's been a long day." He huffs, but moves from me to sit back down. The confused look on his face disappears, but I can nearly smell the gears burning rubber inside his brain. I guess I better ease him down a bit.

"Ryan, it's a good thing, I promise. We'll talk about it later. Maybe some sushi before dancing? I hear the hotel has an awesome bar with delicious sashimi, rolls, and of course sake!"

"Fine, Lex, you win. What time do we head out?" Gotcha!

Hours later we're in downtown Phoenix. The club is amazing and situated right across from the hotel's sushi restaurant. Ryan and I enjoy watching the club goers arrive and either find themselves swept right in or standing in a long line with others who are also fidgeting with excitement. I hate lines, but really, who doesn't?

After enjoying our dinner and plenty of sake shots, we meet with the club manager and tour the nightclub meeting various employees, from bartenders and DJs to dancers and muscle. Ryan happens to know a couple of the security guys and one or two dancers, surprise,

surprise! While he gets into some *back in the day* conversations, I aim myself toward the bar in the house music room and take a seat on an open barstool.

My left leg is hiked up on a rung while my right one hangs down, revealing more leg than most would deem legal. The teensie hot pants I wear underneath my emerald-green dress give me some necessary freedom to dance; nothing should ever hinder a person's body from moving unreservedly with the music. The fabric of my dress gives the impression of a mix between sequins and snakeskin; it clings to my body but has a smooth softness to the touch. The straps hug my shoulders closely, allowing the deep V to show the light smattering of glitter twinkle across my chest before plunging safely between my breasts. Ryan's face was completely blank when he first saw me leave my bedroom. Yes, he can be incredibly quiet most of the time, but this time his eyes targeted upon my body made it perfectly clear what he thought of the new purchase. His reaction brought a smile to my face as I thought "two can play at this game."

The shimmering snow-white, quartz bar top is softly lit underneath and encased in a long unstained, knotted wood. It is a perfect highlight in a two-story room equipped with numerous dancing podiums, a raised stage, and speakers nearly as tall as the first floor. The design is flawless and elegant. I opt for a new cocktail, drinking a couple of mojitos before deciding to get down from my perch, and join the throng of sweaty bodies in the middle of the dance floor.

The current song has a quick tempo that instantly fills the crowd with vibes of happiness and intensity. I enjoy the energy in the room, but the song doesn't move me in the way some songs do. Everyone has a song or songs whose rhythm just meshes and bonds with their soul; it's as if your limbs are being controlled by the beats, vocals, and changes in speed. The music begins to transition into the beginning sounds of one of my favorite songs. A song that makes me feel both longing and sadness for my broken family, before transforming me with its strength and passion into a woman who is thankful for having had the experience of being loved.

Tonight is different though; the song latches onto my very being and I feel no sadness, only love and an intense openness to being loved, and by goddess it arouses me. My body sways, and slowly my head tilts back as my right arm reaches into the air, snaking above me. It slides down, cutting through the air as my fingers move along my neck. They trickle down its length before moving across my chest and gliding down my stomach, finding my hips under the tightness of my dress. I pull on the fabric at the hem, hiking it even higher up my leg to give my body even more freedom to dip and sway. "Sun & Moon" comes in clearer and the Above & Beyond lyrics take hold of me.

"I'm sorry baby. You were the sun and moon to me. I'll never get over you, you'll never get over me.
And when the big wheel starts to spin, you can never know the odds. If you don't play, you'll never win."

The intensity of the melody sends my body into a frenzy as I spin around, feeling the floor under my heels. It's as though my feet are on a swivel, letting my body succumb to the beats. My hands reach for the sky again before taking turns swaying around my body, sweeping over my thighs, and bracing me for the times I daringly arch backwards. Beads of sweat began a sensuous trail down the back of my neck, and I touch the droplets lightly with my fingers, trailing them around my neck and into the cleavage of my breasts.

My eyes are closed for the most part, but I am suddenly compelled to open them. As I look across the dance floor, Ryan is clearly in view. Others are giving him a wide berth, either because of his size or his apparent inability to completely conceal the waves of power rolling off him. His eyes lock with mine, and I feel his lust and desire drill through me as his eyes spark. A second glow from his hip causes me to glance down his body. Oh, damn. There's a glow coming from the ring on his hand. He wears it all the time, but it never seemed out of the ordinary before.

Ryan suddenly moves toward me quick as a panther, immediately extinguishing both silver glows before reaching me. He keeps some distance at first, moving with me. Damn, it's so sexy to not have a man grab at me right away on the dance floor. It's a dance, damn it! Even in the wild lions tease and play, oh, and then there's the whole jaw on the back of the neck thing, but hey, I have a point, right?

Ryan's dark V-neck shirt clings to his chest, revealing his muscles as they ripple with his movements. His arms move lightly despite their muscularity. Hell, I could watch him move forever but my hands want to touch instead. I move my fingers down his chest before they take hold of his hand, drawing him toward me.

We find our perfect dancing position again as I move to the right quickly, keeping his left leg between mine and arching backward. When I curl up, his hands travels down my hips, grabbing both sides of my barely covered backside and squeezing possessively before lifting me up so I wrap my legs around his waist. He moves with directness, holding me until my back is against a towering speaker. I slowly slide down to touch my heels to the floor as the motion of the beats continually force the speaker to vibrate. I feel the wind created by the movement pulsing against my back while the throbbing electronic sounds take hold.

"We were in heaven, you and I. When I lay with you and close
my eyes our fingers touch the sky.
I'm sorry baby. You were the sun and moon to me. I'll never
get over you, you'll never get over me."

Ryan stares into my eyes, his unfurling power and body moving against me. By everything meshing together, this song, the thrumming on my back creating waves throughout my body, the feel of Ryan's skin against mine, and the fiery licks of moisture once he begins to kiss me along my neck, feverishly has me wishing we were alone in this place. I can truly let go and be with this man, this man who knows my secrets. I feel I can trust him, and that has a way of making my body respond in the most unusual ways. His hand drifts up along my arm before wiping a strand of hair from my eyes. I catch the glow of the ring again, but my question is halted as he kisses me passionately. His grip brings me even closer to his body and I feel his desire for me as well. I press deeper into his mouth before the world begins to get hazy. What in the world? This place needs to get a grip on their fog machine.

The music dulls to a hum, and I bolt upright in the hotel bed, noticing the growing darkness creeping underneath the blackout curtain. The green glow shines from my eyes, lighting the room as I scan around quickly. A second spark comes from across the room, and my eyes focus on the shape of Ryan's body in the doorway. His eyes are ablaze and the ring glows on his left hand. I see his bare chest rising and falling heavily, as if he were still pressed against me in the club.

What, a dream? Damn it! Oh shit, my nipples are alert and clear as day through my sheer tank top. My sleep shorts don't help either as goose bumps break out all over my exposed skin.

Power crackles, and I move onto my hands and knees and crawl closer to the edge of the bed. Ryan crosses the distance between us, and I lift to my knees to touch the skin on his shirtless chest. My body tingles against his just as my power reaches and pulls against his, tempting me.

He leans in, making my skin vibrate in waves of excitement. Warm lips brush mine, followed by Ryan's hand landing lightly on my back. Inside my body, senses buzz wildly as if synapses are firing on overload, sizzling and popping under my skin. It is close to how I feel when pulling from the earth, but with Ryan's force mingling with mine I feel somehow even more alive, even stronger, and oh boy, a tad hotter and very excitable. With a lustful moan into his lips, he responds by pressing his hand firmer into my back, causing my nipples to burn against his chest. Without thinking, I pull him down and flip him over so I am straddling him, my arms wrapped around his neck.

Our lips and hips move in sync as I kiss his mouth then draw back slightly, keeping him just a breath away from being able to kiss me fully. I trace his mouth lightly with the tip of my tongue before nibbling on his bottom lip and pulling it gently. He growls sensuously and his strong hands pull me back toward him. Lips parted expectantly, I wait for a full-on assault but instead he barely brushes my lips with his own, teasing me into a kiss and then pulling away. He finally lands a light kiss before continuing to my cheek, ear, neck, and collarbone. My arousal shoots up a notch when his lips reach the tops of my breasts, the energy shooting through us increasing exponentially—intensifying my need even further. Ryan's hands gently move up my back, grazing my neck before grabbing hold of my hair and tugging my head back in a slightly rough, yet hot damn, a pleasurable way. Nothing has ever felt like this before.

Suddenly, his body stops its melting chocolate motion against me, and he becomes the rigid-as-stone Ryan I have come to know. His hand lets go of my air and I whimper at the loss of the sensuous tension.

"Lex?"

"Mmmm . . ." I manage with my head tilted towards him and a sloppy grin on my face.

"I hate to say this, and please know there isn't a single part of me that wants to interrupt any of this, but I think someone is coming to the door." Boy is he right. I feel his hardness against me while I continue to roll my hips, causing the friction that is setting both of us off.

" Um, no, that's not what I mean. Something's up, Lex." Smile fading I realize he's not talking about the fire between my legs.

"What's wrong? Oh damn, are you reading my mind? I wasn't really expecting to do that." I move my hands to my head, trying to stop the visions of us in my mind. His laugh is light and sweet as he gently pulls my hands towards him.

"I don't think I need to read your mind to know what you're thinking right now, Lex, because it's exactly what I'm thinking. But to answer your question, I'm not sure what's wrong, but I need to find out."

I am kind of stuck in the desire to rip our clothes off, but I manage to get the gist of what he is saying while also create a mental sticky note reminding me to keep my shields up around him. Mr. Nosey doesn't need to know everything I am thinking, and hopefully I can keep him out of my dreams, even though my mind is having a hard time not being creative right now. I look down at him and give a lusty smile that leads to his hands giving my thighs a warning squeeze before he slowly lifts me off him, giving me one last kiss and moving to the door.

"Where are you going?" Yep, my brain has checked out.

"Hold on, let me get the door?" His tight butt moving away from me brings a pout to my lips.

"What door?" Yep, I'm in a lust coma. A knock sounds on cue, followed by a voice on the other side.

"Ms. Conner? Sorry to bother you, but it is rather urgent I am told." Crap, of course it is. I'm far off the radar in the middle of the desert, and something urgent is afoot.

I stay where I am, too underdressed to hurry out. I hear mumbling and some agreeing words and then the sound of the door closing. Ryan returns a few moments later, pulling a shirt over his head and looking at me with an obvious change in his demeanor. I blow out my held breath, shifting a stray curl from my eyes.

"Let me guess, something has come up, and you have to leave. Oh, and you can't tell me everything yet but I need to trust you, right?"

"I need to make a phone call. I'll be right back. It's seven now. I'll grab us something to eat downstairs and then we can head to the club. That way you have time to get ready and maybe even rest a bit more." Ugh, the whiplashing change in intensity of my mood makes my head spin. Being turned on to off does make me feel that a bit more sleep would be okay. Plus, that hike and spa did wipe me out. Maybe a few more minutes won't hurt.

"You'll tell me everything when you get back, right?" As I move to the edge of the bed, I clutch a pillow to my chest as the cold settles in from his absent warmth.

"Yes, I just need to know what it is so I can tell you. I need to call my family. Apparently they've been trying to reach me. Guess we've been a little busy." He comes to where I am sitting with my legs dangling off the bed, and reaches down to place his hand gently on the side of my neck before moving it back and curling his thumb around my ear.

"The last thing I want is to leave you right now, but I'll be right back. Try to get some sleep." He kisses me softly and full of promise, but it ends too soon.

I'm not sure how much time passes, but I must have fallen asleep quickly, maybe even before he left the suite. I think he came back in to see me before he left, but that may have been another dream.

The sensation of him next to me isn't a dream though; his warm, solid body is curled against my back, and his left arm under my neck. The heat radiating off him is soothing and makes it hard for me to wake completely. When I finally open my eyes, I glance at my right hand cradled in his left hand. It takes me a second, but then my breath catches as I see and feel the weight of his ring in its new spot, on my right ring finger. It's magically melded there, and the warmth of its presence soothes me. My eyes begin to flutter and I know I am going to fall back asleep, but before I do I notice the engravings circling the well-worn silver ring—suns and moons chasing each other for all eternity.

CHAPTER 16

The Council

Journal Entry:

Carmen, Sandra, Shane, Nic, and I were having a blast at a late-ass event, one that was actually for us as opposed to the countless months of back-to-back-to-back events for clients. Carmen left earlier than the rest of us, I thought to retreat home, but her text a few minutes later let me know she wouldn't be home that night. Curious—where was she going at three in the morning!?! Nic and I stumbled to share a cab, my wobbling attributed to my hours of dancing versus Nic's "martini I love you" evening.

When I finally made it home, I went to open my door but something was blocking it. My power reached out, and I knew it was Bear; he was alive, but sick. I could sense the poison in him: auto coolant. There had been stories of other dogs in Encinitas getting sick from coolant poisoning, and it was beginning to feel like they were not accidents. I had to get to Bear so I could heal him. I ran around the side of the house, threw open the fence gate, and barreled into the back door. His breathing was labored, so I knew I had to act fast. Bear was eleven years old and so large that I knew that fighting this off would not be easy for him. I drew sharply upon the Earthen energy inside me and sent healing tendrils into Bear. He growled in pain when I shifted him to see if I could get his weight under me. Holding his head to my forehead, I splayed my fingers hard on the wooden floor, pulling on the Earthen energy and calling upon it to heal him.

"Heal him now!" I cried out, demanding power from Gaia. I reached into his body with my force, seeking out the poison, following the traces from his stomach through his veins, heart, and away again into his arteries. I pulled the evil substance with a vengeance, back into the earth and away from Bear's body. The floor sizzled and burned as the poison dripped out of Bear, pooling and then disappearing into smoke. My big lab threw up where he lay, and his breathing started to slow to a normal and less-labored rhythm. I eased off my pull on the earth and allowed a small trickle of it to spread all over Bear, searching one last time for any trace of poison. Finding none, I bent over him, easing my arms under his body and using all my might I lifted him off the floor. Finding his dog bed in my room, I lowered him slowly, covered him with a blanket, and kissed him before leaving the room.

I leaned against the door in exhaustion before my hands hit my knees and my head slumped toward the floor. Small drips sounded below me, and I opened my eyes to the sight of drops of blood hitting the floor. My nose was bleeding, something very rare for me; I don't think I'd had a nosebleed since I was in college. The ferocity I used to help Bear had taken its toll on me, and I quickly cleaned up in the mirror before heading back to the spot where Bear had nearly died. I touched my fingers to the remainder of his stomach contents on the floor, and used my power to search the sickening remnants. I found pieces of a soup bone that had apparently been soaked in poison; a trap, a cruel snare for any animal that stumbled upon it, wild, lost, or visiting. I cursed myself for the times Bear had strolled away from the house while we spent time in the front yard. Our neighborhood was open and friendly, but there was someone amongst us who was sick, sick enough to poison any animal that smelled the delicious bones summoning them to their death. I searched deeper into the sickness and found hints of the fingers that had touched the bone and rage began to build inside me again.

It was a vicious thirst for payback that sent me searching harder and faster, using the power of the earth to seek the person out. The energy was a guide inside my mind, showing me flashes of where I'd find the perpetrator. Ah yes, there, outside the neighborhood, a large plot of land with a singular house. In there I found her, sleeping in her bed, next to her husband, while two small children slept in the room next to theirs. She lay at peace with her hands tucked under her head. The same hands that placed the bone in coolant, the bone, like many others, that had poisoned other dogs, cats, even wildlife from the

160

unpopulated areas in the hills. My nose began to bleed again, and I eased off on the power. My sight went a little hazy when I got up too quickly from the wooden floorboards.

Stumbling, I found the couch and tried to breath in and out, calming myself and preparing for what I was about to do next. What was I going to do, exactly? I felt myself spiraling a little out of control with my anger at that woman. The power from the earth cycled in and through me so fast I had to keep a hold on it and let it swirl inside, becoming one with my hair, skin, bones, and cells. It found its place within my building anger and intensified the need I had to make that woman pay. I hadn't felt that much fury since I rid this plane of Steven, but I didn't feel in control this time. The lack of a moment to plan my reaction could be part of the boiling outrage. Steven had been a long time coming and involved a great deal of preparation, but the woman would be dealt with immediately if I had my way, and it might not be pretty.

A tugging sensation pulled on my awareness as a light scratching came from the back door. I opened the door, cast my eyes to the ground, and wouldn't you know, that little twitchy fox Vex strolled right on in.

"Where is he? Ah, never mind, Eila, I can smell him from here." His golden tail fluffed and flicked as he ran to the room where Bear lay. I followed him robotically, my mind fuzzy like walking in a dream. "Excellent healing, Eila, not a drop of that hideous poison left in him. He will be just fine, maybe a little weaker since he's an older dog, but it's better than dying as painfully as he would have today. No, this dog deserves another good couple of years." His words were encouraging yet also made me instantly sad as life is life, and we cannot escape death whether at the end of a long, well-lived life, or even a short and vicious one.

"Thanks, Vex. It was close I think." Wiping my nose again, I hid he small drop of blood and instead smoothed back my curls, when did they get so sweaty?

"So, Eila, where are you rushing off to? Gaia was weakening in the pit of her stomach from the amount of energy you were pulling. It's getting a little dark, don't you think?" Dark? Of course it was dark; it was the middle of the night. Oh wait; I knew what he meant by dark.

"Wait. Hold on a minute, Vex. I'm doing something good by going after her. This isn't evil. She's the evil one! What am I supposed to do? Just let her go? Give her a small warning? Hope the cops will take care of it and give her a slap on the wrist and maybe a fine? What

*about the other animals that will suffer if I choose to do nothing? No!
She needs to pay, and in more than a monetary way. She has been
taking life, innocent life from Gaia. Doesn't the goddess care?" I am
not dark, I'm not.*

*"Easy there, Eila, of course she cares, and we will take care of this
little woman's misguided attempt at keeping animals out of her trash.
She isn't well by any standard. On her own, she might not have a
chance at getting the help she really needs, but we can make sure this
woman gets placed in a facility where she can't hurt another living
thing again. What we need is finesse, Eila. A little bit of finesse, and
some really good timing." Vex gave Bear a tickle on his nose with his
own and walked out of the room.*

*Vex's plan was pretty easy, and something I wish I had thought of
myself, damn it! I guess that was the point; I needed to see the ease
amongst the trees and keep my angst for revenge in check. Vex was
right, I could see and taste the darkness in that need to make her pay.
It was alluring and made me feel powerful beyond anything I had ever
felt in my twenty-three years. There are those who were born
Protectors and Healers, those who may not have the predisposition to
do good, who weren't born with a heart to fight for those who cannot
fight for themselves, but were born instead out of hate, deceit, and
selfishness. Or, maybe they were so beaten down by the world that the
power was the only thing that made them feel alive. I saw how those
wielders of our power could easily be led to the side of evil. Something
I tasted myself that night, and I could only hope that despite Vex's
magical appearing act, I would have been able to shut down the urge
on my own. Vex turned to me at that thought.*

*"Eila—Alex—that's the point, you aren't on your own. It may feel
like it sometimes, but I promise you, you will always have someone to
watch over you. Steven's ability to keep you hidden was the only lapse
in your protection, and I'm deeply sorry for all that happened during
that time. It will never happen again. Now, let's go get this bitch." I
was shocked for only a moment by his words, but with a shrug I smiled
at the craziness of my life.*

*The timing had to be perfect. The cops needed to show up at the
exact moment. Sheila Bart's house was still dark at four A.M., as most
houses were. Vex snuck around the back to the garbage cans and
found the bowl, a freaking dog food bowl, full of several bones dipped
and soaked in coolant broth. Vex growled silently at the dish; his lips
pulled back and baring some pretty sharp-ass teeth.*

162

"Easy Vex. I'm heading around front now, the cops will be here any minute, and we need to act fast." I lightly touched his fur. I knew he didn't really like that, but his golden head—softer than it should be on a fox, so it had to be the whole mystical being thing—was so damn cute, I had to. Giving him a nod, I slipped out of the backyard, hiding on the side of the house so I could hear Sheila and even catch some glimpses of the show.

I heard the banging and yelping as Vex started to make a ruckus out back. If we were right, Sheila would come out first. The back door opened and I heard the cock of a gun. Shit we didn't think about that. No way would she shoot him! Would she? Then again, Vex didn't seem too concerned as he started talking shit to her right away.

"What the hell, woman, you poisoned me? Why? What did I do to you?" Sheila gasped and pressed her back against the door. Even from around the corner, I could smell the alcohol and cigarettes on her reeking breath.

"What? What did you say? I must be dreaming! What the hell is this? Die already, you fleabag." Her quivering hands still held the gun, as she tried her darnest to keep it aimed on Vex. "Oh god, I really need to stop the drink and the pills. I told the doctors those pills wouldn't work, damn it!"

"Yeah, they don't work well when you drink your ass off with them. Dumb human. Don't you read the labels? Oh God, it hurts! Why? Why did you do this?" Vex was an impeccable actor as it turned out, and I knew he would keep her going. Tires crunched on the gravel driveway. Red, blue, and white lights lit up what was left of the night as dawn started to chase it away. I met the officers out front and told them I heard a commotion around back. They made their way with weapons drawn as they came upon Sheila ranting and raging at a dying animal on the ground, screaming for it to tell her the meaning of her life, as if he was sent to her from above like some sort of furry deranged angel.

One officer lowered her weapon and moved toward Sheila while the other one kept his steadily aimed at her heart.

"Mrs. Bart, you need to drop your weapon and put your hands behind your head." Sheila saw the cops, registering only long enough to point and repeat two words over and over.

"Fox talking. Talking fox."

Yes, yes, I see the fox ma'am; no I don't hear him speaking." Sheila dropped the gun, but kept ranting on and on about the fox talking to her and about her penance to God. It was too late for her. The only thing waiting for her was a padded cell and some heavily

organized visitation from those in her family that might want to see
her.

Our deranged neighbor was placed in handcuffs as other officers
arrived and kept the rest of the family at bay. I felt bad for her children
who would become aware of the fact that their mother was a monster.
I could only hope her mental illness didn't pass on to them; you know,
that whole apple not falling far from the tree thing. Before they could
get Vex tranquilized and into a cage, he perked up and took off.

Vex stayed with me for a while to make sure Bear was doing well
before he gave me a proverbial tip of his hat and slipped away. I lay
on the floor next to Bear and slept with him into the daylight hours,
soothed by the rise and fall of his body, weeping for those who hadn't
been saved because I was too late.

I wake up in the darkness wrapped in the sheets of an empty bed and
with a growling stomach. The clock on the bedside table glows
brightly, letting me know it's ten. Man, I was hoping to get to the club
around now. I wonder if I should just scratch the whole plan seeing as
a lot has changed. I jump out of bed, giving myself a long stretch and
then a once over in the bathroom mirror. A murmuring and rustling in
the common area between the two bedrooms grabs my attention, so I
quietly lean against the door in an attempt to discreetly overhear what
is happening on the other side.

"No, you told me to locate her and to do what I could to assist in
finding the truth, and helping her is supporting that very mission. No.
No, I'm not bringing her in! What? No! I will not ask her if she wants
to speak to the Council. She barely knows about our world, and you
want me to throw her to the hounds? It's out of the question!" Silence
followed, except for the sound of shoed feet pacing as Ryan listened to
whomever he must have been speaking to on the phone. "Don't you
think they were the ones snooping around the house? It seems like the
most logical explanation to me. They're trying to find me, to find her.
No! No, Mom! I understand, and I will check in with you when we get
back. Yes, we'll leave now. Promise me you won't tell them, okay?
Thank you! I love you, goodbye."

I step away from the door with my heart thumping in my chest.
Was someone at my house? His house? What was Ryan trying to find

the truth about? Steven? Me? Before I can answer any of my own questions, I hear a light knock on the door.

"Lex, hey, can I come in?" Ha, his question seems hilarious to me and I laugh hysterically. He didn't ask me that question a few hours ago.

"Just a minute."

My renewed modesty, and the rising doubt about Ryan's intentions have me changing out of my tank and shorts to fling on a shirt and pull on my jeans. I reach for the doorknob and open the door not even caring about the state of my hair.

"What? Time to go already, but we were having so much fun, weren't we?" My hand is on my hip, and I don't budge to give him access past my door.

"I guess you overheard me. Look, Lex, I can explain in the car, but we'll have to pick another time to check out the club. Right now, we need to head home." Did he just give me orders?

"Why is that, Ryan? Whose house is being poked through and what truth are you trying to seduce out of me, huh? Why don't you just ask me? No need to go through the motions and act like you care about me and want to help me! What is it, Ryan? What do you want to know? You sure as hell aren't sharing much with me about you, about how or why you're even in my life! You have no problem leaving me in the dark, do you? It's time for you to start talking or I'm out of here, and I mean *now*! "

Ryan sighs and backs away from the door, turning his back on me and heading into the common area. As he moves away from me, my power perks up and turns on its defensive systems again. I see his back and neck faintly tense when he feels the charge in the room. He turns toward me slowly with an appearance of complete calm on his face. It's obvious that he's worried, not worried about my feelings, but worried about what I am capable of doing. Well, good.

"Lex, you're jumping to conclusions. I'm not acting, I'm drawn to you, and you know that. Don't you think you'd be able to tell if I was faking all of this? You're a powerful Earthen Protector, Lex; you need to trust your instincts and those on your side. Don't you remember what Dana said?" Moving out of my room, I add my other hand to the opposite hip and give him my "and" look.

"Okay, look. That was my mom on the phone that you so sneakily eavesdropped on. My dad was the one I called earlier from the lobby, but she was the one with the information I needed. She was tied up trying to cover our asses by the time I was able to reach her. My mom found some traces of someone snooping around our family home and called immediately to warn me. She didn't want to leave a message, and we were only able to connect just now. Someone took great care to try and cover his or her tracks, so it has to be someone with great skill, perhaps someone on or close to our Council."

"Who or what in the hell is this Council?" Another tidbit my grandmom left out of my training.

"The Council oversees the Earthen Protectors, and the US based group sent me to find you and observe. I wasn't supposed to interact with you as much as I have, because I was only tasked to bring you back to them. Call me cynical, but the power in the Council has always put me on edge. I don't trust them, or at least some of them." I don't sense a lie, but I keep forgetting I don't know Ryan really at all, so how could I really know?

"So, you were sent to find me by some group you don't trust, and now I'm supposed to go with you to the very people you don't trust? So they can what? Take me against my will and do what with me? Really, Ryan, how am I supposed to trust you when you keep things from me? Yes. I will head out now, but I'll find my own way home, thank you. I think it's safer if I don't travel with you, don't you agree?"

He raises his chin, looking at me as anger sparks in his eyes. It's a reaction I haven't ever seen from him, and it terrifies me. I sure do hope he is on my side, as I pity those that oppose him. He can't deny my line of thinking though, and I know he'll concede, but before we leave, I have more questions.

"How did you find me in the first place? Won't they just do the same thing you did to locate me? Really, how hard is it when they know who I am? There is the Internet, you know. All they have to do is google me! Great, now I'm going to have to change my name." I rub my hands up and down my arms, realizing goose bumps had broken out at the thought of someone again controlling what I do. Ryan sighs and then sits down on the couch, asking me to join him instead of storming off right this instant. I choose to sit across from him on another chair instead.

"The Council had only heard rumors and stories of a girl your age who was able to use both of our inherent Earthen powers of protecting and healing. No one knows you are that girl. My parents were tipped off by a cryptic message claiming that the stories of the girl were true, and that the girl was actually Stacy Conner's daughter, who was living on the West Coast. We didn't share this information with the Council, and I asked them for the assignment to find you. With my history of tracking those that others can't, and my record of following orders, or at least appearing to, they let me go alone."

I look into his eyes and begin to feel that familiar humming coming off his skin. It makes my body want to ease my shoulders down from my ears, and release the bundled-up muscles in my back. But my swirling power that had engaged at the feelings of being left out of the loop isn't backing down that easy, instead keeping my senses on high alert. Even though my brain is listening and trying to make sense of all of this, it is also calculating its best methods of survival as the notion of being sought after by yet another player in this game comes to light. Either Ryan doesn't notice I am not backing down fully, or he is only trying to appear unaffected in order to keep me from going off.

"Once I used the Internet to find out that you went to school in Southern California, it only took a few hints of your healing ability and what I knew of your family power's signature to finally focus on your trail in San Diego. You keep such a low profile, over your gift I mean." What is that supposed to mean? Recalling the emerald green dress I was supposed to wear tonight, I guess he had a point.

"You really do have amazing control for someone so young, someone who has been on her own and away from the support of your kind. It wasn't until I felt something resembling Steven's power signature resonating from the Gaslamp area that I found you. At first, when I reported back to my family we were worried you had turned to his side, but there is no truth to that, I know. In fact, I think the power I sensed was either from Steven himself, or someone working with him."

"You mean you can feel him, like I can in my nightmares? Oh goddess, he must have a way in already! He's already breaking through, isn't he?" This is bad. Everything being tossed at me makes my body go into power-saving mode. With my hold on the Earthen energy lessening, my muscles reflexively release even more of their tension. I look into Ryan's eyes and he gives me a look of thankfulness knowing that I've taken it down a notch, but that doesn't mean he has good news for me.

"Yes, I think so, but my dad doesn't think he can do it alone. He asked me to watch you from a distance and see if you were breaking the bind yourself. I took observations and immediately reported back to him that there was no way you were doing what he feared. Steven is lucky. If it had been me, he'd be dead from brutal means rather than

167

bound away alive, even if he is in some hell dimension." Ryan's eyes give a silver flicker, and once again I sure as hell hope I can trust him to be on my side. This man is one powerful-ass dude. I think I'm in shock, because I can't talk, my tongue and lips can't seem to move.

"Lex, when I first felt your power I confirmed what the anonymous sender thought to be true. You're the girl we've heard so much about. You have unbelievable strength and magic, and now that I'm here to help you, we can stop Steven for good this time. I know I keep saying it, but you have to believe me, you aren't alone anymore. Do I look like I need to answer to some Council? They don't know who you are yet; your family kept them in the dark about you, and you in the dark about them for good reason. My parents have kept my progress vague, but I guess those who sent me are getting restless. They expect me to stay out of sight and report your location back to them, or to have brought you back by now. But don't worry, we have some time, and I have ways to keep them searching. We're in this together, and we will see this through."

"But won't they find us? Can't they just follow your energy signature or something?" Oh, I can still talk, that's a relief. I'm following his tale and logic at this point, I think.

"What they don't know is that I can change it. I can mimic someone else's power, or even a plant or animal. It's something I've always been able to do." This takes me aback a bit. What Ryan is explaining is exactly what I did to Steven; I mimicked his power, so he didn't even realize I was taking hold of him. It is something he had inadvertently taught me when he trapped me the very first day. I knew that was what he must have done to catch me off guard, so I taught myself. Steven was too much of a cocky jackass to think a scrawny little girl like me could possibly have the ability to do something so difficult. People truly do underestimate me way too much.

Now, here's Ryan telling me he can do the exact same thing; either it isn't as unique as I thought, or he has even more abilities than he lets on. As much as this intrigues me, it also sets me on edge. What if he is tricking me? Making my scan of him come back all good when he is really hiding something sinister from me. Despite another spike of concern, my mind signals my body to dial down my hold on Gaia's power even more, it's exhausting despite having caught up in a nightmareless sleep, and this back and forth on what I really know and trust about Ryan is beyond irritating.

I should have eased off a bit since both my desire and ability to hold the energy at a high level of alert for so long will drain me completely, and who knows what's in store. My immediate protective power surge inches off a bit once again as I take control, letting it bubble slowly under the surface, but it has already cost me by washing away my hours of rest. Standing up slowly, I move over to the couch, collapsing next to Ryan.

"This sucks, do you know that? The whole thing sucks." I'm one with the words right now, aren't I?

A stinging hits my eyes and coldness tumbles down my cheeks. Damn it. I don't want to cry in front of him. Uncaring of my desires, tears trickle down my cheeks while Ryan's eyes follow their movement as he takes in my appearance, and I'm sure, registering the level of safety. To some people, it may seem like he is being tentative, but I'll never use that word to ever describe Ryan's actions, ever. I don't think he is ever tentative—graceful, rather, cunning and calculating, like a jaguar.

He touches my face lightly, wiping away my tears. Normally I wouldn't allow anyone to do something so comforting, let alone see me this way, but right now I am a little exhausted from the intense power uptake, and with Ryan, it somehow seems natural. Maybe it's because I don't want to be alone with my secrets anymore. It has been a long time since my grandmother passed. I haven't been around anyone like me since she left, at least not someone who wasn't evil. Maybe I take comfort in Ryan because of the vision I had with my grandmom that my power is even greater now, and that using my "radar tracker of good" on him is still coming up as all systems go.

"In two ways you have been my mission, Alex. I was invested in the life of Alex Conner from the closeness you have with my family as much as finding the girl with the amazing abilities. I know I was only supposed to either hunt you down or watch you, but you have to know that the instant I met you I knew who you were and that I had to help you. There is no way you are siding with Steven; and your power resonates in a way that connects perfectly with mine. The slight change I sensed when you came back from the spa hasn't even knocked us out of alignment. It's something I've never felt or even heard of before with anyone who wasn't part of my family. And yet, this feels different than that. I can't explain how, but it is."

I have to agree with him. His left hand touches my right one as he traces the ring where it sits upon my finger. I had totally forgotten about it. It sparks at his touch, warming my hand instantly.

"I'm not sure how it got there. Do you want it back?" I don't want to give the ring back; it seems to belong to me now.

"No, no, it's yours. I think it always has been."

CHAPTER 17

Going Under

Ryan and I agreed that with the Council's noses up our asses, it was best to separate on the way home. After catching a late flight home to San Diego and leaving Ryan to drive alone, I scoop up Pitter and pack yet another, more long-term, suitcase and take off for Sandra's house. Once bringing my Seer BFF up to speed, she demands that I stay with her until we feel I'm not in danger from Ryan's a-hole Council. Maybe someday I will tell the Council my secrets, but it will be on my own terms and not because I'm being forced to.

Pitter is ecstatic when he realizes we are at Sandra's house. This is a nice change from his crazy rampage in the car, where I swear he was climbing upside down, and I have a couple of scratches to prove it. I have to admit I am pretty darn happy to see Sandra as well, but my reaction is far removed from meowing and tail flicking, instead it is tears and shoulder shaking.

Sandra moves me to the couch and just holds me for a while. I cry for the secrecy and the anonymity I once had that is slowly being stripped away. I cry for the piece of my heart that I gave to Ryan and the feeling of guilt in my heart. I cry for Justin and the part of me that feels I should have been smarter than that. Sandra soothes me through the tears and helps me to bed with promises of a better day tomorrow and some fun that night. Thursdays are awesome in La Jolla, so my itching for dancing will be sated for sure. I could use that before the first session with Dr. McAdams on Friday.

After working from Sandra's house all day, I am ready to go out. I borrow some of her clothes since the woman has one hell of a closet, and we head out. As we walk toward the sushi restaurant that has become the club of choice for Thursday nights, I hear an intake of breath from Sandra as she grabs by arm and picks up the pace.

"What in the world, Sandra? You know I can walk on my own, no need to drag me. What? What is that look for?" I turn around and glance back the way we had just come. We passed right by a coffee shop that stays open late, so I head back in that direction and Sandra speaks up before I reach the glass window.

"Alex, don't jump to conclusions. You know we're all friends." I inch toward the glass and peer in to see Carmen and Justin at a table. I jump back as if a bee had just stung me, then look again. Why the hell am I hiding anyhow? They're both my friends, right? But why didn't they tell me they were meeting out? Oh, ya, I did tell them to pretty much back off, didn't I?

I peek at them again just as Carmen rises from the table. Justin says something to her, and she turns back to grab his shoulder. Her hand rests there, and she gives it a squeeze. It happens too quickly for me to stop it. The energy rushes into my hands, matching the amount stored inside me, and the glass begins to shiver. I feel Sandra's hand on my arm and even though the sound of her voice touches upon my awareness, I can't make out what she is saying. The green eye is up, and I am not in control. Little sleep last night and some pre-partying at Sandra's may be the cause, but I also keep replaying the dream of Justin and Chey in my head. Mistrust and jealousy join the party, dancing around and poking at my nerves. Sandra manages to at least move me away and into an alley before the glass shatters and the screams begin.

"What the hell, Alex? What were you thinking? What if you hurt someone?" Sandra is right, I can't believe I completely lost control; it has been an accident of course. Thankfully the window shattered outwards, attracted to my unleashed energy.

"Everyone's fine, even Justin and Carmen. I don't know what happened! I just snapped. Seems to be happening a lot lately with my emotions, but this is the first time with my powers. What are they doing there together, anyhow?" Sweat drips down my temple and a shiver rolls up my spine and down my arms.

"We're all friends, Alex. I'm sure it is nothing, maybe for work? Carmen does need to keep going on new projects, you know, and who has the most unique greenhouse in the area? Justin, that's who, my little over reactor. Now, let's get out of here before the witch-hunt begins."

"Sandra, you really are the only person in San Diego I can trust." After I speak the words, her response rings true and in line with Dana's, and my grandmother's, warnings.

"And therein lies the problem, Alex, because that is exactly what Steven wants you to feel. You're handing him his escape on a silver platter!" She's right of course. I need to get a grip.

I take some deep breaths and try to rein in, trying hard to stay focused and present. Justin and Carmen just doesn't make sense. It's not that it isn't possible, but why would they do that to me? Not only personally on Carmen's side, but professionally as well. Carmen is my partner, and I do trust her, right? More than Justin, but mainly because I have known her longer, and we have been through so much together, remaining so close throughout it all. Maybe this is the trick? Maybe she really isn't my friend or maybe, just maybe, Justin is the issue. If not, perhaps my fears and strain are making something out of nothing. I touch my small purse, which holds Dana's potion, and think about drinking it to take a real look at Carmen and Justin again. Then realization hits me: not now, this doesn't feel right, taking it now would be a waste.

What I need to do is to move forward and take control of this night. It is time to dance! We begin to walk toward the bar again when I feel warmth above my top lip. I wipe my finger under my nose and see that it is wet with blood. I dab quickly again without Sandra noticing, but there is no doubt that my intense, over reactive use of power has not only weakened me, but is obviously too far into the darkness for the goddess's liking.

Despite the drama, Sandra and I have a blast dancing the night away. And when I say dancing the night away, I mean dancing until the wee hours of Friday morning! Damn it, I hope this doesn't affect my meeting with Dr. McAdams tomorrow, or this morning.

Wishful thinking. My night out causes me to be particularly sleepy in Dr. Reynolds' office. My evening had consisted of enough drinks to down a horse, so the nightmares hadn't been the issue as much as the lateness of the evening. The power wielding I used to break and repair the glass last night was absolutely exhausting. Even though my power appears to have replenished, I'm not feeling my grandmother's gift as strongly today. I didn't have any more nosebleeds last night or this morning, but I still feel chills through my body when I think of the place my jealousy took me to and the power I wasted and abused based upon my reaction to the situation. My guilt over feeling this way toward my two friends, plays a tug-of-war with the guilt over my feelings for Ryan. Ah, can't my life just be boring and normal for a while? Please?

Dr. Reynolds sits across from me, working at her desk. After taking a good look at me, talking a bit and then realizing I need some peace and quiet, she moves to her desk as we wait for Dr. McAdams.

I am tired, but I feel prepared. I have a good deal of Earthen energy stored and on alert for the process. This was the plan even before my grandmother visited me, and I know I was strong enough then so the absence of her power boost shouldn't cause any problems. Not to mention, I am amped up at the idea of ridding Steven of some control over me by erasing his worst sins and taking a better look at the past with new, more practiced eyes. I drink some more water, lean my head back, and close my eyes while we wait. Dr. McAdams comes in moments later, and I try to shake the sleepiness to look alert for him.

"Long night, Alex? Are you ready for today, or do we need to reschedule?" Oops, busted. Time to sit up and look bright eyed and bushy tailed.

"Tip top shape, doc. Ready when you are." My cheesy grin seems to appease him and I fight my face as it tries to turn my smile into a yawn.

"Okay, if you are certain. You know revisiting times of trauma can be quite draining, so I need you on your toes. Remember, you must be aware enough to anchor yourself in the present in order to navigate the moments in the past without living as that child, rather, you need to be the strong woman you are now."

"I'm all good, Ian. I'm ready." He motions me over to the chaise lounge and sits next to me in a chair, pushing it close to my side. I close my eyes before being told and heighten my awareness to the present as he guides me through meditation to anchor me in the now. Once my mind is a blank slate, rid of various jumbling concerns and worries, I bring up my power to encircle and protect me from being completely in someone else's control, or from saying something I shouldn't. My body feels warmer as I use the magic, but otherwise there is no sign, nothing a normal human would pick up on, anyhow.

I hear Dr. McAdam's voice in my head as I listen carefully and allow a part of me to reach back and touch a memory of Steven, weeks before he met me by the tree. I have worked on this moment many times during my preparation, and it is easy to find, with no hint of fear, sadness, or pain. Dr. McAdams is talking, tuning me to him and to my present self, scars and all. He asks me to describe where I am in the past by taking a sidelong glance at it. He tells me not to commit to it, not to lose myself in it, just to take a peek.

We were all at the dinner table; Chey, Greg, Irene, and I. Steven wasn't home yet, which was normal for him, but my mind knew he would be there soon to make his entrance carrying a boxed cake in his hands. It was a night I thought he was a decent father, a night to celebrate Chey's birthday with a man I thought was good to his children, even to me, a girl that wasn't really his but was still considered part of the Nestrour family. It wasn't a perfect family, but at the time I thought it was a happy one, a safe one.

This is where I can leave my memories, right here at this point in time, and remove every memory from there on until his funeral. Everything he did to me, his attempt to harm Chey, it will all disappear. But I need to somehow hold on to the memory of the binding and the feeling that he was evil enough to deserve it. I still feel that removing that altogether will somehow prove disastrous. This is the tricky part. I have to basically separate myself into three parts: in the present, in this vision, and to touch on the moment I exiled him without all the scars of what led me to that act.

I continue to feel the chaise's cushion under me while I also feel the warmth of the wooden chair at the Nestrour house. Steven places the cake in front of Chey, and we all begin to sing Happy Birthday to her. Chey sits on my right and Steven stands behind her, hovering with his hands on her shoulders like a proud, protective father. She is smiling with glee before blowing out her candles. When she leans back, Steven moves to kiss her on the cheek and that's when I see it, the slight movement in her neck as she inches away from him, shuddering in such a faint way that only the Alex I am now would notice. My eyes shift to her left hand where it rests upon the table, curling into a fist and shaking slightly before releasing to reflect a calm demeanor, one rare for an eight-year-old child.

My head begins to shake back and forth on the lounge, and I feel my stomach lurch while the tears burn my eyes.

"No! No! This didn't happen! No! No!"

I grip the chaise, and Dr. McAdam's voice begins to speak in flowing tones, telling me to stay in the memory, asking me what I am seeing.

"Alex, don't change the memory based on what you know now. Careful, you may be tricking your mind. Remember, this was a time you had vividness for what you saw and felt and it was a safe time for you."

"No, no! I was wrong, he, Steven, he was either hurting or working toward hurting my sister! I just didn't see it before. No, does this mean? Oh, Chey!"

"Hold on, Alex, this could be you morphing the past. Don't lose focus. Let's slowly ease you back and we can reset and try another time. Wait! Relax your breathing, relax Alex, it's okay."

My body does not think everything is okay. The thrashing in my mind causes my muscles to flex and release. The dining room becomes more of my focus, and I feel myself losing the sight, smells, and feel of Dr. Reynolds' office, along with my hold on the memory of Steven's exile. I move my attention away from Chey's hand and see everyone else sitting there as if nothing odd has happened. I look to Chey again and then above her head to Steven. My head starts to throb when my eyes meet his; he is looking directly at me.

"What's the matter, Doll Eyes? See something you like?" What? What the hell? This didn't happen. I shake my head and tears begin to well in my eyes. I hear Dr. McAdams, but his voice is faint, lost somewhere in the distance.

"Yes, yes, go get it. I must have left it in your study. We need to calm her before she gets lost. I'll stay with her."

Stay! No! I don't want to stay here, get me out of here! I grip the table and feel the comfort of soft suede in my fingers. Yes, there it is, the chaise. I'm still with Dr. McAdams, I can fight this and stay grounded.

Steven makes a move, reaching out his hand toward my arm. I am paralyzed in this confusing seat, and I can't keep him from grasping a small portion of skin on my inner elbow and pinching me roughly. I bite my lip to keep from screaming as blood trickles down my arm. My foster mom and Greg continue to eat across the table, asking Chey what she wished for, all three of them oblivious to what is happening. Willing my muscles to respond, I try to struggle again, nothing happens at first, but then I feel the strength in my inner being, the power wrapped inside me uncoiling and preparing for a fight. I regain control of my body and rise from my chair, making a move to escape this haunted dining room. The vision of the room shifts, fading, as I instantly feel light. My view of the room changes as I sense my body lifting above the floor.

The wooden panels of the house transform instantly to the soft, carpeted floor of Dr. Reynolds' office. The scene below me is of my body shaking uncontrollably while Dr. McAdams leans over me. He is struggling to get a grip on my arm and I hear him calmly asking me to come back to the office, to the chair, to the day, time, anything he can think of to trigger my awareness.

"Ah, this is it." Dr. McAdams's words tumble quickly out of his mouth, and I can't follow everything he is saying. It's like I am getting feedback from two places, one in the distance above him, and one under his restraint on the lounge chair. He finally gets a good hold of my arm with his left hand and I notice a small bag he produces on top of his lap. As his fingers zip back the opening, he removes a syringe from its contents. Ah, hell no!

"I found it, Sharon!" Dr. McAdams yells out, and I attempt to holler from my vantage point, but all I feel is the tiniest movement of air past my lips, my words coming out in a breathy whisper. Dandelion seeds float across my awareness as I feel my grandmother's power return to me.

"No, no, I'm fine, I'm here." I urge the power to calm my body and to move my arm away. The door to the office opens, and Dr. Reynolds runs back in holding a bag.

"Here it is! Oh, you found it. Wait, I think she appears to be calming down, she's lucid, Ian, she's okay." My bird's eye view fades, and my eyes flick open to look right into Ian's. His crinkled forehead shows a second of strain before it disappears, relief mixed with concern taking its place.

"Oh, good." His hand moves to place the syringe back into place in the small bag. I look at my arm and see a small trickle of blood; he wipes it away with a cotton ball and affixes a bandage.

"Good, Alex, very good. I was hoping you would come back around, and I wouldn't have to push the plunger, and here you are. Sorry about that little poke, I rarely have to use a sedative, but I didn't want you to harm yourself. There have been times a patient just can't move away from the fear and the trauma in their memories, even if it wasn't an accurate account of the event. The body can't handle the strain the mind puts on it sometimes, so we have to relax the patient pharmacologically. No need this time, though. You did great coming back to your grounding point. Very good! How are you overall? Do you feel okay?"

He lays his hand on my arm and the tingles running along my body are as if I'd gone temporarily numb. I nod my head, taking a glance back into the vision I had, and shiver.

"I don't know what happened! Either I was remembering that night differently, or I really missed all the signs the first time. It's so weird; I practiced that memory over and over just like you said, and it seemed perfect. I'm sorry, I guess I'm not ready, or maybe it just won't work on me." Dr. McAdams gives me a consoling look and moves back to sit in his chair next to me.

"It's different for everyone I work with. Sometimes the memories are easier to erase because they have been repressed for so long that they are compartmentalized into a nice package and thus, easy to remove. In other cases, the memories are woven so deep into who the person currently is that it's hard to control the way the psyche manipulates the past. It appears you are the latter, but that doesn't mean all is lost. We may just have to go back further in time, maybe even before you met him. Do you want to try that next time?"

"Alex, it's really okay, we don't expect things to go perfectly the first time." Dr. Reynolds speaks before I can answer. "Why don't you and I keep our regular appointment next week and talk about it then? We can come up with a different memory to work on, if you like."

It's unusual for her to jump into a decision for me like this, and the obvious change in her approach leads me to notice a slight tenseness in her shoulders. She immediately realizes my appraisal of her and maneuvers to her desk, taking out her date planner to busy herself.

"Yes, that sounds good. Sorry Ian, perhaps next time?" But something in me knows there won't be a next time. I don't think Steven is going to let me escape the memory of what he did to me, no matter where I go in my timeline. It is time to prepare for a fight with all my baggage and scars intact, and for the first time in a long time I am ready to accept that. What choice do I have?

I swing my legs around the chaise and gracefully stand up before taking a not-so-ladylike stretch. Dr. McAdams rises as well, smiling at me with his tanned face while slight crinkles from years of squinting into the sun's glare frame his eyes.

"Yes, until next time, Alex. I'm still very hopeful that this process will work for you." I give him my best all business and absolute confidence smile while shaking his hand warmly. I like the guy; he just doesn't have a chance against what I'm really dealing with. Not his fault by a long shot, and I hope he won't see this as a defeat. Dr. Reynolds comes around her desk and gives me a hug. She doesn't give many of those, but I think today warrants it. As she pulls away, she hands me a tissue and points to her nose. Oh, great. Now I can't do anything without one of these popping up. I dab slowly and thank her.

"You had me a little worried for a moment there, Alex. I should have known better though. You are a very strong young woman. Even though today didn't lead to the exact outcome we anticipated, I think we have reached some sort of a turning point. I very much look forward to talking about it next week. Take it easy today and shake off this experience."

Roger that! I am planning on a nice run and then a Bloody Mary at the beach. Not only do I need to release some of the tension from the session, but I also need to get my power reserve under control and cycle some of it back into the earth. It is coiling tight and then releasing over and over in my body, almost making me sick with the motion. My grandmother's extra boost must have finally rebooted and triggered my protective system big time, and now I'm on a little bit of overload. I give them both my final goodbyes and leave the office building.

After a good run and the previously planned Bloody Mary with Nic, I am ready for a nap. I tuck into Sandra's guest bed, alone since apparently Pitter prefers her bed now, that little turncoat. I bundle a pillow in the crook of my arm and snuggle into it, hearing the faint sound of the La Jolla waves as they rock me to sleep.

The dream is fast, over really before it begins. It seems more like flashes of spastic light, movement, and sound with small replays of the dream of Ryan and me in the club. The lights flicker madly as I dance alone looking across the floor trying to find Ryan. Instead, my eyes land on a male figure with two girls dancing around him, rubbing against him and touching his chest and back before dancing suggestively with each other in front of him as he watches with a cold, calculating stare. Justin doesn't blink when he shifts his gaze from the dancing nymphs to land upon me. His cold stare becomes a horrid grin as the words "Doll Eyes" fall from his lips. The girls immediately stop and turn my way, the shock of their true faces forcing my body to slam into the wall of speakers behind me. The intense beat of the music pulses with my heartbeat, and I realize I am trapped, unable to move away as Chey and Carmen make their way toward me. I feel warmth in my hand; Ryan holds fast to it as he appears next to me, staring wildly at the girls and smiling.

"Why didn't I feel you? I should know when you are here, but I didn't feel you this time." Ryan turns to me, a nauseating smile spreading across his face.

"Oh, Lex, don't you recognize your own handiwork? Just as you did to Steven, so have I done to you. Easy to mimic a power source you recognize, easy to camouflage mine with yours so that you trust me. You really are a stupid, silly girl, aren't you? So easy to trick." His hand moves too quickly for me to follow as it grips my neck in a bone crushing fashion around.

Sparks dance in my eyes when the oxygen stored in my lungs vanishes, unable to be replenished quickly enough.

Carmen and Chey move closer into view, Chey with a white rabbit in her arms and Carmen with a black one, dark as night, in hers. They laugh and stroke the animals' fur before they disappear, and Ryan's face is all I see before the dream ends and I wake to my screams and gasps for air.

CHAPTER 18

Friend or Foe?

Journal Entry:

I thought I had lost Bear once, but Vex was right on point when he told me Bear would have a couple more good years left. Even the vet kept telling me how incredible it was that a dog as big as he lived for fourteen long years. No matter how many years a loved one has, I swear it is never enough for those who are left behind. I insisted on celebrating Bear's life; there was no way his beautiful loyalty and love would be left to constant tears and heartache. Although I could not control both of those all the time, I tried to celebrate more than lock myself away within my grief.

Carrying Bear's ashes in my backpack, I was determined to take the same trip he, my grandmother, and I took when he was barely a year old, to the Ruby Mountains outside Elko, Nevada. Grandmom had found out about the amazing location in one of the hundreds of National Geographic issues we had stockpiled in our home. This time, Carmen was joining me, our first vacation time used in two years, and it was well worth it

Bear was my best friend who stayed by my side only to venture off when the wilderness called for some scouting, or to playfully interact with a dog or chase off a rabbit. In that moment, safely upon the ground, I held him tight telling him over and over again that he was such a good dog, my most trusted companion, and my best friend.

In the years that followed, he was my only constant, my protector, even getting hurt by Steven in the process. I had thought he was lost to me once. Now, as Carmen and I looked out upon the lake, I could see images of him prancing proudly around the edges of it as we made our way back from the harrowing ordeal. Bear saved me that day, and he saved me every day thereafter.

The San Diego Zoo may very well be the most amazing place for animals in captivity, and even though some will never agree with caging animals, one can't ignore the amazing work they are doing with conservation. Many species on the endangered list have been successfully bred here, and it goes without saying that the zoo is truly an awesome sight to behold during a grand event celebrating those accomplishments. The city planned this fabulous event, bringing in scientists, animals lovers, and important personnel to mingle from all over the city and the world.

The security is top notch tonight, with my usual muscle and eye candy. Before tonight, I hadn't seen or heard from Ryan in days as he spent his time retracing our steps and covering all our tracks to keep us hidden from the Council. After the nightmare last night, which by the way I might have been spared had he been around, I find myself once again worrying about whether I can trust him. I think he senses my unease as he is giving me a wide berth, only checking in briefly before moving back into action as lead security for tonight's event.

I knew Justin was going be here. He sent me a text with the heads up last night. Seeing him all dressed up, an unusual sight for him, to say the least, is difficult for me while I deal with my jealousy and mistrust as well as my own guilt about my feelings and actions with Ryan. On top of all of that, I am also worried about being around him, for fear of his safety. All things considered, I know I have good reasons for keeping my distance. Who knows what I might do or say? Part of me wants to grab him and kiss those amazing lips while moving my hands through his thick, dark hair, and the other side of me wants to confront him and his relationship with Carmen. They are friends, of course, just friends. Right?

Nic breaks through my inner turmoil with his giggling ramblings about monkeys throwing poop at all these pretty people in their pricey get ups, especially the scientists with their poking and prodding. I smirk at his colorful language and the pictures it makes in my head. The party is going well; I think it's safe to say that Nic and I can leave now. Maybe Carmen will want to stay longer so I can head to Sandra's house and get some sleep; I didn't get another wink after that mother of all nightmares. But before I leave, I need to ask Ryan when I can go back home because I definitely miss my own place. As I make a move in Ryan's direction, I hear Justin call my name and I freeze while he walks my way.

"Alex, are you getting ready to head out? I haven't had a chance to talk to you all night. There are some very interesting people here, and of course, you've done an amazing job with everything." He smiles at me with that beautiful, honest smile that makes me feel safe, that makes me want to melt into his arms. Not that terrifying look of menace that haunts my dreams. But I have to say, as I think back, the nightmares have truly reared their ugly heads since I met Justin. Maybe there isn't a correlation at all, but I can't ignore the fact that he may be a trick in my life. Not to mention, he and Carmen seem to be getting closer with no regard to letting me in on the development. Of course, with my many absences I haven't given them much of an opening for that conversation.

"Thanks, Justin, it's good to see you. This is the perfect event for you to be a part of; maybe you can even find some more people to back your projects. I'm sure they'd love to have you here instead of at SDSU." The grateful smile on his face suits him, he's charming, there's no doubt about that.

"Yeah, well, you know me and academia. I can't escape its clutches and the money just rains down in buckets." We both laugh, and it feels normal, right, and something I miss. His eyes move from mine, and I see a smile in their glint. When I turn, I notice who he is looking at as Carmen maneuvers around the room with such grace that only I can tell there is a slight urgency. Jealousy rears its ugly head and I step away from him.

"Well, it looks like I'm done here. Nice to see you, Justin." I begin to move away, but he grabs my arm.

"What was that, Alex? I know you need your distance, but why do I get the impression something is bothering you and that it has something to do with me?" Oh, ya think?

"Look, Justin, you're an adult. Do what you want with whomever you want. I don't care." Oops, not really keeping it in check, am I? I bite my tongue and carefully remove his hand from my arm.

"What are you talking about, Alex? You're the only woman I want to be with, but in case you've forgotten, you're the one pushing me away." The charming smile is gone now, but I could care less. "Yes, you disguise it with all of this working on yourself crap, but I don't believe for a minute that that's all there is to it. Oh, I'll play dumb and hope so, but really, the ball's in your corner, right? It's not like I have a say in what Alex does." I guess he has a point and my lips part as I try to interject, but he moves on full throttle. "No, you've always been so damn independent. Something I love about you, but right now you may have to start thinking about whether or not you just prefer it that way. Permanently." His words sting, but I have to give him credit for hitting the nail on the head in some ways. He has no idea I am trying to keep him safe. Maybe letting him go for good would be best; he seems to be giving me an opening for just that.

I look into his eyes, ready to send him on his way either out of concern for him or that lingering lack of trust I have floating around in my head. Either way, it's better for him. I'm sure I'm going to be a constant liar to him all of our lives, keeping things hidden that he wouldn't, couldn't understand, or never let him get as close as he hopes to be. But, if he is the trick, one of us is really going to get hurt.

"Okay Justin, have it your way. Let's cut the crap, shall we? I think it's best we keep our distance, don't you? I'm obviously not in a state to be what you want or need, and you, well, you may be a better liar than I've ever given you credit for." My power sparks and tries to wrap itself around him to seek out treachery. All I sense is the calming feeling of the earth, her plants and flowers, ocean, the wind, and the sand. It swirls around him in the usual way, the way in which I know him, and there is nothing to worry about; my suspicions were just being too suspicious. Man, I must be exhausted by the nightmares Steven is sending me, sending me on purpose to keep me from trusting people who love me. It seems to be working.

I exhale so deeply that even the look of shock and anger on Justin's face disappears as he looks at me with concern. He reaches for me again, but I have crossed a line that will keep him safe from me, and holding it for now is the best choice—for both of us.

I move out of his reach, only shaking my head at him as the tears form in my eyes. Tears for losing him, and tears of joy that maybe, just maybe, he hasn't been deceiving me all along. I can feel his eyes on my back as I walk away. Carmen has been watching us, and her eyes flick back and forth from Justin to me with a look of worry and confusion.

I ignore her and walk to where Nic waits for me. Forget about going home to bed, this calls for a night out with Nic because now I really need a drink—make that drinks. Thankfully, Nic is always down for drinks, so my night ends in a haze of alcohol and no thoughts of Carmen or Justin.

The knock on my door is way too early for my liking. The amount of drinks I consumed last night may not have given me the type of hangover most people get from that level of consumption, but the lack of sleep created by this early-ass wake up certainly rattles my head. What the hell? I was having a nice dreamless sleep, too. The knock comes again, a little impatient this time and accompanied by Sandra's sleepy voice.

"Alex, honey, can you come out here, please? We need to talk to you." We? Eh, yep, I sense her. Carmen is definitely waiting in the living room. I can feel her nervous energy and obvious annoyance as well. Shit, someone pissed her off. I didn't get any calls last night about the event, so it has to be something else; it has to be me.

"Just a minute, geez, there isn't any chance this can wait, can it? I'm working on some good z's in here for once." Hey, it is worth a shot.

"No, no Alex, I think we need to take care of this now." I get up and grab some clothes off the floor. As I pull the tank top over my head, I catch a glimpse of my purse on the table. Remembering the potion that is in there, I think about reaching for it and getting this over with once and for all. Erase all doubt or mistrust, or erase Carmen and Justin from my life completely. The power inside me ignites. My mind moves to memories of my grandmother and instantly her energy mixes with mine, tingling in my fingertips. I can faintly make out the sight of dancing dandelion seeds shimmering in the light creeping through my curtains. In my anger last night, I had forgotten about her gift. Maybe that is all I need for now; I have to believe that she would have sensed evil in Justin, so perhaps she can give me insight into Carmen as well. I have a feeling this potion is for another time, so I leave it where it lies.

"Okay, okay, I'm coming! Keep your pants on!" I open the door and Sandra gives me a once over.

"Haven't I told you nothing good happens after two in the morning? Maybe it needs to be midnight for you! Wow! I'll meet you in the living room. Carmen is here, as I believe you already know, but it looks like you could use a few moments in the bathroom, girlfriend." She takes a chunk of my hair in her fingers and shakes her head. I smack her fingers playfully and groan when I catch a look at my reflection in the mirror. A few more hours of sleep and this would

185

have all looked *much* better, at least the darkness under my eyes if not the insane bird's nest thing going on in my hair.

After brushing my teeth, not bothering with my hair besides putting it up in a haphazardly messy bun, and giving myself a quick five minute meditation to both calm my nerves and wake me up, I am ready to face the music with Carmen. It is obvious that Justin must have told her what happened, and with Carmen's intelligence she must have figured something out. I take one more deep breath before turning the corner and seeing Carmen. She is sitting on the couch, leaning her head back with her eyes closed. I don't think I'm the only one who didn't get much sleep. Of course, she is in full workout get up so at least she woke up on her own accord, able to get some of the anxiety out before heading over to confront one of her oldest friends.

"Good morning, ladies. To what do I owe this early morning meet and greet?" So what, the clock reads one P.M., who cares!

"Hi, Alex, sorry about waking you. I didn't know you had such a late night. Since I'm here already though, I really think we need to talk." Here we go. "I spoke to Justin last night; he was pretty shook up after you left, and I couldn't help but notice the conversation you two were having. We've both been worried about you, as you know, but Alex, you don't think Justin and I are more than friends, do you? There's no way you can possibly believe that either of us would do something like that to you. That I would risk our friendship!" I stare at her, eyes not showing any of my emotions. "Damn it, Alex, you're my best and oldest friend. We've known each other since we were teenagers, for nine freaking years, and nothing, not a guy, money, or anything will be able to come between us, ever."

She is shaking slightly. I can understand her being upset, but I would be more upset with her if the roles were reversed than trying to prove it wasn't true. No, she is also pissed. I can tell; she may be good at keeping her cool at work, but I know her tells. Hell, I would be pissed at her if she thought I was being an absolute dipshit and risking our friendship and our company. But I'm not her, and I'm not living a normal human life like she is! No, I'm pretty much fighting for my life here and watching my ass is a requirement, no matter who I upset in the process.

"Okay, yes, you're right. I had some concerns, but last night I knew I was wrong. It's these nightmares, the lack of sleep has led to such an edginess that I can't think straight sometimes." As I continue to take the blame for the tension and for the grief I have caused both of them, I send my power with its new tendrils of my grandmother's magic in tow to Carmen. I work the tendrils up and around her, searching her mind and body for deception. No, I've never heard of somebody being completely under mind control, but hey, evil hath no boundaries, and I have to make sure. I feel a sharp kick to my shin, bringing my attention to Sandra. She gives me a scowl, obviously alerted to my power surge and wondering what I am up to. I give her a look signaling her to chill out and kept the scan going, thankfully coming up empty handed. Dana told me to trust myself, and I do, even more now with my grandmother's power within me as well.

So that was it, at least one of the tricks, and not one that meant my friends were out to harm me. No, it is Steven's trick. He is clearly playing with my emotions, with my heart and mind, hoping I will lose myself to the pain of losing my friend and "boyfriend" to each other. Of course he would try to use the mistrust and anger I felt toward them to open the doorway even further, but I've caught it in time, right? I suddenly realize something. While Carmen is in mid-sentence, I think about how crazy it is for me to actually think she or Justin would ever do such a thing. I jump up, startled, and make some excuse to use the bathroom. I yell out for Sandra and wait for her to come with me.

"What the hell, Alex? Acting all jumpy and wielding that much power around right now is definitely going to alert Carmen to something. I have a feeling you want to keep it as much a secret as I do, so tone it down, will ya? What? What's wrong?" I am shaking now, feeling suddenly cold and vulnerable.

"He knows, it's too late, he knows." I turn from her gripping the sides of the sink. Staring into the mirror I see confusion on her face.

"Who knows? What are you talking about? Shit girl, you're freezing, goose bumps are all over you."

"Steven! He knows about everyone, about all of you! I can't protect anyone, not even myself. How can he not know? He's making these dreams in my head. He's the one that kept putting Justin in those mind-screwing situations with Carmen and Chey. My God, what if he does something to Chey?" Sandra grabs my shoulders firmly, trying to still the rattles while turning me back around.

"Alex, calm down, you need to keep your cool. Look, you've already beaten him at this little game. Trick one has been revealed, so you need to focus on the positives. You can still keep your distance from Carmen and Justin. You now realize that your crazy notion that they're forming some relationship behind your back was all a Steven-formed hallucination. He'll lose that grip on you. Remember, it's the loss of trust that will set him free." She is right, but did I figure this all out too late? The power I used to break the glass the other night made me weaker than I thought possible, even before that, in Arizona with Ryan when I struggled to keep on alert and check him out. Maybe I am already losing a grip on the binding, or maybe the door is already open.

"What if I came to my senses too late? I feel weaker since that night the glass broke, like he took it from me when I reacted that way. Like he won some part of his freedom already in that moment of mistrust." Leaning over, I put my hands on my knees, nearly wobbling to jelly.

"Okay, let's take a second and breathe. We can still keep Carmen and Justin safe. We will just come up with another plan. I know I can keep an eye out and stay even more tuned in to them, and maybe Ryan has some ideas. Can't he have some people keep watch or something? I mean, the man looks like he could have an army at his beck and call for all we know." Hands still on my knees, I look up at her tilting to my head. "I know, I know, he didn't share all the facts, but didn't you tell me your power cleared him as well?"

Ryan, in all this madness today I had forgotten about Ryan. Sandra is right in some respects, but I hadn't told her about the dream I had, about the ability he may have to mask his true nature from me, to trick me like I did to Steven. And why wouldn't he be able to master it? He is definitely strong enough to do it and really the only person I've been around lately that has power like mine—at least that I know of. One trick down and the second and final one will reveal who is working with Steven. If it isn't Ryan, then I'm out of ideas as to who in the hell it could be.

CHAPTER 19

Potions

Journal Entry:

I felt safe with Justin. Don't ask me when the last time was that I could say that about man. There had been very few times in my life that a man held my heart or my trust so the number can be counted on one hand. Some should count, but I don't even know because I never even met them, my father and my grandfather were both nonexistent except for pictures and stories my mother and grandmother told me.

It was the first time a man seemed real to me, like there wasn't deception lingering in the wings waiting for me to drop my guard. I'm not saying I was completely unguarded around Justin, but all my scans of him using the goddess's power came back nearly giddy. I mean, why shouldn't she be, this man was basically an extension of her very being. He was more at one with nature than anybody else I knew; sometimes I wondered if he was more in tune than I was, and I chose to leave the type of work he loved and continued to do.

Justin grounded me, more in harmony again as I had begun to drift further into the nightlife of party planning and away from the acts of taking care of the goddess. Although I never stopped completely, I did feel myself drifting away from using my power, from tapping in and helping her when I could. I had been engaging more with the outdoors by hiking, learning to surf, snorkeling, and even camping again—all of the things my mom and I did when I was young, and sometimes even with my grandmother.

I cherished those times in my childhood with my grandmother, traveling to out of the way places no one had even heard of, going off the grid, being one with Gaia, losing myself to the sights and sounds around me, and forgetting the worries that were always in the back of my mind. Justin brought me closer to that, he brought my power out in me more, not that I let him know anything about it, or that he ever noticed me doing it, but he made it important again. It was as if being around him brought out the need and the ability to connect with my old life without all the suffering.

Sleep had become hectic now that I'd been starting to wake in the middle of the night, which really wasn't my style. Once I fell asleep, I stayed asleep and usually had some pretty vivid dreams. But, lately there had been nothing. No fleeting memories of a dream whatsoever, just blackness. I would wake in darkness with a feeling of being watched; the fear was enough to make me turn the lights on in my new loft and stare around the room. Pitter, my new kitten, often gave me a sleepy look before mewing and hiding his eyes under his paw.

Getting Pitter had been Sandra's idea. Losing Bear the year before was enough to keep me from ever bonding to another animal again. Vex dropped by every now and then, and once he even stayed the night curled up at my feet. I cried myself asleep that night, missing Bear and everything he was to me—a protector, more a brother than a child, my best friend.

Carmen and Sandra thought it was living on my own in the loft that was bringing about the fear; I had never lived on my own before. But having Nic in the same complex had sealed the deal for me. The love of his life was very generous with the loft he sold to me, and I couldn't have been happier. With lots of upgrades and open space, it didn't feel like the loft was the issue. It felt like something else, something familiar, but absent from my life for a long time.

A couple of months later the darkness and emptiness of my dreams began to shape into realistic vicious assaults. I would dream that insects and spiders were crawling all over my room and all over me. Justin nearly jumped out of his skin when I woke up screaming and smacking at the pillow and myself. I turned the lights on, instantly blinding him, but at least he had the sense to grab Pitter before I pitched him off the bed.

"What? What, Alex? What is it?" It took me a few seconds to realize I had been dreaming. It felt so real. I could still feel the spider legs all over my arms and back. I had to search again to shake the memory of them crawling all over my ceiling, dropping down toward

190

me attached to their silken webs. I gave myself a stern mental headshake, not wanting to appear completely out of my skull to the man I had only been dating for a few months.

"Just a bad dream, sorry about that. I haven't had a nightmare like that since I was a kid." Saying it out loud made the memory of those years come rushing back. I had those dreams before, back when the Nestrours took me in; in fact, they started right before Steven showed his true self. I made my way to the bathroom in silence. After closing the door behind me, I leaned my back against the door and slid down its length. I didn't think of Steven, I didn't think of what he did to me and certainly not what I did to him.

Steven was a chunk of my past I had neatly carved out of my memory and stored away in a hidden section of my brain. Having the dreams trigger the trauma I had endured before I bound him away shocked me deep inside. The tears wouldn't come though; I never cried in that house, I never wanted him to see me weak, even though at times that is just how I felt. At first I had been unable to stop him, unable to break through his power over me, but eventually I found a way.

Twelve years later and I had never spoken of how Steven really went away. He wasn't really the type of man who would take his own life. Don't get me wrong, Steven was truly sick, but not in the way those suffering with depression and other mental disorders are. No, he was just a power-hungry asshole who used his power to destroy innocence. I know it's awful to say, but part of me felt no one really mourned Steven's death; rather, my foster family was set free. Chey and Irene smiled and laughed more, my foster brother Greg came home more often, called more, and Chey and her mother visited him more often. All I knew was that all of it made Chey and my foster mom so much happier.

I never told any of them what Steven had done to me, and I would never repeat what he almost did to Chey. It took a while, but I did finally open up to Sandra and Carmen, but I only told them about his abuse, not about my abilities. I'd never told a soul what I could do, who I really was. It was too dangerous for everyone. Besides, what would I say? Even though my mother had contacted me when I got to college, she only barely touched on overcoming something unmentionable. I could only speculate that admitting more than that would be too much guilt for her; even I believe it never would have happened had she come back for me. Something I don't and may die never understanding.

I picked myself off the floor after hearing Justin lift off the bed. His footsteps sounded, and I ran the water to try and avoid having the awkward conversation. If it kept up, he was either going to run for the hills, or I was going to run to the nearest therapist. Maybe that wasn't a bad idea after all. Therapy was something I didn't engage in. Oh, I spoke to many social workers and doctors when my grandmother passed, but I think my main goal there was to somehow keep Bear with me at all costs. Something I managed to do, even though that had been at a great cost to my childhood.

After Steven's "death" I tried support groups but never opened up. My high school counselor called me in. I was fairly certain my foster mother, Irene, asked her to check on me. She was easy to talk to and even though I hid a lot from her, she didn't press, she didn't push

Some of our most important conversations centered on being myself, trusting myself, and to grow from my past and not to stay stuck in it. What I didn't do is follow up with counseling in college and not a single time thereafter. Moving through life had been enough of a distraction, enough of a barrier to the memories of the evil scars Steven left within me. I guess what I didn't remember from my talks with Ms. Dine was that if people don't work through the trauma they experienced, it would come back to haunt them, it would invade their personal life, and wreak havoc on their relationships—both friendly and intimate. At the time, I thought forgetting seemed the best idea, but those nightmares surfacing might have been my brain finally telling me I needed to deal with what he did to me, and get help. I wasn't sure what was happening and why the dreams were back, but I wasn't going to be traumatized by that man's memory. There was no way he would have power over me again.

Tonight is shaping up to be pretty damn exciting. One of the older restaurants in the Gaslamp was finally gutted to become one of the largest downtown clubs, and the Grand Opening is tonight.

The walls dividing the restaurant from the club were torn down to create an amazing open space with a massive bar at differing levels to break up the area and allow for tables, podiums, and some comfy niches where couches and overstuffed chairs are strewn. On the left of the club, a late night restaurant is open for the partygoers. The best part of the renovation is the fact that Shane is the new owner. It took some major maneuvering, but with the connections between Nic's partner and our company, Shane had finally been able to persuade the original owners to sell. The transformation of the club had been an idea Shane and I had concocted years ago when we were mere patrons at the restaurant. Seeing our late night ramblings and dreams come to life is so exciting. No wonder we're all ready to party! Shane asked me to help him with the name, and we finally settled on Rapture.

With everything else that has been going on I feel I deserve a night off from worrying about it all; about Steven, Ryan, tricks, and all things that come from nightmares. Tonight is a celebration, a time to be with friends, to let loose, and to pour my soul into dancing the night away. My best friends are joining me tonight, Carmen, Nic, and Sandra. We promised Shane we would be there early, and that we would promote the crap out of the event to help pack the house. It didn't take much since word of mouth travels fast in our industry, and most people were chomping at the bit to come.

I sent a text to Justin asking him if he would come celebrate with us. For the most part, this was more my scene than his, but it was a special occasion, and he knew it was a big deal to Shane and me, so maybe he would show up. Carmen had helped me smooth things over with him after the zoo debacle, but he and I haven't spoken since.

The good vibes start rolling early and right when we arrive. Shane greets us before taking us straight to the bar for a shot, toast, and drinks before we go on a tour. At the end of the jaw-dropping trip, we sit at our VIP table and as Shane stands in what I think is a motion to leave, he asks me to stand up and join him. We walk a little ways away to a private area, and he places a cool metal object in my hand.

"Alex, you're the one person I trust more than anyone in the world, so these are for you to keep. I'm not asking you to do more than you can right now, but one day I hope we can sit down and talk about a partnership, if that's okay with you. You and I spent countless nights dreaming and planning about owning a club, and now I have one and I want you to be a part of it. I didn't bring it up before since you were in the infancy stages of your production company, but I think so we can manage it all, together."

I open my hand and stare down at the two keys linked together by a silver chain with an owl pendant. The owl's eyes are glowing green stones, and they stand out against my shiny sapphire mini dress. I look up at him, and we both have the biggest smile on our faces. I feel like I am in college again, ready to take on the world with grand plans and visions. I embrace Shane and kiss him on the cheek. He's one of my few friends who still treat me like I'm normal.

"You're awesome! This is so exciting! I can't wait to celebrate with you tonight, and when the time is right we will talk about everything, but for now, I'm honored to hold the keys to this amazing place. You really have outdone yourself, haven't you? Well, you know what this calls for, right?"

In college, we would start our celebrations with a couple of rounds of shots, and now was no different. Except he really needs to be on his toes tonight, so even though two or three won't affect me, I know he needs his best judgment, we only take one more.

We party into the early morning hours, and Sandra and I are nearing the sweaty mess stage from all our dancing so we head to the bathroom. On our way there I see Ryan over the crowd of people, but opt to hustle into the girl's room rather than say hello. It's no surprise he's here. I know Shane has been consulting him on security; hell, it was my recommendation. My mental blocks go up, just in case. No need for Mr. Nosey to be all up in my business tonight.

When we walk out of the bathroom, I feel someone touch my arm. I had expected Ryan, but thankfully it is Justin instead. I don't know what comes over me, but I just feel instantly happy to see him, figuring out he's not the bad guy has overwhelmed me after how we left things the last time we were together. In a un-Alex like fashion, I fling my arms around him and kiss him full on the mouth. I quickly backpedal, feeling like that was probably really inappropriate, but I couldn't help it. This whole night seems magical for once in a long time, like old times, normal even.

"Sorry about that! I'm just so glad you're here. How are you? Thank you so much for coming!" He give me one of his panty dropping smiles and nods his head.

"Of course, Alex. I wouldn't miss this for the world. Sorry I'm so late. I had a bachelor party, and it took me a while to convince the guys that this would be an excellent move instead of staying at a crappy strip club all night."

"Well good. We have a table over there if you want to join us, bottle service and all."

"Absolutely! Do you think we can fit six other guys as well? I promise they'll behave, or I'll boot them out." Oh, boy, Nic and Sandra will have a field day with a bunch of bachelor party boys. This should be interesting.

194

"Sure, no problem. Why don't you come over now, have a drink and say hello first, and then go grab them." I lead the way to the table and notice our bottle is nearly empty. After making Justin a drink, I offer to go to the bar instead of waiting for our server while he chats with the crew. I wish things could always be this way; it's so easy, like it was before the nightmares began.

After putting our request in with the bartender, I turn to lean my back against the bar and look out among the crowd. I feel him coming, but I'm startled nonetheless when Ryan appears beside me; even more so when he grabs my arm and holds it up to his face. My mental blocks are still in place although I kind of feel like sending him a "What the f..." thought right now.

"What in the hell is this? What happened?" For a second, I have no idea what he is talking about. The puncture mark from my near sleepy time injection didn't even need a Band-Aid, so how the hell does he even see it?

"I'm fine! Nothing to worry about, just don't think the hypnotherapy is going to work out as well as we hoped, is all. I kind of lost some control in the process. Can we talk about it later? I'm trying to have a normal, fun night here." I look at him full on for the first time and damn does he look tired as hell. "What the hell happened to *you?* You look like hell! I mean you look tired, I don't think you could ever look like hell." Damn fumbling tongue, as usual around this man.

"I've had a busy few days trying to keep our asses safe, and sorry I can't let it go, something isn't right. I can feel it. I felt it even before I touched your skin. Can't you? I can even feel something odd here in the club. I knew exactly where you were when I got here hours ago, but now it's like I feel you in two places, like it's hard to trace where you are exactly. You have to tell me exactly what happened in that session."

"Hold your pants on, geez. I'm sure it's just my grandmother's energy mingling with mine that is throwing you off..."

"No, Lex, it isn't! I was able to pick up on you with your new power signature after our night in Arizona. My job is to protect you, and if you aren't going to help me do my job, then I'm going to haul your ass out of here right now."

"The hell you are!" What the hell crawled up his ass? Okay, I know I should be grateful and all, and maybe a little worried as well. I mean I did have the Council on my ass now, but for goddess's sake can I have one night? "Look, we can talk about this later. Right now I'm going to bring this beautiful bottle of vodka to my table and enjoy

195

a drink and even more sweaty-ass dancing. I'll catch up with you later." I make a move to leave when he grabs my elbow.

Now I hate being grabbed, so this royally pisses me off. My immediate reaction is to physically get his hands off me, but I don't want to make a scene. I lower my voice to a hiss as my power tingles and sparks inside me.

"I will talk to you later, Ryan. Now let go!" My power zaps him, causing him to immediately open his fingers and release my elbow. He seems a little shocked that I actually used my ability on him, but nods.

"I'll be close by, Lex. Don't leave the club without me, not even for a second." He answers me in an equally sinister voice before I walk away.

I nod to him like a good soldier and smile brightly. I feel a little bad about the zap I gave him, but I like my boundaries, damn it, and they pertain to everyone, even my own Earthen Protector. Not to mention he is acting a little crazy, and he's not off my "possibly the bad guy" list either. I give him one last glance, trying to read him with all I have. My power scan comes back empty once again, but the irritated look in his eyes tells me he knows I searched him over, and he is not happy about it. Hey, if he wants to keep things from me then he shouldn't be surprised that I don't trust him completely. I give myself a little that's right "humph," turning around just in time to avoid hitting a girl in the back with the vodka bottle as I make my way to our table.

Shane stops by to see us as we gather around, laughing our asses off about crazy event stories and Nic's horrid impressions of some of our most troublesome clients. Justin and the bachelor party have gotten into the mix just fine, partaking in multiple shots from the bottle and enjoying the sights and sounds of the club. One of Sandra's jams comes on, and she dashes off to the dance floor, hauling me after her so fast I nearly spill my drink. I motion for Carmen to join us, but she looks comfortable right where she was, right next to Shane. I give a long glance at Justin as I am pulled away. I feel my heartbeat thumping as I stare into his eyes; he seems so genuine, and unbelievably handsome. He could be mine if I could only get my head right.

The song has the beat to move my body, but it's the words that really get to me. The DJ is masterfully mixing "Sweet Dreams" by the Eurhythmics and "Tell Me Lies" by Fleetwood Mac, as if on cue, to make me lose the euphoria of the night and worry about the horrors lingering in the wings. I tell Sandra I have to use the bathroom, and she shouts out that she will wait right here as I make my way.

I notice Ryan leaning against the wall near the restroom, watching me like a hawk as I come toward him. For a moment I think I see a flicker of sadness or even longing, but it is gone in an instant, replaced by the statue of stone I am used to seeing. I feel his power stir, causing me to tingle inside with excitement. Why is that? Maybe it's like Ryan said, he doesn't feel this way with anyone but his family, and he knows how to change his power signature to camouflage himself. Maybe he's tricking me into feeling this way about him, to want him and trust him.

Enough with all the guessing! I feel around in my purse for Dana's potion and step into the bathroom to drink it down. The waxy, red covering unravels easily in my fingers. The cork is a bit trickier due mainly to my two-fold shakiness. I don't want to spill a single drop so I either need to be very careful opening it or hold the damn thing over my mouth as I wiggle the cork loose in case a drop falls. The second option is too awkward a position so instead I painstakingly take my time to maneuver the cork free. Am I ready for this? Am I ready to see the truth?

The swirling cosmos inside the bottle twinkles at me as I take one look before drinking it down. Please don't grow into a huge Alex monster; oh, and please don't shrink either! It has a surprisingly sweet taste and is smoother than I would have thought with the crazy looking contents inside.

I give myself a few minutes in the bathroom, gauging how the liquid will affect me. My vision starts to sharpen and then haze a bit in the bright bulbs of the bathroom vanities. It's a little disorienting, so I pull on some Earthen energy, hoping to balance things out a bit. That makes the state of things even wackier as I see the green vines of my power flickering while my grandmother's dandelion seeds drift in and out of my vision. I ease up a bit and decide to return to the table before I discreetly track down Ryan.

As I exit the bathroom, I see some commotion near the bar. Ryan's frame stands out to me in the fray. He is far away, mixed up with so many other people who appear to be helping a woman slowly lie down on the ground. There is a flurry of action, and I curse myself for some good old-fashioned shitty timing. There is no way I am going to get myself over there and face Ryan in this mayhem. I look at our VIP table and don't see Sandra. She must still be dancing, but no surprise there. I should be joining her right now, but no, I have to decide what to do after my perhaps rash action of taking the potion. I don't want to track her down; she'd want to get involved, and I can't risk anything happening to her. Nope, I'm on my own.

My head is swiveling back and forth trying to decide my best course of action when suddenly something tugs at my awareness and my power jolts into action. When I focus on the exit, my stomach drops and my heartbeat races in my chest. For one millisecond I swear I see Steven walking out of the glass patio doors and onto the sidewalk. I can't get the best view so I find my feet and allow them to propel me toward the door in pursuit. Shit, I should probably get Sandra. I look over my shoulder at the commotion by the bar and try to locate Ryan, but I can't see him anymore. The woman is being lifted and carried outside now, and he's nowhere to be seen.

My heartbeat pumps rapidly, causing the blood to rush and thump inside my ears. This may be it. It is a real possibility that right now I might be tracking whoever has been behind all of this! Maybe it is Ryan. Am I ready for this? My heart hurts a little at the possibility of Ryan betraying me. Even though he is a suspect, I never really felt it in my soul; it just doesn't make sense with how I feel around him. Of course, none of this makes any sense, does it?

The flashing lights are not helping the new fogginess that has developed in my sight. Looking at the crowd, many people have a subtle glow surrounding them; perhaps this is the Earthen energy that we all have within us, visualized. Even though the ability to use the force isn't innate in all of us, it is still there all the same. Maybe this is what people mean when they talk about auras. Right now I wish all their glowiness would tone it down a bit as I try to maneuver my way to the door.

I pick up the pace in my heels and rush out the patio door, turning to the right where I thought I saw the figure go. Besides the normal giggling and jostling on the sidewalk from those taking a smoke break or waiting for a cab, I don't see anyone that looks like Steven or anyone I know for that matter. The woman who apparently had some sort of episode is sitting in a chair outside with her friends cooing around her while a paramedic takes her vitals. Ryan is nowhere to be seen nor is the Steven look alike. I begin to walk down the sidewalk in the direction I thought he went casting out my power again. This time it seems to ricochet back at me, not giving me a clear indication of where to go or how far away he has gotten.

A thought comes to me. Maybe I can send just my grandmother's power out to locate him. I've done this in the past with my own power solo, hoping to bring the culprit to light, but I always came up empty. It is time to try something new. I continue to walk, focusing on the new presence of my grandmother's energy while pushing mine deep down, attempting to send only her powers towards anyone that feels like Steven. I feel a change, recognition of something, but it can't be. It's as if I am up ahead; my power signature is bright as day and it sure as shit isn't me. What the hell? My power tries to react within me, sensing an imposter, but I have pushed it aside to solely use my grandmother's. My force lags like a slow computer reboot, and I feel exposed, realizing that I probably should have thought about trying this out sooner. Cursing myself inwardly, I slow my pursuit in an effort to get to my power's full strength back. As I pass an alley on my right, a familiar voice stops me in my tracks, and I jump at the surprise greeting.

"Hey, Alex, I mean Ms. Conner. Hey, I thought that was you." I stop in my tracks as my spine goes rigid but then releases when I put a name to the voice. When I turn around, I see Dr. McAdams leaning against the entrance to the alley. There's a club down the alley a ways, and I can hear the hip-hop music pulsing through the walls.

"Hi, Dr. Mc... I mean Ian. Guess I didn't peg you as the late nightclub goer. Where are you...?" I stop mid-sentence as I take in his features, which are beginning to morph, not into Steven though, but into someone who looks a lot like him. Steven's son, my foster brother, Greg. My breath hisses. Apparently Greg can use Earthen power to change his appearance, just as I have on many occasions. Before I can react, he grabs my arm, my disbelief and power lag making me an easy mark. The previous puncture of his needle poke blazes hot, causing me to cry out.

"Greg? Greg is that you? But why?" I try to call upon my stored earthen power to the surface once again, pleading in my mind to break me free, but it is entangled with his own potent energy that I don't even sense before it starts to engulf me. It creeps up my leg, squeezing every muscle into a spasm. It oozes into my chest, pushing the wind out of my lungs and causing me to gasp. Within seconds it is over my mouth, silencing my whimpers as it continues to crawl over me, giving me shock-like jolts and warnings as Greg holds me. He is looking into my eyes with an expression of smug satisfaction and revenge, his smile, a snarling nightmare on his face, beginning to break as he speaks.

"Does this feel familiar, little sister? My father told me how you tricked him into being trapped by mimicking his power, only letting yours creep in and take hold at the last possible moment. My dad didn't have a chance, did he? It's too bad I need you, or this would all end right here, right now!"

He squeezes my arm at the point of his previous mark, and it becomes apparent that more went on that day than a mere accidental poke of a needle. I curse myself for not taking Ryan's warnings more seriously, and, more importantly, for not trusting him. Unable to talk, I can only cause strangled screams in my throat and beg my limbs to move.

"I see my little draw on you worked perfectly. Taking blood from you while you were deep in my father's nightmare not only served as a great way to locate you so I could take you when no one else was around, but will also serve to invoke our little ceremony this evening." Greg's voice is so different, sinister even. I can't believe it is actually him.

"Funny you are all alone out here tracking me even though you are surrounded by powerful assistance. What a stupid girl you are. Those dreams really got to you, didn't they? Never knowing who to trust, and now look where all that fear and doubt has gotten you. Now, be a good little puppet and let's walk all cutesy hand-in-hand to my car. Dad is expecting us." Greg is obviously enjoying this all too much and for the life of me, I still can't call upon my power reserve to overcome his strength.

My body is shaking with both fear and unpreventable physical reactions to his painful jolts of power, but it stops rattling when he takes control of my body. I find myself walking hand-in-hand with him away from the alley, away from the lights and sounds of Rapture's Grand Opening, away from Ryan, Sandra, Justin, all of my friends, and anyone who could help me. In a last futile effort, I send a jolt of my energy into him, trying to distract him while carefully pooling a small portion of my grandmother's power into my free right hand. Greg immediately realizes what I am doing and squeezes my left hand so hard I think he may have fractured at least one of my fingers, but the pain is overridden by a small glimpse of hope as my right pinky moves on its own.

Even with that small glimmer of hope, I can't believe this is happening. I'm stronger than this, smarter than this. Why in the hell did I tear out of the club alone? I should have found some help, but from who? I had thought Ryan was the "who" I was chasing, and there was no way I was getting anyone else involved.

We make our way to a parking garage and to what must be his car. I quickly scan its license plate into my memory before he opens the door and throws me inside.

Before he gets in, I try one last-ditch effort. I wiggle my grandmother's power into my awareness, dropping the shields on my mind and sending a piercing, desperate mental scream to Ryan.

"Ryan, I know you can hear me, *help me*! Steven's partner is my foster brother Greg. He has me in his car in the parking garage on Market and 5th. I don't know where we're going, but he's known as Dr. Ian McAdams, license plate number DKE247, red Jag. *Hurry! Please.*"

The door opens, and Greg slides in, giving no hint that he knows what I have just done, assuming I was even able to reach Ryan. We are far from the club and well beyond his stated reach. Greg turns slowly to me as he closes the door.

"You thought you got away with it, didn't you? Well, now it's time for payback, you little whore!" Pain lashes through me over and over again as his power tears through my body, electrocuting me into a state of convulsions that make me smack my head repeatedly and painfully into the glass of the window. Sparks appear in my vision, which is blackening to claustrophobic proportions. I know I'll lose consciousness soon.

"I'm coming, Lex. I have you. Just hold on, please Lex, hold on!" Ryan's voice suddenly breaks through the pain, bringing me hope just as the darkness consumes me.

CHAPTER 20

Truth & Lies

Journal Entry:

The night's fundraiser was a benefit to raise money for cancer research. It was also an evening for me to once again recall all the reasons I despise cancer's vicious, menacing ass. I thought of my grandmother every day, but not like that, not by remembering why she was taken from me and how the awful disease assaulted her over and over again. No matter how many remissions she endured, how many organs were removed, healed by Earthen energy or transplant, it always came back, in the same spot, the same size and with the same result—pain, sadness, despair, and the ongoing fight.

I had never known about Grandmom's numerous remissions and healings until her last one. I remember the exact position of the sun on her face, and the sound of the wind in the trees when I asked her to allow me to heal her, and my heartbreak when she told me no. I was livid, beyond angry, and confused by a woman I thought to be stronger than a thousand men and yet she was saying no to life, to being with me. But then she explained why, with the tale of endless years. Fifteen years of back and forth of reliving the horror again and again, of the hope and promise leading to the subsequent re-scans and despair. She couldn't live like that anymore; it was taking away her control over her life and, most importantly, over her death.

My anger was first directed toward cancer itself. I spent hours poring over research, finding out how it attacked us, whether there was a rhyme or reason, a cause to why cancer happened, but I found nothing to assist me in my quest. The illness didn't discriminate, not for the young or the old, the rich or the poor, the recluse or the famous. It was merciless in its destruction, and in its wake of those of us who were left behind.

After my research led me to not a single answer but "I don't know," I turned on the goddess. I concentrated on the very energy she allowed me to harness, the one that I could not use to permanently heal the woman who took me in, who gave me unconditional love, who not only accepted me for what I am, but who was also the only person I could learn from who was like me but hadn't left me.

I cursed at the sun, the moon, and the stars. I pulled from the goddess' red earth, from her rock formations, rushing rivers, and trickling creeks. In my rage, I did the unthinkable and pulled the goddess's energy right out of thin air. I teased out the molecules of hydrogen and oxygen flitting in the air, and caused starbursts of matter to suddenly be created and destroyed, resulting in spectacular rumbles from the earth that caused Bear to whimper in unease. I too felt a shock and awe at myself, but it only lasted a moment before I pressed on, threatening to take down the stars from their home. I demanded from our goddess an answer. I pleaded with her to save my grandmother, to ease her suffering, and in response she did. The bells rang in the hospice, the harps played, the staff wept, and I draped myself across Grandmom's bed, holding her hand, whispering I love you, and singing to her softly.

"You are my sunshine, my only sunshine.
You make me happy when skies are grey.
You never know dear how much I love you.
Please don't take my sunshine away."

The air surrounding me is warm and dry, smelling of wood with a touch of rust and wine. Without the smells, I would have thought I was sitting in a warm sauna with sweat dripping down my face as the toxins leave my body. But the stinging sensations stemming from my head and face remind me that I'm not that lucky.

I startle myself awake only to scream as the flesh tears on my wrists, where the binds holding my arms behind my back, dig in harshly with each movement. My heels are off, lost who knows when or where and my dress is disheveled and torn. Scratches run along both legs, what in the hell, did he drag me down here? No other sounds reach me, nothing else but the echoes of my own shrill noises and the quickening of my breath. Looking around, I struggle to see anything in the darkness. Sweat continues to drip from my hairline down the right side of my face. On second thought, I'm guessing it is either a mixture of sweat and blood or, knowing my luck, it's probably all blood. I remember Greg or Ian, or whoever the hell he really is, smashing my head into the car window over and over again. My mind begins to fill with terror and a sickening sense of impending doom at my predicament. I have no earthly idea where in the hell I am, and nobody will have a clue as to who would have taken me, let alone think to look for the good Dr. Ian McAdams.

Damn it, Alex! Going rogue and leaving the club was a stupid-ass idea! I mean, I thought I was tracking Ryan, which is probably just as bad knowing his level of power. Wait, Ryan! His last words drift with a sliver of faith into my mind.

"I'm coming, Lex, I have you. Just hold on, please Lex, hold on!"

He has to know where I am or at least be working it out, but I've been out of it for who knows how long, and I'll venture a guess that he may need a coherent mind to read to get some sort of lock on a person's location. I can only hope he was able to pick up on my power signature and that I didn't shut everything down completely like my grandmother taught me to do when I was little. Apparently my years of being alone in my abilities softened me, that and Steven and Greg's onslaught of vicious dreams and mind-splitting headaches that have been keeping me sleepless and off my game.

My grandmother's face flashes across my mind, and I know I have her power in my back pocket, but right now I have no idea where Greg is, and I don't want to risk letting my ace in the hole slip away just yet. With how dark it is in here he could be in this very room, at this very moment.

I glance around again, trying to get an idea of where I am, so when I try to make contact with Ryan, I can give him some form of intel to follow or he will never be able to find me. The smell of wood is obvious, and as I squint into the darkness, it seems as if the entire room is covered in wood from top to bottom. It feels like a small room, maybe the size of my bedroom. I'm helplessly confined to a chair in the middle, and there doesn't appear to be furniture anywhere else. What I can make out are numerous shelves adorned with bottles—a wine cellar, but more like one in a home and not a restaurant. Oh, if I could only be so lucky as to be in a house that is traceable to Dr. Ian McAdams. Please have him be so cocky and confident to have brought me to his known address.

I begin to wiggle my fingers and then my toes when pins and needles shoot up my legs and arms from being unconscious and immobile. Even though seeing Greg right now will scare the hell out of me, I'm starting to think that maybe if I can talk some sense into him he can be reasoned with. I mean, he can't be all bad with what he's done for his life's work, right? Greg has healed people; he's brought them back from the brink of insanity, given them normal lives, or at least better than before. There is no way he faked it all, not with Dr. Reynolds knowing so much about him. Oh shit, what if she is in on this as well? What if the last year working with her has been the ultimate set-up? I refuse to believe it, but I guess anything is possible. Greg fooled me; he even used my own trap for Steven on me by mimicking my own power signature to cloak his own, but how? It took me months and months of close contact with Steven to learn how to match him. I haven't even known the good doctor for a month.

The coward knew exactly how to make me feel safe and to trust him, his power disguising him, leading his introduction with a tale of surfing with his dad to throw me off completely. Not to mention my power's read on him; the connection I felt wasn't because he was good at all—it was because he felt familiar. The fact that I didn't even sense power in him shows the amount of control he has. He must have leaked just enough to trick my own power into being duped, to convince me that I was safe.

I haven't seen Greg in over ten years, and we never knew about each other's abilities. Back then, I didn't even think about the possibility. How can Greg even stomach helping his father when he has to know what he did to me? Greg read my file when Dr. Reynolds allowed him access once I agreed to the hypnotherapy, and everything about the abuse would be in there, I'm sure of it.

We were never close though, so maybe he is just as wicked and evil as Steven; maybe he is the same or worse. The thought makes bile rise in my throat, wondering about all of the time he may have been alone with Chey. My mind starts to be bombarded by thoughts of other young girls.

A low thump from above breaks into my thoughts. Okay, so either I am in a basement or perhaps the first floor of what I hope to be his house. Footsteps sound above and behind me, passing over my head going forward. A door opens somewhere in front of me, creating a soft glow of light. I can see much better now. A stairway heading down into the room comes into view and the room is a bit bigger than I thought, maybe the size of my loft's downstairs. It is definitely a basement converted into a wine cellar, and the breeze created by the opening door moves the warm mahogany smell around me.

I start to shake, but quickly get a hold of myself and raise my chin in defiance. I will not let Greg see fear in my eyes, nor will I accept any form of defeat. As far as I am concerned, this is just the beginning, time to stall and time to get some answers. Maybe I can even set him straight, or help change his mind. I can only hope he doesn't already know and simply not care about how much of a monster his father really is, because that will make him just as evil. I have faith that perhaps there is still a good person in there.

His whistles go in time with his footsteps as he heads down the stairs, all cheery and light as if he is on his way to some happy occasion. Well, if Daddy is being set free, I guess he's preparing for a family reunion. Yet if he doesn't already know what Steven is capable of, then he is in for a rude awakening. That man is a conniving snake. I wouldn't trust his ass for a second, even if I were his own flesh and blood.

Greg's form steps into the dimness of the room, still appearing as Dr. McAdams. I wonder if he has somehow made himself permanently look this way, and only Dana's magic revealed the truth. The glow from the open door above splashes shadows across his face, causing his wicked smile to appear even more frightening. A chill runs through me. His smile grows bigger as he relishes my fear. I can see something glinting in his hand. It is dark as night one second and glowing in an onyx stone–like fashion the next. Twirling the object in his hand while taking slow steps toward me.

"You know why I chose to go into my line of work after I lost my father? I thought the trauma my family and me, even you, had endured was something I could help others live through, not to mention help me understand my own loss. Understanding grief, longing, and sometimes the inability to go on in life was all I focused on for my patients. I was so good at it that it didn't even occur to me that I had my father's power, and that was influencing and healing. Then I moved away from the mere death of loved ones, and ventured into those who had actually killed others. I mainly focused on soldiers returning from the many wars in the world, and the veterans still suffering decades later. It was during my work with them that I had my first dream, or visit I should say, from my father."

He moves the object in his hand and holds it close to his face. I make out the black stone handle and the long blade of the knife he cradles. Glancing from it to me, he takes in my appearance with a look of disgust.

"He came in flashes. At first I could only hear him, hear him screaming in pain and asking for help. I thought it was my mind imagining what he must have been going through while in the depths of depression and suicidal ideations. But it was soon apparent that it was him, actually him being tortured over and over in the hell dimension you trapped him in and that he never, not even once, had thought about killing himself."

"That bastard deserved it!" I spit at him. He moves too quickly for me to get another word out before he strikes me across the face. My power tries to react to him, to lash out and trap him, but I am met with a paralyzing force that squeezes the flickers of magic out of my awareness. I grasp for a hold onto it, to bring it back, but it is gone, or trapped away by Greg's own.

The feelings of electrocution in my body are replaced by the sensation of bugs crawling over me, biting and pinching me under my skin. It is terrifying, and it takes all I have just to breathe and try to calm myself down under the pain and fear. "This isn't real, this isn't the end of me, I will persevere." I speak my mantra over and over:

"I don't want to hear your lies, you little bitch! You came into our house, this broken, sad little waif of a girl who no one thought would ever be capable of such treachery, but I know the truth." Pacing with a mad glint in his eyes, Greg runs his free hand travels absently through his blond hair. "My dad was finally able to speak to me once Valant came to me for a trade."

"Who the hell is Valant?" I scream at Greg, losing a bit of self-control over the situation as my nerves continue to grate. He moves to strike me again but stops himself when he catches sight of his hand covered in blood from the last blow. He wipes his hands on his jeans, snarling at the mess.

"As if you don't know Valant! The demon you gave my father to, you disgusting piece of filth!" Oh shit. The demon has a name? "Through the torture he inflicted on my father, Valant was able to find out about me and to get glimpses into my life and work. I didn't know much about demons until Valant, but what I know now is that they feast off of not only those trapped away in hell dimensions, but also upon the suffering of others in this plane. That is, as long as he is invited to watch while the trauma is relived or, better yet, as it actually happens. Lucky for him, and lucky for my father and me, I work with those whose lives revolve around the traumatic events they continue to suffer. I would invite him into my place of business disguised as one of my office staff, and he would feed on the suffering, the loss, and the pain as I guided them through their tragic events with hypnotherapy." Greg paces back and forth movement, looking around at some imaginary annoyance before stopping in front of me again.

"Valant, a demon no less, helped me make a name for myself as my clients were instantly healed. Their pain disappeared as he absorbed it, and they could finally live normal lives. I had taken hypnotherapy to a whole new level, growing my power in other ways each day. Soon, therapists were seeking me out every day, even your own Dr. Reynolds—my BFF, the dumb bitch just like you."

Well, that sure is one hell of an answer. My stomach clenches at the thought of Dr. Reynolds as a loose end. The authorities will go to her when they can't find me, but I'm guessing Greg will never let that happen. She has to be in danger, if she isn't dead already. Once again another person is in peril because of me, and not someone I ever thought I had to worry about.

"For payment, Valant let my father and me visit from time to time, but never, ever would he agree to let him go. You are the only one who can do that, but I'm guessing you already know that, don't you?" I shake my head at him, but it doesn't stop him for a second. "Well, our visits were long enough for me to hear the real story. You tried to win him over with your wiles, and when he wouldn't yield to your whoring or agree to leave his family and run away with you, you threatened to ensnare him into a hellhole with Valant. He never thought you would really do it, or even that you were that strong, but you had even more incentive to get rid of him, didn't you?"

He stops his pacing, his back facing me. The tension is unnerving; Greg's behavior is so erratic that I fear I wouldn't have time to block him if he suddenly decided to stop his revelations and just take me out. I can only hope that there is some sort of ritual thing he needs to carry out, taking my blood to break the bonding. If I'm in luck, it will take more than him slicing through my carotid artery without any warning to do the job right. Thank goddess he keeps rambling on, Hopefully he will continue long enough for me to work on my freedom from this dungeon.

"You sure fooled us, didn't you, Alex? You and your druggie mom are the same, sponging off men, tramping from place to place. My dad told me you threatened to bind him and my mom away if he didn't give you a large amount of money. He begged you to take the cash he had hidden away, to just take him and to promise that you would leave my mom and family alone. Your little payday allowed you to do what you always wanted to do, to be back in San Diego, and it even paid for your college and business venture, didn't it? I never thought you were smart enough to get the money you did for school, and I knew he would have left more to my family, but you took it. You fucking thief!"

I have had just about enough of this crazy-ass talk spewing from Greg's mouth. His repetitive movements and fitful speeches are freaking me out, not to mention the big ass knife. I take a second to search for my grandmother's power and then quickly send it out, away from Greg and down through the wooden floor, entering into the soil in search of Ryan. I can only hope he is close enough to feel me. I have to keep Greg talking, and I know I should probably start by telling him just how much of a daft idiot he is.

"You're either incredibly dense, or maybe you have more screws loose than some of your mental patients. Are you telling me you bought that bullshit story? I know you and I weren't close, but you know about my relationship with Chey, you know I took care of her and how much I love her. And something you never knew, and a memory I saved from Chey herself, was that your fucked-up creep of a father tried to abuse her! Sexually, you stupid fuck, just like he did to me." That got his attention. His eyes bulge like he just got slapped across the face. "You actually believed his story? A fourteen-year-old foster kid tries to take a forty-something-year-old away from his family? Now, which makes more sense, Greg? Don't you think it's more believable that maybe, just maybe, he belongs where he is with his buddy Valant, someone I've never met for your information. But you two seem chummy enough." Veins begin to bulge out from his neck and along his temples.

"You're lying!" Greg spits the words at me, seething in anger. Geez, I'm starting to think maybe there is no getting through here.

"Look, Greg, I know you want him to be alive, to be with you, he's your dad. I get it, I really do. If I could have my grandmother back, my mom, or even have a chance to meet my dad, I would jump at it. But your father is evil, he is a dangerous Absolute Protector hell bent on destroying the way of life we have now. You must know something about your power, about our history, his history. He's even too evil for the Absolute Protectors, which is why they kicked him out. He was hiding out, acting like *Mr. Family Man* to keep from being imprisoned

209

by Earthen Protectors and the Council. I'm sure you've heard of them. If it hadn't been me who exiled him away, it would have been them because he's bad news, Greg. Get out now, while you can, because if you think this is going to end badly for me, you had better check in with reality. He doesn't care who he uses or hurts, not even his own family. He only cares about himself."

It looks like he's listening to me and I think I see his eyes drop in thought, finally thinking about what I am saying. I have to keep going.

"Greg, you're a good person, you're an amazing doctor, think about how much good you have done. How many people you've helped! Don't throw that all away because of Steven's lies and some Demon. Don't do this. I can help you. I know people who can fix everything—we can put an end to all of this."

Greg's voice is a whisper and I think that maybe he is coming around.

"He tried to hurt Chey?" He pauses and my breath catches, this is it, he's listening. And then my confidence wavers as his eyes turn cold.

"Do you really expect me to believe that?!" His says as his voice raises to a thunderous yell. "You really are fucking out of your mind, aren't you?"

I don't flinch at his madness. I know what I saw, he is listening, and part of him has to know what I am saying is true. There is no way he was as separated from the world of Earthen and Absolute Protectors as I was. Was there? If his dad is the only one he ever knew, it may just be the case. What I know for sure is that he is a manic mess, and I'm guessing messing with that Demon Valant probably has something to do with that; maybe Valant is even his "mentor" leading to this dark power he's been wielding. It's frightening, less calculating than Steven's was, or is, wilder and possibly uncontrollable even by Greg himself if he continues to spiral out of control.

Without warning, I watch in horror as a dark grey shimmer crawls along his arms, oozing my way, drawing my once-beautiful glowing green vines and taking them hostage before blinking them out of existence altogether. The visualization of his power is terrifying. I have never seen Greg's before because up until now, he held it in his control just like my grandmother had.

Watching Greg's magic work its way toward me, I feel a sense of loneliness and emptiness, like I will never feel the sun on my face again, or sand moving between my toes. I will never be held or kissed again, and thoughts of the family I will never have drift away, leaving only my wish for the pain to end. It reminds me of the hopelessness and emptiness I felt when I was trapped by Steven, something I had vowed would never happen again. I try to break free, knowing these feelings aren't mine, they aren't real, but Greg only pushes his force against my will more strongly, more fiercely, breaking me down. What is this madness? It's as if he heals in reverse, completely the opposite of what I can do.

"I don't even want to hear your lies, bitch. I read your bullshit file. I know girls like you with your attention-seeking stories of made-up trauma just to get someone to care about you, to replace the void in your life from Mommy abandoning you, or Grandmother kicking the bucket. Oh, poor Alex, partying little lush, fucking two oblivious men at once, dealing with Daddy and Mommy issues. I know all about your kind. Too bad your mom's genes passed down to you, or maybe you would have been a decent Protector for our cause. But I think your lifestyle proves loud and clear what you are all about: all partying, sex, and frivolity. Look where it's gotten you! You're nothing, Alex, you're broken, worthless. You are *nothing!*"

Unbidden tears fall down my face, mirrored by the sweat dripping down Greg's temples.

He's right. What? No, he isn't! Oh, great, now I'm arguing with myself. Can this day get any worse? Greg's force is trying to take over my mind bit by bit, and I fear he is winning and I don't know what to do. I could bring out my grandmother's power in full force now, but what if it doesn't work? I need help. I need Ryan. I also need to find out what Greg intends to do.

"You're right, Greg, I'm nothing, I'm worthless. You should just kill me now and get it over with. But what you're not right about is what your father is. I know you're a good person. You were helping me when we began prepping for my hypnotherapy sessions. You have saved hundreds of others and you're still helping people, even if your co-worker is a Demon." His vicious snarl lets me know he doesn't find any of this funny. Well, neither do I, buddy. "You must know that your dad is evil. Is that the side you want to be on? I don't know how you learned about your powers, but you did learn what good you were capable of before Valant and Steven started fucking with you. I know Daddy dearest was never there to help you find your way, so let me help you. I know what we are, what we can be, but your dad, he is the darkest Protector out there. Everyone on the side of goodness and peace wants him either to stay where he is, or dead. Which side do you want to be on? He's tricking you, Greg. You have to at least think about it." His power eases up a bit; I can tell doubt is chewing away at him slightly.

From what I recall of him, he was never home all that much. I would venture to think that he and his dad were never really close, so that is one of the very things driving him now, the ache of needing to have a relationship with his father, to have his approval. This may even be the first time Greg ever felt Steven wanted or needed him. Top that off with finding out that he is alive and I am responsible for his torment, no matter the reason, would certainly be enough to make him take Steven's side. I get it, I understand, even if it means my life.

"Why don't we ask him? There's no time like the present to make this easy on all of us. So now, sister, you will do what you are told. Don't make me force you, because you know I can. Just a few more seconds of feeding you the emptiness you are being consumed by, and you will be begging me for this knife." He moves behind me and I squirm to try to see what he's doing. "I'm going to release your right hand from the back of the chair so you can hold the knife. We have to use your blood, drawn by your own hand, to call the Demon Valant to you. Now, be a good girl, and slice open your left arm and call Valant. I can't kill you, not yet anyway, so get on with it. I'll take care of the rest." Greg's directions are clear and of course, there always has to be blood, damn it! Well, at least he isn't planning on letting me die, well, not yet at least.

The instant he cuts my hands free of its bondage and loosens his powerful hold on my hand I take advantage of the little freedom I have to use my thumb to caress the silver ring attached warmly to my right ring finger. I don't know why I hadn't thought of it before; it has to be a way for Ryan to sense me. Sending my grandmother's energy into the metal, I fill it with her power, praying to the goddess that it won't give me away by starting to glow or spark. I plead for my actions to reflect a dormant use of magic so Greg won't sense or see what I am doing. My hopes are answered as I feel the ring warm in response, and I know Ryan is nearby. For the first time, I have a feeling that I might actually be able to get out of this alive.

CHAPTER 21

Demons & Fathers

Journal Entry:

I just wanted you to hold me close. I couldn't feel the ground below, and I didn't sense the world above. I only had you. I only had the lightness of your touch, the feel of your breath on my skin, and the beating of your heart against my back. I just wanted you to cradle me in the darkness. But not to leave me— not to leave me here.

The cool obsidian stone touches my palm, and I swear I hear a sizzle as it makes contact with the ring. I don't think I'm going to get out of what Greg is asking of me, but hopefully Ryan will get here before it is decided that I am no longer needed. Holding the knife, I strike it across my inner arm and watch the warm blood trickle down, moving in streams along my fingers, losing their fight against gravity, and falling to the ground. Greg's eyes turn black as his power takes in the sight, and I know he can taste victory coming. I don't think there is any way to continue stalling and try to keep Steven exiled where he is, so instead I hold on to the belief that Ryan is coming. Now I can only hope Steven will be easy work for him. But truly, his exile has been anything but easy to deal with, so I doubt this will be simple for anyone. This Valant is the wild card, but that is something that we will have to figure out along the way.

"Ok, good girl, now call for him! Call for Valant, call for the Demon you've gifted my father to. He's been waiting for you. A little too reverently, if you ask me." Oh, great, a Demon groupie, well, maybe he can be reasoned with then, or at least kept out of things. I don't think he can harm me unless I'm in his dimension, but then again, I don't know shit about Demons. I didn't even know Steven was being held by one.

"Okay, okay, hold your little boy pants on. This doesn't exactly tickle, you know. Just wait till Daddy dearest gets here, Greg! There is no way he can hide his true nature, and you'll see the mistake you are making soon enough, brother." Yep, I can get smartassy at very inappropriate times, and apparently being faced with meeting a Demon and possible death is one of those times. Greg grabs the knife from my right hand and takes a new zip tie to lock me back in place in the chair. Silence takes over the room until sounds of my blood plopping into the pool on the floor breaks the quiet apart.

"Shut up, and call for Valant! I don't want to hear your filthy mouth say anything else, or I'll bind you to him instead of letting you out of your miserable excuse for a life, and see how much you like that." I guess this is it, no Ryan yet, just me and a small room that's about to get pretty crowded.

"Valant, I call upon you." That sounded appropriate. I mean how do you call a Demon anyhow? "I'm here with your buddy, Greg. He asked me to call you, hope this is a good time." Greg obviously doesn't like my creative scripting and lets me know it by digging his fingers into the open cut in my arm, causing me to scream out in pain. A whoosh makes my eardrums pop, and I know we are no longer alone.

"Perhaps it's just me, but you may want to gag her, Doctor. I'm sure your neighbors will be able to hear her soon if that keeps up." The voice comes from behind me, as cold as ice and as smooth as oil. A smell like death and lilies assaults my senses, and I struggle to turn my head around, nearly knocking myself over in my chair. I want to see what is back there. The binds on my wrists dig in deeper, but I don't care, I do *not* want my back to a Demon.

"Let me help you with that." I am suddenly launched into the air, chair and all, and turned around to face the Demon named Valant. No horns, no red skin, no scales, or tail. Valant is a normal-looking man, dressed in a business suit and tie, looking more like he leads a boardroom meeting than a hell dimension. He smiles, and his teeth twinkle at me, sharp and deadly. Yep, that's more like it, all Demony and freaky. His hair is platinum blond, long, and straight as it brushes along the tops of his shoulders. The dark grey suit makes his hair stand out even more in the darkness.

"There, that's better. Let's ease up a bit shall we, Greg? I think she'll behave, won't you, Alex?" Hitting the X hard, he moves around me and his sharp nails trail along my left arm, smearing the blood there before Valant lifts his fingers to his mouth, slowly licking the redness off each one of them. Eww.

"My name is Valant, but you know that already don't you, young Alex? My, don't you taste delicious, such power and strength; you will make an excellent addition to my collection." I squirm in the chair to no available. "I have thoroughly enjoyed this past year, feeding off your fear and mistrust—nothing personal, as you know. Creating nightmares is Steven's specialty and my, oh my, did father, son, and your own innate mistrust of others give him such fuel to create them. What fun this has been, so thank you, Alex, really, thank you." What in the hell? There is no way I am going anywhere with this guy.

"No one is doing anything with her until she releases my dad." Greg jumps in, before I can protest. "Now, tell her what to say and bring him to me." Valant turns his head slowly away from me, holding my eyes with his own until the last possible moment.

"Yes, of course, Greg, this is the deal, isn't it? Alex for your father. You did promise me a powerful Earthen Protector and boy, you weren't lying. Gaia will be most upset to lose her. How delightful." Damn, Greg does plan to give me to him; maybe I should have chosen death. Valant turns his attention back to me, kneeling before me as if I were a child. "I must say, I can't thank you enough for sending Steven to me, such a bad boy he is, and when you were only a child. Such power."

Eyebrows raised I smile at him. "I was happy to gift him to you, so what do you say you keep him and show me your gratitude by letting me out of here." Valant's head flies back in his laughter. I have a feeling him saying thank you was all the appreciation I would ever see or hear.

"And you're funny. Don't worry, I won't hurt you, much." Yeah me. "Okay, Ms. Conner, repeat after me. Steven William Nestrour, I release you from my bind. My blood is my proof of this wish, my words the seal to the removal of your entrapment to the Demon Valant."

I tremble a little in front of him. What in the hell am I doing calling Ryan into this? What if something happens to both of us?

"Don't worry, dear, you are safe for now. Once Steven is free, and Greg binds you to me… well, then that's another story, isn't it?"

He gives a little wink and swiftly moves away from me, taking a finger to spin my chair back around to face Greg and the stairway. It's as if Valant read my mind or sensed my fear. I hope he doesn't Ryan? If he does, he isn't saying, not even to Greg. I guess I shouldn't be surprised; he seems to like a good show, and maybe he even hopes he will be able to gorge on other people's distress for weeks after this confrontation in this cellar. I can only hope that is the case. I take a deep breath, sending a prayer out to Gaia, and then another subtle power surge into the ring before I repeat word for word after Valant. Greg has been busying himself with a bag in the corner; clothes appear in his left hand, shoes in the other.

I see why in an instant as Steven's form appears curled in a fetal position on the floor in front of me. His movements are slow at first as he unwinds himself and starts to stand. I avert my eyes, not wanting to see his gangly, naked form. The years seem to vanish and I am that young teenage girl again, trapped with him, by him. He stretches, appearing to relish in my unease as he slowly takes the clothes from Greg and takes his time putting them on. Once he's dressed, Greg makes his way to embrace him, but Steven coolly moves form him, walking towards me instead. I see the hurt in Greg's eyes and only pray that now he may be able to see through his father.

As Steven reaches me, I shed my terrified girl feelings and look him straight in the eye.

"Hi there, Steve. How was hell? Been having some fun times with Valant? Not enough if you ask me, and maybe this time things won't end so peachy for you after all." Steven, always the cool and calculating one, doesn't try to hit me like his temper-tantrumming son; instead, he barks in laughter while clapping his hands together.

"Ah, forever the feisty one, aren't you? I do hope you've enjoyed all the lovely sleepless nights and days as well as the mental anguish I sent your way. It worked so well to put you off your game and into the arms of your helpful Dr. McAdams, not to mention keeping Valant happy enough to allow me to keep popping into this dimension to break you. Ever the optimist that something or someone will save you. Don't you know we can only save ourselves? Well, I'd love to chat some more but it's time for you to go, isn't it, Valant?" That was fast! I had anticipated some more face off time, hoping to get Ryan here, hoping to show Greg Steven's true colors to maybe convince him that his father is all lies and pure evil. Steven knows better; he isn't going to waste any more time. He walks toward Valant with the question upon his face.

"Of course, Steven, I will free you once she is mine." Valant turns to Greg, and the strength of Greg's power begins to take hold of me again.

"Greg, wait! Look at me! Steven is lying to you! When was he ever there for you? He doesn't even care that you're here now. Look at him! He is using you. Don't do this, Greg, please." The sensation of being pulled into the earth begins to take over my being and I struggle against the zip ties that hold me in place.

Suddenly, Ryan's ring begins to burn as the humming feeling of his power sweeps through my body—he's here. I see Valant's eyes widen a little and a wicked smile spreads across his face, but he stays still, not saying a word. Ryan's silver power races down the stairway ahead of him like a jet stream as he flies down the steps, not making a sound or even moving the air around him. Greg is on the floor in an instant, and his hold on me drops just as fast. He writhes on the wooden boards, convulsing under the weight of Ryan's power, helpless, as Valant and Steven look on without an ounce of emotion. It becomes abundantly clear that Steven doesn't have the use of his power, not yet. I think he owes Valant a replacement toy before anything like that can happen. I look from Steven to Greg, feeling pity as I fear my freedom may mean Greg's demise, one way or another.

"Are you okay?"

Ryan is at my side releasing my hands from the bondage, encouraging me to use my power to heal myself while he keeps Greg under his control. He takes in the room around us, staring at Valant with interest rather than fear, or even surprise. His look of death is focued on Steven. I don't think Steven is getting out alive no matter what he did for Valant, but then again, maybe he will try to go back with him instead of facing death. Hell, Valant might be able to blink him away to "freedom" at any time. If he gets away, I will never be safe; any and every chance he gets he will come after me. I can't live that way again. Ryan isn't about to give Steven a chance, and from the look in Steven's eyes as he takes in Ryan, it is clear he knows it too.

"I'm okay, thank you for coming. I'm sorry I didn't listen to you."

"Let's worry about that later. We have other things to do right now." Ryan's eyes never left Steven as the sicko's cool demeanor starts to shred and he falls to pieces. Turning to Valant and almost pleading with him, he points frantically at Greg.

"Take him! I can bind him to you if you let me free for just a moment. Greg is a worthy trade, he has my blood in his veins, and he may very well be just as powerful as me, some day. Let me give him to you, please." Greg's face turns to me in dismay and cold realization when he feels the impact of Steven's words. The whole thing is sad despite the horror of what Greg nearly did to me, but our focus is on Steven, not Greg, and we need Steven fully free from Valant to touch him.

Ryan has a hold of me now, pretty much holding me up in fact. The blood loss and the physical and mystical battering I took from Greg have almost drained me completely. I try to draw in Earthen energy and nearly fall over, my reserve having been spent on locating Ryan and a half-ass attempt at healing myself. Well, I sure as hell am not going to let Steven know how badly I am hurt, so I push off of Ryan, standing my ground at his side.

I look at Ryan and then at Greg. Steven needs to be destroyed, and I don't think being in a Demon's possession will allow that to happen. Too bad for Greg that he chose to believe in the wrong person.

"We need Steven free from the Demon; it's the only way. Greg made his bed." Ryan whispers into my ear, and I know Greg is officially out of luck.

"I know. It's the only way." Mentally distancing myself from Greg, I have to agree. It is the cold hard truth and even though I still had hope for Greg, this isn't the time to try and help him.

Valant looks at me with something scheming in his mind that sends shivers up my spine. Something is up, but I can only hope it isn't anything nearly as bad as what I would endure if we don't take care of Steven once and for all. Greg is whimpering in the corner, and Ryan eases his hold on him. Greg rolls to a sitting position, attempting to stand.

"How could you? After all I did for you!" and he glares, cursing at his father. "After all I have sacrificed for you! You are just going to give me to him? You are my father!"

"Actually, Doctor, he isn't your real father." It's Valant who speaks, and for the first time I see Steven look down at the ground, but not in remorse, I think he's manically laughing. "You are of his blood though, but Mommy had to get a little naughty with your dad's brother and poof, here you are. He hates you really, a constant reminder of his wife and brother's betrayal, but you did your job, and quite well I might add. It will be a delight to feed off your pain and daddy issues for all time." Valant turns to Steven as Greg falls sobbing to the floor.

218

"I grant you the use of your power to bind him to me, Steven. Don't try a single thing, otherwise I will send you back *home* in a breath."

The quickness at which Steven's power forces Greg to be given to the earth is viciously mesmerizing while his screams are muffled by the wood flooring engulfing first his head and then the rest of his body. In an instant, he appears next to Valant as a wraith of some sort. Greg spats and struggles to be free of the bind, his body arcing toward Steven, using a colorful list of curse words as he threatens his father with every type of bodily harm possible. The Demon laughs at Greg, ignoring his worthless fight and instead addresses Steven over Greg's howls.

"It is done. Steven, you are free. Greg, let's see how this plays out, shall we? Don't worry, you may yet get your revenge," Valant says with a gleeful laugh.

Steven turns to Ryan and me, splaying his fingers toward the ground and attempting to pull energy from the earth. I see his eyes blaze with red fire as his power is revealed. It isn't a smooth flow though; there is an obvious lag in the uptake, as though he used all he had on Greg and is spent from the binding. His eyes widen as he realizes his error. They widen even further when Ryan pulls an intricately molded metal gun from behind his back, leveling it intently on Steven. Magnificent ruins, vines, trees, and animals are cast into the metal, bulkier than any handgun I had ever seen, but Ryan doesn't struggle with its weight. This must be what Dana gave him, a weapon of power, something to take Steven out for good, and the bastard knows it.

Steven spins on his heels to make a run for it, and I swear I see Valant clapping in delight at the mayhem.

"Say goodbye to Steven, Lex. This time there's no coming back for him. He'll never harm you, ever again." Ryan's words are full of force and pride. He wants and needs to protect me—that is clear to me now.

"Goodbye Steven, and this time it's for good. Oh, and just so you know, yeah, this is going to hurt, you sick piece of shit." As I say the last word, Ryan's power pours into the gun and he pulls the trigger. Silver power shaped into multiple bullets tear through the air and find their mark in every part of Steven's body. A red flurry of light engulfs him as we watch his body disintegrate like a dead animal decaying in time-lapse footage, finally turning to red dust on the cellar floor.

Relief, pain, and exhaustion flood me as I turn into Ryan's embrace, refusing to cry in the presence of the Demon or my foster brother with his betrayal.

"Well, well, well, that was just fantastic! I'm full and light as a feather, dear Alexis. You and your friend put on quite a show. I'll be taking my prize now. Oh yes, before I leave, Greg has something to say, don't you, Doctor?" Valant manages to shake Greg's shadowy form by the throat like a rag doll, throwing him toward me, the momentum causing him to slide along the floor on his face, but he leaps to his feet instantly and makes a move toward me. Ryan is there to block him just in case he isn't as trapped as he seems, but I touch his arm, and he moves away.

"Alex, please, you can't let Valant take me! I'm sorry, you were right. I'm so sorry." I shake my head feeling sorry for him, but there is nothing to be done, and no way am I going to trust him that easily.

"I'm sorry too, Greg, but you made your decisions. Now you are going to have to suffer the consequences. Come on Ryan, let's go." I answer as we move to leave the cellar.

"Don't you want to know how I mimicked your power?" Greg's words stop me in my tracks. "I bet you wondered, didn't you? It was your mom. I trapped her and used her to get to you. She knows your power signature backward and forward, and she sang it to me like a little bird under her filthy, drug-induced haze. Poor Stacy Conner, so powerful, but so lost to you for all this time."

I spin back around so fast that I nearly fall on my face, finding time to shoot Valant a glare as he snickers at me. This is such bullshit! How in the hell did my mom get herself into this, and how will I find her if I don't let this weasel go? Greg, forever the loon, knows I won't let Valant take him now and that I must have undoubtedly underestimated him. He smirks at me.

"I bet you didn't see that coming, did you? I'm more formidable than you give me credit for, and if you don't get me out of here NOW, you will never know where she is. What's it going to be, Alex? Are you going to be a good daughter and save your mother? Only I know where she is, and you will never find her unless you tell Valant to LET ME GO NOW!"

"He's lying Lex, he'd say anything to get away from the Demon. Don't trust him; we can find your mom ourselves." Ryan tries his best to intervene. But I can't leave with this uncertainty hanging thick in the warm air. After all, Greg did find a way to mimic me, and having my mom makes the most sense. No matter what, I can't risk it, not

220

now. Maybe this was why she has been silent for so long. This whole time I thought she was still on some super-secret mission, but Greg has had her trapped for at least a year, maybe even more. I shake my head at Ryan and look at Valant. He looks smug and delighted by this turn of events. He's known this all along; he knew this was going to happen, and now I am going to find out what he is willing to trade to give Greg over to me.

"Okay, Valant, let's have it. You've had this ace up your sleeve the whole time, so what will it take to give me the little creep, or can you just be a pal and make him tell me where she is for a smaller trade of some sort?" Valant's chest rattles in time with his laugh.

"Now, that wouldn't be any fun, would it? No, you must give me a trade worthy enough to let this little vermin go, but I will be fair to you. After all, you gave me Steven for over a decade and your own torturous year of fun, so I kind of owe it to you." Somehow I doubt Demons ever feel they owe anybody anything, but I let Valant continue without interference.

"I won't require another binding, something more along the lines of what Greg did for me. Alexis, your chaotic life has been full of suffering, and I know it will only continue for you, as you're a magnet for pain and drama. All I ask is that you allow me to relish in it. You must tell me all that has happened and does happen to you. There may be times I wish to be around during your trials, and you will have to abide me, or you will break our pact, thus giving me power to bind you to me. So how is that? Fair, I would say."

Ryan is on my arm spinning me around to face him.

"Alex, you can't trust him anymore than you can trust Greg to tell you where your mom is."

"I know, you're right, but I can't risk it." I face Valant and nod. "You will have my word Valant, but under some conditions. You cannot demand to visit me without warning or at deeply private times; there are no free drop-ins or peep shows. I have to invite you, and just because you don't get what you want right away all the time doesn't mean you can just sweep me away to your hell dimension. And this agreement *will not* be in effect until we meet again, and we have official and very specific ground rules put in place. And that is not going to happen until I find my mother." Valant's fingers coming together while he drums them in thought.

"Take it or leave it, but that's as close to an agreement as you are getting from me tonight. Now, I need your word, Valant. Agree to my demands or the deal's off the table." I hope I know what I am doing.

For some reason this seems like a good choice, but lord knows my choices haven't always led me in the right direction.

"Of course, Alexis, you have my word. So nice doing business with you, my dear, Doctor, and you too, large, hulking man I do not know. I'll be seeing you!"

Valant is gone in an instant, and Greg shimmers out of existence for a moment before he appears right in front of us again, fully formed this time. He takes a moment to pat himself down, making sure he is really all here. I move toward him as his hand comes away from his side, a dark ball of energy in his palm. Before I can get my power to respond and latch on to him, a wall of darkness appears behind him, like the void I had seen in his eyes and along his arms. I lunge for him, screaming out.

"No, no! Greg, please! Please tell me where she is!" Greg takes a step back and begins to disappear as the darkness folds around him, and then, he is gone.

Epilogue

"Humankind has not woven the web of life.
We are but one thread within it.
Whatever we do to the web, we do to ourselves.
All things are bound together. All things connect."
~ Chief Seattle

Pitter continues his stubbornness, climbing atop my suitcase, no matter how many times I provoke annoyed "meows" from him each time I push him away. He knows I am taking off, maybe even that it is open ended, and that is just not acceptable to him. Ryan expects a quick turn around on his end after dropping me off at home to pack. We already stopped by Sandra's to get the important items I needed from my stay there, but with this having an unknown timeline, I need to pack additional things from my loft. Sandra wasn't home, but I left her a note telling her I would be in touch and to please come by the house to take care of Pitter. I would have kept him at Sandra's house, but I want him with me right now. It just doesn't feel right to leave him there while I plan my departure.

The decision to hunt down Greg wasn't even a question; we know finding him is the key to finding my mother, and we also know that wherever he has her, she isn't safe.

When I hear the knock at the door, I can't believe Ryan is back already. I rush downstairs to open it, calling out that there is no way he can expect me to be ready yet, and how in the hell is he back so soon anyhow. I'm shocked that he even bothered to knock! Come to think of it, I don't feel his presence at all. That's odd. I tense at the thought of who it can be, or why anyone else would be here when dawn is barely breaking outside.

When I open the door my dark god-like avenger isn't in the doorway, quite the opposite in fact as Dana who stands in the coming light, her flowing white hair ablaze with the rising sun.

"Dana, what are you doing here?" I stutter in surprise, as well as thinking about how rude I am for not greeting her properly. I quickly motion her inside, giving her a warm embrace before holding her in front of me to tell her the news of what happened in the last few hours.

"Dana, Steven is gone, for good this time, but it's my mom who needs my help. She's being held somewhere, my foster brother Greg has her, and he's been using her all along to trick me. She's in trouble and Ryan and I are going to find her." Dana smiles brightly with a clever glint in her eyes that only means she has something up her sleeve.

"What is it, Dana? Do you know where she is? Is she okay?" Dana gathers my hands in hers.

"Oh, what a clever boy that Greg is," she says excitedly. "He had us all fooled, and saved his smartest trick for last, in hopes of saving his own skin. That snake never had your mom. I doubt anyone could have held her against her will, unless she wanted them to think just that. No, my dear Alexis, I have come to take you to her. She needs our help. It's your father, dear, we need to save your father." My jaw drops, and bees buzz in my head with the confusion created by her words.

"My dad? But he's dead. No one ever told me who he was and never that he still might be alive, and now I need to save him? What about Ryan? We're supposed to be tracking Greg, together. I guess the fact that he doesn't have Mom makes it less urgent, yes, but I have to tell Ryan. He saved me. He means something to me, something I've never felt before." My voice looses some of its vigor as the look on her face turns to one of pity.

"Alexis, he may not have chosen to tell you, but I think it's best you know now. There isn't a future for you and Ryan, not more than friendship I fear. His family is part of the Council, and they are very specific about acceptable matches for the Earthen Protectors. Their goal is to continue bringing more Protectors into the world and they feel the best way to do that is by spreading themselves out to breed with humans, not with others of their... your kind. It's a doctrine, and one Ryan knows very well."

The air is knocked out of me, and my heart thumps wildly with despair and disbelief. Why didn't Ryan tell me? How could he keep this from me? He knows I have feelings for him—feelings I thought we shared. At that moment, I lock my thoughts down and lift my chin, meeting Dana's eyes while successfully holding back the heaviness of my tears.

"Okay, Dana, let's go."

Thank you for reading my first book
Trust: The Alex Conner Chronicles Book One

Now, check out the 'Note to the Reader' and enjoy a sneak peek into

Truth: The Alex Conner Chronicles Book Two

Available now on Amazon

A Note to the Reader

Trust wasn't the first book I attempted to write, but it's the first one I actually finished. From the pages of the story, I'm sure you can gather that I spent a lot of time in the Western part of the United States, mainly San Diego. I moved there after college, and the six years there brought this series to life. San Diego is vibrant with people from all over the world, and being in my 20's, I was open and eager to learn, observe, and dive into the diversity of the city.

Now, after five more books, I decided to pick up *Trust* again and look at it with fresh eyes and a new look. Starting out as a first-time writer I made a lot of mistakes, and this was my chance to redeem myself and make this book even better. I wanted Trust to come out of the gate stronger to keep readers invested in the other stories from the Alex Conner series, so I hope I've done a worthy job of it all.

Yes, some of these pages are somewhat autobiographical; mainly the death of the grandmother figure and the grief and loss Alex endures was my own way of dealing with the passing of my mother from cancer in 2010. I was angry for years, not enjoying life, being fearful and sad. When I went to Arizona in 2014 with a good friend (my mother loved the desert) and had the same experience Alex does at that spa, but with my mom. After coming home to the East Coast, *Trust* poured out of me as if she was guiding my words, fueling my brain and body as I wrote into the late hours even though I had to wake at 5:30 a.m. for work on mere hours of sleep. I've felt more connected to her than ever since then, the anger and sadness had blocked her for so long, but not anymore.

Other parts of Alex and her friends, and foes come from imagination and people I can call friends, while others I only briefly met. The Stephen character is based on a real-life, abusive foster care situation one of my friends still struggles with today. I wanted to give her a dash of revenge and prove to her that what happened doesn't define her, doesn't make her weak, and that she is worthy of love. I hope Alex's story reflects those goals, and I hope the layers of revenge were sweet for her as well.

Writing about abuse of any kind is difficult. Whether someone has been sexually harassed, betrayed by someone who was supposed to be a caregiver, or pressured by a partner who was supposed to show us love, it affects us all differently. But, the truth is, it does affect us, it isn't okay, it cannot be tolerated, and it isn't our fault. Abusers thrive on the ability to flip the switch, to make us feel like we made them do this or that, or that it's just the way things are. Well, not anymore. People aren't staying silent, and not being threatened into silence and submission. Voices are rising up, and help is there for all of us.

Not realizing I was writing any of my experience into this story at first, it wasn't until this recent read-through that I felt the stinging in my eyes as it made me think of my past. I stayed with an abusive boyfriend when I was a teenager. I never believed anyone, not my friends, my sister, mom, none of them when they said that I was in an abusive relationship. It took years to get out of it, to say enough, but the effects of the abuse didn't end there. He had altered my perception of love, of what it should be or should feel like, how I dealt with my own anger, and he screwed with my trust of others. Becoming a counselor myself, I went through a grueling program that made me take a deep and invasive look at myself. That was when I started to truly heal. Pieces of that process are in Trust, bits of the wonderful friends I've had over the years that got me out of jams, that loved me no matter what, and that are still there for me if I need them, Alex has them all and more.

If these pages help anyone else, even a little bit, I feel I have done what I set out to do. Yes, I love fantasy, I love kick-ass female leads, and I love the Scooby-type gangs, but these stories, and the ones after, also breathe emotion, real human scars, triumphs, mistakes, and tragedies.

I love to write and to entertain, but I also love to help people. My hope is that parts of the stories do just that for each of you.

Thank you!
Parker

CHAPTER 1

Warrior

The constant banging against my chest is my own damn fault. I should really try to get rid of this blasted ring again, but for some reason I can't seem to make such an absolute decision. Desert sand flows around me as I exert more force, arcing and sending my staff into a spin, smacking glowing balls of fiery light out of the air.

At first, Dana sends them to me all nice and sweet-like, spinning the bright balls of light the size of a racquetball around me lightly, giving me a chance to whack a few. Though, I think she's trying to get me dizzy, off my game and on my ass. I lift my wooden staff up then down to the left, sending a red ball sparking off into the distance. Spinning with the end of the staff making a circle in the red sand, I use it to leverage myself into a kick with my right leg and shattering another orb into sparks of purple and blue. The ring whips around on its chain once again, this time fly free from its place inside my shirt to crack me on the cheek. Damn ring. Damn Ryan. The beautiful sterling silver ring with the endlessly chasing sun, moon, and stars constantly remind me of Ryan's deceit. The anger gives me enough motivation to spin kick into the air and take out three more balls as I realize Dana is now dive-bombing me with them instead of playing solar system.

I leap to the right when a raging red ball of fire comes flying at my face. Where in the hell did that come from? I break my fall, saving my face from skidding along the red sand by a fingernail when I manage to get both hands down in time to hold myself in a plank with my staff pressing uncomfortably into my right palm. The momentum still manages to spray dirt in my face, and I spat it out, cringing as bits crunch between my teeth.

"Ha! Nice try, Dana. Is that all you've got?" I snarl, trying to rise when a smack reverberates through my leg from where another ball hits its target. "Son of a. Come on!" The motion pushes me over just enough to lose my balance and shift my hand right on top of a prickly pear cactus.

"Ow!" I huff, jumping up and gently switching the staff into my left hand and thrust my hand in the air towards Dana's form in the distance. "I thought we were clear of these things." The nasty barbs plunged into the palm of my hand trace an outline of my staff with another protruding painfully from my wrist. I hear a chuckle coming from a small rise; the crazy lady's form is a dark outline creating an amazing sight against the jaw-dropping Pozo Redondo Mountain backdrop. Putting my staff aside, I can't help but smile, wince, and smile again while I pluck the needles from my skin.

"You've gotta pull them out faster that that you big baby," she hollers. "You're just making it worse."

"Oh yeah, I'm making it worse. How about a new rule, no throwing those things at me when I'm down." *Crack* "Hey, what the hell." Another ball smacks me on my left butt cheek making my muscles seize in a damn charlie horse. I jump around on one leg looking for the culprit while looking like an insane person. "That is it, if you're not playing anymore, than either am I!"

Taking in the landscape around me, I'm mesmerized colors in the sky, blues, purples, pinks, and reds look like water colors swirling amongst traces of clouds as the sun begins to set. The desert, though the plant life is primarily muted in color and stunted in growth, is still vibrant against the red, sandy dirt. Tall cylinder saguaro cacti reach into the night sky like long fingers escaping the earth, reaching helplessly for the stars. I take it all in, every part of the Arizona desert, I feel the rustle of wind through the small leaves of sage bush, inaudible to the human ear, but not for me. I sense the scratching sound of burrowing insects in the sand, and scorpions under stones. I even hear Dana's heartbeat; it thumps in time with the pulse of Gaia herself, of the earth's goddess who allows me to harness her Earthen energy.

I splay my fingers towards the earth, willing Gaia to share her power. A tendril, merely a whisper of energy, like static electricity, rushes into my fingertips and I force it to move within my body where three needles remain. Using my ability, I move the Earthen energy

233

deeper inside my skin and force it to push the cactus spines free. *That's better.* The stinging sensation remains though, so I send a softer wave of force into the wounds and heal myself by using the energy to burn out the poison before pulling my skin back together.

Still pulling upon the earth, I drive some of the power into each crevice of my body and into my mind, holding it there, keeping it stored so I don't have to stop and seek out more during this duel with Dana. Looking down, I spot emerald green vines sending off burst of power, the visualization of my power that only Earthen warriors like myself can see, weaving around my arms. My grandmom's icy blue dandelion dances along the twining vines and I smile at her presence.

A buzzing hits my awareness; I'm in tune with my world and can sense everything now, even the sound of Dana's flowing white dress nearly 100 feet away from me. She's sent three Earthen balls of destruction my way, and I'm not letting them get close to me this time. Flashes of blue, purple, and yellow circle me, and I itch to grab my hidden weapons, but I'll hold back for now. Taking off at a run, I go to meet the yellow one head on, it's not stopping and I am close enough to send my power into it, overloading the pain-wielding ball and exploding it into sparkles of golden yellow dust.

The blue and purple cross each other, an inch from my face, and I jump backwards, stumbling over a low sage bush, and falling hard on my side. No cactus this time, and I manage to pop up into a crouch as the purple light zooms over my head. Watching it streak away, I gather my force into my hands and send it after the glowing nuisance, allowing my energy to consume it and extinguish it's light.

"Damn it, Dana. I am filthy, do you know how annoying it is to have to go through a pair of jeans everyday?" I don't hear her response, I hear nothing at all until a ball smacks me in the back of the head and I fall face first onto the ground. Hurt consumes me when I smack against massive flat rocks buried in the sand. My groan sounds as loud as a scream in the quietness of the desert, but I manage to lift myself up, watching with a snarl on my lips as drops of blood hit the rocks.

"You busted my lip," I spat out. "Real nice." Carmen is going to have a lot of questions during our next video call. She's already wondering why I need more of my clothes sent to me already. There was just no fixing scorched denim. Using the back of my hand, it's a mess, but the cleanest part I can find, I wipe the blood from my nose. With dirt, stone, and blood caked against my face; I bring myself up slowly, scanning my surroundings for a ball of light. It's more difficult than sensing things that touch the ground, and I have to rely on the bits of earth and water in the air to locate the flying torture device.

"There." I whisper. I've found it, and I can sense that it's streaking a path towards me from behind, but I don't give myself away. Barely moving, my feet grind into the sand, making grooves to slide within. "Not yet." I whisper while pretending to smack dirt and plant parts off my jeans. "Almost, there you go, come on you son of a bitch." It closes in on me and I spin, reach both hands out with my fingers shaping a ball of green power, my vines twisting and turning within it, growing lighter as dandelion sparks within. I thrust it at the blue ball, and my force instantly consumes it before, causing it to implode like a mini atomic bomb within an indestructible bubble. The light show is fascinating, odd even as my force holds the explosion inside, not allowing any pieces, or a hint of sound, escape.

"Woohoo, there you go, who's your mommy," I shout off while doing a little spin. "Suck it ball, that's right. Suck. It." Fist pumping into the air while jumping up and down brings aches from my bruised side and butt cheek to my awareness. "How about a quick sixty, eh?" My voice calls out to Dana, and I hope she hears me before sending more death balls my way.

"Okay, baby Conner. Lick your wounds while I think of my next attack, and this time, use what I gave you please. We both know you need more practice with the staff." Thanking the goddess for small favors, I take a moment to assess the damage on my body in the dying light.

We've been in this desert outside of Dana's RV park on and off for nearly three weeks now. And let me tell ya, using cell phones as a hot spot to work remotely has been giving Carmen fits. As my best friend and business partner, she is in a constant state of worry about the state of things with our party-planning company, Feelyne Productions. What she worries about the most though, is what she perceives as my deteriorating mental health. Good thing my college buddy Shane is there to help her with Feelyne. With his new San Diego Gaslamp club Rapture opened, there have been plenty of people to cross over and help for both businesses. Shane gave me a set of keys to Rapture on opening night. I still have the keys, but I doubt I'll ever be able to dedicate myself to being the business partner he needs, not since my whole world was flipped upside down. And now, instead of playing in the Gaslamp, I'm stuck out here playing ninja, busting vicious earthen balls of pain in the desert.

I told Carmen that I needed a little break from San Diego after having a successful hypnotherapy treatment from Dr. McAdams. Ya, that's what happened, at least that's what Carmen and my other friends Shane, Justin, and Nic need to think. Only my grandmother's most trusted, and dare I say a tad bit crazy friend Dana, my Seer friend Sandra, my mom, and Ryan know the truth about what really happened that night. This is how it has to be in my world, my world of danger, magic, and hiding the truth. But back to being out here…in the middle of nowhere, waiting for word from my mother so we know where she is, where my dad is, and what in the hell we are going to do next.

Sometimes I wonder if Dana and my mom did all of this on purpose to get me worked up, out the door, and away from my life in San Diego. I thought my life was finally going to start getting back to normal after Steven met his demise and my nightmares came to an end. Oh, but no! Wishful thinking. My life will never regain what I somehow considered normalcy. After all, there is still my wicked-ass foster brother Greg to catch, and let's not forget I have to find my father, who is goddess knows where. I've never known my father. Honestly, I had been told he was dead, but apparently I'm not the only one who keeps secrets. And of course, let's not forget the cat is out of the bag about Ryan and I being forbidden to ever be together because of some stupid Council 'rule.' A rule that requires Earthen Protectors, like Ryan and me, to help spread our abilities through the generations by finding partners outside of our secret world. The Council, bah, some group of Earthen Protector leaders I have never met nor do I ever care to meet.

Yep, I thought things would be all hunky dory after Ryan and I caught up with Greg and saved my mom…ugh, who am I kidding? It was all a ruse. Greg never had my mom in captivity. Now his sniveling ass is in the wind, and my life is in shambles. Being in the desert right now may be the best thing for me and Dana and my mom knew it. Oh, and big shocker. Apparently I am not battle ready yet. I guess the occasional kickboxing, and club dancing doesn't cut it when one decides to join this little good-versus-evil war instead of staying out of the game.

My 'being captured by Greg' stunt didn't really impress the seasoned Earthen Protectors, aka Mom and Dana. Being a descendant of powerful Earthen Protectors and Healers, I have the ability to harness power from the earth and bend it to my will. However, that isn't enough when it comes to protecting others, or in the case of what occurred three weeks ago, even keeping my own ass safe. As a result of my capture, Dana said it was Mom's orders to get me ready for what was to come, and to keep me from getting into that heap of a hot mess again.

In my defense, I was under duress from mind-assaulting nightmares, which didn't lend much room for sleep and made my brain split in two, not to mention they had a Demon on their side. Who has a Demon on their side, anyhow? Don't get me started on that, or him for that matter. I'm still cringing from the idea of Valant coming to 'visit.' I left that topic out of my discussions with Dana, although I am fairly sure she smelled him on me. Yep, I said smelled. She is the Mistress of Potions and Weaponry, and I don't think much gets past her, which is probably why she told me my staffs were badass enough to give a Demon's a beat down.

So, little Miss Weapons and Potions has been kicking my booty day in and day out with her little toys-of-fun while my body screams in agony over newly torn and reformed muscles and burns from various colorful earthen power balls of light. My blisters are finally forming into calluses, accumulated by using my favorite weapon: Dana's hairpin staffs. The weapons master forged and ornately carved hairpins and filled with tough-ass titanium metal. With the tiniest command from my power, these beautiful hairpins transform into two fight-ready staffs. They are twins I've named Serenity and Chaos; the latter defines my life and the former I can only wish for.

Once I take the hairpins into my hands and call their names, they change from elegant pieces of wood into wicked fighting weapons. Their lengths, covered in intricate vine carvings reflecting the nature of my power, are intermingled with dandelion seeds to symbolize my grandma. Cresting waves encircle both ends of each staff, and a fox hiding in the foliage represents my beloved fox friend Vex. I haven't seen Vex in nearly two years. He has helped me more than I would have ever thought possible, bringing me back from the brink of insanity more than once. I wonder where he was during all the stresses of this past year. He always told me I wouldn't be alone, and to accept the help sent to me, but apparently that didn't mean from him.

Aside from being aesthetically beautiful, my staffs are tremendously powerful. They have the extraordinary ability to be magically shaped into various fighter-friendly lengths. My favorite options are to either use them as a couple of two-and-a-half-foot pieces, or meld them together to form a single five-foot ass-kicking staff. Their sickly trick, one that I rarely use, is accomplished by willing the titanium metal running within their center to protrude to a sharp point at either end. Honestly, it scares the crap out of me, but it's nice to know that if I ever need to up my game a notch, I can.

Dana got a kick out of my less than stellar techniques with the staffs at first. My obvious lack of ability to balance the large staff from the very beginning didn't discourage her from sending those earthen balls of light at me at all times of the day and night, searching for ways to send dirt and sand into each and every orifice. When I put my weapons away and try to use my kickboxing skills to take on the barrage of lights with feet and fists, as in just a minute ago for example, she makes the lights dense and painful, like rocks hitting my flesh and bones. This inventive teaching technique forced me to add the weapons to my repertoire more often, unless I want I find myself bloody and broken. However, Dana does tend to my injuries in the best ways possible, with natural remedies in the form of cooling and warming salves, teas, and delicious feel-good foods. Using my healing power on myself wipes me out too much to be relied upon.

A silver ball of light grazes my hip, spinning me to the right and causing a slight growl to escape my lips. Dana has taken advantage of my reverie, and I'm paying for it dearly. The bitch about these balls is their target-reaching addiction, like little torpedoes locked on to me. Their weight not only knocks me in all different directions, but they shock or burn me as well. It really depends on how sadistic the weapons master is feeling.

The sun has set, but the glow from the rising moon silhouettes the weapon's master on the hill above me; she reminds me of Rafiki, that crazy baboon from the Lion King, except I am the one with the staff. That's it. She and her little round weapons are going down tonight.

Looking around, I bend over to pick up my discarded staff. Holding the five-foot staff with both hands parallel to the earth and call upon Gaia's energy. I command it to change into the two short staffs. Spinning them gently in my hands, I take my stance, eyeballing the silver ball as it arcs back my way, while at the same time watching a bright pink ball form in Dana's hand before that too makes its way toward me. Trying to keep them both in sight becomes difficult as they adjust until one aims at my front and the other directly at my back. I need a distraction to allow me to face off with one at a time.

Holding the staffs tightly, I point my fingers to the ground, pulling energy into my being, willing it to grab dead brush and cactus from the ground. Once at my command, I fling the plants at the silver ball heading directly toward me before wheeling around and running to

238

meet the pink ball of torture head on. I swerve and smack at it with my right staff before spinning left to give the pink glowing nightmare a crack with my left staff as it tries to redirect itself. After taking its licking, the ball hits the ground and sputters out of existence. A slight buzzing hits my awareness. I swiftly drop to the ground in a lunge before bringing both arms above my head, moving them in a figure eight as the silver ball attempts to whiz past me before meeting its demise. Sparks rain down around me, illuminating up my eyes before vanishing, leaving me in nearly complete darkness with the only light coming from the ascending moon and a soft glow of green from the visual show of power blazing in my eyes. I stay in my lunge, muscles taut, awaiting another onslaught before I sense the force of rocks being kicked up by tires not more than five miles away.

"Your boy toy is here!" Shit! Dana is so damn quick and quiet she causes me to jump into a crouch and aim my staffs in her direction. She is right, of course. My heart flutters in my chest as I send my awareness outwards, picking up on flickers of Justin's presence.

Journal Entry:

There is always that one recurring dream, one that feels real even when I wake. Even more intriguing is that I can tell I've had the dream before as I am dreaming it again. The darkness of night, moss under my feet, and a glowing blue gown chasing after me as I follow sparks of fairy wings, dandelion seeds, and forest creatures down a winding path. I have never been so free, so unafraid, and so protected. I laugh with the critters as the fairies bid me to follow them. Sparkling dandelion seeds tickle my skin and touch lightly on my nose, causing it to twitch. I am free. There are no worries or fear. It is as if I am one with the earth, Gaia's own child living in nature, within her world, one of magic and beauty, not of pain and man. Oh how I wish I could stay in these moments.

It has been years since I last had this dream, but this time it seems to mean something more than it used to. The tumbling down the trail and the skipping and singing slow to a stop once I came upon the soft glow of a greenhouse in the middle of the woods. I tiptoed on bare feet, feeling the warmth radiating off the glass, seeing the blurring of colors as the steam and age of the building hide the true treasures within. I could never find the door, no matter how many times I tried. It felt like eternity as I moved around the four sides, gliding my hand along the glass and metal bindings, searching for a way in, a secret door perhaps. Maybe if I pushed a pane just right, or hummed the right tune or gave the secret knock, the secret greenhouse—more like a giant treasure box—would open for me. But it never did, not for me anyway. It did always open for him, the boy, as young as I am, twelve, but taller, and with hair as dark as night.

He made his presence known when a small squirrel ran toward him and up the length of him as if he were a tree. The darn thing squealed, squeaked, and swooned over him in each and every dream. Her fellow four-legged creatures and the flocks of various birds nearly rolled their eyes at me and shake their heads, embarrassed by her obvious infatuation with the boy. All the while, these animals hover around my feet and take turns cuddling in the crook of my arm or finding a perch upon my shoulder to give me small nudges and pecks on my cheeks.

His laugh is always comforting, free and innocent; not a man's laugh, but not nearly as childish as I know some may seem at our age. No, he is just perfect and steady. So steady it seems as though an earthquake wouldn't move him, and not even a raging bear would make him flinch. His eyes gazed into mine and I had to shake myself from getting lost in them when I realized he was asking me something.

"What? I'm sorry. Did you say something?" He gave a hearty laugh and a small shake of his head, not in a condescending way, but rather as though he is in awe—in awe of me?

"I've seen you before, here at this moment, in this time. We have been here before, haven't we?" As he talked, he moved toward the greenhouse, laying a single hand upon it as a door became visible and opened for the boy instantly. I nearly stomped my feet in annoyance at the ease at which he had penetrated the secret treasure box. I quickly forgot my jealousy as my eyes gazed upon the glorious array of flowers and water features inside.

"Well, are you going to come with me? You want to see what's inside, right? Come on in; I'll show you." As he said the words, he turned to me with his hand open. I saw the etchings of a tree limb tattooed from his wrist up his arm and into the sleeve toward his shoulder. I had seen that exact tree limb before and in an instant I stumbled backwards as I realized that although I thought I had known someone else over the last year and a half, I may have known him for much longer. I reached out my hand and touched the markings on his arm, Justin's arm. The tree tattoo responded to my touch, giving the

240

impression of limbs waving in the breeze, leaves floating in the air, and I swear I saw a speckling of dandelion seeds floating among the beauty. The boy smiled at me and grabbed my hand, and we are two children together, running into Gaia's greenhouse surrounded by magic, colors, and smells.

The first time I had this dream was when I was twelve. I woke up sweating in my bed in my grandmother's home, wondering what had just happened, my feet still tingling with dew from the moss on the trails, my face still warm from the greenhouse lamps, and the kiss I received on my cheek. A sweet kiss the mystery boy gave me while we gazed upon the orchids.

This time when I wake up, I am much older; I know Justin. Did I just put him into my recurring dream or has he been there all along? And if he has, then what does that mean? And what is he?

Truth: The Alex Conner Chronicles Book Two

Available now on Amazon

About the Author

Ms. Sinclair is an Amazon best-selling author who writes novels in the fantasy, suspense, YA, & romance genres. Parker gives credit to the development of her imagination and passion for writing to multiple childhood destinations lacking indoor plumbing. It may sound odd, yet when your journey to adulthood consists of numerous backpacking, camping, and hiking trips to the most out-of-the-way and breathtakingly beautiful places in North America, the creation of games, worlds, and characters are the results. She would never trade the childhood her parents gave her, and she thanks them for raising her to have her own thoughts, dreams, and bountiful imagination. Oh and she wishes to thank them for teaching her that one should never leave their jeans on the floor of an everglades campground shower—lest they do the dance of the scorpions in the pants again!

While attending college, Ms. Sinclair studied biological sciences and psychology, specifically animal behavior, but her love has forever been to write. There are boxes in her house filled with notebooks, journals, and logs with poems, stories, lyrics, and personal rants scratched into them with pencil, marker, pen, whatever she could get her hands on. Words demanded to be thrown out of her mind and onto paper by any means necessary. Ms. Sinclair's studies have contributed greatly to the worlds, characters, and stories she creates, proving that no matter what path you take, it will all be part of where you end up—sometimes in spectacular ways!

Since 2007, Ms. Sinclair calls Coastal Virginia home where she writes full-time, is a member of RWA, a licensed educational counselor, and enjoys quality time with her children, husband, and fur babies.